BELOVED HONOR

"Don't you love me anymore?" Rene asked quietly.

Cat hung her head. "My God, I have tried not to. But I cannot seem to help myself." She began crying. "I am afraid . . ."

"Of what?"

"I do not think I am worth the sacrifice you are making."

"Oh, Cat." He kissed her nose, very lightly. "My dear Cat. I do."

He tipped her chin up with the tip of his finger, his arm tightening around her. He had the smell on him of summer, of green fields and ling flowers and wide blue skies, and his eyes were silver-blue in the moonlight, like star-spangled lapis lazuli. His mouth when he kissed hers was warm and taut with longing. "I have missed you," he murmured, caressing her cheek, "more than I can say." His hand slipped down to the throat and then to her breast, stroking her softly. Her flesh seemed to flame at his touch, even through the pale nightdress. "God, you set me afire. I thought I would go mad from wanting you while I was away."

He lifted her onto the bed and then climbed up beside her. "From now on, we will be together, Cat, whatever happens. I won't ever leave you again."

PUT SOME PASSION INTO YOUR
LIFE . . . WITH THIS STEAMY SELECTION OF
ZEBRA *LOVEGRAMS!*

SEA FIRES (3899, $4.50/$5.50)
by Christine Dorsey

Spirited, impetuous Miranda Chadwick arrives in the untamed New World prepared for any peril. But when the notorious pirate Gentleman Jack Blackstone kidnaps her in order to fulfill his secret plans, she can't help but surrender — to the shameless desires and raging hunger that his bronzed, lean body and demanding caresses ignite within her!

TEXAS MAGIC (3898, $4.50/$5.50)
by Wanda Owen

After being ambushed by bandits and saved by a ranchhand, headstrong Texas belle Bianca Moreno hires her gorgeous rescuer as a protective escort. But Rick Larkin does more than guard her body — he kisses away her maidenly inhibitions, and teaches her the secrets of wild, reckless love!

SEDUCTIVE CARESS (3767, $4.50/$5.50)
by Carla Simpson

Determined to find her missing sister, brave beauty Jessamyn Forsythe disguises herself as a simple working girl and follows her only clues to Whitechapel's darkest alleys . . . and the disturbingly handsome Inspector Devlin Burke. Burke, on the trail of a killer, becomes intrigued with the ebon-haired lass and discovers the secrets of her silken lips and the hidden promise of her sweet flesh.

SILVER SURRENDER (3769, $4.50/$5.50)
by Vivian Vaughan

When Mexican beauty Aurelia Mazón saves a handsome stranger from death, she finds herself on the run from the Federales with the most dangerous man she's ever met. And when Texas Ranger Carson Jarrett steals her heart with his intimate kisses and seductive caresses, she yields to an all-consuming passion from which she hopes to never escape!

ENDLESS SEDUCTION (3793, $4.50/$5.50)
by Rosalyn Alsobrook

Caught in the middle of a dangerous shoot-out, lovely Leona Stegall falls unconscious and awakens to the gentle touch of a handsome doctor. When her rescuer's caresses turn passionate, Leona surrenders to his fiery embrace and savors a night of soaring ecstasy!

Available wherever paperbacks are sold, or order direct from the Publisher. Send cover price plus 50¢ per copy for mailing and handling to Penguin USA, P.O. Box 999, c/o Dept. 17109, Bergenfield, NJ 07621. Residents of New York and Tennessee must include sales tax. DO NOT SEND CASH.

BELOVED HONOR

MALLORY BURGESS

ZEBRA BOOKS
KENSINGTON PUBLISHING CORP.

ZEBRA BOOKS are published by

Kensington Publishing Corp.
850 Third Avenue
New York, NY 10022

Zebra and the Z logo Reg. U.S. Pat. & TM Off. The Lovegram
logo is a trademark of Kensington Publishing Corp.

First Printing: June, 1995

Printed in the United States of America

For Phyllis Hingston Roderick,
who knows about these things.

I won't be my father's Jack,
I won't be my father's Jill,
But I shall marry the fiddler's son
And have music when I will.

—*Mother Goose*

Prologue

Douglasdale, Scotland
September, 1330.

"Scat, Cat," Jessie Douglas said, fastening rose-colored satin ribbons to the circlet of pristine white heather that was to adorn the bride's brow. "I swear, every time I move to do something, you are underfoot. Fetch me the scissors, Janet."

"I want to help," her sister Cat insisted, reaching for the knife tucked into her girdle. "You can use this. Why won't you let me help?"

"Because you are hopeless in anything to do with clothes, as you know perfectly well," their sister Tess said calmly, confiscating the knife and tossing it to Janet.

"Give that back," said Cat.

"Will not," Janet told her. "You can't wear a knife in a wedding, goose. It isn't proper."

"You see, Cat?" said Jessie, frowning in concentration as she tied the last bow. "It's just as I always say; you've no sense whatever of propriety."

"But what if the English attack?" Cat demanded.

"If the English attack today, Papa will ask them in for a cup of ale." Tess sat very still as Jessie settled the wreath of heather on her black curls. "After all, it isn't every day that a man's eldest daughter is married."

"Only the eldest by a month," Jessie said.

"Four months," Janet put in.

"Ten," Cat said, not to be outdone.

"Still, I am the oldest." Tess smiled with satisfaction. *"And,* need I mention it, the winner of the bet."

"The bet has nothing to do with who marries first," Janet pointed out, her mouth full of pins as she tucked a wayward flounce of yellow damask under Tess's hem. "It has to do with who marries last. There can't be a winner, only a loser."

"Well, I am the first not to lose, then," Tess said complacently.

"Don't count your chickens," Cat murmured.

The bride turned on her. "What does *that* mean?"

Cat's gold-green eyes glinted. "Only that Gill Tullibardine has not yet said 'I do.' He may still come to his senses."

"Fiddlesticks," said Tess. "He is head over heels in love with me."

"He surely seems to be, more's the wonder," said Janet, and ducked as Tess hurled a dainty shoe her way.

"I don't see how you can be so calm, Tess," Jessie said plaintively, trying for the fifth time to arrange her own wreath to her liking. "I swear, if it were I being wed—"

"We would all be extremely surprised," Cat broke in.

Jessie stuck out her tongue. "Just because I don't shamelessly chase every shapely pair of breeches that comes down the lane—"

"I do *not* chase boys."

"Of course you do, Cat," Tess told her. "You have to. Otherwise, what man in his right mind would even look at you when he has *us* to contemplate?" She smoothed her wedding gown over her shapely hips with supreme self-satisfaction.

"That's not fair," Cat said hotly. "I am nearly a whole year younger than you, Tess. I'll fill out. Wait and see."

"No you won't," said Janet. "Your mother was a skinny little slip of a thing, and so shall you be."

"Well, *your* mother was an adulteress."

"Could we leave our mothers out of it, just for today?" Jessie asked, finally getting the wreath settled to her liking. "None of them was any better than she should have been. But they all loved Papa, and that's what counts. Cat, for heaven's sake, come and let me comb out your hair."

"I *did* comb my hair out."

"When, Thursday last? Get over here—and sit still!"

Cat did, for two whole minutes, while Jessie tugged a tortoise comb through her long, fiery curls. "I hate to say it, Cat, but you have got the best hair of the lot of us," she observed.

"I don't think she has," said Tess. "Who wants to be a carrot top?"

"You would kill to have her hair, and you know it," Jessie told her.

"Would not."

"Would too."

"Ouch! That hurts, Jess!" Cat leaped up from the stool. She was rather inclined to agree with Tess, and would gladly have traded her reddish gold curls for Tess's black or Janet's blond, or even Jessie's rich brown ones. Red hair made one too conspicuous; it was the first thing anybody ever noticed. And it carried with it a whole passel of assumptions—that one was hot-tempered, impatient, flighty—which were just not true.

"I'm sorry, Cat. But you have got some kind of *something* stuck in here—"

"Spun sugar," Janet volunteered for her sister, while Cat made frantic shushing motions at her. "She was in the kitchens all morning, pestering Cook for sweets."

"Spun *sugar?*" Jessie wailed. "That won't comb out, Cat; I shall have to wash it, and it *never* will dry in time for the ceremony!"

"Couldn't you just sort of pin that part up, and put the wreath there?"

"Oh, honestly, Catriona," Tess sighed. All three of Cat's sisters came and stood over her, frowning and poking at the offending strands. "Couldn't you have been more careful just this once, for my wedding day?"

"I meant to," Cat told her. "Honestly I did. But you know Cook's cakes. And I—"

All four girls froze at the sound of a familiar knocking on the bedchamber door—two loud followed by two soft. "Come in, Papa," Tess said then, with a withering glance at Cat.

Archibald Douglas strode in in full wedding regalia—his best doublet and breeches topped by a velvet cape lined in saffron silk, chest blossoming with military honors, the blue sash he wore by right of his post as one of King David's councilors slicing his bosom at a raffish angle. Even without the finery, the father of the girls could, at the age of forty-two, still turn the heads of a roomful of women anytime, anywhere. His black hair had gone part white now, but it still swept back with a great wave from the high forehead that Tess had inherited from him; his eyes, piercing blue beneath straight thick brows, marked Janet as his own. Jessie had his cheekbones, strong and planed, and his fine aquiline nose. But only Cat had got the Douglas mouth, full-lipped and wide, quick to tighten in anger, even more quick to broaden in a smile. And it was the Douglas mouth which, rumor held throughout Scotland, had made Archibald and his half brother James so lucky in love—or, at least, in lust.

Just now those blue eyes were sweeping over Archibald's quartet of daughters. "The Douglas girls," everyone called them, for though there were amongst the renowned clan that ruled over Southwest Scotland other females, none were so striking nor so notorious as these, all born within a twelvemonth to four of Archibald's many mistresses. " 'Twar a time o' war," he was apt to say of the year of their birthing—1314, the date of the immortal victory of the Bruce over Edward the Second's English forces at Bannockburn. "And ye ken how in wartime things hae a fashion o' gettin' away fro' a man." He never made any other apology to the world for these living proofs of his excesses. There was no need to—he was a Douglas, and as such as near to deity north of the Tweed as any soul save a Bruce could be. He had brought the girls up under his own roof, here in the family castle at Douglasdale. He had of his own volition offered a stipend to each of the mothers for her lifetime. What more he might have said to them about the circumstances remained their secret. None, at least, had stabbed him, which had been what James Douglas had predicted his brother's fate would be when the girls were born.

"Tess." He came and kissed her white brow, so much like his own, that was crowned with heather. "How stunnin' ye look. Like a right ruddy angel."

"I made her wreath," said Jessie.

" 'N' a fair job ye did," said her father, and kissed her, too.

"I made the gown," said Janet.

"Ye hae got yer mother's touch wi' a needle, Jankins."

"I made a spot on the train where I stepped on it," Cat offered.

Archibald laughed and tweaked her chin. "Well, I bae glad to see, Kit-Cat, that ye bae not o'erawed by the grand occasion o' yer sister's nuptials."

"Nor you," Cat said, smiling back at him slyly. "Tell us, Papa, have you ever been at a wedding before?"

"Never." He gave a mock shudder. " 'N' if nae fer the four o' ye, I ne'er wuld go."

"If you'd prefer," Janet said dryly, "we could follow your example."

"Nae, nae, lass! What bae wild oats in a young man bae the sowin' o' disaster in a woman." They looked at him. "Savin', o' course, yer mothers."

"Oh, Papa." Tess sighed fondly. "You are utterly unqualified to offer moral instruction. All we can try is to ask ourselves at every turn of the road, 'What would Papa do?'—and then make sure we do the opposite."

"Callin' me a hypocrite, bae ye?" Archibald demanded, hands on his hips.

"Of course she's not, Papa," Janet said soothingly. "Just because you do things like profess to hate the English, but had us English governesses all the time we were growing up—"

"There bae gude reason fer that," her father growled. "The bludy English think we Scots bae uncouth savages, dinna they? Sae I made damned sure ye'd talk the tongue sae bludy fair they'd ne'er hae cause t' look down their skinty noses at ye, as they do me 'n' my generation. Wha' o' it? All the Scots today do the same."

"It's no use, is it, though?" Tess crinkled her own pert nose. "We don't sound like them anyway, though we may not say 'dinna' or 'cannae.' "

"Especially Cat," Jess put in, "when she curses."

Archibald grinned at his youngest daughter. "She does hae a fair way wi' a curse, dinna she? Well, scoff if ye like at my words. But as God bae my witness, the happiest day o' my life will come when I see the last o' ye well wed."

"Which won't be me," Janet said promptly.

"Or me," Tess said, fluffing the skirts of her wedding gown.

"Or me, I hope." Jessie's voice was a little wistful.

"We'll see," Cat said. "We'll see."

"Speaking of 'well' wed," said blunt Janet, "you might have upped the odds for one of us, at least, by making her legitimate."

"Wha', 'n' had the others hold it against me all my lifetime?" He grinned that infamous grin. "Nae chance, pet. Ye bae Douglases. That will suffice fer ye."

"Was that meant to be an insult to Gill, by the by?" Tess demanded of her sister.

"Of course not. Gill's perfectly lovely—but he *is* a younger son."

"Well, the older one's a prick," Cat murmured.

"Mind yer mouth, Cat!" her father chided. "Though in God's truth, that he bae. Not to mention a de Baliol man. Damned gude fer him he bain't comin' today. Mind ye, hospitality bae a sacred duty, but I cannae say I'd bae able to stomach such traitors at this feast."

"Speaking of de Baliol partisans, Tess, what did your mother finally decide about coming?" asked Janet, finishing up the hem of the bridal gown.

"She isn't. I had a letter this morning. She wrote she knew she wouldn't truly be welcome."

"Oh, Tess. I am sorry." Jessie squeezed her sister's hand.

"It's all right. It isn't Mother, you know; it's that husband of hers. De Baliol through and through. Mother would have come for your sake, Papa, I know that she would."

"Well, I reckon I can appreciate his feelings," Archibald said judiciously.

"You mean he might not care to be present at the wedding of the child his wife gave birth to whilst betrothed to him?" Janet laughed. "I can't see why not."

"She went ahead and married him, didn't she?" Cat put in. *"And* brought along all her millions. You missed your chance, Papa, there."

"Money means naught to me, darlin'."

"It does to Tess," said Janet. "Did she send you a wedding gift, Tess?"

"Five thousand marks," the bride announced with satisfaction.

Archibald whistled between his teeth. "Whist, pet, ye should bae payin' the pipers today, 'n' nae I."

Tess tucked her arm through his. "But money means nothing to you, Papa, remember?"

"Sae it dinna. Still, five thousand marks—" There was gratification in his blue eyes. "It shows she must still think fondly o' me, wuld nae ye say?"

"Or of Tess, you self-centered old codger." Janet laughed again.

"All you need now, Tess," Cat said, "is for there to be a war between King David and de Baliol, and for Gill's brother to get killed."

Jessie gasped. "Cat, you bloodthirsty thing!"

"Well, she *would* get to be countess."

"He wouldn't have to be killed," Tess noted very calmly. "Only attainted for backing the wrong side."

"Lord, Tess, one would almost believe you had thought it all out!" Jessie still looked aghast.

"Don't think she hasn't," Janet noted, her blue eyes glinting. "Tess always thinks everything out."

"Better that than to gadfly about the way Jessie and Cat do."

"I do *not* gadfly," Cat told Tess. "Maybe Jessie does, but not me."

"Do so."

"Do not."

"You do too, Cat. What would you call it, then," Tess appealed to their father, "when a girl stops dancing in the middle of a dance with one boy to run over and speak to another, leaving her partner gawking in the middle of the floor like a fish?"

"When did I do that?" Cat demanded hotly.

"Last night after supper! You left Gill's cousin Theo standing all by himself to talk to Danny M'Tavish! Gill's mother was absolutely mortified."

Cat squinched her small face. "Lord, did I really? I didn't

mean to. It is just that a single dance with Theo seems to last forever. I am sorry, Tess. I'll try to make it up to him tonight."

"Don't bother. You would only manage to make more of a mess of things."

"Well, if the Tullibardines took more care to teach their clan decent dancing—"

"Don't you *dare* insult Gill's family!"

"On that cheery note," Archibald said hastily, "shall we go in? The guests are waiting."

"Now?" Tess forgot quibbling and for the first time looked a bit flustered. "It can't be six o'clock already!"

"We can't go yet, Papa," Jessie said worriedly. "Cat's got sugar in her hair."

"Has she?" Archibald squinted at his youngest daughter. "I cannae see it."

"Told you," Cat said, and stuck out her tongue. "Just put my wreath on, Jess, and I am ready to go."

"You'll be sticky when you dance," Jessie warned.

"No one will want to dance with Cat anyway," Janet said. Cat poked her in the side.

Tess looked at her father. "Could I have five minutes more? Please?"

"I dinna like to keep the guests waitin'. . . ." But he relented at the pleading in her eyes. "Very well, pet. Five minutes. But nae more."

"Cold feet, Tess?" Janet asked when he'd left them.

"She hasn't got cold feet," said Jessie, arranging the wreath atop Cat's fiery curls. "How could she? Gill is any girl's dream."

"Have you slept with him yet?" Cat asked, causing Jessie to nearly send a hairpin through her eye.

"Of *course* she hasn't!" Jessie was scandalized. "They aren't married!"

"You needn't act as though it never happens, Jess," said Cat. "All our mothers did."

"I beg your pardon. Mine was already married," Janet pointed out.

"But not to Papa. Have you, Tess?" The bride shook her head. "Are you scared to?" Cat wanted to know.

"Only a little. Well, sometimes a lot. It is just hard to imagine how it—how it all fits together, if you know what I mean."

"Much the same as it does with the horses or cows, I reckon," Janet said wryly.

"Lord, I hope not like horses!" Tess's eyes were wide.

"I saw two lizards doing it once on a rock," Cat said thoughtfully. "The female was on top."

"How do you know it was the female?" Janet demanded.

"How do you think? I could see the male's little lizard thing." Tess giggled. "I touched Gill's once."

"Did you!"

"What was it like?"

"Over his clothes or under?" That was Cat.

"Over."

"Where were we? Where was Papa?" Jessie demanded.

"It was in the carriage last winter. Under the blankets. He put my hand on it." She stopped. All three of her sisters were looking at her eagerly.

"And?" said Janet.

"And," said Tess, "for the rest, you'll have to wait till *you're* married."

Archibald pounded on the door. "Girls! Come along!"

"She's only jesting," said Cat. "You'll tell what it's like, won't you, Tess?"

"Girls, let's go!"

"She'll tell," said Janet. "We always tell each other everything."

"Girls!"

"I can't wait," Jessie said, dreamy-eyed.

Tess smiled smugly and floated toward the door in a cloud of silk.

"Well. That's that," said Janet, and snapped her fingers at the boy who was handing the wine 'round. "Over here, if you please!"

"It went beautifully, don't you think?" Jessie gazed across the

Great Room toward the dais, where Tess and her new husband were accepting congratulations from the guests.

"Gill mispronounced two words during the vows." Cat crunched a handful of sugared almonds she had swiped from a passing tray. "He said 'pleet' instead of 'plight,' and 'dearth' instead of 'death.' "

"Did he? I wouldn't know. I had this one—" Janet hooked a thumb toward Jessie. "Blubbering in my ear the entire time."

"I was not blubbering!"

"Were too."

"Was not. Anyway, I can't help it. I always cry at weddings. Papa says 'tis the sign of a soft heart."

"A soft head, rather. Pippin, would you *please* get over here with that wine?"

"I bae tryin', Lady Janet!" the serving boy called to her through the crowd.

"I wonder does that make it invalid?" Cat mused.

"What, mispronouncing words? Of course it doesn't," said Jessie. "Don't you remember Fiona MacNab's wedding, where that skinny Campbell she married stuttered so badly that he never did get the vows out? They've got five bairns now."

"Five bairns?" Cat choked on a mouthful of almonds. "But they have only been wedded—"

"Six years," Janet finished for her, claiming a cup from the elusive wine tray at last. "One a twelvemonth. That's about right."

"Gor, she must be lying in year-round," Cat marveled. "What a bloody bore."

"Mind your mouth, Cat," Jessie said absently. "I think it will be lovely to have children."

"You shall have to find a man to marry first," Janet observed.

Cat giggled. "Not necessarily."

"Anyway," Jessie went on, "Gill always garbles his speech when he is nervy. Don't you remember what he said when he proposed to Tess?"

" 'Will you weed me, Tessie?' " Cat mimicked the groom. They all laughed at the memory of the story Tess had told them— after swearing them to secrecy.

"Well, he's a bit of a fool, Gill is, but he'll do for Tess," Janet said, "for so's she."

"That's a dreadful thing to say, Jan. What are you eating, Cat?" Jessie demanded.

"Sugared almonds. Want some?"

"Certainly not. Look at you; you've got bits of sugar all down your front. Between that and your hair, we'll be picking ants off you yet."

"I should want to marry someone cannier than that," Janet said, "and a good deal older."

"Why older?" Cat asked, letting Jessie brush crumbs from her dress.

"Because women, for the most part, are so much smarter than men that it's wise to let the husband at least have a head start in years. And since I am so much smarter than the average woman—"

"You shall need at least an octogenarian." Cat surveyed the Great Room. "How about Hoot Gibson?"

"Not quite so old as that—and I *will* insist he have some teeth. Someone more like . . . like that fellow there." She pointed to a red-haired man of perhaps thirty who was offering his best wishes to the groom. "Who is that, Jessie?"

Her sister, somewhat nearsighted, squinted. "Charles MacGregor. Already married. Besides, you don't want a redhead, Jan. He'll have a temper like Cat's."

"Quite right," said Janet, and Cat gave her a poke. "How about him, then, talking to Father Joseph by the doorway? Who is he, Jess?"

"Toby Thomsin. I don't know, Janet. He is nearly fifty, I think, and he has never been married."

"Neither has Papa—nor Uncle James," Cat pointed out.

"Even so, the gossip about Toby is that he—you know."

"What?" Cat demanded.

Jessie lowered her voice to a whisper. "That he prefers boys to girls."

Janet laughed. "Honestly, Jessie, how do you find out such things?"

"I keep my eyes and ears open. Someone has got to pay attention for the two of you; you are both hopeless at gossip."

"Because it is boring," said Janet. "Who is that girl over there, Jess, in the horrible hat?"

"Where?"

"Over there, by the table with the crumpets. She looks like a crumpet herself, doesn't she? Or a strumpet. What sort of gown is that?"

Jessie squinted. "French, I think. Good Lord."

"What?" Janet demanded.

"It can't be. And yet—I am almost sure it is."

"Is *what?*"

Jessie took another hard look at the tall, elegant blonde. "I think it is one of the de Baliols!"

"No!" Janet stared at the girl. "Not really!"

"Yes! Look at her! It must be—what the devil is her name? Esther? Eliza?"

"But what would she be doing *here?*"

"I'm sure I don't know. Cat, what is the name of Edward de Baliol's niece, that we met in Edinburgh at King David's birthday?"

"Where was I?" Janet asked.

"You had the chickenpox and had to stay home; don't you recall? Cat, what's the name—Cat? Cat, what are you staring at?"

Janet turned her attention from the de Baliol intruder to follow her sister's gaze. "Oh, my," Jessie murmured.

"Too young," said Janet. "But even so—oh, my! Cat, are you still breathing?"

"Who is he, Jess?" Cat whispered.

"I haven't any idea."

"Well, go and find out!"

"I don't take orders from you; I am not one of the servants."

"I'm sorry. I'm sorry! Go and find out, please."

"That's better," Jessie said, and flounced away.

Janet was scrutinizing the stranger in their midst. "He has got too much hair, I think. And his eyes are set too far apart. There is something odd about his face—he doesn't look Scottish at all, if you ask m—"

"Shut up, Janet," said Cat. "He is the most beautiful creature I have ever seen."

Janet rolled her eyes toward heaven. "Christ, I hope you are not going to humiliate us by chasing after him the way you did Thad MacKenzie at the harvest ball."

"Who is Thad MacKenzie?" Cat tore her gaze from the stranger long enough to glance at how Jessie was faring. "Good; she is asking Lady Alison; if anyone knows, that biddy will. Oh, Janet." She sighed with bliss. "Just look at him."

Tess was beckoning them from the dais. "The dancing is ready to begin," Janet said, pulling her sister's arm. "Tess needs us up in front."

"Tess can wait."

"Papa will be angry."

"Papa is never angry with me."

"He will be if you spoil Tess's wedding by making a fool of yourself in public over some boy you've never even been introduced to!"

"I shall introduce myself to him," Cat said complacently, "as soon as Jessie tells me his name."

Tess was waving at them more frantically. "I am going," Janet declared.

"Wait! Here comes Jess."

"Tess needs us for the dancing," Jessie called as she approached them. "Come along, Cat."

"But—"

"Your sister needs you," Jessie said again, firmly. "I'll tell you what I know on the way."

Three parti-colored birds in bright silk, they fluttered toward the dais, Cat's fiery head close to Jessie's brown one, Janet holding aloof. "We've met him," Jessie was saying. "Lady Alison swears it."

"Impossible," Cat scoffed. "I should certainly remember if we had."

"It was years and years ago, at King David's christening. And you most certainly know his father."

"Who?"

Jessie was smiling, enjoying doling out the knowledge she'd gleaned. "Uncle James' friend Michel."

"Michel Faurer? The great knight?" Cat rubbed her hands together. "Ooh, this just gets better and better. The father is with Uncle James, then, isn't he, on his way to the Holy Land? I shall have something to talk to him about. But where has he been? What is his name?"

"Rene. He's just spent five years in Paris, being schooled there by his grandfather. The father is French."

"Told you he did not look Scottish," Janet put in smugly.

"He's not Scottish at all. His mother is English." Jessie scanned the crowd. "There she is, over there. In the blue velvet. Isn't she exquisite? Her name is Madeleine. And the little girl is Anne, his sister." Cat, looking, saw a lovely woman with curly black hair, smiling serenely, and a small child in a high-waisted white gown, wide-eyed with excitement. "She is ten years younger than he, born the same year as King David, so that would make her six. And there is some sort of story about the parents, Lady Alison said—very romantic, but I hadn't got time to hear it."

"I'm astonished you found out so much as you did," Janet observed. "Lady Alison must talk even more than you do."

Jessie stuck out her tongue, then turned to Cat. "There you are. I did the best I could."

Cat hugged her quickly. "You did marvelously. I shall do your chores for a week!"

"If I'd known that was what you were offering," said Janet, "I would have gone."

They were close to the dais now. "Where the devil have you been?" Tess demanded, leaning over the table.

"Cat's in love," Janet told her.

"Oh, Christ, again? Cat, I am warning you—if you do anything to embarrass me—"

"I won't," her sister promised solemnly. "This is real, this time."

Janet rolled her eyes once more.

"Darling," said Gill Tullibardine, claiming Tess's hand, "the musicians are waiting. Are you going to dance with me or no?"

"Of course I am, darling. Cat, what's his name?"

"Rene Faurer," Cat pronounced, starry-eyed.

"Who?" Tess asked again. But Gill was pulling her away, and the other sisters' partners came and led them into line.

Cat was paired with one of the Tullibardine cousins—not Theo, but this one, too, had two left feet. Keeping him from mutilating the hem of her sea green silk gown had her busy, but not so busy that she did not steal glances at Rene Faurer each time the dancing brought her close by him. He stood leaning against one of the roof pillars, not even tapping his toes, holding a tankard of ale, his blue eyes very cool and aloof. *I wonder what he might be thinking of,* she mused. It was nothing very pleasant, from the looks of him. But that was all right. She was tired of boys with no more in their empty heads but hunting and wenching. If he'd been schooled in Paris, he must be very cosmopolitan. He—

"The music's stopped," the Tullibardine cousin pointed out, eyeing her a bit strangely.

"Ah. So it has." Cat flashed him a small version of the Douglas smile. "Lovely dancing with you." She started toward the pillar on which Rene Faurer was leaning, but was brought up short by Jessie calling her name.

"Wait, Cat! Where are you going?"

"Where do you think?"

Jessie yanked her back. "Not yet you don't. Have you forgotten? We are each to dance with Papa."

Sighing, Cat let herself be led to the dais, where she waited, hopping from foot to foot, while first Tess, then Janet, then Jessie circled the floor with their father. *Last, I am always last,* she thought impatiently. *Everyone expects me to lose the wedding bet, too, I know, just because I am the youngest. But I intend to surprise them. I am going to marry Rene Faurer, and it won't take me long to win him, either; just wait and see!* Catriona Faurer. Lady Faurer. Did the father have a title? Not that it mattered, of course. She wouldn't—

"Cat," Archibald Douglas said for the third time, holding out his hands to her, "anytime ye bae ready . . ."

"Oh! I am sorry, Papa!" Cat saw Tess glaring at her as her

father led her into the center of the room, where he smiled and waited to pick up the beat of the viol and pipe and drum, and then swung her about in a sprightly galliard. He was a wonderful dancer—the best in Scotland, folks had said when he was younger—and she nearly forgot about Rene Faurer in the sheer pleasure of moving with him to the quick, wild song.

"Ach, ye hae got yer mother's feet on ye, Catriona," he told her, grinning as he swung her right up off them, making her skirts sail. "She could step a lively one like nae one else on earth, may God rest her soul." Cat's green-gold eyes glowed at the compliment. "Jessie tells me there bae a boy has caught yer fancy."

"Jessie has got a big mouth."

Archibald laughed. "That she has. Which one bae it?"

They were dancing quite close to the roof pillar. "I'll tell you later."

"Promise?"

"Aye. Promise."

"Well, I pity the poor creature, whoe'er he may bae, fer when my Cat goes after somethin', she gets it. The trouble bae, she rarely wants t' keep it."

"That's not so!"

"Sooth, lass, sooth!" He squeezed her hand, spinning her about. "Ye come by it natural enough. O' all the mothers, yers is the sole one, I suspect, who would nae hae married me had I asked her to."

"Nonsense. She loved you, Papa."

"P'raps she did. But she loved some things more."

"What things?"

"The smell o' peat on the hearth. Gettin' the washin'-up done. Havin' a lock on her door, 'n' her own key to latch it." He chucked her small chin. "Sae. Will there bae another lovesick swain parked upon my stoop, then, when yer fancy moves on?"

"Not this time, Papa. This is real."

The musicians ended their song with a flourish. "Well," said Archibald, and kissed her hand before relinquishing it. "Mind ye behave yerself, Cat."

"Why is everyone forever telling me that?" she asked crossly, then turned to start toward the roof pillar at last—only to find that Rene Faurer was gone.

"Oh, drat." In the torchlight she scanned the assembly, searching for his black head. "Whist! Cat!" she heard, and saw Jessie pointing surreptitiously toward the anteroom where the kegs of ale had been tapped. Cat blew her a kiss of thanks and started there, only to find her way blocked by a strong-set young man with a shock of white-blond hair.

"Remember me?" he asked, grinning. Cat didn't. Not the least discomfited, he made a neat bow. "Malcolm Ross. We danced together at your cousin Emrick's wedding. I was hoping I might have the pleasure again."

"Were you? That's nice," Cat said absently, and pushed past.

He was in a corner, close by a window, with his tankard newly filled; she could see the crown of creamy foam atop it. Cat grabbed a tankard of her own, the one her cousin Fergus was about to drink from. He arched an eyebrow at her. "Thirsty, Cat?"

"Parched dry, thank you ever so much. Dancing always makes me thirsty, doesn't it you?" she appealed to Rene Faurer.

"I wouldn't know."

"Don't you dance? What a pity. I beg your pardon; we have not been introduced." She elbowed Fergus.

"What? Oh! Cat, permit me to present to you—" He blinked. "Who the devil are you?"

"Rene Faurer."

"Ach, Michel's son! It's a pleasure to meet you. I had the honor of serving under your father at Durham in '28. A truly masterful commander. He—"

"Fergus," Cat said meaningfully and stepped on his foot.

"Ouch! Ach! Where was I? Cat, Monsieur Faurer. Monsieur Faurer, my cousin Cat. As I was saying, Faurer, your father—"

"Fergus," Cat said, "your wife would like to dance with you."

"My wife is eight months along with child."

"All the more reason why her wishes should be honored, Fergus. Go!" She shoved him toward the door.

Rene Faurer was looking down at her. Close up, his eyes were bluer than mountain gentian, blazing, breathtaking. "Cat?" he said.

"For Catriona."

"I see. It suits you."

"You mean because of my eyes. Everybody says that."

"Actually, I was thinking of your manner. The way you dismissed Fergus and all. Very high-handed. Complacent."

"I am *not* high-handed!" Cat said, so haughtily that even she had to laugh. "Well, perhaps I am, a little. But you know, all the Douglases are. It's bred in the bone."

"So you are a Douglas."

"Aye, of course." And then her green-gold gaze slanted up at him. "You make that sound rather like a disease. Nothing fatal, like plague, but annoying. Scrofula, perhaps."

He shrugged his shoulders. He had lovely shoulders, broad but not brawny, beneath his earth-brown coat. The collar of his white shirt showed just the merest hint of embroidery, very subtle. The effect was more masculine than just plain linen would have been. "We cannot help our birth," he said.

"No, but I wouldn't want to. Your father is with Uncle James, isn't he? Taking the Bruce's heart to the Holy Sepulchre."

"Is he? I rarely know where my father is."

Rather hard going, Cat thought, and might have given up despite his handsomeness had she not sensed a wary watchfulness in his casual words. It was almost as though he were waiting for something—something he would not welcome. "I like your shirt," she said.

He laughed. It was a low, winning laugh, surprised, as though she'd said the thing he least expected. "Thank you. My mother made it for me. My sister told me not to wear it."

"Why on earth not?"

"She said I would look a pretty boy, and be teased." The thought had made him smile. His teeth were white and even, as perfect as everything else about him. Cat could hear her heart thumping in her breast.

"Did you enjoy Paris?" she asked a little breathlessly.

"How did you know I'd been in Paris?"

"My sister Jessie asked Lady Alison. She likes to keep up on the gossip. And we didn't know who you were. We've met before, though. At the king's christening."

"I must confess, I do not remember."

"Neither did I. But we were children then."

"And here we are, all grown-up."

She looked at him, suspicious. It sounded as if he was mocking her. "Well, we are. I shall be sixteen come October. Tess is getting married. I mean, she is married."

"Lucky Tess."

There it was again—that lofty, half-mocking tone. *Get back onto Paris,* she told herself; *it is a safer subject, not so forward for a first encounter.* And she was about to when a voice purred at her side: "Darling, *here* you are." Turning, she saw the girl whom Jessie had thought was a de Baliol, her frothy hat perched cunningly atop her smooth blond head. It was Rene Faurer that she was talking to.

"Whatever are you doing hidden away in here all by yourself?" the blonde went on, sliding her gloved hand through his arm with easy intimacy. Her voice, smooth as her hair, had a little tinge of French to it.

"But I am not alone, Eleanor. Allow me to present Catriona Douglas. Lady Douglas, Eleanor de Baliol."

The two faced each other. "You must be a friend of the groom's," Cat said.

"The fellow with the peculiar name? Never met him. I am Rene's guest." She smiled up at him. "I have been staying with the family. But I am from Paris, where I live with my uncle Edward."

I know all about your uncle Edward, you little snake, Cat thought; *he has been scheming for years to steal the throne from the Bruces.* But aloud she merely said warmly, "I do hope your uncle is happy there in Paris."

"For now, I trust he is." Eleanor de Baliol smiled again. "But you are one of the famed Douglas girls, aren't you? Catriona. Let me see. Ah, yes. Your mother was the barmaid."

Cat's eyes flickered green-gold fire. "My mother kept a tavern in Craignure, if that is what you mean. She had the inheriting of it from her father. She kept it going, alone, for fifteen years. It served the best victuals in all the Isles."

"Very resourceful of her, I'm sure."

"You're bloody right it was."

"My, my, Rene. You warned me about the Scots' penchant for rough language, but I never expected that you meant the women!" Eleanor tucked his arm closer to her frilly bosom. "Come, let's dance."

Cat stood square in front of them. "I thought you didn't dance," she said accusingly, glaring at Rene Faurer.

"Who, Rene?" Eleanor laughed, a light, rippling sound as frothy as her gown. "He is a marvelous dancer. No doubt he only meant he did not care to dance with you. Pray excuse us."

Cat didn't move. "Why wouldn't he care to dance with me?"

The girl was already stepping around her, pulling her partner along. "Darling, the music is simply too rustic; you will die laughing. *C'est trop amusant.* I—"

The sound of lace tearing apart stopped her dead. Cat was gripping her sleeve. Eleanor de Baliol's pale blue eyes narrowed. "You ill-mannered little minx! This gown was made for me in Paris by Anatole Rémarque himself!"

"Well, he ought to have taken more care tacking the lace down. Why," Cat repeated, "would he not care to dance with me?"

"That would seem obvious enough!" Eleanor yanked her tattered sleeve free. "It is just as Uncle Edward always says, Rene, isn't it? Poor breeding will out."

"I," said Cat, "am a Douglas!"

Eleanor de Baliol eyed her pityingly. "But you are not really anything, are you? Just another of your father's bastardly indiscre—"

"Bitch," Cat breathed, and lunged at her, just as a chorus of voices called from the doorway:

"Stop, Cat!"

Jessie got to her first, grabbing her shoulders, whirling her 'round so that Tess and Janet could steer her back to the Great Room. "But she—" Cat began.

"Hush!" Janet hissed. "Just hush!"

"But—"

"Oh, Cat." Tess was on the verge of tears. "You *promised* me!"

"I didn't—I wasn't—"

"Papa will be so ashamed when he hears," Jessie fretted. "You know what he always says about hospitality being a sacred duty."

"But you don't know what she called me—called us!"

Janet's pretty mouth was grim. "I can guess. Words are only words, though, Kit-Cat. Why must you let them wound you so?"

"I don't know. . . ."

At her back, Cat heard a now-familiar voice purr, "That's a redhead for you—always ill-tempered." She started to turn.

"I'll show you who's—"

"Cat!" Janet clamped a hand over her mouth. "Come! It is time for the toasts now."

"And if you do *anything* else to embarrass me, Cat," Tess threatened, "as God is my witness, I'll never speak to you again!"

From her seat on the dais, Cat had a perfect view of Rene Faurer. He was flanked by his little sister Anne, with their mother beside her, and by Eleanor de Baliol, who looked utterly at ease, not a single pale gold hair out of place; somehow she'd even mended her sleeve. Cat's hand inched toward her own unruly curls and felt a stiff crust of spun sugar. *Damn her,* she thought, *and damn him too!* He hadn't had the decency to intervene while that smug little tart insulted her under her own roof! And she hadn't even been invited! She had said herself that she was Faurer's guest. Surely that made him responsible for her.

He seemed willing enough to take responsibility now. Cat sat and silently fumed as he helped Eleanor de Baliol to the delicacies she pointed to on the tray before them, beckoned a servant to fill up her wineglass, retrieved her napkin when it slid from her lap. It was just as he was straightening up again that the blonde glanced Cat's way, mouth curling in that supercilious smile. Janet saw, and shook her head warningly, stopping Cat from sticking out her tongue. "Why in the world would you care about any man who'd sit with a de Baliol?" Jessie whispered, leaning toward her.

"They have both been living in Paris," Cat whispered back. "It is only natural that they should be acquainted."

"Something more than acquainted, I'd say," Janet noted mercilessly, nodding at the couple. Rene Faurer was eating grapes from Eleanor de Baliol's fingertips.

"Stop whispering and pay attention to Papa!" Tess hissed at them from farther up the table.

Archibald Douglas loved making toasts. He was wrapping up his well-wishes for the newlyweds; everyone raised goblets and drank to their health and longevity and happiness and—with Tess blushing and Gill grinning—to a long line of heirs. In the silence of swallowing, little Anne Faurer's voice carried clearly as she asked her mother, "Cakes *now?*"

"Not quite yet." Madeleine Faurer smiled at Archibald, who laughed.

"Ach, the child speaks truth; I bae long-winded. But it wuld nae bae fittin' fer me to finish without drinkin' to my gude brother, James, who as ye all know bae takin' the heart o' our late King Robert, God rest 'n' keep his brave soul, to the Holy Land. It war the greatest sadness o' the Bruce's life, I know, that he could nae live to keep his vow to go on crusade. But now the best part o' him, the biggest part, the part that led this great nation o' ours to freedom fro' the damnable English—" Archibald paused and spat. "Will gae there wi' my brother, God willin'. Here's to James, 'n' to the heart o' the glorious Bruce!"

"To James and the Bruce!" the company echoed. "To Good Sir James!

When the cups had clinked back on the table, Archibald looked again at Madeleine Faurer. "There bae one that travels wi' James to whom this country owes a debt near as big as to the Bruce. He came to us a stranger, a man without a country—'n' blessed we all bae that he chose us fer his own. He led the horse at Bannockburn, on that great day forever branded in the heart o' every gude Scotsman. He served at Berwick 'n' Byland, 'n' stood by the Bruce's right hand at Northampton, when the treaty sealing the nation's independence war signed. I hae been privileged to call Michel Faurer a friend fer nigh on twenty years now, 'n' fer my money there bae nae finer soldier in all Christendom. I drink to his health now. To Michel Faurer!"

"To Michel Faurer!"

"Michel Faurer!"

Cat watched as Madeleine Faurer smiled and nodded graciously at this honor to her husband. Little Anne applauded excitedly. Rene was leaning over as Eleanor de Baliol murmured something into his ear.

"We bae fortunate," Archibald went on, "to hae Michel Faurer's son amongst us this day. He has been off learnin' what passes fer knowledge there on the Continent this many a year—" A ripple of laughter passed through the guests. "But we all hope 'n' pray he bae come hame to serve Scotland as nobly as his gude father has. Will ye say a few words, son?"

Rene, still bent toward Eleanor, did not seem to hear him. His mother reached to pat his arm, getting his attention, nodding at Archibald, who waited on the dais, cup raised. Rene straightened up on the bench, and his blue eyes, dark as the little mountain gentians, ran slowly over the crowd. He looked at Archibald, at the bride and groom, even, briefly, at Cat. Then he got to his feet with easy, languid grace and held his own cup high.

"I'll give you a health," he said. "I drink to Scotland—when she shall be ruled by boys no longer, but by men."

The guests gasped—Cat among them. "Treason!" she heard someone cry, and saw it was her cousin Fergus, rising from his bench with his sword drawn.

"I'll have him first, Fergus!" Gill Tullibardine clambered over the table and down from the dais, scattering sweetmeats and wine. Tess screamed and tried to hold him back.

"Darling, no!"

"He's slurred King David, Tess, at my marriage, and I'll not sit by!"

"I'll cut *yer* bloody heart out and feed it to pigs!" That was another Douglas cousin, Duncan, who, Cat knew, had served at Bannockburn. "How dare ye shame yer father sae, ye knave?"

Rene Faurer hadn't moved. His mother was very pale; his sister seemed bewildered. Only Eleanor de Baliol was smiling, thinly, coolly, at the chaos around her. "See? I *told* you!" Jessie hissed to Cat.

"I say we string him from the rafters!" Malcolm Ross cried, waving a dagger.

Archibald was standing on the table now, stomping his feet, banging two cups together, calling for quiet. "He bae a guest," he was roaring, " 'n' hospitality bae a sacred duty! Duncan! Fergus! Sit down! Gill Tullibardine, get back here, or by God, I'll take back my daughter!"

"Let me at him! Let me at the traitorous bastard; he bae nae son o' his father!" white-haired Keith Ramsay was bellowing while his wife held his arms. He was so ancient that he could not even stand without a cane. And young Robbie Stewart had stripped down to his tunic; with his scarlet hair flying, he leaped over a bench and made for Rene Faurer's throat, crying, "I'll show ye bloody Scots hospitality!"

The entire room was in an uproar, Cat's father still bellowing at the top of his lungs, every young man in the place and half the old ones calling for Faurer's head, the women screaming, dogs barking, the cups and plates crashing onto the floor, when into the midst of the chaos came a sound that silenced even Archibald Douglas: a shattering echo of hooves against stone. Everyone turned toward the iron thunder, falling silent. Through the open doors at the far end of the hall came a rider atop a horse, both so dust-covered that one could not make out their colors. Then a sudden downdraft from the hearth caught the knight's ragged pennant and spread it; Cat saw the remnants of the three white stars of the house of Douglas glimmering there, and for some reason her heart stood still.

"Archibald," the man atop the horse panted, yanking off his helmet.

"Angus? Bae it ye, man?" Cat knew him too, then, by his head of red hair and the brawn of him: Angus MacPherson, another cousin, distant, who had been the Bruce's valet in battle for more than two decades. But he had gone with Sir James to the Holy Land. What was he doing here?

"Oh, gude m'lord—" Angus MacPherson was crying, wild tears streaking the brown dust on his face. Archibald stepped down from the table he was standing on, his own face very pale. The angry boys and men around him fell back, moved away.

"My brother . . ." he whispered.

"Slain, gude m'lord. God forgive me the bringin' o' such news! Slain by the infidels in Spain!"

Tess stood in her place at the table and screamed, a horrible anguished scream. Jessie fainted dead away; Janet barely caught her before she hit the floor. Cat just sat and stared, disbelieving. Dead? Uncle James dead? No one so brave and strong and noble as Good Sir James Douglas could die.

And yet, she thought, and yet, the moment she had seen those tattered Douglas stars, she knew. . . .

Archibald was faltering on his feet. Cat jumped and ran to hold him, help him to a chair. His skin felt thin as that of an onion, and as papery. The shocked hurt in his eyes was terrible to see. "James. Oh, James," he keened, leaning into her arm, "how am I to go on wi'out ye, brother o' mine?" Cat held him tight, stroking his wild hair, and saw that in all that vast assemblage of folk, one soul only was moving—a small figure in a snowy high-waisted dress, making her way toward the mounted knight in the center of the floor.

"Angus?" the little girl piped, looking up at him. "Angus, where is my papa? He was to carve me an olive-wood boat."

"Annie." The huge knight swallowed. "Oh, Christ, Annie. Yer papa—"

A sudden motion caught Cat's eye: Madeleine Faurer sagging forward in her seat, a hand at her mouth. "Michel . . ."

Without a word, Rene Faurer stood and gathered her up in his arms. Annie had turned to her. "Mama?"

"Come, love," Rene said very softly, very gently. He scooped her up, too, and held them both easily, tight to his chest.

"But what about the cakes?" Annie asked plaintively. "We haven't had our cakes!"

He strode toward the long table that held the sweets. "Which one, pet?" Annie paused, considering, then pointed. "A fine choice," he said gravely, and stooped to let her reach it with her small hand. Madeleine Faurer's face was buried against his neck.

"Rene!" someone called after him—Eleanor de Baliol, rising in her seat. "Rene, what about me?" But if he heard her, he gave no sign; he just kept moving toward the open doors at the far end of the hall.

"Faurer!" Robbie Stewart, still wearing only his tunic, bounded toward his receding back. "By God, I've not finished with ye!"

Rene turned on him with such palpable fury that Stewart stopped dead in his tracks. "Have you no bloody heart?" Rene said in a tight, low voice. Stewart started to speak, then flushed red as his hair. Shifting his mother and sister in his grip, Faurer put his back to the Scotsman and kept walking, straight through the doors.

Janet and Jessie, now revived, had joined Cat and Tess at their father's side. "It is all his fault!" Jessie cried, clinging to Archibald's hand.

"Whose?" Janet asked.

"Rene Faurer's! He has called down a curse on our house with his wicked toast!"

"Jess, that's absurd," Cat told her. "If Uncle James died in Spain, it had to be weeks ago, even months, long before Rene—"

"Jessie is right," Tess declared tearfully. "My wedding day is spoiled, no small thanks to him!"

Cat started to protest again, but was stopped by the searing grief in their father's eyes. The room was filled now with the sounds of weeping, as the women, the dreadful news having sunk in, began to mourn.

"I wish Robbie had smashed his head in," Janet said with venom in her voice. "I don't know why on earth you would want to defend him, Cat."

Neither did she, really. She looked across the torchlit hall to where Eleanor de Baliol was sitting, still without a blond hair displaced but looking guarded, wary. Even as Cat watched, the girl rose and slipped out through a side door.

Faurer hadn't so much as rebuked his guest when she'd been so unconscionably rude. And that toast he'd made—it was the height of churlishness, or of madness, to offer so bald an insult to King David in this company. He hadn't exactly seemed grief-stricken, either, at the news of Michel Faurer's death. She remembered the way, cool, almost disdainful, he'd told her, *I rarely know where my father is. . . .*

And yet . . . she pictured, too, how swiftly he had moved to comfort his mother in her loss, bear her away to mourn in privacy. And he'd let his little sister linger over the cakes—how many men would have known that, in her muddled fear and sadness, with the first glimmer of the awful finality of death flickering in her soul, what that child needed most was a pretty sweet? Into her mind there came an image of herself at that same age, and the English governess, horrid Miss Beadle, who'd brought her word her own mother was dead. "Chin up, girl" she could still hear the woman saying briskly. "You've got your father yet, haven't you? And that hussy never gave a fig for you, you know." What Cat wouldn't have given at that moment for someone or something to sugar the pain. . . .

Aye, Cat mused, despite his faults, there was something more to Rene Faurer worth learning. The question—she glanced at Tess's resentful expression, Jessie's tearful one, Janet's hard reproach, her father's tragic eyes—

The question was whether after all that had gone on this day, her family would let her learn.

Part One

One

November was wild along the west coast of Scotland, where the choppy white waters of the Channel met the swells of the Atlantic and came crashing up against the rock-hewn shore. The incessant slough and thud of the waves reminded Cat of the visits she had made as a child to her mother's home on the isle of Mull. Inside the old, low-slung tavern, the Crown of Feathers, where Marguerite MacLeod had served tankard after tankard of ale to thirsty fishermen and the pilgrims on their way to St. Columba's shrine at Iona, peat smoke and laughter always hung heavy on the air against that same backdrop of ebb and flow. Cat had loved making those visits—and loved, too, coming home to Castle Douglas again, where Papa and her sisters were waiting. Marguerite, she thought, had never really been meant for motherhood. She'd adored Cat—there was never any question of that—but she hadn't much concept of what children needed. She'd always treated her daughter as a miniature grown-up, had her work washing glasses and stirring cauldrons of oyster stew. Cat had long since concluded that her mother's own abbreviated youth—she'd been only thirteen when Cat's grandfather's death left her an orphan, and the proprietress of the Crown of Feathers—had robbed her of all memory of what mattered to a child.

Wind was howling down from the cliffs beetling over the shoreline. Harsh though the weather was, Cat was glad to be gone from the gloom pervading Castle Douglas these days, with everyone still in mourning for Uncle James. Tess had canceled her honeymoon with Gill to stay and comfort Archibald; Jessie burst into tears at the mere mention of their late uncle, and even sharp-tongued Janet was glum and subdued. Cat had no patience for mourning. She'd loved and admired James Douglas as much as any of them, but if she'd had to listen to one more blubbering recital of his mighty deeds, she would, she was certain, have gone quite mad.

Even in his grief, Archibald had sensed how his youngest daughter was chafing. Perhaps, too, he recognized that losing her mother so early had served to inure her to sorrow; no other death could ever touch her so deeply as had Marguerite's. What else could explain his acquiescence to the daring notion she'd hatched as she came upon him in the stables, rubbing polish into a suit of silver-clad armor that was not his own?

"What are you doing?" she had asked.

He'd looked at her, blue eyes rimmed in red. "Wipin' up Michel Faurer's armor, lass. It came back wi' James's things fro' Spain. I thought to send it along to the widow. There bae some other stuff, too—his chain mail, his sword . . ."

"How very kind of you, Papa," Cat said after the merest pause. Amazing how quickly an idea could form itself in the mind. But now she had to tread gently, gently. . . . "She seemed a lovely woman."

"Ach, she bae a bonny soul. Ye'd never in yer life ken she bae English," Archibald had said—the highest compliment, under the circumstances, he could have paid.

Cat had reached out to touch the fine tracery of engraving along Michel Faurer's breastplate. "What was he like?"

"Michel? Very bold. Very grim. A man who lusted for battle. None of us e'er could understand wha' Madeleine saw in the fellow. And yet theirs was one o' the great loves, I reckon, o' my time."

Though dying to know more, Cat forced restraint. "She must be heartbroken."

"Oh, aye. Her sun rose 'n' set wi' the man." Archibald sighed, rubbing oil and sand into the creases of the greaves. "I pity her, poor thing, left wi' naught but th' little girl, 'n' that wild son o' hers."

"Had they a son? Oh, yes. The one who gave the horrid toast."

Cat made a face. "With any luck, he'll have gone back to France and his de Baliol friends."

"I hope sae, fer her sake." Finished the polishing, he covered the armor with a fine crimson cloth. "I'll hae Geordie or Jock make a trip to Ayrshire in the wagon t'morrow; it bae but a two-days' ride."

"She will be glad to have the relics, I'm sure." Cat pursed her wide Douglas mouth. "With no other family here, she must be lonely in her mourning."

"Nae doubt. A family bae the greatest comfort," he agreed, piling the sword and chain mail atop the cloth.

"I wonder . . ."

"What, Catkin?"

"Would it help ease her pain, do you suppose, if I were to go along? Rather than just having Geordie or Jock leave all this on the doorstep, as it were. A servant, you know—I wonder if it might seem a wee bit cold."

"I had nae thought o' that. P'raps I should go myself," Archibald said, frowning.

"Oh, no, Papa. The girls need you too much here," Cat said quickly—too quickly, she feared, as his blue eyes met hers.

"But ye, Cat—d'ye nae need yer family wi' ye to mourn yer uncle?"

She hesitated, then said truthfully, "Papa, I loved Uncle James dearly. But it seems to me—well, he was a soldier, wasn't he? I can't quite understand why it should come as such a surprise that he's been killed in battle. The wonderment to me is that he lived so long!"

Her father laughed. "Ye hae got a point, lass. He war a mad-man, war James. But there bae a soothin', dinna ye think, in rememberin' our dead?"

"I think it hurts to remember."

"Well." Archibald cleared his throat. "It all depends, I reckon." He looked her up and down. "P'raps ye wuld be some solace to the widow, then."

And that was how she came to be bumping along beside Geordie on the seat of the wagon, following the old road up the Ayrshire coast to Langlannoch, where Madeleine Faurer lived.

They'd stayed the first night of their journey at Dalry, in an inn close by the Galloway Forest, and that, too, had reminded Cat of Marguerite: the clattering of hooves in a cobbled courtyard, the bustle of servants come to take your cloak—that had been one of Cat's jobs—even the food they'd shared, plain and hardy, just right after eight hours of riding through damp chill. Her mother was much on her mind of late. Perhaps it was the shock of Uncle James' death—or, perhaps, meeting Rene Faurer again after all these years. She'd searched her mind often for some memory of him at King David's christening, but time and again she found nothing, not even a glimmer there.

Once only, a few months before the fever took Marguerite, Cat had asked her why she and Papa lived apart. "Because we bae nae married," had been the answer, "just as yer sisters' mamas bae nae married to yer father."

Why not? Cat wanted to know. Her mother had waited a long moment before answering, her chin resting on her white hand. "We bae nae right fer each other, yer father 'n' I," Marguerite said finally. "A man 'n' a woman, to marry, should bae like two halves o' a plum. But I bae a berry, and your father bae quince. One wuld nae even serve us on the same plate." Cat remembered looking at her, uncomprehending. "One wuld o'erpower the other," Marguerite explained.

"Oh." How Cat wished, with a decade of hindsight, that she'd asked who would overpower whom! But instead she'd said, "How did you come to have me, then?"

"I'll tell ye all about it when ye bae older." But, of course, she never had.

One of the great loves of my time. That was what her father had said of Madeleine and Michel Faurer. How splendid it would be to have folk speak of one's *amour* that way! Could the passion that had lit up the father's life be ignited in the son? That was what Cat intended to see.

Of course, she reminded herself, he may not even be at Langlannoch. He might truly have returned to France with that horrible Eleanor de Baliol. But she couldn't believe he would leave his mother and sister alone in their grief. He would be there. He *had* to be there.

"There it bae," said Geordie, pointing through the dusk and shimmer of sea mist.

"Are you certain?" Cat asked dubiously. The house that rowned the summit of the hill ahead of them seemed too modest or a great hero like Michel Faurer.

"Ye heard yerself the directions I got in Dalmellington."

"Aye, so I did." Cat nibbled her lip as the wagon rumbled closer, suddenly doubting the wisdom of her grand scheme. What exactly was she to say to Rene Faurer when she saw him? How would she explain what she was doing there?

No lights showed in the windows of the house. It *was* small, Cat saw, but perfectly suited to its site on the spit of land over-ooking the sea—made, like the high wall surrounding it, of na-ive sandstone, buff-colored, with the surprise of a red tile roof and turrets—minarets, really—that gave it an exotic air. The gates were of black iron, and opened when Geordie hopped down to try the lock. Inside the wall was a garden, browned and dry now, but surely lovely in summer, when the roses and jessamine cascading over the yellow stone would be in bloom.

"Wha' should I do now?" Geordie asked uncertainly, reining in the horses at the garden's edge. "It dinna look to me as though they bae at home. And where bae we to stay if they bae nae? I cannae drive that road back to Dalmellington in darkness. And I dinna ken the way on to Ayr. I—"

"Oh, Geordie, do hush. It isn't likely, is it, that they'd go off and leave the gate wide open. Go and knock at the door."

He didn't budge from his seat. "I dinna like the looks o' the place."

"What in the world do you mean?"

"It has the look o' ghosts."

"Don't," Cat said, "be absurd. I shall knock." And she did, standing on the doorstep with dried leaves from the bare trees crackling beneath her cloak hem. She knocked twice, loudly, with a knocker that beneath her fingers—it was very dark now—seemed to be shaped like a demon of some kind. There was no answer. Geordie was muttering gloomily from the wagon seat. She was about to admit, reluctantly, that the occupants must be away when a voice floated out of the darkness, quite close to her side:

"Who is there?"

"Christ!" Cat jumped. "You gave me a start!"

"And you I." A spark flared in the night; she heard the hiss of a lamp wick, and then saw the yellow light point up the angular planes of Rene Faurer's face. She had her hood drawn up, and he held the lamp closer.

"It is I. Catriona Douglas."

"Catriona—who?"

Cat felt still more unsure of herself. Good Lord, he did not even recall her. "Catriona Douglas," she said again. "We—you were at my sister Tess's wedding. The night you heard about your father."

He reached out and pushed the hood back with one long, strong hand. Her hair glittered in the lamplight like red gold. "Ah, yes," he said then. "Cat. What the devil are you doing here?"

She gestured toward the wagon. "I've brought your father's things."

"My father's things?"

"Aye. His armor and his sword, and his chain mail. They came back from Spain with my uncle James', and my father thought it best to send them along."

"Christ. Will he never be buried?" Rene Faurer said, less to Cat than to the night.

She stared, taking him literally. "I haven't got the body. You should have gotten his body."

"We did. My mother threw it into the sea. She didn't eat for a week afterward." In the warm golden light, his eyes were dark. "And now this."

"She threw it into the *sea?*" Cat heard her own voice rising very high indeed.

He nodded. "Some sort of pact they had made. She says I'm to do the same with hers when her time comes. That's the sort of cheery discussion we have been having." He strode to the wagon and poked beneath the blankets covering his father's belongings. "What in hell am I supposed to do with all of this?"

"I don't know," Cat said, bewildered. This wasn't going at all the way she had imagined it. "We thought—my father thought—you would want them. Mementos of him. To treasure."

"I have got enough bloody mementos of him." He stood with his hands on his slim hips, the lantern at a cockeyed angle, and for a long moment stared at the contents of the wagon. "Could you—can you just take it away?"

"Take it away *where?*" asked Cat.

He seemed about to answer when the door before her creaked open, and lamplight fell on the lovely face of Madeleine Faurer, looking very thin and pale. "Rene?" she called. "Rene, I heard a knocking—"

"Damn," her son muttered, stepping away from the wagon. "It's all right, Mother. It is only—"

"You are one of the Douglas girls, aren't you?" Madeleine said, recognizing Cat. "The youngest one. Forgive me; I don't remember your name."

"Catriona. Cat." Cat made a little curtsy, feeling as awkward as she ever had in her life. She had the sense she had stumbled into a pageant in the middle, that there were forces at work in this place which she did not understand. Ghosts, Geordie had said, and perhaps he was right. That was what the woman before her had the look of, anyway.

"I am sorry if you were kept waiting. I heard the knocking, but I was trying to settle my daughter. She—she has not been sleeping well of late."

"It is I who am sorry, for disturbing you."

"Oh, no, not at all," the pale, drawn woman said. Her voice was not like a Scots voice; the vowels were shorter, the endings of the words crisp, and the rhythms were rougher. Rene's voice was much the same. "But all of the folk who came to—our visitors have all long since gone. What brings you here?"

Cat glanced at Rene. There was something very close to hatred burning in his blue gaze. *He is being unreasonable,* she thought, anger flaring in her heart. *If it were I, I would want to have these things.* "I've brought some belongings of your husband's," she told the widow evenly. "His armor and his weapons. They came with my uncle's to Douglasdale, so I brought them here."

"His armor . . ." The woman's gaunt but lovely face shifted, rearranging itself, a sort of mask, pleasant but unnatural. "How very kind of you, Mistress Douglas. Rene, please unload the wagon."

"Mother. Don't you think——"

"If you don't want them, someday your sister will. Unload the wagon, please."

Rene Faurer looked at her a moment longer, then spun on his heel and did as she bade. Cat glanced toward the wagon. Geordie was still sitting on the seat, positively bug-eyed. She had to ask him twice to help with the unloading, and even then he kept darting nervous looks at the darkness around them, as though he expected spirits to come flying at him on the wind.

Speaking of wind, the sea air had grown quite cold. When the two men had carried the last of the equipage into the house, Madeleine turned to Cat. "You'll stay the night, of course. And you must be famished."

"We supped at Dalmellington."

"But that is hours from here. Come along, child."

"Thank you." Cat followed her inside.

Like the house itself, the front hall was small but well proportioned, with a great huge hearth at the far end in which a fire was smoldering, and two staircases, twins, curving up toward the second story on either side. Someone had lit the torches. From a side room she could hear Geordie's and Rene Faurer's footsteps as they moved the mail. On the stone walls hung elegant, intricate tapestries, as fine as any Cat had seen at the royal palaces in Edinburgh and Stirling. "What splendid hangings," she remarked as they passed one that bore a fantastic scene of an Eastern palace capped with minarets and onion domes, its gardens lush with apricot trees.

"How nice of you to say so. Embroidery is my little passion. Michel—my husband—was so often away, and it helped to have something to pass the time."

Cat looked round in wonder at the dozens of hangings, each filled with hundreds of thousands of neat, small stitches. They were, she thought, sad but eloquent testimony to this woman's lonely life as the wife of a great warrior. Perhaps the reason why neither Uncle James nor Papa had ever married was so they would not leave a woman with a legacy such as this. It represented a near-lifetime spent with a needle in hand.

They passed through the hall to a smaller room furnished with a huge table for dining, dozens of benches, and still more hangings. "Please, sit," Madeleine Faurer said, indicating a spot. "We have cold ham and smoked salmon—or I can warm you some stew."

"Haven't you got any servants?" Cat ventured in puzzlement.

"Of course we have." A smile flitted over Madeleine's face. "A man and wife and their two boys and their wives. But they had a family wedding in Troon to go to, so I gave them a fortnight. They'd had a great deal of extra work lately, what with the—with all that's gone on."

Cat bit her lip. "I've arrived at a most inconvenient time, I fear."

"No, no. Not at all. What can I bring you?"

"Cold salmon is fine."

Cat sat and waited, staring at the tapestries. *Lord,* she thought, *I've put my foot in it this time. Rene despises me for showing up with that armor, heaven only knows why. As for the widow—poor thing, she seems not quite all there, and here am I making her fetch me salmon and turn down a bed in the middle of the night. Geordie was not going to be happy when he found out the servants were away, not with his talk of ghosts—*

It was just as she spoke that word to herself that she heard the first bloodcurdling scream.

It was high-pitched and drawn-out and anguished, wild as a banshee wailing, and it made Cat freeze, with terror pricking up and down her spine. Just as it faded away, there came another, equally bone-chilling. Madeleine Faurer came running from the kitchens, not even seeing Cat, calling, "Rene! Rene!"

"I heard," came his voice from the front hall. "I'll go."

"I'll go with you."

They both disappeared. Geordie poked his head into the dining hall. "Dinna I tell ye? Ghosts!" he hissed.

But the scream had been all too human. "Come with me," Cat

told him, heading for the kitchens. "You will feel better after you have something to eat."

A platter of salmon was lying out where Madeleine had left it. Cat rustled about and found bread and butter to accompany it, and the ale keg, from which she poured two mugs full, with perfect heads. Geordie sat at the table and sniffed the foam on his mug suspiciously. "There bae somewha' in this ale."

Cat tasted it. "Brewed with herbs. Woodruff, I think, and borage. Go on. You need something to steady your nerves."

"Naught wrong with my nerves," he sniffed. "There bae somewha' wrong wi' this house, though."

"Of course there is. They've just had a death."

"So hae we," Geordie pointed out, poking with his knife at the salmon as though he thought it might bite him. "But ye dinna hear such screamin' in Douglasdale."

Truth to tell, Cat hadn't much appetite either, though she sought to make it look as though she'd eaten more than she had by pushing the fish 'round on the platter. Geordie ate the bread and butter, downed the ale, and rose from the bench. "Where are you going?" Cat asked.

"To see to the horses. I'll sleep in the stables, if it bae all the same to ye."

"You'll be cold."

"Aye, but at least I'll be amongst familiar company."

He stomped out. Cat sat and kicked the heels of her boots against the flagstone floor, saying to herself, *Well, Cat. Everyone always tells you that you are too impulsive by half, and I suppose this proves it. What in God's name made you think Rene Faurer would have the time of day for you, in a house filled with grief?*

She yawned; she was terribly sleepy. Going to the kitchens to get her own meal was one thing, though; wandering about upstairs searching for a bed was another. There was nothing for it but to sit and wait until someone showed her to a room. Perhaps Geordie had the right idea after all, she thought, leaning her head on her hands and contemplating the salmon's beady, staring eye.

She must have fallen asleep, for she woke with a start sometime later, a terrible crick in her neck from bending over the table. The smell of salmon was strong in her nostrils; grimacing, she pushed the fish away and moved a spoon that had been under her forearm, pressing into her flesh. Rolling back her sleeve, she examined the skin, then began to try to rub the impression of the bowl away. A bit of movement caught her gaze; she turned and saw Rene Faurer standing with his broad back against the door-jamb, a cup in his hand.

Embarrassed, Cat abruptly let her sleeve drop. How long had he been there? The notion that he had been watching her sleep made her dreadfully self-conscious. Had she been drooling? Snoring? He looked at her and crossed the room, opening a cupboard, refilling his cup from a corked bottle. "Brandy?" he asked, extending the bottle.

"No, thank you."

"Are you certain? It is French. Very fine."

She shook her head, then remembered the scream. "Is everything . . . all right? I heard—"

"My sister. She has nightmares since my father died."

"Oh." Cat pictured the tiny black-haired girl she'd seen at Tess's wedding. "Poor creature."

He put the bottle back and drained his cup with rather frightening swiftness. He was wearing a loose white shirt, open at the throat so that she saw the ropy muscles at the top of his chest, the hollows of his collarbone. He looked even taller than he had at the wedding; his black hair was coming loose from the band that held it at the nape of his neck. He picked up a candle. "I'll show you to a bed," he said. "Unless you prefer to join your man in the stables."

Sensing disdain for Geordie in his voice, she jumped to his defense. "The long ride made him nervy. The stretch from Dalmellington is hard driving."

"It is a godforsaken place to build a house, I'll grant you that."

She stood and followed him to the front hall and up one long staircase. At the top he paused, thinking. In the candlelight she saw the flicker of still more tapestries, and a portrait, very striking, of Madeleine Faurer, made, she guessed, a dozen years ago. There was one of Rene, too, as a boy, dressed in blue velvet, two puppies at his feet. Already he'd had that wariness in his eyes.

He moved past them quickly, opened a door, and stood aside

to let her precede him. Candlelight fell on a high draped bed, a chaise, a table holding a pitcher and basin. On the floor was an Arab carpet in a pattern of crimson blossoms and green leaves. The furnishings were far finer than anything at Douglasdale.

He used the candle to light another on the table at bedside. "Is there anything you need?" Cat shook her head again. "Good night, then." He stalked toward the door, then paused with the latch in his hand, looking straight at her. "What brought you here?"

"I—I told you," she faltered, taken aback. "Your father's belongings—"

"You could have sent them with the servant." His voice was brusque.

"My father feared it might seem cold to send just Geordie." It was only a small lie.

"Did he? I would not think Archibald Douglas would be chary of offending a traitor like me."

"The thought was toward your mother," Cat said tartly. "Anyway, you've my father and no one else to thank that my cousins did not shred you to pieces at my sister's wedding."

"I don't recall having asked for his help."

"You didn't have to. He would have done the same for a heathen Moor who was under his roof. The Douglases believe hospitality is a sacred duty."

"Aye. So I think I heard your father shouting as your cousins came at me with their knives." His full mouth had a wry twist.

"Well, it was bloody stupid of you to have offered that toast amongst such company." Cat was getting hot, but couldn't help it. He was so arrogant, so aloof; did nothing touch him?

"What do the Douglases believe, pray tell, about guests who call their hosts 'bloody stupid'—*uninvited* guests?"

Had there been something near enough to hand, Cat might have thrown it. With all her will, she reined in her fury. "My coming here was meant as a kindness," she said, as steadily as she could. "Had I any notion this would be my reception, I'd have stayed at home—which is where I intend to return tomorrow morning, just as soon as I can."

He arched one black eyebrow. "I assumed you would, Mistress Douglas. No one's asked you to stay." He headed for the door.

"Well, I wouldn't even if someone did! I wouldn't stay if you begged me!" Cat shouted at his back, and then felt like kicking herself for the childish outburst. He pulled the door shut behind him with a brief, sharp click; she could picture the disdain for her that must have shown on his face.

"Well, what the bloody hell," she muttered, washing up at the basin. "I *will* be gone in the morning. Next time I get so carried away with a man, I'll listen to those sisters of mine."

Christ, she was tired. Crossing the room, she reached to turn down the bedclothes and saw at close hand the yards and yards of elegant cutwork adorning their edges—more mute evidence of Madeleine Faurer's lonely existence here in this house that her husband—"one of the great loves of my time," wasn't that what Archibald had said?—had built for her here at the edge of the world.

Two

Cat awoke in the morning to find a pair of green eyes—not green-gold, like her own, but green-blue, like aquamarines—staring into hers from only inches away. Startled, she sat up and then let out a cry as a great ball of gray fur leaped from the pillow beside her to the foot of the bed.

"Mama said there was a lady here named Cat," the face that went with the eyes, very small, very solemn, told her. "I wanted Grimkin to see her."

"Grimkin?" Cat said faintly.

Her visitor nodded toward the ball of gray fur, which had rearranged itself atop the counterpane into the biggest, fattest cat that Cat had ever seen. "My kitty. Have you got a kitty?"

"No. I haven't."

"Just as well, I suppose. It would be confusing. Say you lost it. Then everyone would have to go around looking for Cat's cat. I'm Anne."

"Yes, I know. How do you do?"

"Not very well. My papa is dead."

"I'm so very sorry," Cat told her softly.

Anne ran her small hand over the counterpane, tracing the stitchery. "Mama says the hurt will go away, but it doesn't seem to."

"It will take a long time, a very long time. But it will," Cat assured her.

"Yes, well, we'll see." The girl was clearly unconvinced, and only being polite.

"I know, you see, because my mother died when I was just as

old as you are. And for ages and ages I started to cry every time I thought about her. But then one time, I didn't cry. I laughed."

"You did?"

"Aye. I was thinking about a dress that she had made for me, and she had sewn the sleeves in backwards. When I tried it on for her, my arms stuck out like this." Cat demonstrated in her shift. "And I remembered that, and laughed. After that, I knew it would get easier. And it did."

"My mama would never make such a mistake." Then Anne's eyes went wide. "What if Mama died, too, and it were only Rain and me left?"

"That won't happen."

"It could, though. I shall have to pray very hard that it doesn't. Is your papa dead, too?"

"Oh, no. He is very much alive." She paused. "What did you call your brother?"

"Rain," Anne said again. "Would you like to have breakfast with me? Mama never eats anymore, and Rain is never about."

Poor child, Cat thought, with a flash of anger for the absent Rene. "I should like that very much."

"Good. Put on your clothes, then, and come along downstairs."

Cat made a quick toilette while the girl sat on the bed, patting Grimkin and kicking her feet. "You have very strange hair," she told Cat, watching her braid up her long red-gold tresses. "Do you like it?"

"Sometimes I do. Sometimes I don't."

"I would like it, I think. Who sews your clothes now that your mama is dead?"

"A seamstress my father employs." Cat glanced down at the forest-green gown she had chosen with such care for the journey, hoping Rene Faurer would find it attractive. She might as well have worn breeches. "My sister Janet made this, though."

"It's very nice. I wish I had a sister."

"I have three."

"You are lucky."

"But you have a brother."

"Aye, so I have. Are you ready?" Cat stole a peek in the looking glass. She looked peaked, but what did it matter? She nodded, and Anne picked up Grimkin, slinging him under one arm. "Shall we go?"

Anne padded down the corridor to the staircase. She was still wearing her nightgown, and cloth slippers on her feet. *Someone,* Cat thought, *ought to look to this child's needs.*

In the kitchens, light was pouring through the long, leaded windows. While Anne rummaged in the cabinets, Cat looked out over neat squares of gardens at the whitecapped sea—then turned away abruptly, irrationally afraid she might see Michel Faurer's body bobbing on the waves. She watched with amazement as Anne very competently blew up the fire from the coals in the hearth, put a rasher of bacon in a pan, and cracked eggs into a bowl. "I shall make an omelet *aux fines herbes,*" she announced. "If that is all right with you."

Cat, who could not have put water to boil, nodded faintly. "That will be fine."

In no time the kitchen was filled with delicious smells. Anne laid two places at the long table. "If you want milk," she said, "I've got to get it from the cow. Otherwise, I'll see to it later."

"Oh, no. I don't much care for milk."

"Papa drank it every day." The girl's face clouded over. She turned to attend to the omelet. "I really can't imagine I shall *ever* laugh to think of him."

"You will. Tell me, do you like living so close to the sea?"

"I love it," Anne said promptly. "I can swim. Can you?" Cat shook her head. "Mama says every girl should learn to swim, for swimming helped her win Papa." Her lip began to tremble. "I learned to swim all the way to the point and back for him this summer, and now he never will know."

"Don't you believe in heaven?" Cat asked.

"Of course I do. But it is not the same."

"No. I never thought so, either," she admitted.

Grimkin was nuzzling at his owner's skirts. Anne crumbled bacon in a bowl and set it on the floor for him. "Shall we eat?"

The food was splendid—the bacon crisp, the eggs perfectly set, flavored with tarragon and chives. "I could never make a meal like this," Cat confessed, accepting a second helping of omelet. "Much less milk a cow."

"Mama taught me. I don't think she would have servants at all if Papa didn't—hadn't—insisted. She likes to do things herself." She looked up at the sound of footsteps in the doorway. "Here's Rain. Hallo, Rain."

"Hallo, crumpet." In the same clothes he had worn the night before, Rene Faurer strode in, bringing with him the tang of the sea, sharp and salty.

"I found Cat."

"So I see. Good morning, Mistress Douglas."

Cat, her mouth unfortunately stuffed with egg, nodded as haughtily as she could. He looked haggard, as though he hadn't slept, with a ragged shadow of beard across the taut planes of his cheeks and chin. But his blue eyes were as cool as ever as he said, "I saw your man in the stables. He'll have the wagon hitched after he breakfasts. You'll soon be on your way."

"On your way?" Anne cried in dismay. "But you only just got here!"

"Yes, I know," Cat told her, "but I really must be going. I am needed at home."

"I don't understand," the little girl said, brow knitted. "What did you come here for?"

"I . . ." Cat glanced at Rene. There was challenge in those eyes, as though he was daring her, waiting for her to lie. But why should she lie? No one had shielded her when her mother had died. The truth was the best way. "I brought some of your father's things. His armor and sword."

"Papa's armor . . ." Anne, too, looked to Rene. "I want to see it."

"Oh, Annie. No. Don't."

"I want to see it," she said stubbornly. "Where is it?" She bounced up from the bench and through the door toward the front hall, with Rene following her, still arguing. Cat hesitated, then folded her napkin and trailed after them, feeling responsible.

The armor had been laid out, still covered by blankets, in a small parlor with a breathtaking view of the sea. Anne had no trouble finding it. When she did, she pulled the blankets away and looked for a long moment at the steel-and-silver cocoon that had protected her father and, at the last, failed him. Rene stood a little way behind her. Cat waited in the doorway, but Anne turned, seeking her out, beckoning her in.

"He taught me all about armor," the little girl said. "He let me help him put it on. I know every piece's name, from bottom to top. See? Solleret, greave, poleyn, cuish, tasset—"

"A charming legacy to a child," Rene broke in, the sneer very clear in his tone.

Cat could not fathom him. "Are you opposed to war?"

"This wasn't war; it was an escapade. Two aging soldiers dragging their dead comrade's heart halfway across the world—and for what? A promise he had made to a fat French pope—"

"Shut up, Rain," Anne said very mildly.

"Who'd excommunicated all three of them more than once in their lifetimes—"

"Shut *up,* Rain. What will Cat think of you?"

There was a brief silence. Then, "Oh," he said, "Mistress Douglas's opinion of me is sufficiently well formed that I doubt any new revelation could change it."

Anne had turned back to the armor. "Here is where the arrow got him," she murmured, "right under the arm, between the plate and the pauldron. Angus said he was leaning down to reach Sir James after he had fallen. Odd, isn't it, that they should die together that way?" She ran her hand over the break in the steel.

"Anne. Don't," Rene said.

"A storm is blowing in from the sea."

All three of them looked to the doorway, where Madeleine Faurer stood, wraith-pale, her black hair loose and flowing down her back.

"What, Mother?" asked Rene.

"A storm is coming in from the sea. I was up in my rooms and I could see the clouds gathering. What are you doing, Anne?"

"Just looking at Papa's things."

"Well, mind you don't get smudges all over the mail; you know how he hates that."

Cat stared at her with a sense of shock. Did she really think her husband was still alive? She looked so worn and thin. . . .

Anne seemed to notice nothing amiss; "Yes, Mama," was all she said. But Rene, his blue eyes seared with pain, put an arm around his sister and drew her close against him. "Did you sleep at all, Mother?" he asked, unable to keep the desperation from his voice despite the presence of Cat.

"I wasn't tired at all."

"You have got to sleep. Come, Anne and I will see you to bed. I'll read to you if you like."

"I really am not the least bit tired."

"Just lie on the bed, then, and close your eyes for a while." An arm around each of them, Rene ushered his mother and sister through the door. In the hallway he paused. "Mistress Douglas. You'll see yourself out?"

Cat nodded dumbly, longing to help but plainly out of her depth. He did not want her here; that was clear enough. She would respect his wishes.

But Anne looked back, too. "Please don't go," she begged. "I have so much still to show you. And I was going to cook you a woodcock for supper. If Rain caught one, that is."

"I'll come back another time."

"When?"

"Anne. Come and help me put Mother to bed," Rene told her.

"But *when* will she come back?"

For the first time, Madeleine seemed to realize what they were discussing. "Mistress Douglas can't possibly leave now," she put in. "There's a storm brewing. Didn't you hear what I said?"

"I've already been outdoors this morning, Mother," Rene said patiently. "There's no sign of a storm."

"But the clouds—"

His patience fraying ever so slightly, Rene pulled her toward the staircase. "Anne, say good-bye to Mistress Douglas."

Anne dropped a curtsy as she was tugged along. "Good-bye . . ."

"Good-bye, Anne. Good-bye, Lady Madeleine." She said nothing to Rene, but their eyes met briefly, and the coolness was gone from his. So much pain, she thought. Not grief, but pain . . .

"I am not the least bit sleepy," she heard thin, pale Madeleine Faurer insist again, her voice a soft little wisp.

Cat headed for the stables, for Geordie and Douglasdale, for the mourning of her father and sisters. It would seem a welcome relief compared to the tragedy at Langlannoch.

Three

A storm *was* brewing. Geordie saw it as soon as they'd cleared the gates and turned onto the road to Dalmellington, but it wasn't nearly enough to send him back to the home of the Faurers. "He war gone the whole night, ye know," he hissed, glancing back over his shoulder as though he thought perhaps the walls would hear him.

"Who was?"

"That young man. Rode out after I'd already laid myself down—'n' near scared the wits fro' me saddlin' his horse. Came back just at daybreak. Brought me bread 'n' cheese 'n' told me ye 'n' I war leaving. Ye bae bloody right we bae, I tells him."

"Gone all night?" Cat repeated. "But where would he go?"

"Not to midnight Mass, ye may be sure o' that." Geordie spat noisily over the wagon's side. Thick, lofty snowflakes had begun to drift down from the sky. The pounding of the waves on the rocks below the narrow road seemed louder than it had the night before. The water was a strange color, too, Cat noticed—a sort of yellowish gray.

"How far is it to Dalmellington?" she asked.

"Twenty mile."

And more than half of that, she recalled, along this high, treacherous sea road . . . "Perhaps we should turn back, Geordie," she ventured as the snow began to fall more swiftly.

"The hounds o' hell could nae drag me back to that house," Geordie said.

An hour later, they might have. The snow was swirling so thickly that Cat could no longer see the ocean below them; the world was a monochrome white wilderness. The wind had picked up, too, blustering up over the cliff to batter at the wagon wheels and whip Cat's cloak up in waves. "Don't you think we had better stop?" she asked nervously.

"Stop where, lass? I dinna recall any houses between here 'n' Dalmellington, d'ye?"

"We should turn around, then."

"I cannae turn 'round. The road bae too small."

Cat's nervousness turned to fear. "Then what are we to do?"

"There bae naught to do but keep on." He took his eyes from the road for a moment, saw her frightened face. " 'Twill bae all right, lass. I remarked a turnabout on our way in, halfway or so. We can pull in there and wait fer the worst o' it to pass."

Though Cat kept her gaze glued to the wall of rock on her left, she could not find the turnabout. The horses were up to their hocks in snow now, still pulling gamely but gaining little ground. Even Geordie looked worried. "Faith, lass," he murmured, "I should nae hae been sae rash. To set out on my own war one thing, but to bring ye along—"

"It isn't your fault. We were both more than ready to leave."

"Still, I should nae want to face yer father should any harm come to ye."

"We should be safe enough, shouldn't we, once we reach the turnabout?"

"*If* we reach it."

"What do you mean?"

He was clenching and unclenching his fists on the reins, trying to keep some warmth in them. "I cannae tell in this morass how far we hae come. We could still bae far short o' that goal. I bae thinkin'—" There was a sudden jolt; then the wagon took a sickening slide toward the edge of the cliff, making Cat scream and cling to Geordie's sleeve. He let fly the reins, whistling and calling to the horses as they skittered out to the berm: "Gee! Gee! Get on, Jenny, Paint! Pull! Pull, or by Christ, I'll cut yer tails off!" Somehow they gained their footing on the slippery snow and hauled the wagon back from the brink of disaster. Slowly, Cat felt her heart begin beating again.

She'd had enough, though. "Geordie, stop!" she cried. "We cannot go on!"

Through the swirling snow she saw defeat in his eyes. "Aye, lass. I know."

"What will we do?"

He sat and thought, his breath white in the air. "If we unhitch the wagon 'n' turn it about on its side, we can hunker down there wi' the—" He stopped. Cat looked at him, frightened again.

"What is it?"

"I thought I heard—"

And then Cat heard it, too—the sound of bells, coming from behind them. As they both strained to see, a rider appeared, looming up big and black out of the endless white. He drew abreast of them, twisting in the saddle to look down at the marks the wheels had left when they skidded. Cat knew before he pushed back his hood who it must be.

"Mistress Douglas. It appears my mother was right about the storm; pray forgive me. I should not have allowed you to leave," Rene Faurer said.

It didn't matter now; all Cat wanted was to be warm and dry again, and sitting by a fire—even *his* fire. "Believe it or not, I am happy to see you," she said wryly.

"I've brought a saddle for one of the horses; your man can ride him. I'll lead the other, and you can ride with me."

Geordie, faced with rescue by the enemy, was reluctant to admit defeat. "How far to the turnabout?" he asked.

"You haven't come five miles from the house."

"Christ." Without another word, he climbed down and began to unhitch Jenny and Paint.

They put Paint on the lead, and Geordie rode the steadier Jenny, with a rope linking him to Rene's saddle horn; the snow was so heavy now that it would have been all too easy to become separated. Cat insisted on riding astride; sidesaddle was more ladylike, but she felt safer with the pommel between her knees. Rene set out at a pace that was quick enough for her to be nervous, but evidently he knew the road stone for stone. By sticking near the cliffs on the landward side, they were even able to avoid the worst of the wind.

It was strange to be so close to him, within the circle of his arms as he held the reins, and feel the warmth radiating from him at her back. At first she held herself stiffly, but as the road wound on and on she began to sag with weariness despite her best efforts, and leaned into him. He paused once to tuck the edges of his cloak around her, brushing snow from her skirts to do so. Cat blushed as his hands swept over her, and was glad he could not see her face.

And still the storm raged on. "Do you have this sort of snow often?" Cat twisted to ask, thinking how desolate Langlannoch would be if they did.

"Only two or three times as bad as this in my memory."

There was one more question she had to ask: "Why did you come after us?"

"Because I knew you would not make it."

After that there was only the blinding snow and the jolt of the saddle for a long, long time.

Cat thought later that perhaps she had actually slept, tucked tight against him, wrapped in his cloak, but she never was certain. She only knew that one moment the storm was swirling and the next it wasn't; she was being handed down from the horse beneath white-capped eaves, then carried into that lonely house atop the cliffs, past the intricate tapestries and up the stairs. She was eased out of her ice-crusted cape and clothes; there were voices, Anne's, she thought, and others. Naked, she was slipped between Madeleine Faurer's pale embroidered linens. "This is your fault, Rain," she heard Anne say quite clearly, and then her brother's voice, cool and defiant:

"You give me too much credit, Annie. I can't make snow."

Four

She opened her eyes to firelight and a smell, unfamiliar and yet tantalizing, musky, mossy, like tree bark and the earth from deep woods. Someone was holding a poultice to her forehead: Anne, small brow furrowed in worry, perched on the bed with an earthenware bowl at her side.

"Finally." The girl sighed with relief. "I didn't know if you were frozen to the bone or just resting."

Cat tried her voice and found it rusty. "How long have I been sleeping?"

"A day and a half. It is Friday morning."

"Friday . . ." Cat's gaze flew to the windows, which beneath drawn-back drapes showed a deluge of white. "And it *still* is snowing?"

"Aye. Mama says it is the worst storm she ever has seen."

Cat thought back to the treacherous journey. "Geordie—is he safe?"

Anne smiled. "That depends who you're asking. I'd say safe enough, but he seems to think he's in the jaws of Hell. He does, however, enjoy my cooking."

That reminded Cat of the smell she had awakened to. She pushed herself up on the pillows and peered into the earthenware bowl. "What is that?"

"One of Mama's potions. She knows herbs and things."

"You'd best not tell Geordie that. He'll think she is a witch. How is your mother?"

Anne's face turned wan. Cat was reminded that despite all her self-possession, she was only a little girl. "I don't know. Still not herself."

"Mourning takes time. Your servants haven't returned?"

"How could they, with this storm?"

So she had been managing all this house alone. Or, rather— "Does your brother help you to look after her, Anne?"

"Rain does what he can," she said rather defensively. "It is hard for him, too. He has the estates to manage—Papa had land in Strathclyde that the Bruce granted to him. Almost every evening he has business in Ayr. Of course, he hasn't been there lately because of the snow."

"Perhaps you could have someone come to stay with you once it subsides. Just until your mother is better. A relative, a cousin or aunt?"

"There isn't anyone. Mama hadn't anyone left in England. There is Grandpapa in Paris, but he is too old and frail to travel. Nearly eighty years old."

Cat, accustomed to a houseful of kinfolk, could not fathom such a condition. "What about friends?"

"I think Mama would rather not. They would only remind her of Papa."

"Well." Cat clambered down from the bed. "I can spare you the chore of looking after me, at least."

"Are you strong enough to be up?"

"Of course. I wasn't hurt; I was only tired." It was chilly, standing barefoot on the floor. "Where are my clothes?"

"The skirts of your gown were all shredded. Mama said she would fix them, but she hasn't yet. I brought you something of hers." The gown was soft yellow velvet, like butter, like primroses. A color Cat would never have chosen, a shade for black-haired Madeleine, or for Tess, but—"It suits you," Anne said, fastening the sleeves. "Makes your eyes go straight gold, just like Grimkin's. Are you hungry?"

"Aye, but I'll go to the kitchens. No need for you to be carrying a tray."

"I will meet you there, then, after I look in on Mama and tell her you are awake."

Downstairs, the house seemed echoing and empty. Cat won-

dered whether Geordie was still staying in the stables. She made
her way to the kitchens, famished but determined not to add to
Anne's burdens. Surely she could find herself something to eat.
Opening the dairy larder, she saw eggs and milk and cheese and
butter. She had seen Anne cook eggs; it hadn't looked that hard.
She could mix in some cheese. And how did Cook at home make
biscuits? Cat had watched that, too, often enough.

She managed to haul a sack of flour out of the pantry. The
fire had burned down almost to nothing; nibbling on cheese, Cat
stoked it with wood and used the bellows, awkwardly, to blow
up the flame. Then she located two bowls, a huge one for biscuits
and a smaller one for the eggs. Closing her eyes, she tried to
picture the motions Cook went through so effortlessly. She just
scooped out flour, didn't she, and crumbled in lard with her fingertips? Was there lard? Cat couldn't find any, so she used butter—too much butter, evidently, for the mixture didn't look right.
She tossed in some more flour, and then, when it got too stiff,
some milk. That made it too thin, so she went back for another
handful of flour. There would be plenty of biscuits—enough for
everyone in the house.

With the dough ready, she turned to the eggs. How many?
God, she was hungry. Two didn't seem very much, so she pulled
out four, then four more; Anne could always eat some. No doubt
it would seem a treat for her to eat somebody else's cooking. And
children always were hungry . . . Cat took two more from the
cooler, just in case.

Anne had cracked eggs one-handed, carrying on a conversation the whole time. Cat tried to mimic the spare motion the girl
had made against the side of the bowl. Egg slithered down the
front of her borrowed dress. Horrified, she grabbed a cloth to
dab the mess away and found, too late, it was the one she'd wiped
her hands on after mixing the biscuits; flour and butter now
adorned the bodice, too. "Damn," she muttered. There was a
pitcher of water on the sideboard, so she dipped a clean edge of
the cloth in there and rubbed at the stain, which spread slowly
outward but did not disappear.

Well, the dress would have to wait. Cat pushed her hair back
from her face with purposefulness—and, it turned out, a bit of

egg yolk. Then, very slowly and methodically, two-handed, she cracked the eggs into the bowl. Some shell slipped in, and some egg slipped out, but overall, she was quite proud.

Which would take longer to cook, eggs or biscuits? Biscuits, she thought, so she turned the dough out on the table and began to press it with the heels of her hands, just the way Cook did. Only Cook's didn't stick like this—to the wood, to her palms, stretching in great gluey strands between them when she tried to pull free. "Damn," Cat said again. Her hair was in her eyes, but she didn't dare touch it. More flour, she thought, and headed for the sack, trailing strings of dough. What was taking Anne so long? Then again, perhaps it would be best if she didn't arrive until Cat had cleaned up a bit.

Most of the first scoop of flour sifted onto the floor as Cat carried it to the table, so she went back for another, her boots leaving tracks in the powder. Once added, the flour made the dough stiffer but not one whit less sticky. Growing just a tad impatient, she decided to skip the kneading—what was it for, anyway?—and stamp the biscuits out. Trying not to leave handprints on anything more than was necessary, she located the sort of cup Cook used for the task, and a wooden doughboard. But the biscuits didn't drop neatly onto the board from the cup; instead they clung inside, so that she had to fish around with a spoon to try and pull them out. By the time she did, they weren't exactly the handsome circles Cook made, but at least they were ready to bake.

But bake where? For the first time, Cat looked for an oven. At home in Douglasdale, the ovens were built into the bricks above the hearth; here, she found, after a good deal of searching, they were inside the hearth itself, behind latched iron doors. When she reached for one of the latches, she nearly burned her fingers off. "Ouch!" she cried, and added an oath for good measure. She glared at the offending door for a moment, then fetched the cloth she was using to wipe her hands and used it as a shield from the heat. Once the door was opened, she returned triumphantly with the doughboard—only to find that the one she'd chosen was too large, and didn't fit in.

"Oh, damn it to hell!" Cat stomped her foot, then aimed a

kick at Grimkin, who'd come nosing about and was meowing as though in reproach for the chaos in his mistress's kitchens. "That's enough out of you," she warned as the cat scampered away. She found another doughboard, dumped the biscuits onto it—some stuck, but she was tired of fighting—shoved it into the oven, and slammed shut the door with a bang that sent sparks flying. That made her notice that the fire had burned down, so she thrust another log or two onto the coals, gave them a blast from the bellows, and returned to the eggs.

"Cheese," she reminded herself, and crumbled a handful of the tart, creamy stuff into the bowl, then beat the mixture with a spoon. Was it too thick? Too thin? Best to leave well enough alone, she decided, remembering her problems with the biscuit dough. She dumped the eggs into an iron pot, then fished with her spoon at the fireback to find a cleek to hang the pot on. How high should it be? She could already smell the biscuits baking; better hurry the eggs. She set it well down to the coals, so the flames just licked the bottom of the pot. Then, congratulating herself, she went to the keg in the corner and poured herself a tall mug of ale.

After no more than a sip, though, she sniffed the air suspiciously. The biscuits seemed to be cooking awfully quickly. Fetching her cloth, she yanked at the oven latch, but couldn't get it to budge. Meanwhile, steam was rising from the eggs. *I'd better stir them,* she thought, *once I check these bloody biscuits.* But when, after several more yanks, the latch wouldn't budge, she ran for a spoon. The eggs were stuck on the bottom. Too close to the fire, she feared, and tried to raise the cleek. It wouldn't move, either. "What in bloody hell—" She gave it a mighty heave, which resulted in its swinging loose from the fireback, so that the kettle of eggs tipped precipitously toward her. Cat let out a scream and caught the handle of the pot with her spoon. Black smoke had begun to seep from around the edges of the door to the oven. And now Grimkin had returned, to rub against her legs. "Scat!" she hissed, sliding the pot back over the cleek. She had to get that oven open! With sudden inspiration, she grabbed the heavy iron fire poker, wedged it against the latch, and pried. Nothing.

"Come on, you stupid bloody son of a bitch!" Cat grunted, applying more pressure. She felt a little give. Then three things happened in quick succession: the door flew open, letting forth great gusts of smoke; the door hit the cleek, sending the pot sliding off the hook and smack onto the fire, so that sparks and flames jumped into the air; and Grimkin screeched as a spark hit his nose, darting between Cat's legs but catching a claw in the velvet. "Oh!" she cried, caught off-balance, teetering between the fire and the table. She grabbed for the table, missed, and fell with a thud. Grimkin, now tangled in her skirts, clawed his way free by dragging them over her head. Drowning in flour-white, egg-stiff primrose velvet, Cat sat up and pulled her skirts down just in time to see Grimkin jump squarely from the table onto the sack of flour, spewing up a great white cloud that then drifted down lazily over everything around her: floor, table, hearth, bowls, burnt eggs, Grimkin, spoons, hair, dress.

Into the sudden silence that followed, with this interior snow falling just as steadily as the snow beyond the windows, there came the sound of very slow applause. Cat whipped her head about. Rene Faurer was standing in the doorway. "That," he said, "was the most amazing sight I have ever seen."

Beneath the powdery hail, Cat felt herself blush flame-red. Then Anne appeared, ducking past her brother to stare open-mouthed at the spectacle before her. "Cat! What in the world are you doing?"

"Cooking breakfast," Cat said. There was flour on her tongue. She rubbed her mouth with the back of a floury hand.

"But—you told me you couldn't cook."

"I didn't want to be any trouble," Cat told her, and began to laugh.

Anne giggled. "What were you making?"

Through her laughter, Cat assured her: "Something simple."

"Well, thank God for that!" Anne was laughing now, too, helplessly, arms folded over her chest.

Cat pushed herself up from the floor, found the cloth, and reached into the oven to retrieve the biscuits, which were burnt pitch-black. "Care for one? I made plenty."

"Oh, Cat. What is that in the pot?"

"Can't you tell?" Cat fished the kettle from the coals and overturned it on the table. A chunk of crusty coal fell out. "Cheese and eggs."

Anne burst out laughing again.

Cat glanced at Rene. His face was all twisted up, as though he wanted to join in their laughter but didn't know how. His eyes as he looked at his sister burned with so much love that Cat felt a pang in her heart. What would it be like, she wondered, to have him look at *her* that way?

Anne came forward, taking down a broom from the wall. "I hardly know where to start."

"Don't." Cat pulled the broom away from her. "It is my mess. I'll clean it myself."

"Are you daft? Doing it yourself is what caused all this. Besides, you'll have to change your clothes."

Cat looked down in dismay. "I am sorry about the gown."

"It didn't fit Mama anymore anyway, since she's got so thin. Rain will find you something else. Won't you, Rain? Rain?"

But her brother was gone.

Five

"Why do you call him Rain?"

With the kitchen at long last set to rights, Cat and Anne were sitting at the table, sipping a tisane of elder flowers that Madeleine Faurer had made in the spring, when her husband was still living. The sweet scent of the blossoms steeping in hot water was the scent of that season, heady and ripe with possibilities.

Anne pushed the remnants of the breakfast she'd prepared them—sausages, bread, and a raisin pudding—in circles on her plate. "You will laugh. But when I was very small, I thought his name was 'Rainy.' You know. Like the weather. Then I found it wasn't, but it still seemed to suit him."

"Gloomy," Cat said. "Dark." Anne nodded. "But he can't have always been that way."

"For as long as I can remember. Don't get me wrong—I would fight dragons for him. But I wish he could be happy."

"Why is he not?"

Anne pursed her mouth. "Mama says it is just because he takes after Papa. But I think she is wrong. Papa is—Papa *was*—rather grim, too, but only sometimes. When there was a battle coming against the English, or when the pope did something he didn't like. The pope did a *lot* of things Papa didn't like. He and Mama used to fight about the pope all the time. With Rain, though—"

"Yes?" Cat asked, as she stopped.

"The trouble with Rain," the girl said slowly, thoughtfully, "is that he needs a passion."

"A *what?*"

"A passion. Oh, not a lady kind of passion," Anne amended, seeing Cat's surprise. "He has got that—or something, anyway—in old Eleanor. But the sort of passion that makes life worth living. Papa had war for his passion. Truly, he loved it. And Mama has got God. She is so religious, I swear, that sometimes it is more like a convent than a house around here. Nothing can shake Mama's faith."

"She is lucky for that."

"Aye, so she is. She isn't even angry about Papa being killed so far away from home. The Bruce, she says, had made a vow to God to go on crusade, so the vow had to be honored."

"I don't think I would be so understanding."

"No, nor I. But I would have done it for the Bruce. I'd have done anything for the Bruce. He *made* Scotland. If not for him, we'd all be liegemen of the bloody damned English."

Cat hid a smile. It was easy to guess what Anne's passion might be. Her parents may have come here as foreigners, but their little girl was as staunch in her love for the Scots as any Douglas could be.

"Rain, though," Anne went on, "Rain hasn't got a passion. Nothing to live for, much less to die for. And that makes him sad."

Cat pondered this for a moment. Then, "Well, what about Eleanor?" she ventured, hoping her voice didn't betray her antagonism toward the smooth-haired blonde who'd come to Tess's wedding. "Can't the person you love be your passion?"

"No, no," Anne said impatiently. "Look at Mama and Papa. I don't think anyone *ever* loved each other more than they did. But they knew that you need something more. Something that takes you outside of yourself. Something big. Something *grand.*"

Cat frowned. "I'm not at all sure I've got a passion."

"Oh, you must. You're far too wonderful not to. You probably just don't know what it is yet."

"Well, I wish I'd find out," Cat said ruefully.

"Do you know what I wish?" Cat shook her head. Anne glanced toward the doorway, then lowered her voice. "I wish that Rain would fall in love with *you.*"

"That's not likely," Cat said after a moment, hoping her blush wasn't too obvious.

"You never know. You could try to find your passions together." Anne nodded her head, decided. "Yes. That's what I wish."

"What's that, Annie?" asked Rain, appearing in the doorway.

His sister smiled a mysterious smile. "Nothing, Rain. Nothing at all. Excuse me, Cat, won't you? I've got to run and check on Mama now."

Rene watched her go, still lingering by the door. Cat wasn't sure he would come in now that his sister was gone, but he did, going to the keg, pouring himself ale. When he spoke, it was with his back turned to her:

"It was good . . . to see her laugh this morning. I've been worried about her."

"You should be," she told him. "She has too much responsibility here. She is only a child."

"I know that," he said sharply. "But what am I to do? Until the Graysons get back from Troon, there's no help for it."

"I wasn't criticizing. Only making an observation."

"If all you have to observe is matters I'm already aware of, you may as well keep your observations to yourself."

Stung, Cat rose from the bench. "Listen, you. It isn't my choice to be here, you know. I didn't ask you to come after us."

"If I hadn't, you'd be lying dead in a snowdrift."

"Very well. Very well, I am grateful. But the storm isn't my fault. What grudge is it, exactly, that you hold against me?"

"That you came here at all. That you brought those things."

"What would you have had my father do with them?" she demanded, eyes flashing gold fire. "Dump them by the roadside?"

He'd faced her now, coolly sipping ale. "Not a bad suggestion."

"What is the matter with you?" Cat wasn't sure if she was more angry or bewildered. "Your father was a great man, a great hero. The finest soldier in all Scotland—don't you know that?"

"I know he liked to kill people." Cat stared at him. "Do you find that surprising? That is what a soldier does."

"Yes, but—well—not—" Cat's tongue seemed to be moving in several directions at once. "That is part of it, naturally. But—"

"No," he broke in. "That is *all* of it. He killed a lot of other men. Hundreds and hundreds. That is what made him a hero."

Fighting to collect her scattered thoughts, Cat said, "Aye, but he did it for a noble cause. For Scotland."

"He didn't care a hang for Scotland. Did you know he'd been a Templar?" Cat shook her head slowly. She didn't know a lot about the order of warrior-monks outlawed by Pope Clement more than two decades before, but she knew they'd been dangerous men. "That was what brought him to Scotland. The Bruce never published the pope's edict abolishing the order. If it had been Edward of England instead, my father would have fought there."

"You must be wrong," Cat argued. "After all, he stayed here."

"He stayed because he was an outlaw in every other Christian nation," Rene said with exaggerated patience, like a tutor instructing a particularly ignorant pupil. "I suppose he could have gone over to the side of the Moors, but he told me once he didn't like their food."

"God in heaven." Cat felt dizzy on her feet; she slid back onto the bench. "What did he ever do to you to make you so bitter?"

"To me? Nothing. To my mother and Anne—a great deal."

"Rene." Madeleine Faurer had come into the room, with Anne close behind her. "Rene, you are wrong."

He turned on her. "Why don't you admit it, Mother? He was never here anyway; what does it matter he's dead? And now you won't have to live with the fear, the constant agony of wondering whether this will be the campaign on which an arrow finds him, or an axe or sword. He—"

"I did not worry about him."

Rene snorted. "You didn't."

"No! He was in God's hands."

"Was he in God's hands on those nights when I would hear you pacing your rooms, then, unable to sleep?"

Two spots of color showed in Madeleine's pallid face, one high on each sharp-etched cheekbone. "There are some matters between a man and wife, Rene, which you cannot understand. By the grace of God, you will someday."

"Matters such as what? Neglect? Abandonment?"

"Stop it, Rain!" Anne cried out, clinging to her mother. "Don't talk of Papa that way!"

"You could count on your two hands, Anne, the months your beloved Papa spent with you in your lifetime."

"Shut up, Rain!" his sister shrieked, and burst into tears.

"That is enough, Rene." His mother's voice was frail but steady.

"I'm not finished."

"You are." They glared at one another. Then, without another word, he left them; they could hear his angry footsteps all the way to the top of the stairs.

Madeleine hugged Anne close, smoothing her tangled black hair. "What is wrong with Rain, Mama?" the girl asked plaintively, rubbing away her tears.

Her mother had a faraway look in her eyes. "He is more like your father than even he knows, Anne. That is what is 'wrong' with him." She gave the girl another squeeze. "I have lost my good shears, pet. I thought they were in my big basket, but they are not. Could you look for them for me? I may have left them in the solarium, or perhaps in the parlor upstairs." Anne sniffed and nodded. "There's my good girl. And don't be angry with your brother. We all have different ways of showing our grief."

When Anne had trotted off, Madeleine sat across from Cat and let out a wisp of a sigh. "You are seeing all my family's soiled linen, it seems."

"I am sorry," Cat said softly. "I fear much of it is my fault. If I hadn't come with that armor—"

"No, no, child. You were kind to come as you did. My son's disquiet began long before you got here. But I wish—" She sighed again. "It is hard to know what to do for him. I never have understood men."

"Except your husband, surely."

The woman laughed. "Lord, him least of all! He was an utter mystery to me. What was God thinking of, to make such a perplexing creature?"

"My father told me you and your husband had one of the great loves of his time," Cat said shyly.

Madeleine Faurer looked pleased. "Did he? That means much, coming from a Douglas. Your people are no strangers to passion, are they?"

"That is a polite way of putting it." Cat looked at her hostess. She seemed less wraithlike, more substantial than she had since Cat's arrival. Did speaking of her loss help or hurt? "What was he like, your husband?" she asked, ready to change the topic if it proved painful.

"Michel? Rene looks much like him." She smiled. "But that, perhaps, is not what you mean. He was not young when I met him. And his anger—" She shook her head, remembering. "His anger then makes Rene's seem paltry."

"Anger at whom?"

"God. The world. Himself. He was a Templar. You knew that?" Cat nodded. "And the pope had outlawed them, all of them. After they had spent their entire lives fighting for the Church in the Holy Land. It was a terrible tragedy. For a long time, he lost his faith. But he found it again. That gives me hope, you see, for Rene." She spread her thin, lovely hands, so adept with the needle, as though longing to stitch her son's future neatly together. "But I wish Michel were here to help me with him. I wish that every day." She raised her green eyes to Cat. "Michel always said it was strong love that saved him. Perhaps Rene—"

"Perhaps Rain what, Mama?" Anne asked, bouncing in. "I couldn't find your shears. I looked *everywhere.*"

Madeleine felt the front bodice of her gown. "Do you know, I think I have got them right here around my neck. How embarrassing, darling; I'm so sorry."

"That's all right. Perhaps Rain what?"

"Oh! Perhaps he will join us for supper. I believe I feel up to cooking again."

"Do you, Mama? Splendid! Cat and I will help. Won't we, Cat?"

Cat nodded, her mind still on the entreaty Madeleine Faurer had left unspoken. *Perhaps Rene . . .*

She'd been asking Cat to save her son.

* * *

The next night, the snow stopped. Cat was doing the last of the washing up from the fine meal—venison in a sour cherry sauce, braised fennel root, biscuits the way they were meant to be made—that Madeleine had prepared, when an unfamiliar light streamed across her gown: that of the moon, high and bright, three-quarters full and waxing. It cast a neat quilt of black-lined squares across the stone floor as it poured through the leaded casements. Cat stood alone—Madeleine and Anne had gone on to bed—with a towel in her hands and let it drench her, that soft white glow, absent for so long. It wasn't enough; three days of storm had left her light-bereft. She pushed open the door where Rene had cleared a path to the barns. The air was breath-stopping cold, the sky clear black and bleeding stars.

She walked halfway down the path through the buried kitchen garden, snow blown up in great drifts all around her; it was, she thought, like walking on the pocked face of that fat moon would be. To be outdoors again after so long, even in that bitter cold, was revivifying. She hadn't realized what a toll these days of gloom and darkness had taken on her soul. Stretching her hands to the star-scarred sky, she turned in a slow circle, her skirts skimming over the hard-crusted snow.

"I beg your pardon; am I interrupting some pagan ritual?"

Cat stopped in mid-circle, seeing Rene coming down the path from the house, dressed in riding gear, a pack slung over his shoulder. He had joined them for supper again, at his mother's request, but had said little, and left before the sweet was served. "Where are you going?" she asked in surprise.

"To Ayr. On business."

"In the middle of the night?"

"A meeting with my father's solicitor. I was to have been there a week ago." He frowned. "But why am I explaining to you?"

"Lord, I don't know. Common civility, perhaps?"

He arched that brow, the right one, so that it made a steep peak. His eyes were indigo in the moonlight. "My, my. Are all the Douglas girls so tart-tongued?"

"Oh, no. My sister Jessie always thinks the best of everyone. She's a bit of a fool."

"I should say. So long as we are playing question-and-answer, what were *you* doing?"

"As you said—a little heathen incantation. To raise the spirits of the dead." Aghast, Cat bit her tongue. Meaning only to be flippant, she *had* raised a specter: that of his father. "I'm sorry. I should not have said that. How thoughtless of me."

"Not nearly so thoughtless as bringing back the bastard would be." He ran his blue eyes over her, from head to toe. "The moonlight suits you. Tones you down a bit."

Makes me more pallid, he means, Cat thought bitterly, *like that whey-haired Eleanor* . . . "I wasn't aware I needed toning down."

"It's your hair. It looks sometimes as though it would scorch a man to touch it." He'd put out a hand toward the wayward curls her washing up had loosened; now he drew it back.

"No one's been burned yet," Cat said, a little breathless at his words.

"You are young still. There will be." He shifted his pack. "I must be off."

She tasted disappointment on her tongue, sharp as a nail. Fool that she was, she'd thought he meant to kiss her. The chagrin made her curt. "Do you think it wise to leave your mother and sister alone like that?"

"They're not alone. You and that invaluable fellow Geordie are here. And I'm beginning to think, Cat Douglas, you could hold your own against Edward of England." It was then he kissed her: swiftly, skewedly, a brush of a kiss as he passed, that caught her on the edge of her mouth, which was opening in surprise, and then glanced off into the frigid air. As though he were a lodestone, she spun about, her mouth following him. *God,* she thought, *I must look like a fish trailing a lure.* She could not help herself, though; that kiss had been sweet as honeycomb, and she wanted more.

But he was walking away, looking over his shoulder. "Geordie, though—I would not count on Geordie to defend a duck against a dog. Mind you look to your back if he's there. Good night!" He waved. Cat, fighting hard, had stopped following. "I'll be back by daybreak. But please, *please*—don't you make breakfast for me."

The next morning, with the sun glinting off the snow, Geordie announced he was leaving. He came to Cat as she breakfasted in the dining hall, with the Faurers. "I hae o'erstayed two days too long as it bae, lass," he told Cat grimly. "Yer father will bae sick with worry fer ye."

"You'll never make it," Rene said, munching toast. "The drifts will be twenty feet high on the sea road."

"I'll up to Ayr, then, 'n' around by the inland roads. Ye made it to Ayr 'n' back quick enough, dinna ye?"

"When did you go to Ayr?" Madeleine asked her son, astonished.

"Last night. I wanted to see whether it could be done."

"Don't you think you might have told me?"

"I told Geordie. I told Mistress Douglas, too."

"I see." But she still sounded aggrieved.

"If the road from Ayr bae bad," Geordie went on doggedly, not about to be distracted, "ye can put up wi' yer cousin Will 'n' his wife there, and I'll on to Douglasdale to soothe yer poor father."

Cat's heart was sinking. *But just last night,* she wanted to shout at Geordie, *he kissed me! How can you make me leave now?*

Damnably, though, he was right. Archibald would be frantic, even if he'd got word of the storm and figured rightly that she'd stayed on at Langlannoch. It was time to be going. There was no possible excuse for staying any longer. "That's the best plan," she agreed.

"Oh, Cat, don't go!" Anne cried. She sounded truly disconsolate.

"I really must. I'd no intention of staying this long." Cat smiled at the girl. "And after all, I cannot go on wearing your mother's clothes."

"Why not? She's got dozens and dozens of gowns. She's got so many gowns that she—"

"Anne," her mother broke in gently, "that's enough, now."

"But what will I do? There will be nothing to do!"

"Christmas is coming in only three weeks," Madeleine reminded her. "And after that, the New Year."

"Who cares?"

"There will be company in the house. Your father's friends—"

"A bunch of old soldiers," Anne declared, lower lip trembling. "All they will want to do is talk about war, and that will remind me of Papa, and I will be sad."

"If you cannot control yourself, Annie," her brother said, not unkindly, "perhaps you should go up to your room."

"I want Cat to stay!"

Madeleine looked to Cat with a small, apologetic shrug. Then her green eyes turned thoughtful. "The Graysons will be back no later than tomorrow, I'll wager. Mrs. Grayson says her sister doesn't wear well on her. She'll be frantic to be home. I don't suppose . . ."

"What, Mama? What?"

"Well—I only thought, poor Cat hasn't had much leisure while she has been here. She's been so busy helping out and washing up—"

"I haven't minded a bit," Cat said honestly.

"Bless you, Cat, I know you haven't. But I feel we have taken advantage of your good nature. If you would want to stay on through the holidays—"

"Oh, Cat, do!"

"I can promise you that Mrs. Grayson's cooking is splendid—"

"So it is, Cat!"

"And if the snow ever melts, I could show you my gardens. There's quite a lot to see even in winter."

"And we could ride horses!" Anne burbled. "And decorate the house, all of us together, with holly and mistletoe! And Mrs. Grayson will bake queen pudding with the tokens in it. And Rain will shoot a boar for Christmas supper, won't you, Rain?"

"I very much doubt Mistress Douglas will want to be away

from her family for Christmas. After all, they, too, have suffered a loss."

"Of course," Madeleine said quickly. "I only thought—I wanted her to know she was welcome to stay, should she care to. You have helped us all so much already, Cat. I should not have said anything."

"Why not? She's *got* to stay," said Anne.

Geordie was looking apoplectic. "Yer father," he began, and launched into a dire prediction of how displeased Archibald would be if Cat even considered such a thing.

Cat didn't hear him. She was watching Rene, studying his face for a clue. What did *he* want? For her to stay, surely; after all, he'd kissed her. But his blue eyes were utterly inscrutable as he met her gaze.

Perhaps that kiss had been nothing more than a moment's fancy, brought on by the moonlight that had set her dancing. Perhaps—worse—in that moonlit madness she had only imagined it, dreamed it. For if it had been real, wouldn't he show her now, send her some sign?

"Stay, stay, stay," Anne was urgently chanting. Geordie had wound down his tirade and was simply glaring, leaving Madeleine to murmur gentle disclaimers:

"I certainly wouldn't want to anger Archibald, Cat, dear . . . I didn't mean to impose. . . ."

Why did Cat have the feeling the decision she was on the verge of making was as momentous as any she would face in her life? Again she searched Rene Faurer's impossibly handsome face, praying for a sign, any sign, even one of displeasure, to guide her choice. He looked back without a flicker of emotion.

And that, thought Cat, ought to be sign enough for any girl.

Thus it was with some astonishment that she found when she opened her mouth what came out was, "I'd be glad to stay."

"Hooray!" cried Anne, and jumped up to hug her. Madeleine looked relieved, but Rene's expression never changed.

"Will ye excuse us?" Geordie said between gritted teeth, and yanked her into the front hall.

"Ouch! You are hurting my arm." Cat tried to twist away, but he held on tightly.

"I wuld like to break it. Wha' the devil d'ye think ye bae doin'?"

"I've accepted Lady Madeleine's very kind invitation to join her for the holidays."

"Don't feed me that shite, lassie; I've known ye since ye sucked teat. Ye bae headstrong and willful, and that bae where this comes fro'. Ye bae stayin' because o' that boy."

"He's not a boy, he's a—"

"Boy I say, fer boy he bae! I'll nae call him a man afore he learns some manners. Dinna ye hear the kick in the teeth he gave to yer father at yer sister's wedding? To yer father, to Scotland, to the blood o' the Bruce—"

"Hush, Geordie, they'll hear you!"

"Who gives a sheep's damn wot they hear? Yer father sent me wi' ye fer protection. Well, it bae long past time I started protectin'. I will nae leave ye here in this house with that cad."

"Geordie, he saved your life—saved both our lives!"

" 'N' I hae thanked him fer it; so hae ye. Ye need nae be raisin' up yer skirts in gratitude, Cat Douglas!"

Cat slapped him, hard, her eyes glinting straight gold. "Geordie Willis, you forget your place."

"As ye forget yers. Ye bae a Douglas, lass! And the Douglases hae got nae truckle wi' traitors." The look in Geordie's eye was equally fiery. "Ye'll bae comin' wi' me."

It was the wrong tack. All her life, nothing had set Cat's mind faster than opposition. She tossed her red-gilt curls. "I said that I was staying. I intend to stay."

Geordie stood, still stubborn, but bested. What more could he do, short of hauling her away bodily? And she was the laird's daughter, more the rue. "I'll leave it to yer father, then, to fix yer wagon," he said darkly. "He'll hae nae more taste than I fer yer shenanigans."

"I'm sure Papa would never fault me for putting myself out a bit to comfort a bereaved widow," Cat said loftily.

He snorted. "Keep it up, lass, 'n' ye'll talk yerself straight into the condition yer mother did. I only hope fer yer sake that ye ken: wot Archibald Douglas found fetchin' in a light-o'-love, he will not conscience fro' his daughter. As ye love yer father, mind ye dinna put him to shame."

Though Cat hated to admit it, his words gave her pause. But by the time she rejoined the Faurers in the dining hall, her head was held high. After all, she'd done nothing wrong, and she didn't intend to. If Geordie had his thoughts in the gutter, well, too bad for him.

"He was just a bit concerned about my father," she announced, to explain Geordie's ire. "But we've talked it over, and everything is going to be fine. I'll write a note for him to give to Papa." It was then she noticed the peculiar expression on Anne's small face. She was looking up at her brother with something very akin to despair.

"I'm so glad," Rene Faurer said smoothly. "I've just been telling Mother and Anne that I invited Eleanor to join us for Christmas. It should be very cozy, don't you think, with all of us here?"

Six

It had been a mistake, a terrible mistake, to remain at Langlannoch. Cat had known that from the moment Rene announced that Eleanor de Baliol was coming, but what could she say? To back away when she'd only just agreed to stay on would have been humiliatingly transparent. Perhaps she could have based her change of heart on political considerations. But no—Rene would have seen through that. After all, she'd had no problem remaining at the house with *him,* and he'd never made any pretense as to where his allegiance lay.

The fact of it was, she was trapped. She hadn't listened to Geordie—who, she recalled in retrospect, had always shown uncommon good sense—and now she was stuck, skewered like a Christmas boar roasting on a spit. Eleanor de Baliol! The memory of that smooth-haired, acid-tongued beauty made her cold palms sweat. They'd have come to blows at Tess's wedding if Cat's sisters hadn't restrained her. What might happen here, when Cat was on her own?

The pity of it was that the prospect of her rival's arrival had managed to spoil some simply splendid times with Rene and Anne. One morning they'd gone riding, with all the land around them still in the deep snow's thrall. High into the hills they went, stopping atop a crest crowned with pines. All around them, the land fell away in great waves of white; their breath was white, too, and when the horses were still, there came a sudden swell of silence, so dead and utter and perfect that Cat thought for a moment she would cry. Her gaze met Rene's, and his eyes were shining as she knew her own must be. Then Anne shattered the

peace with a snowball scooped from the pine boughs that hit her
brother square in the chest; he yelped and returned the favor,
lobbing one at her. Cat joined in, and soon instead of pristine
white silence there were challenges and screams and squeals,
while the smooth snow was trampled into mush by the horses'
hooves.

Then one evening, Madeleine had been reading aloud in the
kitchens, by the hearth. All of them were listening—the six
Graysons, Anne, Rene. It was a book of Italian love poems, of
all things. Madeleine was reading slowly, translating as she went,
when she sounded out a line that went,

> Caught as I am in the trammels of thy bright hair . . .

Involuntarily Cat glanced at Rene, remembering what he had
said about her scorching curls on the night he'd kissed her, and
saw that he was sitting back in his chair, arms folded over his
chest, looking steadily at her. He smiled. Madeleine read on, but
Cat's heart stood still.

There had been half a dozen such moments—not enough to
make a feast of, but nibbles that kept her famished for more. It
was courtship at a glacial pace—if courtship it was—advancing
by fractions of inches. And on the morrow it would end, for on
the morrow Eleanor arrived.

Someone knocked on the door of her room. "Come in!" Cat
called. It was Sharon Grayson, one of the daughters-in-law, a
round-faced, friendly girl, a few years older than Cat, who was
four months along with her and her husband Dugald's first child.
Her report on the family's extended visit in Troon to Missus
Grayson's sister, confided to Cat in private, had made her howl
with laughter. "Laird in heaven, there bae nothin' like a long
snowstorm," Sharon had summed up, "to make ye see the heart
o' a person. 'N' I bae here t' tell ye, had that snow lasted one day
more, ye'd hae seen Mum's heart 'n' her sister's lyin' red on the
drifts, fer them two would hae torn each other limb from limb."

"Ready fer me to tidy up, Miss, or should I come back later?"
Sharon asked now, feather duster and oiled cloth in hand.

"Now is fine," Cat told her. "I wasn't doing anything, really.

Actually, I was. I was wondering about New Year's gifts. I should like to get something for Anne, and for Lady Madeleine too. Have you any ideas?"

"Ach, surely just havin' ye here to cheer 'em bae gift enough," Sharon said, applying her duster with cheerful zeal. "Still, if ye bae set on it, there bae a shop or two in Ayr with nice things—little toys 'n' wha'not, such as bairns like. Though, truth to tell, Mistress Anne sets little store by such stuff."

"Still, I might find something." The notion of a trip to town was appealing. "How far off is Ayr?"

"Eight or ten miles up the sea road." Sharon pursed her mouth. "Ye could wait 'n' go wi' Young Master on his evenin' journey. By that time, though, the shops would bae closed."

"I'm sure he doesn't want to be bothered by me, anyway, when he is on his way to do business with his solicitor," Cat agreed.

"Solicitor!" Sharon looked at her and laughed. "Solicitor? Well, there bae a new name fer it!"

"For what?"

But Sharon evidently regretted her outburst, for she shook her head. "Never mind, then."

"Never mind *what?* Why did you laugh?"

"Fer nae reason at all."

"He told me he had business in Ayr since his father's death," Cat said doggedly. "Anne told me the same thing."

"Well, if he says it bae a solicitor he sees, then surely it must bae."

Cat was certain there was more to this than Sharon was telling, but the maid had gone tight-lipped; not one word more could she get out of her on the subject. The mystery, if that's what it was, crystalized her decision: she would go to Ayr.

Dugald rode out with her for the first five miles or so, but then she sent him home, insisting there was work enough at Langlannoch for him without taking time to chaperone her. The road was clear; by now most of the snow had melted, and the day was warm enough, with a light sea breeze, to leave one's hood down.

She reached the town an hour past noon by the church bell, and was surprised to see how bustling a place it was. It had a royal charter, for the Bruce's red-and-gold lion flew from the

ramparts of the bridge that ran across the River Ayr. Several
white-sailed ships lay at anchor in the fine curved harbor; there
was a small, squarish castle within the walls, and a whole row
of shops running along the narrow road leading from it to the
quays.

She bought a farthing's worth of roast chestnuts from a one-
armed man, who scooped them adeptly from atop the hot coals
with a funnel of paper. "Bannockburn?" she guessed, nodding
at the stump that stuck out from his shoulder, and he grinned and
shook his head:

"Nae, pet, Antrim Hill. But I war at the Bannockburn, ready
to give this 'un, too, if he'd hae need o' it." There was no cause
for him to say who "he" was; any Scot knew it had been the
Bruce that men made such sacrifices for.

"God bless and keep you," Cat said softly.

" 'N' a happy Christmas t' ye, pet. Mind ye dinna burn yer
tongue!"

Cat heeded the caution; the nuts were so hot she could feel
them through her gloves despite the cone of paper. She juggled
them from hand to hand as she walked, leading the little roan
mare she had borrowed from Madeleine. She felt carefree and
jaunty, strolling along with gold in her purse and the day to herself. Anne had begged to come with her, but Cat promised her
another visit; this one, she'd said with a wink, she had to make
alone.

Her good spirits flew even higher when she found a perfect
gift for Madeleine straight away: a little silver comb set with
malachites that were just the deep green of her hostess's eyes.
But after that, her luck turned: though she searched and searched,
she saw nothing that she thought would catch Anne's fancy. Oh,
there were plenty of geegaws and trinkets, and she hesitated for
long minutes over a cunning little painted horse. But she realized
that Sharon had been right: Anne, self-contained little thing that
she was, hadn't much use for toys. This would be a difficult
holiday for the girl, the first without her father, and Cat wished
she could find something that would help ease Anne's loss.

She thought back to the first New Year's after her own mother's
death, when she had been Anne's age. Archibald had given her

a wonderful gift: the leather apron Marguerite had worn while working at the Crown of Feathers, still stiff with spilled ale and strong, peaty *uisquebaugh,* and smelling so much like her mama that she'd slept with it for months on end. That was what she longed to find for Anne: a memory of her father. But how could she, when Cat knew so little of the man?

At an impasse, she turned her thoughts to Rene. Should she buy him something, or was that too forward? If he gave her nothing in return, she would be embarrassed. But if he had got her a gift and she had none for him, perhaps he would think she didn't care for him, and she didn't want that. She'd get him something safe, something small and noncommittal, she decided. Something like—

Lemon drops. They shone like little buttons of sunshine in the window of the apothecary shop. "Are they good and sour?" she asked the man inside.

"Tart eno' t' pickle yer lips," was the answer. So she bought half a pound, and then some candied apricots for Sharon, who, she knew, was craving fruit in her pregnancy.

But that still left Anne. Cat hurried her steps; night would come soon, and she did not want to negotiate the sea road in darkness. *A memory,* she thought, *I need a memory.* And then, passing a stationer's shop where some gorgeous marbled parchments were displayed, an idea for the perfect present came to her in a flash.

With all her purchases made, she looked about for a place to buy something warm to eat to start her on her journey: a meat pasty, perhaps. There was a likely-looking inn at the end of the lane leading up to the seawall, so she started there. She was about to enter the place—the sign said it was the Speckled Fawn—when she felt a restraining hand on her arm. "Mum," said a voice, "I wuld nae gae in there."

She turned. It was the chestnut seller, a peculiar expression on his timeworn face. "I beg your pardon?" she said in surprise.

"There'd bae nae way fer ye t' know it," he mumbled, "since ye bae nae fro' these parts. But ye cannae gae in there."

"I only wanted something warm to eat," Cat told him, perplexed. "Isn't it a tavern?"

"Aye—it bae a tavern o' sorts, but nae sort fer a lady. There bae a stall just there, where the Dyers Road crosses—" He pointed with his one hand. "Ye can buy yerself a tasty bite there."

"Well. Thank you very much." Cat cast one last glance at the sign—a tavern of sorts?—and then started back down the lane. She turned around once, halfway to the crossing, and saw that the one-armed man hadn't moved; he was waiting there with his cart as though to be certain she would take his advice.

She had a sausage roll from the stall. It was delicious, but too big to eat all at once, so she folded half of it up in the paper the chestnuts had come in and tucked it into her saddlebag. *I really must be going,* she thought; the sun was already nearly at the horizon. She mounted the mare and had just leaned over to check the girth when she heard rapid hoofbeats coming. Quickly she led the horse in under an eave—such very narrow streets!—adjusted the strap, and straightened up again just in time to see Rene Faurer ride past.

She was so surprised that it took her a moment to find her tongue; by that time, he was out of earshot, clattering on down the lane. He hadn't seen her, Cat was sure; he'd been intent on wherever he was riding to. She rode out into the lane and watched. He stopped at the end, beneath the sign for the Speckled Fawn.

Well, no reason why he shouldn't meet his solicitor at a tavern—even a tavern *of sorts,* whatever that meant. *Leave it be, Cat,* she told herself, but knew she wouldn't. She never had been able to restrain her curiosity. And so long as the chestnut seller was gone—

She urged the mare up the lane and tethered her to a post a few yards short of her goal.

Her first thought was to peek in a window, but they were all tight-shuttered. So she took a breath and strode straight up to the door. From beyond it she heard tavern sounds, familiar sounds, ones she'd been raised to: laughter, song, the clink of ale mugs against wood. The chestnut man must have been some sort of fanatic, she thought briefly, to steer her away. But just to make certain—she pulled at the door. It opened smoothly, silently.

How many women there are, she thought with some surprise, staring into the dimness within. And then, How very little they've got on . . . that one there, the dark-haired one, was in nothing but her pettiskirts. And she was sitting on a man's lap, her bare arm draped around his shoulders very comfortably. As a matter of fact, most of the women seemed to be in laps, or balanced on the knees of men who were playing cards or throwing dice.

Oh, Cat, you dimwit, it is a brothel! she told herself with a shock of recognition. With half her heart she wanted to slam the door shut; the other half couldn't bear to look away from those languid, half-naked women, with their farded lips and cheeks and wild, loose hair.

Then she spotted Rene. He was dead in the center of the room, his face in profile. There were *two* women with him, one on either knee as he sprawled in a low chair. He had a drink in his hand; his head was thrown back, and he was laughing. She'd never seen him look so carefree and at ease.

Someone handed him the dice cup. The woman on his left knee, a tall, lithe brunette, kissed him full on the mouth as he shook it. *Perhaps she's the solicitor,* Cat thought darkly; *she is certainly soliciting something, the way her breasts are about to fall out of her gown. If you could call that a gown.* She felt her cheeks burning. More than anything else, she hated being made a fool of. How could he lie to her, and to his sister and mother, and have them all sorry for him for making all those trips to Ayr when the whole time he was holed up in a whorehouse? It was absolutely despicable of him.

And yet . . . he looks so happy, Cat thought, and more than angry, she was hurt—hurt that she had never brought that unrestrained laughter to his sculpted lips, made his indigo eyes glow with such pleasure. She watched him for a moment longer, hiding, craven and silent, behind the polished door. His luck was good; when he spilled out the dice, the women clapped prettily and lavished him with kisses and hugs. She would never in her life have believed it was Anne's grim, moody Rain who returned their caresses, whispering in their ears.

Well, the chestnut man was right, she thought. *I ought not to have come here.*

She closed the door and slipped off into the gathering twilight, haunted all the way back to Langlannoch by the echo of his laughter ringing in her head.

Seven

Eleanor de Baliol arrived for her visit in a cloud of fluffy ermine white as the snow still crusted the land. She rode a fine dainty Arab that must, Cat thought enviously, have been worth four times what her own pretty palfrey back in Douglasdale had cost. Trailing far enough behind her not to spoil the impression she made cantering toward the house were three servants, their mules so burdened with parcels and bundles and baggage that they looked like small mountains moving across the landscape.

"Oh," Anne sighed when she glimpsed the procession from her bedchamber window. "I was so hoping . . ."

"What?" Cat pressed when the girl's voice trailed off.

"Well . . . it is horrid of me, I know, but I hoped she wouldn't come."

Cat watched with her heart in her throat as Rene came out to the courtyard to greet the guest, lifting her down from the Arab. Eleanor's ermine-clad arms slid around his neck; they kissed, and the girl whispered something into his ear. "She is an old friend of the family, I suppose?" she ventured.

"Lord, no! Papa never would have let a de Baliol in the door. No, Rain met her in Paris, and when she came here with him last fall—well, you know Mama; she was too kind to turn her away. Though I daresay if she'd known then all the trouble Eleanor would prove to be—"

"What sort of trouble?" Cat broke in, and then realized that she sounded far too anxious for information.

"Oh, you know the sort. She lorded it over the servants, which is something the Graysons aren't used to. Sharon came near to walking out over it all; Mama had to beg her to stay. And the food wasn't to her liking—too plain, she said, and then I said, If you don't like it, why don't you go back to Paris? And Mama got cross and made me apologize, when I thought *she* was the one being rude. I still think so. And then Rain was so strange around her." She laughed. "Well, Rain is strange anyway, I suppose, but . . ."

"Strange how? With her around, I mean."

Grimkin had hopped onto the windowsill; Anne scratched the cat's ears, making him purr. "Well, sometimes he was nice to her, awfully nice. And then sometimes he'd be perfectly wretched."

Cat's heart sank down again, like a stone. That sounded like the behavior of someone in love. In fact, hadn't Tess told her that was how she'd won Gill, by being perverse?

"I think," said Anne, ruffling Grimkin so vigorously that he mewled in protest and leaped down, "I think she wants to marry him."

"Do you?"

"Yes, I do. I wouldn't mind, you know, if I thought it was because she loves him. But I don't. I don't think so at all. I don't think she loves anyone but herself."

"Then why *would* she want to marry him?"

"For his money, of course."

Cat glanced about Anne's rooms. Like the rest of Langlannoch, they were handsome but by no means lavish. Anne saw the puzzlement on her face. "Oh, Papa wasn't rich," the little girl explained. "I don't think he even cared about money—probably because he was a monk for so long. But his father is a grand *seigneur* in France. And Mama would have inherited a lot of land in England, in Devonshire, except that she married Papa. It is all under attainder now. Rain couldn't claim it unless—"

She stopped, but Cat finished the thought readily enough: unless the de Baliols, Edward of England's allies, were in power instead of little King David.

The information certainly shed new light on Rene Faurer's motivations. Money, Cat thought with dismay. The lowest of all spurs to treachery.

Anne was gnawing on a fingernail, looking stricken. "Oh," she said again, "I *do* wish she hadn't come."

Cat tugged the girl's hand away from her mouth and held it tightly. "Stop that; it's a terrible habit. I know because I do it myself. If you want a treat, come along downstairs and watch her face when she sees I am here."

It was Christmas Eve, and the household's other guests had already arrived. The priest, Father Joseph, who'd performed Tess and Gill's wedding, was there; Cat knew him well, but had never realized he was the Faurer family's friend. Several of Anne's father's old companions-in-arms had come. One, named Tomas, a grizzled, cheerful man who kept a tavern in Oban, had known Cat's mother a little. Another was Brant, who had a wife years younger than he, and three children not much older than Anne. It was nice of them to have come, Cat thought, to keep Anne company. The last guest was the most unusual. His name was Guillaume; originally from France, and a Templar, like Michel and the others, he'd had his tongue cut out by the Inquisition when the members of the order were arrested. He hadn't let the mutilation defeat him, though; he'd married a Scotswoman who had lost her hearing as a girl in a bout of fever. The couple communicated with grunts and motions of their hands, aided in dealing with the outside world by their two strapping sons, Anton and Stefan, who could hear and speak perfectly and were just a few years older than Cat. She admired them immensely, for their good humor, for the robust love they showed their mother and father, for their lack of self-pity. Theirs, she thought, could not have been an easy life. It was something to dwell on when she got to feeling sorry for herself.

Cat and Anne found the whole group assembled in the front hall when they got downstairs. Madeleine looked a bit nervous at the notion of introducing this de Baliol anomaly into their midst. But Eleanor did not notice; she swept through the doors, her arm in Rene's, all aburst with smiles and kisses for her hostess. Then, shrugging off her ermine cloak into the hands of a scowling Grayson to reveal a dainty riding habit in a gorgeous shade of sky-blue velvet, she scanned the room.

"Annie!" she called throatily. "Where's my little Annie?"

Anne left Cat's side as though she was going to meet the executioner, but submitted to Eleanor's coos and kisses and remarks about how much she'd grown "just in two months!" with good grace. Cat told herself firmly that if a six-year-old could hide her feelings that well, so could she.

Of course, she hadn't reckoned that Eleanor, upon being led 'round the room by Madeleine for introductions, would stop dead upon seeing her and say, in the sort of tone that might be used by someone who had just found a large insect in her portmanteau, "My God. What is *she* doing here?"

Before Cat could think of what to respond, Rene was at the blonde's side, saying smoothly, "Mistress Douglas has been acting as a sort of companion for Anne for the past month or so."

You bastard, thought Cat. *What about the times that we have spent together? What about that kiss you gave me?*

"Really? As a governess?" Eleanor tittered as though the notion was preposterous.

"Nothing so official as that," Rene told her.

"Well, thank heavens. I know you Scots have some peculiar ideas about education, but honestly!"

Cat balled her hands into fists in the folds of her gown—the yellow one that Madeleine had lent her, spotless now. Remember, you are a guest in this house, she told herself. "I'm here," she said, "as a friend. What brings *you?*"

"Why, the chance to spend the holidays with dear little Annie, and Rene's mother, and, of course, Rene." She tucked her arm through his with easy intimacy. Cat looked up at him and saw satisfaction in his blue eyes. It was infuriating. *He is enjoying this, the son of a bitch,* she realized. *He is taunting me. Nothing would please him more than for me to lose my temper now. Well, by God, I won't do it, then, just to spite him!*

"What a lovely riding habit that is," she told Eleanor, and saw the girl's face register wary surprise, as though waiting for the insult she expected to follow—that surely would have followed had the compliment giver been she. But Cat said nothing more, simply smiled. In the moment of silence that stretched, she heard the odd burbling sound that meant Guillaume was laughing.

"Th-thank you," Eleanor said at last. "I had it made in Paris, of course. Your gown looks familiar to me somehow, though I can't think why."

"How very observant of you. It is one of Lady Madeleine's; she was kind enough to lend it to me after Rene found me in the snowstorm. I hadn't got a stitch of clothes."

It was not precisely an accurate statement. But the carefully worded half-truth was worth it, for the chance of seeing Eleanor de Baliol's elegant jaw drop open wide. *"What?"* she said in a sort of screech, turning to the man whose arm she was holding so possessively.

"It *is* nice to see you again, Eleanor," Cat said warmly. "Merry Christmas." Then she walked across the room toward Anne, who was giggling with unabashed delight.

"I guess you showed *her*, Cat!" the girl whispered. Father Joseph was grinning at Cat; the broad shoulders of Missus Grayson, who was carrying in cups of hot spiced cider, were shaking so with silent laughter that she had to set down her tray.

But though she hated to admit it, most gratifying to Cat had been the sudden gleam of unmistakable, bemused admiration that had glinted in Rene's gentian-blue eyes.

"As if I dinna hae better things to do wi' my time than press out her gowns," Sharon Grayson said darkly, running her feather duster over Cat's bedposts with ill-disguised vengeance. "Got three servants o' her own she dragged here from whatever corner of Hell she war in last—"

Cat stifled a laugh. "Sharon, you mustn't say such things!"

" 'N' why nae?" the maid demanded, hands on her hips as she faced Cat. "Says worse than that about me, dinna she, the moment my back's turned? Tellin' Mistress I bae lazy 'n' cheeky—"

"Oh, Sharon. She didn't!"

"She did! 'N' all because I would nae bend down to wipe her bludy damned shoes after she'd been to the stables—me, nearly five months along with a child!" The duster flew across the top of Cat's dressing table; her rooms, she thought wryly, had never been so clean.

"I cannae for the life of me understand wha' Young Master sees in that 'un," Sharon muttered, " 'specially when he could have a gude, kind lass like ye fer the askin'—"

"Who says he could?" Cat asked, aghast.

Sharon faced her again. "Ach, will ye deny ye bae sweet on him, wi' the way yer eyes turn all moony when he walks in a room? This bae me ye bae talkin' to, pet, nae his sister or mother."

Cat knew her cheeks were turning a giveaway pink. "I did not think I had been so transparent as that."

"Sooth, *he* will nae hae noticed, if that bae wha' flusters ye."

Sharing her secret with the maid proved a tremendous relief. Had she been at home in Douglasdale, Cat realized, she would have hashed over every minute detail of Rene Faurer's looks and behavior with her sisters each night. "It is not exactly that I am sweet on him, Sharon," she confided, perching on the edge of her bed. "I mean, half the time he infuriates me so, I can't even see straight. But there is something about him . . ."

"His looks," Sharon said promptly. "Just like his father. The handsomest set o' men I ever laid eyes on—*if* ye like that dark, dangerous kind. Myself, I'll stick to my Dugald. He bae a plainer sort, p'raps, but at least ye ken straight out what ye get."

"It isn't just his looks, though, Sharon." Cat screwed up her face, anxious to explain. "There is something in him that seems so angry and unhappy. As though he is suffering—"

"Hmph," said the maid, shaking out the drapes. "What wuld he hae to suffer about, I'd like to know?"

"That's just it. It seems to me he has got everything a young man could want. So why isn't he happy?"

Sharon shrugged. "There bae some folk just born that way."

"But not him." Cat spoke with conviction. "Don't ask me how; I just know it. I can feel it inside. He just needs someone to save him. I want to save him." She laughed, hearing how grandiose that sounded, as though she was Jesus himself. But her green-gold eyes were solemn as she looked at Sharon. "He is in love with Eleanor, I know he is. But do you think—do you think that I have any chance?"

The maid looked at her for a long moment, then laid her feather duster down. "I'll tell ye wha' I think. I hae known Young Master all his life. 'N' I've known ye—what bae it, a fortnight now? 'Twould seem clear eno' where my loyalties should lie. But if I wa' to offer up a prayer in the matter, I'd pray that ye should nae have a chance. Savin' bae all well 'n' good, but Christ knew Judas war beyond redemption, dinna he?"

Rene was baiting the Templars as Cat came into the dining hall for supper on the eve of the New Year. It was a popular pastime for him when he found the aging warriors together; he would run through a litany of old battles in which they had served with his father—and lost. His command of the history of the Crusades was astonishing, and extremely rude.

"Your defeat by the Grand Mameluke at Tripoli, Tomas," he was saying now, "what year was that? 'Ninety-six? 'Ninety-seven?"

Tomas sucked on a peppermint lozenge. " 'Ninety-eight, Rene, as you know full well."

"And the Templars blamed that defeat on—what?"

"We were betrayed by the pasha of Egypt, with whom we'd made a treaty."

"Odd," Rene mused, as Missus Grayson set a huge stuffed goose before him for carving. "I've a history of the battle which claims one of your own knights did the betraying."

Guillaume, sitting at the far end of the table, made a low noise deep in his throat. Cat, slipping into her seat, saw one of the tongueless man's sons pat him on the shoulder in a gesture meant to placate. The son's eyes when he looked back at Rene were filled with pity. It was remarkable, Cat thought, how forbearing they all were with him.

His mother was less so. "Rene," she cautioned as he picked up the carving knife and began to whet it against his thumb.

"What? I have got such a history."

"The goose looks grand, Madeleine," Brant's wife said quickly.

"Written by the church, no doubt," her husband told Rene in

an even tone. "Much history has been revised since the order was disbanded."

Rene began to carve the goose, chopping off the legs and wings and then slicing the breast meat in neat pieces. "Annie, you like the wing, don't you?" He offered it to her on the tip of the knife, smiling, and Cat dared to start breathing again, thinking trouble had been averted. After filling the platter with meat, Rene held it for Eleanor, who was seated on his right. Cat was farther down the table, between Father Joseph and Anne. For a time the company was busy filling trenchers with the magnificent meal Missus Grayson had prepared—mashed turnips, a chestnut dressing, beans baked with bacon and thyme, three different boiled puddings, and besides the goose a haunch of venison, a roasted salmon, woodcocks in pastry, and quail eggs preserved in a tasty brine.

But with everyone settled in to eating, Rene began again. "There's another thing that perplexes me, Tomas. The pope is God's voice on earth, isn't that so? Yet my father often said, and now you tell me, too, that the accounts of the Templars sanctioned by the pope are in error. That would mean the pope is in error. Now, how can that be?"

"Rene," his mother said again, sighing.

"Well, you can see how it confuses me, can't you?" Rene appealed to the guests.

"Rain," his sister said, "why don't you shut up and eat?"

He grinned at her and did. Cat, enjoying her food, if not the conversation, immensely, took a huge bite of crisp-skinned goose, and then noted that Eleanor de Baliol was picking at her meal with dainty little nibbles. Self-consciously she finished chewing; it seemed to take an awfully long time. To make matters worse, no sooner had she swallowed—resolved to be more delicate—when Father Joseph beamed approval at her and remarked, "So nice to see a young lady who truly appreciates food." Eleanor tittered, so that Cat wanted to crawl beneath the table in chagrin. Why, oh why wasn't she home in Douglasdale, where even if Tess and Janet and Jessie poked fun at her, she knew she was loved?

After that, the conversation turned to safer topics: the weather, which was so unseasonably warm that Madeleine was worried her jonquils and fritillaria would be fooled by the thaw into blooming prematurely; some horses Guillaume and his sons were breeding from stock the Templars had brought in from Araby; and, of course, Missus Grayson's cooking. But the usual source of conversation at Scottish tables—politics—was notably absent. Cat, like everyone else there, was acutely aware of Eleanor de Baliol seated at the head of the table, taking little sips of Madeleine's apple wine while, across the Channel, her uncle Edward was plotting to overthrow the boy-king.

For Cat, at least, the appearance of the sweets was a blessed relief. Anne had helped Missus Grayson with the baking; as Rene made a fuss over his sister's almond cakes, Cat thought again how strange it was that he should be so prickly with the rest of the world and so tender toward the girl.

After the sweets, they retired to the larger of the parlors, where a fire was roaring and the presents to be exchanged were piled atop the sideboard. Rene poured port for the men and cider for the ladies, except for Eleanor, who asked for brandy. "Annie, darling, do come here and see what I've brought for you!" the blonde commanded imperiously. Anne was bright-eyed with excitement; what child could resist gifts?

And what gifts these were! There was a riding habit just like the one Cat had admired upon Eleanor's arrival; and a cloak of crimson wool, hooded and lined in downy miniver; two gowns, one of green shot silk and the other of blue damask with otter fur trim—"Because I simply couldn't decide," Eleanor explained with a pretty moue—and calfskin boots, tanned soft as velvet, with gloves to match; and a chain of real gold, the tiny worked links set off by a pendant decorated with curving leaves and flowers and centered with a bloodred gem. "A garnet, for my birthstone?" Anne asked, admiring it in the firelight.

Eleanor shook her blond head, smiling. "A ruby."

Madeleine, sitting on a tapestry stool by her daughter's side, drew in breath. "My, my. I fear your bounty will spoil her for her other presents, Eleanor."

"Well, Annie knows how very fond of her I am. Don't you, Annie?"

Cat watched as Anne, torn between the splendid surfeit of gifts and her animosity toward her brother's friend, hesitated, then nodded. "I suppose so." Then she shot an apologetic glance at Cat, who smiled in reassurance. It would be a rare bairn Anne's age, Cat knew, who could have resisted the pull of such loot.

"Here's my gift to you, Anne," Madeleine said, rising from her stool to go to the sideboard.

"Wait!" Eleanor cried gaily. "There is still one more of mine. That big one in the copper-colored sack. Bring it to her, Rene." The command had a ring of familiarity that pulled at Cat's heart.

Dancing a little with anticipation, Anne unfastened the cord at the neck of the sack, tugged it open, and reached in to withdraw a poppet, the finest Cat had ever seen, with porcelain hands and head, painted with blue eyes and pouting mouth, and long, silky gold hair. "She's beautiful," Anne said in shy awe.

"I am so glad you think so. My uncle Edward gave her to me when I was just your age, and now I give her to you."

The little girl blanched. "Your—your uncle Edward?"

Eleanor nodded. "He truly is the *sweetest* man. Just ask your brother."

Anne raised stricken eyes to her mother. "I can't keep it," Cat overheard her whisper. "Can I?"

Ever the gracious hostess, Madeleine smiled at Eleanor. "Why, dear, of course you can."

"But he has *touched* it," Anne hissed, and Cat felt a surge of hatred for the blonde for having put the girl in such a spot. She hadn't had to tell Anne where the doll had come from, but of course she did.

Anne looked longingly at the beautiful poppet—then resolutely slid her headfirst into the sack, tightened the cord, and presented it back to Eleanor with a curtsy. "You are very kind. But I think—I think that such a special gift to you from your uncle should stay with you." Her small hands were trembling with the effort of that speech.

Madeleine reached out and gave her daughter a tight hug.

Eleanor, smiling with thin lips, simply shrugged. "If you like. I'll hold on to her, shall I, until you are older? Perhaps you'll change your mind then."

After that, everyone seemed in a hurry for the gift-giving to be over; the mood had been spoiled. Madeleine seemed touched by the comb Cat had chosen for her. As for Rene, he raised one black brow when Cat came toward him with a ribbon-tied sack. "You shame me, Mistress Douglas," he drawled. "I've no gift for you, I'm afraid."

"This is more of a medicine than a gift," she told him. Tomas, sitting beside Rene, burst out laughing when he saw what the sack contained.

"Jesu in heaven," the old Templar said, "will those further tarten his tongue?" Cat couldn't tell what Rene thought of her little jest; his indigo eyes were inscrutable as he thanked her and popped a lemon drop into his mouth.

Then Cat took her present for Anne from the pile. The girl saw its square shape beneath the damask wrapping, felt its heft, and smiled knowingly. "A book. It is a book, isn't it, Cat?" She slipped off the ribbons and wrappings, then held it up triumphantly. "See? I knew it was a book!" She opened it at random, blinked at the pages, turned over several more, then looked at Cat in puzzlement. "But there's no writing in it. What sort of book is it?"

"I made it for you," Cat explained. "It is for you to write in, about your father. What you remember about him now, so you can't ever forget."

Madeleine made a little noise like a sob. Guillaume put his arm around her thin shoulders. Anne's eyes were shining. "Oh, Cat," she breathed. "It's the most wonderful gift. I shall begin right now, tonight. I'll put in about last New Year's, when Papa gave me Grimkin and then took me outside with him, under his cloak, to look for shooting stars . . ."

Standing by the fireplace, Rene slammed his cup down atop the mantel and left the room.

"Oh, Rain." Anne sighed unhappily, clutching the book to her chest.

Tomas put his hand on Madeleine's shoulder. "Shall I go after him?"

"What is the use?" She gave a small shrug of helplessness.

For Cat, though, Rene's rude departure was the last straw. She rose from her stool. "Will you excuse me, please?" she asked the company. As she left them, she heard Eleanor's voice, sounding peevish:

"An empty book? What a peculiar present that is!"

He'd headed for the kitchens. Missus Grayson, finishing the washing up, glanced over her shoulder as Cat came in, and nodded her toward the back door. "That way. Though why ye'd want to bother bae beyond me." Cat thanked her, pulled a cloak from the row waiting on hooks, and stepped into the night air.

He was all the way at the end of the garden, leaning on the stone wall there, looking over the sea. He did not move as Cat came up beside him; she got very close before she asked, her anger barely restrained, "Have you some quarrel with my choice of gift for your sister?"

He turned to her then. It was the second time she had seen him in moonlight; she'd forgotten how the silver darkened his eyes. "I just don't happen to believe there are any memories of our father that warrant recording."

Cat's own eyes narrowed, slanting like Grimkin's when he spied prey. "What has made you so hard and uncaring?"

"What has made you Michel Faurer's champion? Christ, you never knew the man."

"The book's not meant as tribute to your father. It is meant for Anne."

"The best thing for Anne would be to forget that he ever existed."

"You are wrong."

His lip curled in a sneer. "And what makes you so sure?"

"My mother died when I was six years old."

"I am sorry," he said after a pause.

"Are you? Why? You never knew the woman."

He looked back at the sea. "She will fill it with all manner of drivel about him. Blow him up big as Hercules."

"And what if she does? Does his being big make you so small?"

"Christ, I'm not jealous of him, if that's what you're thinking."

"No?" Cat asked coolly.

"No! I just don't see why everyone has to act as though he

were some sort of bloody god. He was a mercenary, a bought sword, a hired killer—"

Cat was getting so mad that she could feel her hands shaking. She tucked them into fists. "It's rather odd to hear the moral high ground being taken by someone who spends his nights at the Speckled Fawn."

She had surprised him. He arched a brow. "How do you know about that?"

"I saw you there one evening when I went into Ayr. But it's no secret. Sharon knew."

"I never made it a secret. I saw no reason to."

Cat raised a brow of her own. "You are proud of being a whoremonger?"

"Are you proud to be the daughter of a tavern wench—"

She gasped.

"And a man famous throughout Scotland for being unable to keep his prick in his breeches?"

Cat hit him, hard as she could—not a slap, but a good sharp punch that landed on the side of his chin and actually snapped his head back. "How *dare* you speak that way of my father!"

He put his hand to where the blow had landed, working his jaw back and forth gingerly. "Did someone teach you to do that, or does it just come to you naturally?"

"You take back what you said about Papa!"

"Take it back? Why? It's God's own truth." Suddenly he laughed. "We make a peculiar pair, don't we? You love your father despite all the reasons you shouldn't, and I couldn't stand mine despite all the reasons I should." The words were spoken in jest, but Cat saw in the moonlight that his eyes were sad. Who was it he reminded her of? Then she realized—her sister Janet, so prickly and tart-tongued, but inside so uncertain. Somehow the comparison made Rene Faurer seem less formidable. Nonetheless—

"Take back what you said about Papa," she told him, "or I am never speaking to you again."

"There's a sobering thought." But he made her a little bow. "Very well. I apologize. Evidently he did learn to keep his breeches closed eventually. There haven't been any more, have there, since your sisters and you?"

Words are only words, Cat reminded herself. There was good in him somewhere. Think of his love for Anne. . . . "Not that we know of. So you see, people can change. Who knows? There might even be hope for you."

He laughed again. "By God, Cat Douglas, you do hold your own! Tell me, then. *Why* do you love him?"

"Lord, I could give you ten thousand reasons."

"Give me one."

Cat thought about it. "I suppose . . . well, I suppose because he *wanted* me. He didn't have to take me in, nor Tess or Jan or Jessie either. But me especially. Their mothers all had titles and money. Tess's had *tons* of money. But my mother hadn't anything. She wasn't anybody. Yet he has never made me feel that I am lesser than they."

Rene turned from her to look out over the dark, roiling sea. "You are one up on me, then, for my father did not want me."

She joined him at the seawall. "That's absurd. Every man wants a son."

"Not mine," he said with great certainty.

"How would you know?"

"I heard Mother talking about it once." He drew his breath in sharply. "Christ. I have never told anyone that."

Hesitantly Cat laid her hand on his arm. "Go on."

"I . . . it was at Christmas. I must have been a little older than Annie—not much. Brant and his wife were here, and she was with child. Her first. There was some sort of problem. I think they thought the baby might die before it was born. Mother was tending to her. I woke in the night and went to look for her. That was when I heard her."

"Well—what did she say?"

His eyes were on the sea, his voice distant and low. "That Father hated her when he found she was pregnant. That he said she had conceived on purpose to trick him. That he . . . struck her. Terrible things."

Cat shivered in the moonlight. "I don't understand. My father said your parents had one of the great loves of his time."

Rene laughed, a cold, bitter sound. "He only married her because he had to. I was born a month after their wedding. I went through his desk and found the certificate, to check the date."

She still could not believe it. "Perhaps you misunderstood what you heard. After all, you were young—"

"I made no mistake. I heard my mother say she prayed every night that I would die in her womb."

"Oh, my God, Rene!" Beneath her hand, his arm was shaking. He realized, and pulled it away. "But . . . but she loved him. There is no question about that; see how she is suffering."

Rene Faurer nodded. "That is the most pathetic part of all. No matter what he did to her—neglected her, abandoned her, abused her—she loved him still, the son of a bitch."

Cat felt she was looking into a fog-clouded mirror, rubbing with her hand to try and clear the glass. If what he said was true—and she had no doubt he believed it was, believed it heart and soul—then no wonder he'd hated his father. But—"What about Annie?" she asked softly.

"What about her? Accidents happen."

"But . . . what did he say when she was born? Was he angry then?"

"He was in Kintyre, fighting for the Bruce. He didn't see her until she was five months old." He paused. "I think he did love Annie, in his way."

"He must have loved you, too."

"You think so? Let me tell you what he did for me on my sixth birthday. He took me out in the hills up there—" He gestured back toward the vast stretches of empty moorland beyond the house. "Gave me a knife and a skin of water, told me to find my way home, and rode away with the horses."

"Jesus," she whispered, horrified. "Why?"

"He thought I lacked nerve." His handsome mouth was twisted with the memory.

"What did you do?"

"Sat on the ground and cried. Mother finally sent Grayson out for me at dusk. Father would have left me there to die, I know he would." He shrugged his shoulders, a great hard shrug, as though he could shake off the memory and its pain. "But as everyone says, he was a mighty hero for Scotland."

"I'm so sorry," Cat began to say, but he broke in:

"I don't know why I'm telling you these things. Please don't ever repeat them."

Repeat them? She was wishing she'd never heard them herself. Lord, little wonder Langlannoch had such an air of tragedy! "Have you . . . did you ever talk with your mother about this?" she asked hesitantly.

"You've seen what she's like when it comes to him. The great Michel Faurer could do no wrong."

"What about to your father?"

"You didn't talk to my father. You listened. And if you weren't good with a sword or quick with an ax, he had no use for you. He had little enough for me." He grinned without mirth, his teeth white in the moonlight. "Well. That's my family. Rather different, isn't it, from the jolly Douglas clan?"

"We—everything isn't perfect for us, you know," Cat said defensively. "We have our troubles. Sometimes we even argue or fight." The difference suddenly struck her. "But we would never attack one another in public, as you do your father. Don't you know how that hurts your mother and Anne?"

"I cannot help it if the truth hurts them."

Lord, he was stubborn. "What about being de Baliol's man? Is that just to spite your father, too?" she demanded.

Bemused, he looked down at her. "What if I said yes?"

"Then I should conclude you are a fool beyond redemption," Cat told him primly, spinning back toward the house. Then she gasped as he caught her arm.

"Redemption? Do you think you can save me?" His voice was harsh. "How?"

"I—"

"This way?" He brought his mouth down on hers with rough force, pinning her to the wall.

Cat meant to push him away, she honestly did. But she had spent so much time wondering what it would be like to be kissed by him that way that she let it go a moment longer, just to feel the urgent press of his lips against hers. His hands slid beneath her cloak, drawing her tight to his chest, caressing the small of her back through the velvet gown, moving up to her shoulders and then to her throat while the kiss grew in passionate intensity. And somewhere in that moment, while his fingertips stroked her cheeks, while his eyes, dark as the sky arching above them, looked deep into hers, the impetus to give him fight was lost. She parted her lips in a sigh; his tongue thrust between them, tasting of lemon drops and port wine, strong and bittersweet.

She felt cold stone at her shoulder blades, and then a rush of chill air at the front of her cloak as, still kissing her, his tongue pushing inside her, he yanked at the laces fastening the bodice of her gown. His palms closed over her breasts. Her nipples had grown hard with the wind; he found them with his fingertips and pulled at them, gently, gently. Cat let out a sharp, involuntary moan.

It was more liberty than she had ever allowed any of her beaux, far more—but then, none of the boys at Douglasdale had ever quickened her heart so; their hasty, covetous kisses had been as different from this embrace as dark from light. Rene Faurer's mouth was hungry, yes, but what it seemed to hunger for most was Cat's tremulous response, a sign from her that she did not want his caresses to end.

End them she must, she knew. And yet—what would happen if she let his hands linger there for just another heartbeat?

What happened was that he knelt before her on the frozen ground and put his mouth to her breast.

"Oh," Cat whispered on an indrawn breath. "Oh—" He had his hands on her waist, his big hands, nearly circling it, and his tongue was teasing her taut nipples, playing over first one and then the other, sliding from side to side. She leaned on his shoulders, arching her back, her blood pounding heavy in her head. How could anything feel so mysteriously marvelous?

He moved his hands lower still, so that they cupped her buttocks. "Don't," Cat whispered. "Stop." He paused; she heard his ragged breathing. Beyond his broad shoulders, the candles in the windows of Langlannoch were glowing. "Anyone might see us—"

"No one will see us." He was pulling off his cloak, laying it across the frost-rimed earth.

"But—"

He drew her down beside him atop the cloak, and silenced her with his mouth on hers.

She lay utterly still, with her eyes wide open. She had always closed them tight when boys had kissed her back at Douglasdale; it was, Tess had told her once, what a girl was expected to do. But she wanted to see him, watch him, did not want to forget how he looked in the moonlight, bending over her with his eyes ablaze.

He was leaning on her sleeve, so that she could not move her right arm. She tugged at it to free it, and he drew back for a moment, smiling apology, adjusting himself. "Sorry," he murmured.

"I shall need that hand to fight you off."

"Will you?" He claimed it with his, holding it to his chest so that she felt his heart against her palm. It was beating as furiously as her own. Then he drew her hand downward along the edge of lace his mother had made for his shirt, to his waist and then lower still, until she felt the taut bulge of his manhood beneath the soft tanned-leather breeches he wore. He held her hand there.

Cat would not have moved it anyway. Her cupped fingers tightened on that strange, hard mass straining against the skin breeches. Like a live thing it was, pulsing, throbbing with a rhythm to match his heartbeat, erratic and wild. She felt its power, but felt her power too, and saw it in his face; he was biting his lip, his head pulled backward as he groaned his pleasure. "More," he grunted, thrusting against her. "Touch me more."

"I dare not."

"Then I will touch you."

She heard the scratch of velvet on frost, and a rustle of silk as he raised up her skirts. *Cat, Cat, stop him now,* she told herself, but she did not move. His hand inched up her legs, past her knees, and played along her thighs that she had clamped tight together. "Let me in," he whispered, his mouth warm at her ear, and by Christ, she might have if at that moment, from the door to the kitchens, they had not heard a sharp, impatient voice calling:

"Rene! Rene, are you out there?"

It was Eleanor, starting toward them across the frozen gardens.

What happened next went so smoothly that Rene and she might have rehearsed it a dozen times. He stood up, pulling his cloak around him. "Eleanor! Be careful where you are walking. There is ice on the path; Mistress Douglas has just taken a nasty fall."

"Oh, has she?" Eleanor did not sound convinced.

"Aye, that she has. Lie still, Mistress Douglas. Don't move until you catch your breath." All this time, of course, Cat was frantically fastening her laces, untwisting her stockings, seeking to make some order of her disheveled curls—no easy task when one was lying on one's back in the darkness, trying very hard to look as though that was precisely *not* what one was trying to do. "Would you go and fetch Dugald, Eleanor, please," Rene went on, "to help me get her back to the house? I think her ankle is sprained." He bent over Cat, who in her rush had lost one of her bodice laces. "Here," he hissed, pressing it into her hand.

"Thank you," she hissed back.

Eleanor kept coming, not so easily dismissed. "I can help you. What the devil were the two of you doing all the way back here?"

"Uh—stargazing," Rene said. "Mistress Douglas pointed out to me that Orion was particularly bright this evening." Cat, who would not have known Orion from the Seven Sisters, prayed earnestly that Eleanor would not pursue that subject, even as she finally got her laces threaded and tied. There was still something wrong with her stockings, and her hair must have looked disastrous, but at least she was dressed.

And thank God, for Eleanor was upon them, glaring down at Cat as she lay in the snow. "Which ankle?" she demanded.

"The right one," Cat said, just as Rene helpfully supplied:

"The left one."

Eleanor's pale eyes narrowed.

"Is it my left?" Cat asked innocently. "I suppose it is. I never have been very good at telling left from right. You know, it doesn't hurt nearly as badly now as it first did. I think that I could walk on it."

Rene frowned. "I'm not sure that is wise. Perhaps I had better carry you to the house."

"Oh, by all means, let's see her walk on it," Eleanor said with an unpleasant little smile. *Definitely* suspicious, Cat thought, just as another voice, clear as a bell, pealed out over the frosty yards:

"Rain? Rain, what's going on?"

"Ca—Mistress Douglas has fallen, Annie!" Rene called back.

"Oh, no! Mama, Cat's fallen! Are you all right, Cat? Where is Dugald? Dugald, come quick and help!" After that, everyone came tramping out of the house, and Cat, torn between guilt and laughter, rode back inside in Dugald's brawny arms, for Eleanor insisted that Rene hold *her* hand lest *she* fall, and got set down in front of the fire, and tried very hard to remember which ankle it was that was supposed to be hurting while Madeleine and Tomas and even Father Joseph poked and probed at it, and winced at what she hoped were appropriate times, and wished devoutly, for she dared not look too closely, that she'd gotten her bodice laces right, and finally managed to convince everyone that what she needed most was a good hot soak in a tub and then straight into bed.

Rene and Eleanor, she noticed as Dugald hoisted her once more—he insisted—to take her upstairs, had disappeared somewhere. No doubt the blonde was still trying to worm out of him what had gone on in the gardens. Cat wasn't worried. Rene could look after himself.

The hot bath was wonderfully restorative. As she washed her throat and breasts with sweet lavender soap, Cat kept thinking: He kissed me *here*. His hands were on me *here*. There seemed scarcely an inch of her body that he had not touched, and remembering his wild, impassioned lovemaking was so enticingly arousing that she longed for him to hold her again.

He wanted her. *Perhaps he will come to me tonight,* she thought, and slipped between the soft linens naked just in case he did—then slipped back out and put on a nightgown instead, so that she should have the pleasure of letting him remove it. She wavered, too, about her hair—long and loose, or tied up, so that he had to unbind it? And would he dare come to her room? Why not, if he'd had the nerve to try what he had out-of-doors, right under everyone's nose?

She was in such a fever of anticipation that she was certain she would never sleep. She lay in bed trying to decide what position he might find most alluring when he entered—on her side, with her hair spread across the pillows? On her back? Hands folded over her breasts, or arms thrown over her head? Perhaps she should pretend to be asleep. In her mind's eye she replayed the scene in the garden over and over again, from their first rude, angry words to one another, to the secrets he had shared with her—*I have never told anyone that,* he'd said wonderingly—to their initial kiss, so passionately perfect! Lemon drops and port wine on his tongue, and the smell of his skin, all musky and warm . . .

She felt sore all over from his kisses, but it was a delicious soreness. She lay and reveled in it—the tenderness of her nipples where his mouth had teased them, her lips bruised with the force of his need. *Lord, let him come soon,* she prayed. *Lord, I want to be lying beneath him, locked in his embrace.*

Do you think you can save me?

Oh, God, Rene, yes!

Lost in a daze of longing and love, she waited for him to come and make her dreams come true.

Eight

Had it all been a dream?

Cat woke up and feared so. It was very early in the morning, dawn barely broken in the sky, and he was not beside her. So he had not come. Perhaps, then, what had happened in the garden wasn't even real—

But no. Testing her lips, still tender with bruises, made it clear she hadn't been dreaming. Shrugging off blankets, she ran to the window and looked out over the yards toward the sea. There, there by the wall—that was where he had made love to her, set his seal upon her for all time.

Despite the early hour, she could not bear to stay in bed a moment longer. She was bursting with energy; she could not wait to see Rene again, and if she could not see him, if he was still abed, then she wanted to gaze upon things that were his—the chair he sat in at table, his boots by the door, the cloak he'd wrapped around them both the night before. She dressed with special care, in the same yellow gown that Anne had told her once made her eyes go gold, pulled back just the front of her hair—let seeing it loose remind him of how he'd caught his fingers in her curls as he'd kissed her—and hurried down the stairs.

Missus Grayson was already up, and stoking the fire in her hearth. "Mornin', Miss!" she greeted Cat. "Happy New Year's to ye. How bae that ankle o' yers?"

"My—oh! I forgot all about it, to tell you the truth. Must have been soaking in the tub that fixed it."

"Nae doubt, nae doubt." Was there a twinkle in the cook's gray eyes? "Keep me company, then, while I beats up the oatmeal. It bain't often anyone stirs o' this hour save me. Did ye—how now, who's this?" Footsteps, airy and light, were dancing down the hall. "Good mornin' to ye, too, Mistress Annie, 'n' a happy New Year's."

"Happy New Year's, Cook. Happy New Year's, Cat. Cat is something going on?"

"Whatever do you mean?"

"Well, last night after you went to bed, Rain and Eleanor were off somewhere for ever so long, and then Rain came back by himself and asked to talk to Tomas, and they went off to Mama's study, and that's the last I saw of them before Sharon made me go upstairs."

Cat could not force back the smile that came to her lips. So he'd broken it off with Eleanor, had he, and then spoken to his father's oldest friend in private . . . there was only one thing that might mean. Catriona, Lady Faurer. She imagined the first presentation at court. How proud she would be as Rene's wife! Of course, there was still her father to deal with—

"Cat, have you heard a single word I said?" Anne demanded crossly.

"Of course I have." But she could change Rene, she was sure of that. She already had. And once he supported King David, Archibald couldn't possibly object to him.

More footsteps. "Busy as mice hereabouts this mornin'," Cook observed, stirring the oatmeal porridge.

It was Rene. Cat's heart went to her throat as she saw him; he was handsomer even than she remembered. And the look in his eyes, blue as the sky, true as the promise of the future, was so solemn and grave—

Rene and Eleanor. The blonde tossed her head and laughed, seeing Anne. "Oh, Annie, isn't it exciting?"

"Isn't *what* exciting?"

"Of course, how stupid of me. You haven't heard. You tell her, Rene.

"Tell me what?"

Cat shifted on the bench, suddenly apprehensive. Why did Eleanor look so pleased with herself?"

"Eleanor and I are getting married, Annie," Rene said.

Anne stared at him, stricken. "But—but—"

"Lord hae mercy," Missus Grayson said very quietly.

Cat couldn't speak, couldn't breathe. There was a tightness in her chest that was so constricting—what did he *mean*, Eleanor and he were being married? *But you're in love with me,* she thought.

Anne was finally getting around to finishing her sentence: "But I thought you were going to marry Cat, Rain!" she wailed.

"Marry Cat?" said Eleanor, holding tight to Rene's arm—that arm which had lain across Cat's naked breast as he pulled her to him. "Marry *Cat?*" The blonde laughed as though it was the most amusing thing she had ever heard. "Imagine! Marry Cat!"

Somehow, Cat got to her feet. Somehow she made her legs move forward. She crossed the room—she could not bear to look at Anne—with her head held high, Archibald's words singing in her mind: *Ye bae Douglases; that will suffice fer ye.* "Congratulations," she said, amazing herself with the steadiness of her voice. She held a hand out to Eleanor. "I wish you every happiness."

Two days later, she reached Castle Douglas. Dugald had ridden with her most of the way, but she sent him back as soon as their horses' hooves touched Douglas land. She wanted no reminders, not even his relentlessly cheerful countenance, of what had taken place at Langlannoch.

Archibald met her in the Great Hall before she'd even time to take her cloak off, with Janet and Jessie trailing anxiously behind him. His expression was thunderous. "What meant ye by that letter ye sent back with Geordie?" he roared at her, shaking his fist. "Stayin' on to look after the girl—I ken fair enough who ye stayed on to look after, dinna I? D'ye take me fer such a fool? That traitorous devil-eyed son of a bitch—if I'd nae had my hands full wi' the king's business, I'd hae ridden there and dragged ye back myself. By Christ, Catriona Douglas, if I find ye hae disgraced me . . ."

"Papa," Cat whispered, and the tortured look on her small

face silenced him in mid-roar. "Papa, I am so glad to see you. I am never leaving you, ever again." Then she dissolved in tears.

Archibald relented, holding out his arms, and she ran to him, burrowed against his warm, worn doublet, shoulders shaking with sobs. "There, there, Catkin," he murmured, stroking her wind-tossed hair with clumsy tenderness. "Sooth, little Kit-Cat. Ye bae safe home wi' yer papa now. All will be well. Ye'll see."

Part Two

Perth, Scotland
November, 1331

Nine

"What do you think of my hair this way?" Jessie Douglas asked, twisting and turning in front of the looking glass hung on the abbey wall. "Does it make me look worldly-wise?"

"No," Janet told her, "but even if it did, no man who spoke to you for more than two minutes could possibly think you are worldly-wise."

"I don't see why you say that." Jessie tucked a stray brown strand back into her carefully constructed chignon. "I am certainly as sophisticated as you."

Janet snorted. Tess, drying her fresh-washed face on a bit of toweling, reached over to pat Jessie's shoulder. "Never mind her, Jess. Janet's notion of 'worldly-wise' is to be so cynical that no man dare approach her lest he be lashed by that sharp tongue of hers."

"Men do too approach me," Janet said calmly. "They approach me all the time. I had more dances than you at the ball last night."

"I didn't feel like dancing."

"Oh, I'm sure."

"It's true!"

"Do you mean you think I am naive, Janet?" Jessie was still worrying her hair.

"Of course you are naive. Stop pigging the glass and let someone else have a chance."

"I wasn't pigging," Jessie said as she moved.

"Were too."

"Was not."

"Not that it matters anyway," Janet noted, "since we can't go to supper until Her Majesty here gets dressed." She glared at Cat, who after a moment looked up from the book she'd been reading, surprised not to hear her sisters bickering.

"Did you say something to me?" she inquired, seeing Janet's irate stare.

"I did. I was just wondering how long you intend to make us all wait for our supper."

Cat turned back to her book. "Go ahead without me. I am not very hungry."

"Papa will have a fit if you don't show up, Cat," Jessie told her, chewing on a hairpin.

"No he won't. Besides, Tess wants to eat my share."

"She is right about that," said Janet, eyeing their eldest sister. "What has happened to your appetite of late, Tess? Do you think now that you have snared Gill, it doesn't matter if you get fat?"

"What a horrid thing to say!" Jessie leaped to Tess's defense. "She isn't fat."

"She will be if she keeps packing in food the way she did last night. Little wonder she wasn't dancing. You'd not feel much like dancing either if you'd just ingested a whole joint of mutton and eleven biscuits."

"I did *not* eat eleven—"

"It may have been ten. I lost count after a while."

"I really don't see what concern my appetite is to you, Janet," Tess said archly, splashing water from the basin onto her face and reaching for a towel.

"Christ, that's the third time in an hour that you've washed your face!" Janet declared.

"I can't help it; I'm hot."

"How can you be *hot?* It is bloody freezing in this drafty old place!"

"Well, I am hot!" Tess peered at her sisters over the edge of the towel. "Can you keep a secret?"

"Of course," Jessie said immediately. "What is it?"

"I mean *really* keep it. Even from Papa."

"Yes, yes."

"Well . . ." Tess's blue eyes danced. "I think I'm with child."

"You *what?* Oh, Tess!" Squealing happily, Jessie showered her with kisses.

"What makes you think so?" Janet wanted to know.

"Janet, you are such a squelch!" Jessie cried indignantly.

"Well, there is no sense getting all excited, is there, if it isn't true?"

"I am hot all the time—"

"That doesn't prove it."

"I am hungry all the time—"

"Neither does that."

"And I have missed my monthly twice in a row," Tess finished in triumph.

"That would seem to cinch it," Janet admitted.

"Or is it just once? I don't know. I never paid much attention to such things."

"This is so exciting! Isn't this exciting?" Jessie was hopping from one foot to another. "But why in the world don't you want to tell Papa?"

"Oh . . . you know how he is. He'd be so worried about me that he'd lock me away in bed until it is born, and I would miss the coronation and everything else."

"He likely wouldn't let you do any dancing," Janet agreed. "Have you told Gill?"

"Not yet."

"Don't you think you had better?"

"I will—*after* the coronation. I am not at all sure he wouldn't want me staying in bed, too!" Tess looked across the room. "Aren't you going to say anything, Cat?"

Cat got up from her chair and came to kiss her. "Of course I am. I'm sorry. I'm so happy for you, Tess."

"Think of it—Papa's first grandchild!" Jessie burbled. "Do you want a boy or a girl, Tess?"

"She wants a boy, of course. Everyone wants a boy first," said Janet.

"I don't," Tess contradicted her. "I want girls—all girls. Sisters, to love each other just as we do."

The three of them—Tess, Janet, Jessie—were all talking at

once now. Cat went back to her chair. She hadn't meant to be rude, but Tess's announcement had brought back to her with a rush her return from Langlannoch, and Archibald's frightful fury: *If I find ye hae disgraced me . . .* The wonder was that she hadn't. Christ, it still gave her chills to think how close she'd come to giving herself to Rene Faurer. If Eleanor hadn't come into the gardens just when she did, Cat very well might now have been the mother of a child by "that traitorous, devil-eyed son of a bitch."

And the worst of it was, there was no one, absolutely no one, she dared confide in—not even her sisters, with whom she'd shared everything all her life. For they'd known long before she had what Rene's true stripes were. They'd warned her, hadn't they, to stay clear of him?

After his initial burst of bluster, Archibald asked no questions about Langlannoch; it was as though he didn't want to know. Her sisters did, of course, but Cat continued to insist it was only her lengthy absence from home that had put her in such a state. Were they fooled? She wasn't sure. Jessie, she thought, suspected something. Janet was right; Jessie *was* naive, but she also had an inborn sympathy for the troubles of others, and she sensed that Cat was suffering. Madeleine Faurer had sent Archibald a letter thanking him for Cat's long visit and mentioning, in passing, Rene's betrothal to Eleanor. After Jessie read it, she was very kind to Cat.

"Get dressed, Cat, please." Jessie's pleading voice broke into her thoughts. "All of us should be together on this night, celebrating with Tess. And besides, what about Malcolm Ross?"

"What about him?"

"He is sweet on you, Cat."

"He doesn't even know me."

"The way to remedy that," Janet pointed out, "would be to come down to supper."

"He is sweet on you," Tess agreed with Jessie. *"And* he is very rich. Not to mention well-connected. Did you know his uncle the earl led the Bruce's Highlanders at Bannockburn?"

"He has mentioned it to me," Cat said wryly, "a few dozen times."

Malcolm, she supposed, was what folk called a small mercy. She vaguely recalled having met him at Tess's wedding. On the short side for a man, though of course still much taller than Cat, he was built solidly, like a soldier; he had thick hair so blond it looked white in sunlight, and pale gray-blue eyes. Jessie insisted he was handsome, but Cat thought his squared-off jaw and narrow nose were, like the man himself, nice enough and no more.

In the past four months, though, since she'd encountered him again at the funeral of his aunt, the countess of Ross, Malcolm had been pursuing Cat: stopping by Douglasdale on the slightest pretext, giving her the sort of presents custom dictated he could—a pair of silky doeskin gloves, a feathered fan, baskets of fruit—writing her long, breezy letters full of news about his doings, to which she had not the slightest idea what to say in reply. Tess thought she was mad; Malcolm, she'd pointed out more than once, would be the third-largest private landholder in Scotland upon the death of his uncle, the earl. Janet, too, despite her cynicism, seemed impressed by their youngest sister's "catch." Jessie fretted and nudged and urged Cat to be more encouraging of Malcolm's suit. "He won't wait around forever while you play hard to get," she liked to say. Cat found her beau's attentions mildly diverting. She had nothing against Malcolm, but neither did she feel anything special for him. He was just . . . there.

"Come to supper with us," Jessie said again. "I'm sure there won't be . . . anyone there whom you don't wish to see."

"Who wouldn't I want to see?"

"I don't know. Why else would you go on staying cooped up in here?"

Cat could not afford to arouse her sisters' suspicions. "I am just not hungry. But I'll come along if it is that important to you." She stood up, closing her book. Jessie was right. A man who was about to marry a de Baliol would not likely come to little King David's coronation. Not even Rene Faurer would be that brash.

Supper in the Blackfriars abbey was a grand affair, with three meats, four fishes, bread white as linen, and a host of extravagant side dishes to be passed amongst the company. Though the coronation itself would be held in Scone, some two miles south, there was little accommodation to be found in that town. Those who were not putting up with friends were staying, like Cat and her sisters, at the abbey in Perth.

Archibald was always in his element at such gatherings, greeting everyone he knew—and Archibald knew everyone—with effusive warmth, drinking too much claret, sitting late into the night singing by the hearth to the sound of the pipes. He expected the same sort of performance from his daughters, with the exception of the claret. Cat had never before minded the way he put his girls on display, but since her mistake with Rene, she'd felt conspicuous in public, as if folk could tell just by looking that she had nearly lost her maidenhead to Scotland's enemy.

It was different for Tess now, of course, since she'd married; her place was beside Gill. As Cat let a delectable roast capon pass her by, she glanced sidelong at her eldest sister farther down the table. She certainly seemed happy. Cat's cheeks suddenly flushed as she recalled the night, not long after her return to Douglasdale, when Tess had taken it upon herself to inform her about lovemaking. "After all, you've no mother to tell you," Tess had said, "and it's better you should know ahead of time when you marry, so there will be no surprises. Really, it isn't bad at all. Sometimes it is quite pleasant." Cat, burning with shame, had listened in silence while her sister explained the raw mechanics of the act of coition. "Any questions?" Tess had asked brightly when she'd finished. Cat had just shaken her head. . . .

"Are you feeling ill?" Jessie whispered anxiously to Cat. "You look all rosy."

" 'Tis the wine," Cat told her, pushing her cup away. "It's gone straight to my head." She would have dearly loved to leave the table, but one look at Archibald, digging into a huge hunk of capon while he held forth on his memories of the coronation of the Bruce, reminded her of how he'd frown on such a retreat.

"Well, it is not unattractive," Jessie observed of Cat's reddened cheeks. "At least, Malcolm doesn't seem to think so. He is staring at you." Cat raised her head and saw that he was looking at her, though she wouldn't have said staring. He smiled. She smiled, weakly, and hastily looked back down at her plate.

Always a dreamer, Cat had never had any trouble picturing herself marrying this young man or that one, whoever most recently had caught her eye. She used to spend hours at it, in fact, imagining what she would wear at the wedding, what her sisters would wear, her shoes, gloves, flowers, ring. She tried now to imagine marrying Malcolm—clenched her eyes shut and really tried, hard as she could. Her mind remained blank. It had been like that for her ever since that night with Rene.

He has spoiled me for anyone else, she thought bitterly, and it was for that she hated him most of all.

There was to be a pageant the following afternoon in the Church of St. John the Baptist, portraying the history of Scotland down to King David's time. Archibald had had a hand in the planning, and could hardly wait for the spectacle to come off. He headed for the church hours early, leaving his daughters strict instructions that they follow promptly, so as to secure good places in the sanctuary. Janet was grumbling about the long wait they would have, and Jess was urging Cat to get moving, when Tess appeared in the bedchamber doorway; she, of course, had separate rooms with Gill.

"Christ, you are prompt," Janet said in surprise.

"I didn't want to anger Papa; you know he is all agog about this pageant of his. Besides, the monks brought someone to me by mistake. You have a visitor, Cat."

Cat turned from the window and saw the small face of Anne Faurer, framed in black curls crowned with a red velvet cap. She looked very shy, very nervous. "I—I hope you don't mind my coming, Cat," she said hesitantly.

Cat conquered the rush of emotion the sight of her engendered—Lord, there was much in her of her brother; that thick black hair, the set of the eyes, not quite Scottish, the fine strong chin—and went to kiss the girl, taking her hands. "Of *course* I don't mind, Annie! It is wonderful to see you again. Tess, Janet,

Jess, this is Anne Faurer, that I spent the New Year's holiday with. Anne, these are my sisters." She introduced each in turn.

"You are the duchess's daughter, aren't you?" Anne asked Janet. "And you are the one whose mother came from Argyll." That was for Jessie. "Mama said she met her once. I asked Mama about you all."

"Evidently," Janet said. Her dry tone made Anne flush.

"Oh, not because of the gossip," she hurried to explain. "I didn't even know about that until Mama told me. Just because I thought it must be nice for Cat to have so many sisters. I haven't got any, you see."

"You have a brother, though," Janet noted.

Anne's eyes went to Cat, looked away. "Yes. Yes, I have. Just the one."

"Then you are one up on us," Jessie said kindly, sensing the girl's shyness, "for we don't know what that's like."

"Oh, well. I should have liked to have a sister just the same." She eyed their gowns, the cloaks laid out for them. "Are you on your way somewhere?"

"The pageant at St. John's," Jessie explained. "Are you going?"

Anne shook her head. "Mama says 'twill be too much of a crush. But I'm to see the coronation on Sunday." She stole another glance at Cat. "I have picked a bad time. I'll come again, shall I, when you are not so busy?"

It was hard even to look at her, to be reminded so of her brother. "I . . ."

"Actually," Jessie broke in with great cheeriness, "we were all ready except for Cat. Why don't you stay with her while she dresses, Anne? See if you have better luck than I in getting her to hurry. And we'll go on ahead."

"Leave *now?*" Janet groaned. "We shall be the first ones there!"

"And just think how that will please Papa!" Jessie told her brightly, grabbing up both their cloaks and steering her toward the door.

"Try not to be too tardy, please?" Tess appealed, then trailed off after the others, leaving Cat and Anne alone.

"I should not have come," Anne said miserably. "You don't want to see me. You are angry with me—"

"Oh, Anne, that's not true!"

"It is too. You hate me because of Rene. But that is what I came to tell you, Cat. There is something going on with him."

"He's not *here?* In *Perth?*" Cat asked in alarm.

"No, no. We don't know *where* he is. He was in Paris, but then Grandpapa wrote that he'd gone off somewhere without so much as a by-your-leave."

"With *her*, no doubt."

Anne shook her head. "I don't think so. Neither does Mama. We got another letter—but here, I've brought it along. You can see for yourself." She dug into her purse and pulled out a sheet of rag paper, handing it to Cat.

She'd never seen Rene's handwriting before. *It is like him,* she thought: elegant, strong and yet impatient, the letters rushing to the right as though he was in a terrible hurry to set his thoughts down. "Dearest Mother—and, of course, Annie," it began. "How I've missed you! That is what such a long visit will do—spoil a man for living without the women he loves."

Cat looked up from the letter. "I shouldn't be reading this, Anne. It is personal, to you and your mother."

"Don't be a goose. I can show it to whomever I please. Besides, it is important. Read this part here."

" 'Did you get the skeins of wool I sent you, Mother?' " Cat obediently read.

"No, no. Farther down. Here." Anne pointed again.

" 'By the by, Mother, about that bedding you were going to embroider for Eleanor and me.' " Cat swallowed, a sudden image of it rising up in her mind: Rene and that damnable blonde lying entwined on soft French linen decorated with Madeleine's exquisite stitchery.

"Eleanor wanted it," Anne supplied. "With both their initials. Mother said she would do it."

Cat started to fold up the letter. "Anne, I don't—"

"Keep reading!"

"I wouldn't start on it just yet," the letter continued. "There has been a hitch in the wedding plans."

" 'A hitch in the wedding plans,' " Anne quoted in triumph. "There, Cat, you see?"

"But that could mean anything at all—that they have postponed the date, that they have had to change the location—"

"No it can't. He wouldn't have written Mama not to start the 'broidery just for that. It means he isn't marrying her. I just know it does!"

Cat did fold the letter then, into clean, neat squares. "Even if you are right, there are—things you don't know about, Anne. Things you don't understand between your brother and me. I would never marry him."

"But you have to, Cat!" Anne was so earnest she was nearly in tears. "You have got to marry him. You will, I know you will. It is what I pray for every night."

Cat shook her head. "Wishing something doesn't make it so. I used to pray every night that my mama would leave Mull and come live with Papa. But she never did. God doesn't work that way." She handed her the letter. "Does your mother know you are here?"

"Of course she does. She sent me."

"With that?" Cat indicated the letter, astonished; it did not seem like Madeleine.

"Oh, no. Mama doesn't know I brought this along. She says we are to say nothing about Rain's betrothal until we hear more from him. She sent me to ask if you would come to supper with us tonight. We are staying over on the High Street. The house belongs to an old friend of Papa's, but he's had to go to Edinburgh to look after someone who is sick. So it is just us. Say you'll come, Cat, please?"

"I can't. I—I have other plans."

Anne's lip was trembling again. "You do hate us, don't you?"

"Of course I—"

"You do! Well, let me tell you this: I am beginning to hate Rain for whatever it was that he did to you."

"Annie, don't say such things! You cannot hate your family. They are all you have, the only people you can truly count on to love you no matter what."

"That's an easy thing for you to say. You haven't got a brother who's a—a traitor."

"I'm sure Rene's not—"

"Yes he is! And a mother who does nothing except sew and think of Papa all day! I swear, we have so many bed linens and hangings already that we could put new ones out every morning and never see the same ones twice!"

Cat couldn't help it; she laughed. "Is your mother still so bad off as that?"

Anne nodded morosely. "I know that I should be more patient. And I miss Papa too. I miss him terribly. But there's no sense in—in wallowing about in it, is there? He is gone, and that's all there is to it."

Cat kissed her furrowed forehead. "You are very wise for your years, Anne Faurer."

"You always made Mama feel better," the girl recalled with longing. "Even now, when she is sad, I tell her about that morning when you made biscuits, and she always laughs."

"Wise *and* manipulative." Cat tweaked Anne's nose. "You little devil. You've gotten what you want from me. I'll come to supper, then, just to prove I don't hate you."

"You will? Hurrah!" Anne enveloped her in hugs. "At four o'clock?"

"At any time you wish. Which house on the High Street?"

"The big one just before you reach the crossing for the road to Scone. The doors in front are painted blue. You can't miss it. It looks very peculiar." She handed Cat her cloak. "Now you had better hurry. Your sisters will be looking for you."

"How did you get here?" Cat asked. "Shall I walk you home?"

"No need to. It's the opposite way to St. John's." Anne was skipping along the corridor of the abbey. At the gate, she hugged Cat again. "Four o'clock? You won't forget?"

"I won't forget." Cat waved and set off for St. John's. She had all of a five-minute walk, she realized, to think of how to explain to Archibald where she'd be dining that night.

Ten

But Archibald, flush with the success of his pageant—King David had been moved thrice to tears, although, as Janet pointed, he *was* only seven, making that no great feat—didn't mind at all when Cat told him her plans. In fact, he seemed pleased to hear that Madeleine would be attending the coronation. "Only fittin'," he grunted, "since it bae nae little thanks to her husband that David's got the crown. Give her my best love, Catkin. I'll call on her tomorrow. Nay, nae tomorrow; there bae that meetin' of the parliament tomorrow; the blasted thing will likely take all day. On Friday, how bae that? Nay, nay, wait; Friday bae the review o' the troops. Well, tell her—when I can."

"I think it would mean much to her, Papa, if you did," Cat said gently. She knew all too well how her father's best intentions could be consumed by the sort of excitement the coronation was creating—especially now that Uncle James was dead, and Archibald the head of the clan.

"And I said I shall!" he barked back at her. "If only to delve a wee bit more deeply into what went on in that house o' hers last Christmastide. That son which bae such a grief to her—*he* bain't here, bae he?"

"No."

"I should hope nae! I should hope he'd ken better than to let his pretty face bae seen hereabouts." Archibald nodded, clearly relishing the thought of what he would have done to Rene had he dared appear.

His cordiality toward Madeleine made Cat quite ashamed of her first instinct, which had been to lie about where she was going. Of course, she reflected as she walked up the High Street from St. John's, there wasn't any reason why her father shouldn't let her go; so far as he knew, naught but homesickness accounted for the odd way she'd behaved when she returned to Douglasdale. And if she'd been a bit withdrawn since then—well, Archibald had much on his mind these days, and didn't everyone know that young women her age got into such moods? Only Jessie had looked at all askance back at St. John's as Cat had bid her family good-bye—and Jessie hadn't said anything.

The door *was* blue—blue as the sea, as the sky, as a loch edged by forest. It was the blue of Rene Faurer's eyes, Cat thought as she raised up the knocker and let it fall. The door swung open, and she found herself looking straight into those eyes.

She didn't—couldn't—move for a moment. Then she spun on her heel and walked off as fast as she could.

"If you are looking for my sister and mother," he called after her, "they have gone to the market. The fish they planned to cook for supper was bad."

Cat stopped in the street. "Anne swore to me you would not be here," she said, still facing away from him.

"She didn't lie. They did not know I was coming—did not even know where I was. I rode in not an hour ago."

She believed it; even in that brief instant in the doorway she'd smelled the scent on him, leather and cold air and horseflesh, that he'd had when he bore her before him in the saddle through the snowstorm. And the scent had brought back to her in a rush the sensation of his arms around her, his thighs tight against hers as they rode through a world composed of wind and white. Had she fallen in love with him, irrevocably, there on that ride? She took three more steps away from him, toward family, toward peace.

"Cat! Cat, come back. Please. I must talk with you."

"I cannot imagine what you might have to say."

She heard his bootheels coming after her on the cobblestones. "I need to explain—dammit, Cat, stop walking. I'd rather not discuss this here on the street."

"I had rather not discuss it at all."

He caught her arm. Cat caught her breath; she had not realized he was so close. "I have broken my engagement to Eleanor."

"Bully for you." She tried to pull away; she still would not look at him.

His grip was so strong. "Come into the house, Cat. I know that I wronged you—"

"How very gentlemanly of you to admit it," Cat said as coldly as she could.

"If you'd just let me explain—"

"Let go of me."

He glanced about the street, crowded with visitors come to town for the coronation. "Cat, people are staring."

"They are about to do more than stare. If you don't take your hand off me, I shall scream."

"I think I love you, Cat."

That brought her round to face him; she slapped his cheek, hard as she could. "You've a bloody damned nerve."

A pair of old women going past them tittered. "Ye tell 'im, dearie!" one called back to Cat.

"You are making a spectacle," Rene said between gritted teeth.

"No. *You* are making a spectacle. I am going home."

"You leave me no choice, Cat." He clapped his hand over her mouth, swept her up in his arms, and carried her back through the blue door. The last thing she saw before he kicked it shut were the two biddies who'd passed them; they were staring at her, all agog.

He took his hand away from her mouth as soon as they were inside. Cat let out a scream, a great, good, long one. "Scream your head off if you like," he invited, "there's no one else here."

She twisted in his grasp, trying to get free, while he strode along the front hall. "Do you intend to force yourself on me again?" she demanded.

"Force my—" Incredulous, he laughed. "Oh, really, Cat. That isn't worthy of you."

He was right; it wasn't. But she felt she had to say something, find some way to regain control of the situation. For with his arms around her, the scent of him filling her nostrils, the two of them alone in the house, it would be so easy to fall victim to him again. *I think I love you,* he'd said. . . .

"Where are you taking me?" she asked in alarm; he'd started toward the staircase.

"Someplace where we won't be disturbed. Where you will listen to me."

"Stop! I will listen down here."

Surprised, he did stop. "You will?"

As his grip relaxed slightly, Cat turned her head and sank her teeth into the meat of his shoulder.

"Jesus!" He dropped her in a heap. "Jesus, I think you've drawn blood!"

Cat didn't say anything in return; she was already on her feet, racing for the blue doors, her skirt caught up in her hands.

He hauled her down from behind before she even reached the front hall, sending her sprawling across the plank floor. "Ouch!" she cried as she banged her elbow.

"If you are going to play rough, you'll have to take the lumps, Cat." He'd straddled her knees and was hauling her around to face him.

"Get off me."

"No."

She spat at him, teeth bared, her loosened hair a wild red-gold mane.

"Christ, you are well named." With her hands pinned above her head and his thighs pressing down on hers, there was little she could do to get free. He settled himself comfortably, grinning down at her. "Now, suppose we start all over again from the beginning—and this time, let's be civilized, shall we? Good day, Mistress Douglas. How lovely to see you again. Have you been well?"

Tears burned Cat's eyes. How dare he mock her! "I am glad this is all such a fine jest to you."

"It's not a jest at all," he retorted. "I just don't see why we can't discuss this like two sane, rational people."

"When you happen to be neither of those things? Dragging me off the street into an empty house—do you know what my father will do to you when he finds out?"

"Your father has better cause than this to hate me. Did you tell him, Cat?" She hesitated, contemplating lying. He took the pause for his answer. "You didn't, then. I owe you thanks for that."

" 'Twas not for your sake I didn't. 'Twas to spare him the pain of learning his daughter nearly let herself fall into shame with such a—such a snake as you."

"See there—you've just admitted that I didn't force you. Now, won't you please listen? God knows you've every right to be angry. I can imagine how it looked to you when Eleanor announced our betrothal—"

"How it *looked?*"

"How it felt, then. But, Cat, I never would have asked her to marry me if I hadn't been in love with you."

"I see. And I suppose you reckoned that after the wedding would be as good a time as any to tell me."

He laughed and kissed her, full on the mouth. "Christ! I have missed you, Cat, as I would miss my right hand."

Cat began to cry in earnest. "You think that just because my mother and father—you think that you can treat me any way you please!"

He sat back abruptly on the floor and pulled her into his arms, this time holding her gently, close against his chest. "Oh, no, love. Never that. When I was born a scant month after my parents were married? 'Twould be calling the kettle black for me to think such a thing. No. If you'll listen, I'll explain why I asked Eleanor—"

"I don't care. I don't care at all."

"Don't you?" He put his hand to the side of her face. "Say it again. Say it so I believe you."

"I don't . . ." But she did; she knew it showed all over her, dammit. She looked away, fighting back her tears. "What difference does it make?"

"All the difference in the world, Cat. You don't know what that night meant to me. I'd never made love before, and—"

She let out a harsh laugh. "Oh, really. All those nights in that brothel—"

He stopped her with his finger on her mouth. "I said 'made

love.' I have had plenty of women. But on my hope for heaven, I never had made *love* to any of them before you." He drew a long breath. "And it scared me, Cat. Suddenly it seemed much safer to wed Eleanor. I knew she wanted it, and—well, there was no risk I would ever feel that way about her."

"What way?"

"This way." He kissed her again, the touch of his mouth so tremulous and soft it might have been a whisper. "Thus. So." His hand found her breast beneath her cloak and covered it, gentle as a bird's wings folding over its nest. "As though without you, I will wither away."

Cat heard her own sigh, low, involuntary. "By God, if you are a liar, you are a good one," she whispered.

"Do you believe me?"

"No."

"Let me think, then, how I might convince you." His fingers moved against her breast, tracing slow circles. He put his mouth to hers, tasting her lips and then her throat and hair, groaning his pleasure. "I have dreamed every night for—Christ, how long has it been since I held you? Almost a year. Of finishing what we began at the seawall." He pushed open her cloak and reached for the edge of her gown, his eyes locked on hers. "Time is wasting."

The latch on the blue doors rattled. "Soon," Rene whispered into her ear, with one last caress. They were upright again by the time the door opened to reveal Madeleine and Anne, in matching black capes with red foxtails at the throat. Anne's eyes went to her brother, then to Cat, and then back to Rene.

"We got the fish," she explained. "But I suppose it doesn't matter. You won't be supping here now, will you, Cat?"

"Don't be so sure of that, Annie," her brother said.

"Stay."

Cat laughed. It was the tenth time he'd made the whispered suggestion in the past hour. "I can't." It was already after midnight; she would have a hundred questions to answer from her father and sisters as it was.

"You can say you stayed with Mother and Anne."

"It is not so simple to lie to my sisters. They can always tell. At least, Jessie can."

"Come upstairs with me now, then, before you go."

Scandalized, Cat looked to Madeleine, who'd been sewing in a chair by the fire but had dozed off, head nodding on her chest. "What, under your mother's nose?"

"Over it, rather. Come on." He tugged her arm, and she laughed again, holding tight to her own chair. Madeleine stirred, sending her embroidery hoop crashing to the floor. That woke her completely; she yawned and smiled at her son and their guest.

"I feel like an old woman, but I must to bed."

"And I was just leaving," Cat said quickly. "It was a lovely supper."

"Yes, it was, wasn't it? Good company makes for good eating. Rene, you'll see her home?"

"Of course."

"Well, go and fetch her wrap. Are you walking or riding?"

Rene looked at Cat, one brow raised. "Walking," she decided. "It isn't far." He nodded and went to retrieve their cloaks.

Madeleine was winding up a skein of thread. Cat looked down at her hands in her lap, shy of a sudden. "Are you going to tell your father?" Rene's mother asked quietly.

"Tell him what?" Cat asked a little too quickly.

"About you and Rene, of course."

Cat felt her color rising. "You know, then?"

"It shows all over the two of you. And I am not so old that I cannot recall being seventeen, and in love. Will you tell Archibald?"

"I thought—not yet."

She nodded thoughtfully. "I think that is wise. Cat, I would never presume to tell another person how to live her life, but—"

"Here you are, Cat." Rene had come back in with the cloaks. "I beg your pardon, Mother. Did I interrupt you?"

"It was nothing important." Madeleine rose from her chair and held her hand out to Cat. "My dear. Do go slow."

"It's not a bit icy out, Mother," Rene said with bemusement, but Cat understood what his mother was saying.

"Don't worry." She kissed the older woman's cheek, still so smooth and fine. "Thank you again."

"You're welcome. Don't forget to lock up when you come upstairs, Rene. Events like this always attract the worst element to town."

"Ever the optimist, eh, Mother?" He kissed her, too. "Good night."

The air outside was crisp and dry and cold; there was a ring around the moon. "This way," said Rene, steering her into the alley that ran beside the house.

"No, it's this way."

"I know a shortcut. Come on." He was pulling her by the hand, across the cobbled yard toward the stables.

"This is no short—" He cut her short, though, with a rough, brief kiss.

"Cat, I've been waiting a *year.* I need you."

"It is so late already. . . ."

"Exactly. What difference can a few more moments make?" She laughed despite her apprehensions, and let him pull her into the mews.

She could hear the horses milling in the darkness. The hay in the loft above them smelled summer-sweet. He closed the door and leaned against it, pulling her close to him, his mouth finding hers as he groped for her bodice strings.

"Oh, God. Oh, Cat. I have been wanting you for so long—"

"Don't pull at the laces that way, Rene; you will break them!" She pushed away from him, but he drew her back, his kiss frantic and wild.

"I need you, Cat."

"Well, I need to get home with my clothing intact! Rene, please." His hands were all over her, caressing her breasts through the gown, sliding down to her waist, to her thighs—

"Rene. Stop," she pleaded, frightened by his unbridled passion.

"Come on, Cat. You know you want it too." He'd turned her about so that her back was against the door; he was leaning into her, pressing his groin to her. Forgetting the laces altogether, he yanked down the front of her gown so that her breasts were freed.

"Oh, Cat." He put his mouth to her flesh in the shadowy stable, tasting her, teasing her and then sucking eagerly. The sensation was heaven. She circled his neck with her arms and nearly sagged to her knees. She could feel his urgency in her fingertips, in the taut knots of his muscles, and knowing that he wanted her so made her desperate for him.

But, *Go slow,* his mother had warned her. And even in the white heat of passion, she heard Archibald's voice, cold with fury: *If ye hae disgraced me . . .* "Wait," she begged again.

He raised his head from her breast, his breathing quick and harsh. "What the devil is it?"

"What if I . . ."

"What?"

"You know," she whispered. "A baby."

He paused, his loins tight against hers. "Christ, Cat. What are the chances?"

"It happened to my mother. *And* yours."

"That would seem to make the odds less, not more. How could three women be so unlucky in a row?"

"I am serious, Rain!" she cried, stung that he was jesting. "If my father found you'd dishonored me, I think he would kill you. Truly I do."

He laughed. "What, with his record of debauching? He'd be dead four times over, at least!"

"It is different with his own daughters."

"I am not afraid of Archibald Douglas."

"You should be."

His hands had been gathering up her skirts, raising them to her waist. "Does this feel like dishonor?" he whispered, and once more put his mouth to her breast. Cat drew in breath as his fingertips played at the edges of her drawers. "Or this?" His thumbs were tracing the contours of her mound of Venus through the sheer linen. Against her thigh she felt the bulge of his manhood, rigid and pulsing with life. "I love you, Cat," he whispered.

"Then why not wait until we are married?"

She sensed the sudden stiffening of his shoulders beneath her hands. "What makes you think your father will ever let you marry me?"

"Why—once he knows that you have broken your betrothal to Eleanor and are here for the coronation . . ."

"What difference does that make?"

"It is proof that your politics have changed."

"But they haven't."

She stared at him in the darkness. "They must have. Why else would you be here?"

"Were I a Roman, I'd have gone to see the coronation of Caligula—even if I were assured his reign would be as disastrous for the empire as David's seems likely for Scotland."

"But—Eleanor . . ."

He let her gown edge drop to the ground with an impatient sigh. "Breaking off with Eleanor had everything to do with you, Cat Douglas, and naught with crowns or kings." He touched her cheek. "Most women would be flattered to know that. Would you rather I'd left her for David's sake than for yours?"

"No," she said faintly. "No, of course not. Only I assumed . . ."

"Never assume with me, Cat." There was an edge of warning in his tone.

Cat's head was all in a whirl. Would Archibald ever welcome a suitor whose sympathies lay with the de Baliols? No; never. There was no room for negotiation there. What was left to do? Hope and pray that Eleanor's uncle Edward fell from a horse and broke his neck. Or else, change Rene's mind . . .

"Why think you de Baliol would make a better king than David?" she asked with studied evenness. If she knew why his sympathies lay in the enemy camp, she might better know how to convert him.

"I have met them both. Edward is a great warrior and statesman, his skills honed by years spent surviving in exile. David is—a child my sister's age."

"But he's the blood of the Bruce."

"And what the hell does that mean? Does the fact his father was a decent soldier prove that he will be, too? Blood." The way he spoke the word, so coldly scornful, was alarming. " 'Tis no more than water thickened with a little color. I don't believe it has got some magical power to confer greatness that a man's blood be mingled in his children—nor, for that matter, to confer ignominy. We are what we make ourselves. No more, no less."

So it cut so close to home as that. Cat felt a great wave of hopelessness sweep through her. Did everything in this man's life hark back to his father? And how could she fight against a hatred so illogical, so deep?

Then his voice gentled, his arms coming around her. "If you care for me, Cat, what difference does it make who I want for king—David, or Edward, or the pasha of Egypt?"

"It will come to war," she whispered. "Papa always says that it will come to war. What then?"

"Your father could be wrong. Or is it heresy to suggest that to a Douglas girl?"

"Forgive me for loving my father. But I always believed that was the natural way of things."

She hadn't realized how sharp her tone was until he laughed. "There are the claws on my Cat! So what if Archibald doesn't think me fit for his daughter? We can still meet in secret."

She was silent for a moment. "I can't," she said finally. "I cannot lie to him."

"Very well. I'll tell him I am courting you."

"No! He'd lief as not kill you."

He took her hands in his, pressed them to his mouth. "It has got to be one way or the other, Cat. Unless . . . you do not want to see me." One by one he kissed her fingertips.

Cat felt a flutter of fire in her belly. Not see him again? She could never bear that. Besides, if she didn't meet with him, how was she to change his mind, make him see reason about the king?

But if she saw him, there was always the danger she'd give in to his impassioned embraces. And if she tumbled to him and Archibald found out, Rene would be dead; Cat was absolutely certain of that. Christ, what a dangerous game to play!

I can hold out, she told herself. *I won't give in to him unless he changes.*

He was stroking her breasts, thumbs plucking at her nipples. She fought down a hot surge of longing, pushing his hands away. "I must go home now."

"Christ, Cat, how can you leave me—"

"I will see you tomorrow."

He let his forehead sag against the stable door. Cat swore she heard his heartbeat racing. *What if he will not let me go?* she wondered, suddenly afraid.

"Where?" he asked, and she let her tightly held breath out. "When?"

"I don't know." Archibald had mentioned that the parliament meeting would likely last the whole day. "In the afternoon?"

"Here at the house?"

"No." Gossip traveled too fast; it would not be long before her father learned Rene was at Perth.

"At an inn?"

She shuddered in his arms. "Are you mad? Everyone in Perth right now knows Papa—*and* me."

"Damn. There has got to be somewhere. . . ." He snapped his fingers. "On the river. I can get a boat; we'll row to some secluded place. Be walking on the promenade near the South Inch, just after noon. I will find you there. Will you do it, Cat?"

"I'll try. . . ."

He kissed her, his mouth warm and winning. "Good. Then I will let you go home."

Cat had never been out of doors so late in her life. The moon had long since vanished; only a few revelers dotted the streets, most none too steady on their feet. Rene tucked his cape protectively around her, pulling her close to him beneath its sheltering cover. There was one bad moment when the city watch approached, but Rene pulled her into a doorway and kissed her, and the guards laughed and passed them by without challenge.

There was a monk on duty at the gate to the abbey, his cowl pulled low against the wind. Cat stopped a few yards short of him, turned to Rene, and held her hand out. "Please tell your mother that I hope she is feeling better," she said loudly. "And mind you keep the compresses hot. A twisted ankle is a nasty thing. I'm glad I was on hand to help her nurse it."

"As am I, Mistress Douglas. I'm forever grateful to you." She could feel him laughing as he kissed her curled fingers with utter propriety. "Good night."

"Good night."

No one else could have heard him whisper, "Tomorrow . . ." as he moved away.

"His mother took a fall while I was visiting," Cat told the monk as she came closer. "For a time, we feared her ankle was broken." He said nothing, just watched her through dark eyes that caught a glint from the lamp he held. She yawned enormously. "Lord, but I am tired! Good night." Then, completely unnerved, she bolted past him and ran all the way to her rooms.

Eleven

The bed Cat shared with Janet and Jessie was big, but not so big that she dared climb into it on that night and risk waking them. Let their questions wait until morning, she thought wearily, shrugging out of her gown and into her nightshift. Instead she curled up on the window seat beneath her cloak, moving as noiselessly as she could. She was so certain both her sisters were sleeping that she started with fright as a voice hissed out of the darkness:

"Where have you *been?*"

"Jessie! Lord, you scared me to death!"

"And you me, to disappear that way!" Cat heard her slipping out of the bed, coming toward her. "Do you realize how long you've been gone? Where were you all this time?"

"At Madeleine Faurer's. Just as I told Papa." She hesitated. "Does he know how late I've been out?"

"No. He came by at midnight to say good night, but I told him you had an upset stomach and had gone to get a cup of wine from the kitchens."

"Bless you, Jess."

"He was there, wasn't he?"

"He? Who?"

"You know perfectly well. That son of hers that broke your heart at Christmastide. The one who is marrying that de Baliol creature."

"He isn't marrying her," Cat said. "He has ended the betrothal."

"Oh, Lord," Jess said beneath her breath. "Then he *was* there. Cat, what are you doing? Don't you know what Papa would say?"

Suddenly Cat longed more than she ever had in her life to confide in Jessie, tell her all that had happened, share her wonder, her precarious joy. "Jessie. Listen," she said.

But just then Janet stirred on the bed, rolling over. Confiding in Jessie was one thing; risking Janet's tart tongue was another.

Jessie was waiting, breathless. "What?"

"Nothing." Cat got up from the window seat and pulled her toward the bed. "I'll tell you in the morning."

"Janet will surely be awake in the morning!"

"Then I will tell you sometime."

"No you won't," Jessie muttered, climbing onto the high mattress, pushing close to Janet, who mumbled and turned onto her side.

She was right; already Cat regretted having spoken. This secret was too big, the consequences too grave, to share. But, "We'll talk more in the morning," she repeated.

"Hmph. That's the last time I ever lie for you," Jessie said huffily, and promptly fell asleep.

In the morning, though, Janet got up, dressed in her best blue satin day gown, arranged her gold hair in what was, for her, a remarkably elaborate fashion, and headed for the door. "Where are *you* going?" Jessie demanded.

"That's none of your concern." Janet's pale eyes skewered Cat, who was still lying abed, watching curiously. "Nor certainly none of *yours*. Exactly when did you see fit to come in last night?"

"Your hair looks very nice, Jan."

"That's what I thought—*very* late. Papa would skin you if he knew."

"Well, what about you?" Cat retorted. "Where *are* you going, all got up like that? Meeting somebody, are you?"

"Don't worry your pretty little head; Papa knows all about it. I'll be back in time for supper." She gave them a brief wave and disappeared, closing the door with a sharp, clean click.

"Well!" Jessie flopped back on the bed beside Cat. "What do you make of that?"

"I don't know. What did the two of you do last night?"

"Got Tess and Gill and went to the ball the Randolphs were giving at the castle. What did *you* do last night?"

"I want to know about Janet. Whom did she dance with?"

Jessie screwed up her nose. "Nobody in particular that I noticed. Malcolm Ross once or twice. Perhaps she is stealing him from you."

"If she is, she is welcome. Anyone else?"

"Robbie Stewart, but you know that is only because she adores arguing with him. The Randolph boys. Durward MacLean." She and Cat shared a groan.

"I think we can count Durward out, even considering Janet's peculiar tastes," Cat noted, and Jessie, nodding, agreed.

"And Papa a few times, and Marjory Quillan's father—his gout seems to be better, Marjory says. By the by, she's being courted by William MacEuan, that everyone thought would marry Julie Campbell but didn't. But Marjory says she won't wed so long as she has her father to take care of since her mama died. Malcolm asked about you." Jessie paused for breath. "He asked at least ten times where you were. He seems quite frantic for you, really."

"Malcolm frantic? Please. Malcolm has never been frantic about anything in his life."

"I don't know. I think if I had someone as much in love with me as that, I wouldn't brush him off so quickly." Jessie's voice was wistful.

"How can Malcolm be in love with me? He doesn't even know me."

"Not the way Rene Faurer does, I suppose." The depth of Cat's blush shocked and surprised her sister. "Dear God, Cat. You haven't—you wouldn't—"

"Of course I haven't!"

"Well, thank God. I didn't think even you could be so stupid as that."

"I am going to wait until we are married."

Jessie choked on laughter. "Married! Papa would never let you marry him."

"Why not, if he supports David Bruce?"

"Does he?" Jessie's blue eyes were sharp.

"Well, no. Not yet," Cat admitted. "But he will. I am going to change his mind; just wait and see."

Jessie looked at her for a moment. "I take it back. You *are* that stupid, if you think that he will change for your sake."

Stung, Cat struck back: "What would you know about it? You have never been in love!"

"What would I know about it? Christ, Cat, I am living proof of what comes from falling in love with the wrong man—and so are you."

"The wrong man? What are you talking about? How could Papa be the wrong man?"

Jessie stood up, pacing the floor in her stocking feet. "Don't misunderstand me, Cat. I love Papa more than I can say. But did it never occur to you that my mother, and yours, and Tess's and Janet's—that they'd all have been a good deal happier if they had never met him?"

Cat stared at her, green-gold eyes wide. "That's absurd."

"Hah! And Janet calls *me* the romantic!" Cat had never seen her soft, silly sister so impassioned. "Did you never stop to think about their stigma, their disgrace?"

"What disgrace? Tess's married, and Janet's stayed married—"

"Aye—but Tess's mother was rich. And Janet's has spent the past seventeen years licking her husband's boots. What do you think makes Jan so angry and bitter? And your mother—do you honestly believe it made her life easier to have the great laird, the great Douglas, dance into the Cock and Bull—"

"The Crown of Feathers!"

"Whatever. Dance in, leave you, and dance out again? In that little town, on that tiny island? Can't you imagine the shame?"

Cat felt oddly hot; her chest was constricting. "The way you are talking, you'd think they wished that we had never been born."

"Well, of course they did! Christ, why do you think they all handed us over to Papa?"

Cat could not look at her; she turned away. "I never knew you thought about such things, Jess. You always seem so happy. . . ."

"I think about them a lot. Do you know what Mama told me once?" Reluctantly, with a sense of dread, Cat faced her, saw the intensity in her gaze. "That she'd have killed herself if she had had the nerve." She crossed the room to Cat, took her hands. "Kit-Cat, listen to me. It isn't worth the risk. No man is worth the risk. Wouldn't you rather be like Tess, have the birth of your child a proud, joyous event, something to share with your family, instead of a disgrace?"

"I haven't slept with him," Cat said indignantly.

"You will, though. He will make sure of that."

The bitterness in her sister's voice made Cat jerk up her head. "What do you mean?"

"Has it ever crossed your mind that he might be using you, Cat?"

"Using me for *what?*"

"To try and discredit Papa. How do you think it would look if the mighty Douglas himself had his daughter disgraced by a man the whole court knows is a traitor to Scotland?"

Cat was appalled. "Christ, Jess! Rene would never—"

"Why not? He has already jilted one woman. Or so he says."

"What is that supposed to mean?"

"Whose word do you have that he isn't still betrothed to Eleanor de Baliol?"

"Why—Anne told me."

"And how did Anne know?"

"Rene wrote it in a letter."

Jessie smiled in grim satisfaction. "Exactly. For all you know, you're no more than a dalliance while he is here in Scotland. He—"

"Stop it!" Cat cried angrily. "You are wrong, Jess! You don't know him the way I do. Nobody does. Nobody understands him."

"Maybe I don't. But I do know this. There are a thousand men in Scotland you could fall in love with and not break Papa's heart. So why Rene Faurer, Cat? What makes him so damned special?"

"It is no sense trying to explain. You have made your mind up about him already," Cat's voice was chilly indeed.

"Do you think I want to hurt you? Do you think I enjoy it?"

Jessie asked plaintively. "But I cannot stand by and watch you ruin your life—"

"Are you going to tell Papa?" Cat broke in.

"Are you going to see him again?"

Cat hesitated. Then her chin came up, and she nodded. "Yes."

"You are making a mistake, Cat. Probably the biggest mistake you will ever make. I know it; I feel it in my bones."

Coming from her sensitive sister, that did give Cat pause. But she shrugged it off. "I don't think so. If I am, though, it is my mistake." She bit her lip, hard. "I wish . . . I wish you could be glad for me, Jess."

"Don't count on that." Then Jessie's voice softened. "I won't tell Papa. Not yet." Cat came to hug her, but Jessie held up an arm to forestall her. "Only because I'm absolutely certain you will come to your senses about him, Cat. That he will show his true colors." She began to make up the bed, smoothing the sheets, straightening the coverlet. "I only hope for your sake it happens sooner, not later."

But Cat had seen his true colors, in a moonlit garden, in a pitch-black stables, and she wasn't afraid. "You are wrong about him, Jess. I swear it. He is gentle and loving, and kind."

Jessie looked at her, her fist sunk in a feather pillow. "I wish I believed you, honestly I do. But all I am is sorry for you, Cat."

At noon, with the pale, wintry sun as high in the sky as it would reach that day, the promenade near the South Inch was more crowded than Cat would have expected. Half the visitors in Perth for the coronation, it seemed, had come out to take the air. *It doesn't matter,* she assured herself; *if someone I know sees me, I won't get in the boat with him, that's all.*

She tried to relax, forced herself to move more slowly, as though she, like the others, was out for no more than a carefree stroll. But her gaze kept straying toward the river, dotted with pleasure craft and supply barges. He was out there somewhere amongst them, her own true love . . .

The hours she'd had to reflect on Jessie's words of caution had only served to strengthen her resolve to meet Rene. Her sister, she was sure, was jealous. Well, why shouldn't she be, with Tess married and Jan rushing off to meet some mysterious suitor, and now Cat fallen in love as well? What would help bring Jessie around fastest would be to find her a young man. She'd spoken well of Malcolm. *Perhaps I should sound him out,* Cat thought, *let him know I am taken, but that Jessie finds him attractive. They would be a good match,* she reflected. His stolidness would prove a fine foil for Jessie, who could be so positively flighty at times. Take what she'd said about Rene not really having broken his engagement to Eleanor. Why, that was positively insane.

A barge had slowed beside her on the riverbank, the drover thrusting his pole into the mud to hold against the tide. Cat's heart began thumping. "Ride, pretty lady?" the fellow called to her. It wasn't Rene's voice; she saw now that the bargeman was too short and stocky to be he. Shaking her head, she kept walking between the rows of bare-branched, black-barked larch trees framing the promenade.

Another barge was coming. She watched from the corner of her eye, meanwhile nodding politely to the men and women she passed. Plenty of them were hiring the barges to observe the scenery along the Inch; there would be nothing conspicuous, she assured herself, in her doing the same. Of course, he'd said a boat, not a barge. Perhaps he was in one of the small sailcraft tacking back and forth across the inlet. *Don't worry, Cat, he'll find you!* she thought, and smiled. All this clandestine coming and going was so new to her. But not, the disquieting idea intruded itself, to him. Well, he'd admitted he'd had lots of women. Surely it was rather flattering, then, that he had fallen for—

"Catriona Douglas?" The thick Highland burr, coming close to her ear, made her jump guiltily. Whirling, she saw the elderly face of the earl of Ross, a good friend of her father.

"Lord William," she stammered, "what are you doing here? I mean—Papa told me there was a parliament meeting."

"So there war." His gray eyes twinkled as he bent to kiss her hand. "But, wonder o' wonders, we wrapped the bludy thing up early." Lord, Cat realized, that meant Archibald, too, would be on the loose. "It seems odd to see ye without yer sisters," the earl went on. "Bae ye waitin' on them?"

"No," Cat said. "Yes. Yes, I am. That is, we agreed that we *might* meet here after dinner. So I'm not sure . . ." She stood on tiptoe, scanning the promenade. "I've not seen them yet."

"Nor I." The earl, to Cat's chagrin, settled into step beside her. "A fine day for a walk, though, bain't it? Gude cold wind after all the hot air that war blowin' about the chambers o' the parliament." Cat laughed politely, even as she scanned the riverbank with nervous eyes. "Seen Malcolm, hae ye, since ye came t' Perth?"

"Who?"

There was the merest pause. "My nephew. Malcolm."

"Oh! Of course. Yes. I have, Lord William. Yes, indeed I have. I saw him—" She tried to remember. Had she seen him? "At the castle, two nights' past," she said a little too triumphantly. "And at Papa's pageant. What did you think of the pageant?"

"Too lengthy," the old earl said, grinning. "It makes my bones stiff to stand fer sae long. Strictly betwixt ye 'n' me, Catriona, I wuld nae be surprised if Malcolm had ideas fer ye."

Far out on the Tay, a smart little skiff was skimming and darting among the pleasure craft, its single sail trimmed tight, to catch the least swell of the landward breeze. Its lone occupant was balanced on the taffrail, hanging far out over the water as he brought the bow about and tacked toward Cat.

"Did ye hear me, Catriona?"

"What?" Black hair streaming on the wind, and white shirt billowing . . .

"I said, I think my nephew Malcolm has ideas toward ye, lass. Wha' bae ye starin' at?" He followed her line of sight. "Ach, it bae a bonny wee skiff, bain't it? Bae ye fond o' sailin'? Malcolm has got as fine a hand wi' a rudder as ye e'er will see."

Cat put her back to the water. "No, actually. I detest sailing. Always have." Surely Rene would have more sense than to say anything to her while she was with the old lord.

"Pity," sighed the earl. "Still, surely ye 'n' Malcolm hae much that bae in common betwixt ye. I—Christ, wha' a bludy fool!"

"Who?" asked Cat.

"That sailor there on th' skiff. Just ran his bow straight across that o' a craft three times the size o' his. It bae God's grace he war nae killed." Cat dared to peek, and saw the skiff still skimming hell-bent for shore. "Ach," said the earl, and spat. "Nae wee wonder. It bae that black sheep son o' Michel Faurer."

"Is it? I don't know the fellow," said Cat.

"Sure ye do, lass. 'Twar he gave that loathsome toast at yer sister's weddin'. De Baliol's man, he bae. God knows wha' he bae doin' here. I hope the bugger drowns."

Unable to resist, Cat turned to watch the skiff. It came careening toward the bank; at the last possible moment, Rene swung it about and sent it flying back across the river, missing by a matter of inches a bargeman, who cursed him roundly and tried to knock him with his pole. "Bludy idiot!" the bargeman bellowed. "Mind where ye bae goin'!" Rene grinned cheerfully and made an obscene gesture at him.

"A bad 'un," the old earl muttered, shaking his head. "I pity his poor mum. God be praised, our Malcolm ne'er gave us such cause fer concern. Sae, Catriona, lass, d'ye think ye might luv him?"

"Love who?" Cat cried in alarm.

"Why, my nephew Malcolm! Who in old Clootie's name war we speakin' o'?" Ross put a hand to her forehead. "Ye look right pale, lass. Bae ye feelin' ill?"

" 'Tis the sun," Cat said weakly. "I think I'd best get out of the sun. Good day, Your Grace." She caught up her skirts and ran.

"I'll tell Malcolm I saw ye, shall I?" the earl called after her. "Aye, 'n' that speakin' o' him made ye go all over clammy!" Chuckling to himself, he stomped off along the promenade in the opposite direction from Cat, back toward the town.

She herself was heading for a stand of larch close by the river's edge; Rene and the skiff had disappeared behind them. She stopped running once she saw that the earl wasn't following her, carefully slowing her pace to a nonchalant stroll. Just before she reached the grove, she stopped, kneeling and pretending to adjust her shoe while she scanned the path in either direction. There was no one near.

She ducked in among the low branches of the trees. The earth beneath them was soft and loamy, bright with fallen leaves and dappled by the sun. Rene had pulled the skiff in among the roots exposed by the river; he was waiting for her, whistling. "Are you mad," she hissed at him, "to have come so close to me as that?"

"You were talking to a man. I wanted to see who."

"Well, he saw you, too!"

"Aye, and made a face as though he'd bit a bad egg. What compliments did he pay me?"

Cat couldn't help giggling. "He called you a black sheep, and said he hoped you'd drown."

"Did he? How charitable of him. Is he a close friend of yours?"

She was picking her way through the trees toward him. "Nay. Of my father's. But his nephew Malcolm—" She stopped, then went on. He'd given her a scare; why shouldn't she give him one? "Malcolm is courting me."

"A rival, eh?"

"You don't sound terribly concerned," Cat said with just a whiff of pique.

"You aren't skulking about to meet Malcolm on riverbanks, are you? You are meeting me."

He looked very self-satisfied, Cat thought—and terribly handsome, in his white shirt and high boots and leather breeches, his black hair tied back against the wind with a thong. "Aren't you cold in just your shirt?" she asked, shivering herself as he held out a hand to help her over the last hummock between them.

"Not anymore." He pulled her into his arms and kissed her. His mouth tasted clean, like the scent of the river. Cat melted against him, warmed by his embrace. "I wasn't sure you would come."

"I told you I would try." His hands were busy at her bodice buttons. "What are you doing?"

"I want to see your breasts in the daylight."

"Stop it, Rene!" She was looking over his shoulder; the figures strolling along the promenade were far-off, but in plain enough view through the larches. "Anyone might see us." But he'd parted the halves of her bodice and was kissing her breasts.

Cat felt a tantalizing frisson of pleasure as his tongue caressed her. The dappled sunlight, the soft loam, the rippling river, the unheeding pleasure-walkers trotting to and fro only yards away, made what they were doing seem somehow at once innocent and daring, naughtily delightful. He laughed and slowly moved his mouth upward to her shoulder, showering her with kisses. Just at her collarbone, he paused and raised his head.

"What's this?"

Cat tilted her head to see the small raised line that marred her white skin, then covered it with her hand. "Janet struck me with the fire poker when we were four."

"And this?" He'd seen another scar, smaller, on the underside of his chin.

"Tess pushed me off a horse. I was six. So long as you are taking count of all my imperfections, Jessie gave me this one." She raised the edge of her skirt to show him her left calf, where two round welts lay close to one another. "With a pair of scissors. But at least that was an accident."

He grinned. "Such an eventful childhood! One wound for each of your sisters. Where shall I leave mine?" He caressed her thigh, let his hand drift upward to her waist, her breast, until it covered her heart, which was beating fast and hard, like a regiment drum. "Here, I think."

"You will only wound me if you prove untrue," Cat whispered, watching his sky-blue eyes.

"Then you will have no wound from me after all."

Slowly he drew her down to the soft earth, pillowed with leaves and moss. As his mouth closed over hers, Tess could hear voices from the promenade drift toward them on the wind. The danger of discovery heightened all her senses, made her feel taut as a drawn crossbow, ready to fire at a finger's touch. When he pushed his tongue against her lips, demanding entry, she thought she would explode with longing; when he ducked his head to kiss her breasts, she arched her back and sighed in happiness. Above the treetops the high white clouds were forming and re-forming. A wheeling flock of starlings darkened the sky with their wings. His thigh was inching over hers, so that she felt his manhood hard against her leg. Quickly she caught her fists in his tangled black hair, pulling him up to kiss her mouth again.

"I want you, Cat. I want you now," he whispered to her throat. "We have so little time. . . ."

"Are you leaving?" she asked in alarm. Where could he be going? Please God, not back to France . . .

"No, no. But until you see fit to tell your father about me, who knows when I'll be alone with you again?"

"You are not bold enough to scale the walls of Douglas Castle?" she asked, smiling.

"I would if you bade me to."

He seemed quite serious—so serious that Cat hated herself for the thought that had popped into her head. Her sister Jessie's warning . . . "Poor Eleanor," she murmured, watching his face. "What said she when you broke your betrothal?"

"What?" He was twisting her curls 'round his fingers, watching them catch the sunlight falling through the trees.

"I only wondered . . . what Eleanor said when you told her that you would not marry her."

"Good God, I don't remember. What makes you ask that?"

She nestled close, but still her eyes did not leave his face. "Only that I should be utterly desolate if you told me you did not love me."

"Not Eleanor. She was a fury. A virago, swearing eternal revenge."

"You said you did not remember," Cat said after a moment's pause.

He swung over to look up into the sky. "Well, why in God's name would you want to talk about her? Women really are the most unnatural creatures."

"You . . . you *have* ended it with her, though."

He swung back. "I said I had."

He seemed so brusque of a sudden that she felt the need to explain. "I am sorry. It is just . . . when I told my sister Jessie about you, she—"

"You told your sister about me? About us?"

"I had to tell someone, Rene. I felt about to burst if I—"

"Can she be trusted?"

Cat stared at him. "Trusted? Of course she can. She promised not to tell Papa."

"And what else did she say?" Cat dropped her gaze; he cupped her chin, forcing it up again. "Go on. Tell me."

"She . . . does not think me wise."

"Very delicately put. And she pointed out you had only my word for it that I am no longer engaged to marry Eleanor." She nodded dumbly, and he cursed beneath his breath, sitting up cross-legged on the leaves.

"I did not believe her!" Cat cried, sitting up beside him.

"You had doubt enough to question me."

She said nothing to that; what could she say? He stared out over the water in silence. Then he reached toward her, to pull a dried leaf from her tangled hair. "Cat," he said, and he kissed her forehead, "if you listen to what others say about me, you will never be happy. You must listen to your heart instead. Without you to believe in me, I have no one at all."

"You have your mother —"

"I am not so sure of that."

"And Anne."

"Anne still believes in Father Christmas and the Fairy of the Forest," he said with a wry grin.

"Oh, Rain." She felt so ashamed. "I do believe in you. Honestly I do."

"Then nothing—not your father, not Eleanor, not God himself—can ever come between us, Cat, so long as you do."

He kissed her, holding the sides of her face, the touch of his mouth on hers hard and fast, like a promise. She put her hand to his heart, beating like the river in the forest's hush—

A thud and the rustle of leaves made them spring apart in surprise. Cat clutched for her bodice, and Rene reached into the leaves at his feet, bringing up a red wood ball. Cat stared at it, puzzled, then heard a child's high voice pipe: "Mummy! Mummy, there's a man and a lady in the woods here, and the lady hasn't got any top on!"

"Get away from there, Pauly!" a woman answered from farther away, on the promenade. Rene grinned at Cat, who was frantically fastening her buttons, then hurled the ball back toward the small boy who had chased it nearly into the larches.

"A secluded spot, you said," Cat hissed, her nervous fingers fumbling with the tiny bone buttons. "Jesus, why not on the floor of the Parliament House?"

"We could, you know, tonight. It will be quite deserted."

"Do you think I'd take your word on that now? Go on, get out, get away!" She pushed him toward his boat.

"Come to the house after supper."

Cat shook her head. "I can't. I have got to spend *some* time with Papa. There's the king's reception this evening—are you going?"

"I will if you'll be there." He waded into the river, pushing the sailboat ahead of him. "I know a little room just off the Presence Chamber where hardly anyone ever—ouch!" Cat had thrown a stone at him. "Well, I do!"

"I am sure you do."

"Mummy, do come see! They have got a boat!" Pauly's excited voice rang out. "She's put on her gown now."

"Pauly, I said come away!"

"Until tonight," Rene called, jumping onto the skiff, throwing her a kiss as he hauled the sail tight. *He looks like a god,* Cat thought, with her heart in her throat as she watched him lean away on the ropes. His hair caught the wind just before the sail did; sun glinted on his strong brown arms. How could any girl not love him?

"The boat's gone away," Pauly mournfully reported to his mother, who was bustling toward him from the promenade. "The lady's very pretty."

"How many times do I have to tell you, young man, that your curiosity will land you in trouble someday!" Grabbing him by the elbow, she dragged him back to the path, casting baleful glances into the trees. "Honestly, young people today have no respect for anyone or anybody! Such carryings-on in broad daylight!"

Cat pulled her cloak low over her face and watched Rene fly over the blue water, growing smaller and smaller in the distance until he finally disappeared.

Twelve

"What are you doing with that, Cat?" Janet asked as her sister pulled her new crimson velvet gown from the wardrobe. "I thought you had it made for the coronation."

"Aye, so I did. But I changed my mind. I'll wear it tonight."

"That will leave you with nothing but your blue damask tomorrow," Tess noted critically from the window seat, where she was braiding Jessie's hair, "which is not nearly so attractive."

"I know. But in all the bustle and crunch of the coronation, who is going to notice what anyone save the king and queen is wearing?"

"Whereas tonight, there will be dancing. You've a point," Tess conceded. "Perhaps I'll go and change as well."

"Oh, no you don't." Janet, already with her cloak on, looked mutinous. "No more changing for anyone, or we shall all be late. 'Tis a miracle already that Cat is this far along." Her sharp blue eyes considered Cat again. "And quite her old self, when it comes to that. You've not been this cheerful since you left for Langlannoch before Christmas last year. Is there something you're not sharing with your beloved sisters?"

Strange, Cat thought, how dissembling grew ever easier. She smiled sweetly. "It makes me happy, Jan, to know that you have got yourself a beau at long last. When are you going to tell us who he is?"

"He is speaking to Papa tonight, so it shan't be a secret much longer."

"You mean asking for your *hand?*" Jessie squealed. "Good Lord, Janet Douglas, how can you sit there so calmly?"

"If you don't sit calmly," Tess told her, yanking her brown braids, "I'll never get your hair done. This is all rather sudden, Janet, isn't it?"

"Not particularly. We've known one another for years."

"And only just now realized you were in love." Jessie gushed a sigh. "It is so romantic! Do tell us who, Jan, please, please!" And Cat and Tess echoed her:

"Tell us, Jan!"

"Oh, very well." She made them wait a moment longer, while she fiddled with a loose bit of braid on the front of her cloak. "It is Rawley Quillan."

There was a long space of silence. Then, "Marjory's *father?*" Jessie asked, with a squeak of disbelief in her voice.

Janet nodded. "That's right."

Jessie looked positively appalled. "Why, he's older than Papa! He's so old he's got gout!"

"Hush, Jess!" Tess said sharply.

But Janet only shook her head, bemused. "I expected that reaction from you, Jess."

"I didn't mean to be rude," said Jessie, sounding bewildered. "I just don't understand—why? Why him, of all people?"

"Well, for one thing," Tess noted crisply, "he has got two thousand acres of the finest farmland in all Scotland over in Strathclyde. Not to mention crofts in Aberdeen and Argyll and Dumfries."

"*And* that reaction from you," Janet told her. "Though I did not expect you'd know the acreage!"

"But Janet doesn't care about money. Not the way you do, Tess," Jessie said plaintively.

"You are right. I don't, as it happens. I care that Rawley is a strong man, and kind—"

"And *old,*" Jessie said again.

"He is thirty-eight. That is hardly ancient. Besides, younger men bore me silly. All they want is to get in a girl's skirts. I can talk to Rawley. He likes the things that interest me." She looked at Cat. "I haven't heard from you yet, little sister. Have you nothing to say?"

"Do you love him, Jan?"

"I'm not certain," Janet said, brutally honest as always. "I'm not sure I know what love is. I mean, I know I love all of you, and Papa, and I suppose my mother. But love for a man?" Her blue eyes were thoughtful. "I know that when I am with him I feel safe, and cared for. Is that love?"

"No," said Jessie, just as Tess said, "Yes."

Janet laughed. "We must have a vote to break the tie, then. Cat, what do you say?"

Cat thought of how her heartbeat had quickened that afternoon when she saw Rene come sailing toward her, of the way her flesh seemed to burn at his slightest touch. "I think that when you are in love, you know it," she said slowly.

"Maybe." Janet shrugged. "But I have never been one to fall in and out of love at the drop of a hat, like you and Jessie. Whatever it is that I feel for Rawley, it is stronger than anything I've felt for any other man."

"But if you waited, perhaps there would be someone else for whom the feeling would be stronger still," Jessie suggested.

Janet grinned at her. "Worried about losing our bet?"

"Of course not. I only want that you should be happy."

"You can be happy with anyone, almost," Tess put in. "Within reason. I mean, it's not as though there is one special man out there whose name is written next to yours in the stars."

"You don't think so?" Jessie asked, frowning.

"Good Lord, of course not! How could there be? Life is just too dicey. What if your one man and you never happened to meet? What if he married someone else? What if you walked right past one another in a crowd somewhere? It simply isn't practical to think there is only one fellow in the whole wide world who can make you happy."

"Does Gill know about your theories on this?" Cat asked curiously.

"I am sure he shares them. Gill and I are happy together because we work at being happy, at loving one another—not because Fate decreed we should be."

"You make it sound so horribly sensible." Jess was chewing her lip. "Like choosing a new gown."

"Well, it is like that, rather. You look for a cut and color that will suit you, something that will wear well—stylish, but stout, too, so it will last."

"Oh, I think you are wrong," Jessie told her, eyes round and earnest. "I think love, real love, hits like lightning, like a bolt from the blue."

"If you believe that, then why—" Cat began, and broke off abruptly.

"*Real* love, I said." And she gave Cat a meaningful look. "Naturally, there are some men whom it is simply inappropriate to love from the start. Criminals, for instance. Traitors. Anyone who is utterly unacceptable to your family."

"But what if your name and his are written in the stars?"

Janet looked from Jessie to Cat, then back at Jessie again. "Am I missing something here? Is something going on that I am not aware of?"

"Of course not," Cat said.

Tess had finished with Jessie's hair. "There! That should earn you a bolt from the blue tonight, pet. You couldn't look more lovely. Oh, do you know what? Esther MacInley said she and her brother were sailing on the Tay yestreen and saw that wretched Rene Faurer, who ruined my wedding."

"Really? I thought he was in France." Cat went and kissed Janet's cheek. "I am glad for you and Rawley. Though it will be rather strange, won't it, to have Marjory for your daughter?"

"Marjory will be happy," Jessie noted. "She can look for a husband now."

"Which," Janet said complacently, "should make her grateful to me."

"Only you and Cat left at home soon," Tess teased Jessie. "I hope you won't be too lonely."

"Not likely. There will be room in the wardrobes at last."

Janet opened the door. "Speaking of last—do put on your cloak, Jess; we are late—I wonder who will be the last one married, Jessie or Cat?"

"Cat, I hope," said Jessie, casting a meaningful glance over her shoulder at Cat as she left the chamber. "I truly, honestly do."

* * *

"Dance with me."

The low voice from behind the pillar at Cat's back nearly made her spill the cup of wine she held. She glanced toward her sisters, gathered in a small knot with Gill and Rawley Quillan and his daughter Marjory, and then at her father, who was discussing some detail of the morrow's coronation with the regent, Thomas Randolph, the earl of Moray.

"I can't," she hissed back to Rene. "My father would kill me. Or you. Or both of us."

"Not out there with the others. Back here." His hand snaked out to grab her wrist just as Cat said loudly, "Well! Hello, Malcolm!" Drat, what a time for him to show up! Had he seen Rene?

If he had, he didn't give any sign. "Good evening, Catriona," the blond young man said, bending to kiss her fingers. "May I say how bonny you are looking this evening?"

"Of course you may. What girl would refuse such a compliment?" She forced a smile at her persistent suitor, just in case he had glimpsed that disembodied hand.

"A new gown, isn't that?"

"Why, Malcolm. Fancy your noticing."

"I always notice you. Besides, the color puts a spark to your eyes. It is really quite . . . bonny."

"Thank you." Cat heard, or imagined she heard, a short derisive laugh from behind the pillar. "Have you been enjoying the festivities?"

"I am now." He came and stood beside her, looking out at the throngs crammed into the castle's reception hall. *How differently he moves from Rene,* Cat thought; *he is so stolid and graceless in comparison.* Something brushed the back of her skirts. She aimed a clandestine kick at the pillar, smiling all the while.

"My uncle told me he saw you on the promenade this noon," Malcolm said softly.

"Yes. Yes, we had a little chat."

"Aye, so he said. I wish I had been there. Perhaps you will walk out that way again tomorrow?"

From behind the pillar, Rene's hand was stroking her thigh. Cat caught her breath and brushed those eager fingers away. "Oh, I doubt it," she told Malcolm. "We are leaving so early for Scone for the coronation, you know."

"Pity. It is splendid news about your sister Janet, isn't it?"

Cat nodded. "She and Rawley seem very happy." Archibald had made an announcement of the betrothal earlier at the reception.

"You will be next, I trust."

"Well—either me or Jessie. Have you seen how Jessie is wearing her hair this evening? It is especially bonny." Lord, now he had got her saying "bonny." "Jess is such a wonderful girl. She—"

"Say, I know this step!" he broke in as if he hadn't even heard her. "Would you do me the honor of dancing with me?"

"Oh, Malcolm. I would rather not."

He nodded, eyes cast down. "You'll be remembering I am not much of a dancer."

Had they ever danced together? Cat truly couldn't recall. "It isn't that," she said hastily. He meant well; though God knew he was a pest, there was no reason to hurt his feelings. "The truth is that I turned my ankle a bit out on the promenade this afternoon."

"I saw you dancing with your father earlier." There was no accusation in his voice, merely observation.

"Aye, so I was. But that aggravated it."

He nodded. "Perhaps you would like me to fetch you a chair?"

"Oh, no, that isn't . . . oh!" Rene's hand had slipped under her skirts. "It just gave a twinge," she said in response to Malcolm's curious look. "Perhaps a chair would be helpful."

"Wait here, please." Malcolm hurried off across the crowded room, a man with a mission.

"Christ, what an imbecile," Rene muttered from the pillar. "So he's the one who wants to marry you."

Cat found herself illogically angry at Malcolm for being such a damp rag. "He is a very fine soldier," she whispered defensively.

"I'll wager he is. He bores the enemy to tears."

"Would you stop touching me, please?" Cat smiled at her father as he looked at her across the sea of shoulders and heads.

"Come with me and let me touch you more."

"I cannot go now! Malcolm will—"

"A pox on Malcolm. I want to hold you, Cat, now. Come away."

She hesitated, looking fearfully at Archibald. He seemed quite intent again on his conversation with Moray. Malcolm was nowhere in sight. Her sisters were still buzzing together about Janet's betrothal.

"Well . . . just for a mo—" She gasped as he grabbed her wrist and yanked.

Behind the pillar, in a darkened vestibule, he kissed her, arms tight around her, mouth eager and warm. "What is wrong?" he asked, pulling away, looking down at her face.

"I am sorry, Rene. But with Papa so close, all I can think about is what he would do to you."

"Come with me, then." He pulled her toward the corridor.

Cat hesitated, hearing Malcolm's puzzled voice from the reception room: "Catriona? Catriona!" If he found her again, who knew if she would ever get away? She turned to follow Rene, and together they ran, their footsteps loud against the flagstone floor.

He led her to a little room beneath one of the stairwells—some sort of closet, hooks on the walls, and shelves, and a wooden trunk, empty, the lid propped open with a length of log. "You were not jesting, were you, about knowing a place?" Cat asked breathlessly as he grabbed a cattail torch from the hallway and stuck it into a sconce, then pushed the door shut.

He shook his head, grinning. "My father spent much time at court with the Bruce. I think I know every inch of every royal residence between Berwick and Inverness." He kicked the log from the trunk, let down the lid, and sat on it, his legs spread, holding out his arms. "Come."

She started toward him shyly. The torch threw fantastical shadows up against the close walls with every move they made. "What is this splendid news about your sister?" he asked, drawing her down on his knee, pushing her hair aside so he could kiss her throat.

"Oh—Janet has got betrothed. To Rawley Quillan. Do you know him?"

"I know who he is." His tongue was teasing at her ear, tracing circles.

"I wish," Cat said, and stopped. What was the sense in wishing?

"Do you know what I wish? I wish I knew what sort of idiot remarks a woman's gown and not what's in it." He bent his head to kiss the tops of her breasts where they swelled above the crimson velvet. "Bonny," he murmured, his face buried against her.

"All right, Rene; you need not laugh at him." For some reason, Cat found herself short-tempered with him on this night. He sensed it and turned grave, pulling away to look into her eyes.

"I am jealous of him, that is all. Because he is free to dance with you in public, and I am not."

"You could be." He would only have to denounce Edward de Baliol.

"I don't see how. Unless by some miracle your father comes to his senses."

His ready assumption that it was Archibald who needed to be brought to his senses irked Cat even further. "Or you could," she said.

"You forget, I am not Scottish. If anyone who is could see beyond his whiskey-reddened nose, he'd realize union with England is the best thing that could happen to this godforsaken country." He leaned against the wall, drawing her close to him. "Christ, let's not argue politics, Cat. Let's make love."

"I find I'm not in the mood," she said stiffly, and felt the muscles all along his body tighten as he held her.

"Well, I find I am."

"I want to go back to the reception."

"No."

She laughed, rising from his knee. "No? What would you do to stop me?"

"This."

He caught her wrists and pulled her back to the trunk in a

whoosh of bloodred velvet. "You are hurting my arms," she told him with her teeth clenched.

"Then leave off fighting me."

"I told you, I want to go back!" She was trying to push him from her, but he still held her hands. She could feel his manhood, thick as a sapling, thrusting at her thighs, and she scrambled to turn in his grasp. The tiny room was stifling; she was breathless, and her head was pounding. This was far different from dallying with him on the riverbank, with half of Perth strolling nearby. This was frightening.

"Men have a name, you know, for girls who lead a man on and won't finish what they've started." His eyes were narrowed in the torchlight.

Christ, he was strong. Cat willed her hands to stop shaking. "And there's a name for forcing a woman to your will. It is 'rape.' If I cry it on you here in this place, you are dead."

"You would not do that to me." But she heard the faint uncertainty in his voice.

"I will, if you don't let go."

He released her abruptly. Cat backed away from him, rubbing her aching wrists. "Bastard," she said evenly.

"I'm sorry," he said in a harsh croak. "God help me, I'm sorry. But I am burning for you, Cat. I can't help myself. To see you standing with him, laughing up at him—"

"Malcolm means nothing to me!"

"And I do?"

She nodded slowly. "Yes."

"Then why won't you prove it to me? And let me prove my love for you?" He sounded hurt, bewildered, like a puzzled boy.

"How? By getting under my skirts in some—some broom closet?" Cat held her chin high. "No, Rene. If you love me—"

"You know that I do!"

"Prove it by renouncing de Baliol."

There, she'd said it, given him the ultimatum. She edged closer to the doorway, half-expecting him to become angry again. But he was staring at the floor; when he raised his eyes, they were dark and sad.

"You don't know what you are asking, Cat."

"Of course I do! It's not so great a matter!"

"What if I made the same demand of you—that you choose between King David and me?"

She looked at him, startled. "But—that is different."

"Is it? How?"

"Why, King David has the right on his side!"

"What makes you so sure?"

Cat felt her temper rising. "He—is—the—son—of—the—Bruce," she said with exaggerated patience.

"And the Bruce was a usurper. He murdered Red John Comyn and stole the crown. Christ in heaven, Cat, what has any of this to do with you and me?"

The image of Rawley and Janet standing together, accepting congratulations, was still burned on her mind. "I want," she cried, and swallowed a sob. "I want what my sisters have, dammit! I want a—a husband, and a home, and children. I want a wedding at Castle Douglas, with Papa giving me away. Are those things so unreasonable?"

He shook his head, smiling a little. "No. But if I cannot give them to you—do you still want me?"

Yes, her heart sang. *No*, her head insisted. Cat stood without moving, torn down the middle, frozen with indecision. Was love worth so great a sacrifice? Her father would disown her. Her sisters would not receive her. She would never be able to go home again. The thought chilled her blood.

A voice from the corridor made her head jerk 'round. "Catriona! Catriona, where are you?" Malcolm . . .

"He can give you what you want," Rene said softly.

"But I don't love him," she whispered.

"Maybe love is a luxury you can do without. Try it. Go to him."

"Catriona! Catriona!" Malcolm sounded increasingly puzzled; she could hear his footsteps now, pacing the flagstones.

"It is you I want," she told Rene faintly.

"Not enough, I'm afraid."

How the devil had this happened? Cat wondered. She had given him an ultimatum, and now *she* was the one being forced to choose.

"Catriona?"

Rene's eyes burned with a low, steady blaze. "Who will it be, Cat?"

"I—" She turned to the door, turned back. "Rene, I—"

"Never mind," he said. "I always knew the answer." He got to his feet so abruptly that she cringed in fear. But he only moved past her and lifted the door latch, bowing politely. "Good-bye, Cat."

The reception hall seemed exactly as she'd left it; she saw her father and sisters, Gill and Rawley, all in their places. Someone touched her sleeve from behind. She whirled about, startled.

"Catriona." It was Malcolm. "Where in the world have you been? You see, I brought you a chair."

"How very kind," Cat said breathlessly. "Could you move it here, though, please? Far away from that pillar. There's a terrible draft from back there."

She did not see Rene again until the guests moved into the dining hall for a late supper, after midnight. Poor little King David, looking half-asleep, led the procession from the reception hall, holding tight to his wife's hand. Cat was walking beside her father when she felt him stiffen. "Great bludy Christ," said Archibald. "See who has come here." She glanced up. Rene was lounging in a doorway not ten feet away.

His eyes met hers, and she saw that he was still angry; his irises were stormy blue. Her father's grip on her elbow tightened. "If 'twere up to me," he barked out, "there wuld be nae place at Scone tomorrow fer such traitorous knaves."

"Come, Papa," Cat urged, trying to tug him onward. He took a few steps with her, but then turned back, wagging a finger at Rene in threat.

"I'll tell Moray I saw ye, shall I, ye scurfy knave? 'N' bid him mind the young king's back."

"Papa, please!"

"Faith, if I dinna ken his mother sae well, I'd swear th' boy bae a bastard," Archibald grunted, "fer there bae none o' Michel Faurer's gude blood in him, that's sure." He trudged on toward the dining hall. Cat followed, not daring for the world to look back at Rene, and not at all certain she wanted to.

She did glance his way once or twice during supper, when she thought it safe. He was not seated with Madeleine, but stood a little behind her table, taking great draughts from an ale mug he had refilled more times than was wise under the circumstances. Well, she thought, looking at her own dining companions, it seemed to be something in the air that night. Gill was downright giddy; Archibald's nose had a familiar red gleam to it, and even Malcolm—thank God he wasn't seated next to her, but by Jessie; Cat had the antique earl of Ross on her left, and Archibald on her right—seemed to be getting light-headed on the good Rhenish wine.

The king and queen were let go after the fish course; Thomas Randolph, the earl of Moray, who was the Bruce's nephew and the regent for young David, led a toast to their health just before they retired. They looked jolly glad to get away to their beds. That started a whole festival of toasting by the lords who were present. Cat listened nervously, her gaze darting toward Rene more than was probably safe. She could not help herself; she just kept thinking of the toast he'd made at Tess's wedding. Surely, surely he would not do anything so rash and reckless here, on this night.

Big, red-headed Robbie Stewart, circling the room in search, Cat reckoned, of girls, saw Rene standing with his ale mug and stopped dead still. As Cat watched surreptitiously, with her heart in her throat, Rene looked straight at Stewart and raised his mug, with a small half smile. Stewart's hand went to the hilt of his sword with an audible *chink,* but just then Madeleine turned to say something to her son, who leaned close to hear her. Stewart hesitated, then turned on his heel and stalked off again.

Leave, Rene; leave now, Cat prayed soundlessly. *There is no place for you tonight, amongst this company.* She felt dreadfully guilty for having quarreled with him. Coupled with her father's harsh words to him, it seemed sufficient to cause him to scowl in her direction more than once as the meal wore on.

Robbie Stewart had wended his way to their table and was murmuring to Malcolm. Cat pricked her ears to hear them, but just then Archibald let out a belch so hearty that everyone laughed. By the time Cat looked back, both Malcolm and Robbie had disappeared.

"Ye seem tenty t'night, Catkin," said her father, rubbing his stomach in satisfaction as the last course—apples, dates, and walnuts still in the shell—was presented. "Bae ye lookin' fer someone in particular?"

"Looking for someone?" she echoed.

"Aye. Yer eyes keep dartin' all about." He cracked a walnut in his teeth, earning a brief lecture from Jessie farther down the table about the dangers of such behavior at his age. Cat hoped that might distract him, but when he'd finished laughing off Jessie's dire warnings, he turned to Cat again. "Did ye ken young Faurer was in the city, then?"

"I—" God, it was hard to lie to him so baldly. "No. I didn't."

"Dinna see him at his mother's house the other night?" Cat shook her head dumbly, picking at a sugary date on her trencher, afraid to raise her gaze to his.

Jessie, chewing her lip, had been watching them from her seat. "Papa," she said reproachfully as he reached for another walnut and raised it to his mouth, "do you want to end up a toothless old man?" Cat threw her a blazing smile of gratitude, then noticed how awfully worried her sister looked—more worried than could be accounted for by fear for Papa's molars. She'd been sitting by Malcolm, Cat remembered, when Robbie Stewart came and spoke to him. There was suddenly a great uneasiness, a heaviness, lying on Cat's heart. All around her, the gay company was drinking, dining, singing, making merry—and all she could think was, Where had Malcolm and Robbie got to? She gazed across the hall to Rene, who had his nose buried once more in his mug of ale.

Just then she saw them: Malcolm and Robbie, fists on their sword hilts, moving slowly, steadily behind the long rows of tables and benches at the far end of the hall. Something about

their faces, the grim purposefulness of their strides, made her
rise to her feet involuntarily. "Catkin, where bae ye goin'?" her
father asked at her side.

Jessie had risen, too, and came to stand beside Cat, putting a
hand on her shoulder. "Sit down, Cat," she said softly.

Cat whirled on her. "What is going on?"

"It is nothing to concern yourself about. Really."

Cat stared at her sister, her sweet, kind, disingenuous sister
that she always had trusted. "Jesu, Jess. What have you done?"
She turned again to search for Malcolm and Stewart. There was
no question in her mind now; they were headed for Rene.

She started to call a warning to him, but Jessie's hand on her
arm forestalled her. "Think of Papa," she murmured to Cat.
"Would you embarrass him in front of all his friends?"

"But—" It didn't matter now; Rene had seen them coming.
He set his ale mug down atop the nearest table and waited, silently, patiently.

Then Malcolm said something to him in a low voice, mouth
curled in a sneer. Rene drew his sword so quickly that Cat gasped.
Malcolm smiled and began to draw as well, but Robbie Stewart
beat him to it. "Stand off, Malcolm," he warned in a voice that
carried all the way to Cat. "This bastard's mine."

Anyone in the hall who hadn't seen already what was happening certainly knew now. Cat saw Thomas Randolph, at the king's
table, stumble to his feet in disbelief. As for Archibald, his eyes
were glowing. "Gie him one fer me, Robbie, lad," Cat heard him
say beneath his breath.

The revelers around them were drawing back, clearing a space
for the two men. Madeleine Faurer took a step toward her son,
but he waved her off impatiently, the bright tip of his blade dancing a little, back and forth, in the glow of the torches. Robbie
had shrugged off his doublet, was rolling back the cuffs of his
white shirt. Rene didn't bother. He feinted toward Robbie, making the onlookers draw in their breaths. Stewart circled warily
away.

"See here, now," Randolph blustered from the dais, "ye twain
cannae do that here, now! Get off wi' ye, now, both o'—"

Rene struck the first blow, a buffet to the right shoulder that sent Robbie reeling.

"Hoy!" Randolph cried in outrage. "Hoy, stop that right now!"

Robbie regained his footing, boots gripping the flagstones, and answered the blow with a quick, darting thrust that very nearly sliced through Rene's doublet, close by the heart.

Randolph was coming toward them, his lined face red and wroth. "In the name o' David, king o' Scotland, I command ye to stop!" he bellowed at the duelists.

"He does not believe David *is* the king," Robbie said grimly. "That's what the bloody fight's about."

Randolph signaled to the guards closest to the two men. "Separate them," he barked out. But the soldiers took their sweet time coming; they too, it seemed, were hankering for this fight. "Stick him through fer th' sake o' his father," Cat heard one man mutter, "that wuld sooner hae died than see his lane son bring him such shame."

There was a furious burst of thrust-and-parry from the two men, the hard clash of steel on steel seeming to rattle the windowpanes. One of the Templars Cat had met at Christmas— Tomas, the tavernkeeper—came forward to lead Madeleine away, but Cat saw her shake her head, rooted to the spot where she stood.

Rene's expression was like nothing Cat had ever seen on him; it seemed the fighting had transformed him. He looked far older than his seventeen years; his face was fierce and thunderous. Robbie, too, looked different, older, crueler. "Come on, Faurer," he taunted, blade tip glistening as he teased the air with it. "Come on and get me, ye bloody coward."

"I'm no coward, Stewart," Rene growled, and rushed at him. Cat clenched her eyes shut, and only opened them again when a clamor of steel told her the blow had been met.

What could one hope for as an end to this clash, she wondered? If Rene should die—but Rene couldn't die. That meant Stewart must, and she had known him all her life. He was the king's uncle, son of the Bruce's daughter Marjorie. Oh, why in heaven did the soldiers not stop them? But the moment for that was lost;

anyone who tried to step between the two wild men now risked losing an arm.

Perhaps if I were to appeal to Rene, Cat thought . . . She took a step toward him, only to find herself restrained by her father, his grip on her arm very strong indeed. "Where d'ye think ye'd bae gaein'?" he demanded of her.

"Papa, I," she began, ready to confess everything to him if only it would stop the fighting.

"Shut up, Catriona," he told her, thrusting her down into her chair and then holding her there.

She could scarcely see across the hall from there; too many folk had crowded forward to witness the duel. With each ringing of steel they all would ooh, or gasp; some of the men were cheering Robbie on. "Let me up, Papa," she pleaded, but he either did not hear her in the clamor, or did not want to. Cat began to cry. "Let me go, Papa! Please! For the love of God!" Another burst of fighting, boots scuffling across the stone floors, swords clashing, and then—

"Robbie!" her father shouted, loosing his grip on her. Cat leaped up and saw that Rene had struck first blood. It was only a little blood, near the redhead's left temple, but the sight of it as it dripped to his shirtsleeve seemed to enrage him. He fell on Rene with a fury, sending him reeling back against the chamber's far wall. Cat wished herself back in the chair, but dared not look away.

Slash! went Robbie Stewart's sword. Rene was bleeding too, now, from a cut on his wrist—not his sword hand, thank God, but the left one, raised to ward off a blow. *Slash!* His thrust caught Robbie's shirt buttons, slicing them loose to skitter onto the floor. *Slash!* Christ, they were going to murder each other; why did no one stop them? Unable to bear the horror of anticipation, Cat made a break for it, darting forward through the crowd. "Rene!" she screamed.

In the split second in which Rene looked toward her, Robbie pierced him in the side, below the arm, running him straight through.

Cat screamed again, a long, wordless wail of terror. Malcolm was smiling at her. Robbie Stewart had stopped cold, wiping sweat from his brow on his sleeve. Rene was still standing, with Robbie's sword skewered through his belly. As Cat watched, he reached down and pulled it free. There wasn't any blood.

His doublet. It had caught his doublet, not his flesh. Relief made her sink to her knees. Rene hesitated for an instant, catching his breath before he tossed the sword, end over end, back to where his opponent stood. "Let's finish it, then."

That would have been the moment to step between them, but no one moved; they were all too stunned by the vision of a man run through come back to life again. Stewart grinned coldly, catching the blade by the hilt. "As ye like, Faurer," he grunted, and they fell on one another once more. Their dance of death was bringing them closer and closer to Cat; as she knelt on the floor, fist at her mouth, she could see only their legs, leaping, twisting, turning, and the occasional flash of a blade.

She struggled to her feet, not daring to call Rene's name again. His face was dark, mouth taut with the hatred that burned, too, in his stormy eyes. She thought of that mouth kissing hers, suckling so sweetly against her breasts, and very nearly fainted; only the press of the crowd held her up. "Oh," she whispered, "Rene . . ."

He had backed Robbie into a corner, hard between two pillars. A hush fell over the crowd; it grew so quiet that one could hear the two men's short, harsh breaths. Robbie's eyes were narrowed as he parried a flurry of strikes.

Then Rene knocked away his sword.

Robbie's dark eyes followed it as it clattered to the floor. He made a lunge for it, but Rene stopped him with his blade at his throat. Slowly, very slowly, Robbie edged backward. Just as slowly, step by step, Rene moved in for the kill.

"Now!" Thomas Randolph bellowed. "Now, gae on, take him!"

At long last the soldiers moved, swarming over Rene in a mass, tearing his sword from him, yanking him around, arms pinned behind his back, to face the regent, who had thunder in his eye.

"Bludthirsty, vaunty boys," old Randolph barked out. "Who in God's name d'ye think ye bae, to break the sanctity o' this coronation wi' yer glinty blades? Ye, Stewart!" Soldiers dragged him forward, bleeding, sweating. "Gae hame to yer daddy's castle. Stay there until ye learn yer manners. Ye bae banished fro' the court. A sentence o' one year."

Robbie started to protest, but the old man's fiery countenance stopped him. He shot one last look of pure, abject hatred at Rene, who returned it; then Robbie lowered his head and let himself be led away.

"Now. Ye, Faurer." The regent considered him. Rene did not look contrite. "Ye hae been a sore grievance to me fer a lang time, my laddie."

"I am not your laddie, old man," Rene growled. "I am no man's laddie."

"Nae yer father's, on th' face o' things," Randolph agreed. "At least, ye hae nae his feelin' fer this country, nor fer its rightful king. 'N' since that bae sae—I hereby order ye banished fro' Scotland, Rene Faurer, fro' this moment on to the end o' yer natural life."

"No," Cat whispered. Banished? Forever? Oh, Christ!

"Then I'll gladly go," Rene said shortly, coldly, "and leave you fools and your snot-nosed king."

Randolph reached out and slapped him, hard. Rene, his arms restrained, spat in the regent's face in return.

"Take him away," Randolph told the soldiers. "Put him on th' first ship at Dundee that bae sailin' o'erseas."

"No!" Cat cried out. Rene's gaze went toward her; he shrugged a little, as a man might at losing a round of skittles. She swallowed what more she had meant to say in a rush of hot red humiliation. Was that all she was to him—a game, a plaything? Lord, but his eyes were cold as they rested on her.

Someone was pressing her hand—Jessie, she saw, glancing 'round, with Archibald beside her, and behind him Malcolm, looking triumphant, pleased. "Come, Cat," Jessie whispered.

"But I—" Wildly, she looked again at Rene.

"Come," Jessie said again. "Malcolm has very kindly offered to see us home."

Smoothly, swiftly, he was at her side, insinuating his arm through hers. "This way, Catriona," he murmured.

How dazed she felt—as though she'd been kicked in the head.

Malcolm's eyes were gravely solicitous. "I'll take care of you, Catriona; never fear."

Cat caught a glimpse of Madeleine then, surrounded by her husband's old friends. She was weeping; they were speaking to her quietly, urgently. She did not see Cat.

Jessie and Malcolm were leading her away. Rene had disappeared.

She turned on her sister. "This is your fault. You planned this, you and he—" She glared at Malcolm, trying to pull free of his arm. "And Robbie. You planned it. You deliberately baited him—"

"Nonsense," Malcolm said crisply. "Faurer is a notorious hothead. The kingdom's better off without him. Let him hie his black hide back to France."

To France. To Eleanor.

Cat collapsed in a heap. Malcolm bent and gathered her up in his arms, held her tight to his chest. She could feel his heartbeat, measured and steady, against her cheek.

"I'm sure it is all for the best, Cat, really I am," said Jessie.

"Of course it is." Malcolm pressed a kiss, very light, to her forehead. "Just wait and see."

Part Three

Edinburgh, Scotland
July, 1332

Thirteen

"And another score," Janet Douglas said, passing the last quiver to Cat with a sigh of relief. "Christ, what a deadly dull job Papa has set us to!"

"Everyone must do his part if we are to be victorious," Jessie replied, tongue between her teeth as she made another slash across the parchment. "That makes fifteen—nay, sixteen hundred score. Papa will be pleased."

"Will he?" Janet plucked an arrow from one of the hundreds of quivers lined up in the storeroom. "Half of them are so old that the shafts are brittle. See?" She snapped it over her knee, demonstrating.

"Even a weak arrow can stop a cowardly traitor," Jessie said stoutly—then threw a quick, worried glance at Cat. But her sister went on methodically loading the quivers into sheepskin bags. "Well," Jessie went on, rather more loudly than was necessary, " 'tis a pity, isn't it, that Tess isn't here? Then it would be like the old days, when we used to get Papa ready for battle. How much longer is it till her churching, anyway?" That was the ceremony, forty days after a woman's confinement in childbirth, that marked her reentry into the community.

"Another week, I think." Janet sat back on her haunches, rubbing pine resin from her hands with a cloth.

"I cannot wait to see the baby again, can you? I think she is the loveliest thing ever," Jessie said dreamily.

"I think she looks like a pig."

"Janet, for heaven's sake!"

"Well, I do," Janet reiterated, unembarrassed. "She has that little pig nose, and she is pink like a pig, and she makes pig noises when that wet nurse feeds her." Cat made a little noise herself, of harsh bemusement.

"Oh, you are both terrible," Jessie told them. "All babies are a bit peculiar-looking at first. And those noises are the nurse's fault, not Baby Jane's. If you ask me, she isn't holding Jane at all properly." Her eyes took on a faraway glaze. "When I have babies, I shan't farm them out to a wet nurse. I shall nurse them myself."

Janet snorted. "If you do, you won't ever get anything done. That nurse works hard for her wages, tied down to that mewling brat practically every hour."

"My, you are just bursting with maternal feelings, aren't you, Jan?" Jessie shook her head, laughing. "No wonder you are marrying Rawley, who has already got himself an heir.

"That is another advantage of marrying an older—where are you going, Cat?"

"Out," Cat said shortly. "Out for some air." She left the storeroom abruptly, leaving Jessie chewing anxiously on her lip.

The stone-walled storeroom had been comfortably cool, but as Cat climbed out onto the parapets of Edinburgh Castle, the summer heat enveloped her, stifling and weighty. Still, better here than in there, she thought, fanning herself with her hand, where those two have nothing better to talk of than husbands and babies and such. On the whole, she had to agree with Janet—baby Jane *did* look a bit like a pig. Though of course Cat was glad that all had gone well for Tess and Gill. *Someone* might as well be happy, she thought morosely, looking down into the castle yards.

Thomas Randolph, the Earl of Moray, was drilling the royal guard some fifty feet below; she picked him out easily by his white beard and crimson hat. How much harm, she speculated, would a rock thrown at him from this distance be likely to do?

She was still angry at her sister Jessie and at Malcolm Ross for their roles in getting Rene banished. But her hottest fury was reserved for the regent Moray, who'd pronounced the sentence with such quick finality. Why exile Rene for life and give Robbie

Stewart but a rap on the knuckles? Even after eight months, the utter unfairness of it still brought tears to her eyes.

And then there was Archibald. She saw him now in the yard below, standing beside Moray with his arms folded over his chest, reviewing the troops as they readied for the coming invasion, and a flush of humiliated memory flooded her cheeks. She had actually gone to him, swallowed every bit of her pride to ask her father to intervene for Rene, ask Moray's mercy. Her father had struck her—the first time ever in her life—and confined her to her rooms for a week.

When he'd let her out, she swore she would not stay in Douglas Castle. She'd written to Madeleine, offering to come to Langlannoch for as long as they would like her there. The note she got in response was not encouraging. Madeleine wrote that she felt too unwell for anyone, even Cat, to visit. Besides, she explained, she had not yet decided how to tell Anne about her brother's banishment, and thus feared it might be awkward to have Cat there.

In a postscript, she added that she'd heard from Rene; he'd written to say he was in Paris, staying with the de Baliols. This confirmation of Cat's worst fears plunged her into such grief that she did not feel capable of making any change. As time went on, she resigned herself to staying on in Douglasdale. If Madeleine did not want her—and clearly she did not—then where else would she go?

It was easy enough to stay busy; at least the rumors of a coming war were good for that. Everyone seemed to agree that Edward de Baliol would make his move soon now that the coronation had taken place—before King David's advisers had time to consolidate their power, and while resentment amongst the English from the Border Counties, who'd lost their lands in the Bruce's wars, still ran high. The questions confronting the Council were *where* de Baliol might land, how great a force Edward the Third of England might throw up to aid him, and how the Scottish army, which in the face of truly historic battles was apt either to triumph against all odds or completely go to pieces, would fare this time.

And on top of all that, there had been the fuss over the birth of Tess's baby. Lord, what a dreadful ordeal her poor sister had gone through! Three days of labor, with the midwives trying frantically to turn the breech baby in her womb while Tess had screamed her head off . . . it was enough, even star-eyed Jessie acknowledged, to make a girl forswear men for life. But at last the wives had succeeded, and Jane had popped into this world, pig-pink and wrinkled, and all the pain had been swallowed up by joy. Of course, Gill *had* wanted a boy, which meant Tess faced going through all that again at least one more time.

Now there was Janet's wedding, scheduled for the first of August, to make ready for. Rawley Quillan was anxious that the marriage take place before de Baliol could land, and his astrologer assured him that an early August date would leave plenty of time for the honeymoon. Janet, bemused, acquiesced to her betrothed's wishes, though she had pointed out to Rawley that August in Edinburgh could be beastly hot.

Cat and Tess and Jessie, along with Rawley's daughter Marjory, were to be Janet's attendants. The wedding would be much smaller and simpler than Tess's, both because of the war and, of course, because Rawley had been wed before. Janet didn't seem to feel cheated, though—and neither did Archibald, who could funnel his funds into defending his sprawling estates.

So, Tess, and now Janet. *In a fortnight, only Jessie and I will be left,* Cat thought glumly, raising her gaze from the panoply of soldiers in the courtyard to the tree-crowned hills backed up against the Firth of Forth. *How dreadful that will be, now that I know she cannot be trusted. I shall lose the bet. I never will marry, despite that pesky Malcolm. How he thinks he shall win me when it is his fault my true love has been sent away, I never will know.* Well, perhaps at last he was coming to his senses; she had noticed him spending more time with Jessie since they'd come to Edinburgh three weeks past.

That *would* be a match, she thought—Jessie and Malcolm, the two snakes who had ruined her life. She wished them on each other.

"Cat?" Jessie, with the worried-yet-hopeful smile that was habitual with her these days around her youngest sister, appeared in the doorway. "We are going downstairs now to find something to eat, Jan and I. Do you want to come with us?"

"I'm not hungry."

"You have got to eat, Cat," Jessie chided fretfully, "or you will just—" She stopped, seeing Cat's stony face. "We'll bring you up something, then, shall we?"

Cat shrugged. "Do as you please."

"Oh, Cat." Jessie was wringing her hands. "I've told you again and again that I'm sorry, and 'tis God's truth, I am. But all I did was tell Malcolm that I thought Rene was sweet on you. It isn't my fault! How long do you intend to punish me?"

"The banishment is for life," Cat told her, very quietly.

"I think you are horribly cruel, Catriona Douglas!" said Jessie, and burst into tears.

Two days later, Cat saw Madeleine Faurer again. She'd come to Edinburgh Castle at the earl of Moray's request, just for a week, to help stir up a poison for the Scots to paint upon their arrow tips. "I learned the mixture from one of your kinswomen," she told Cat in the castle yards, where she was directing a bevy of serving girls stirring great iron vats. "Linnet MacPherson, that is married to your cousin Angus."

Cat nodded; Linnet's expertise in all matters medicinal was famous throughout Scotland. "But is Linnet here?"

"Nay. One of her bairns is sick. She waited long enough for those children of hers that she is not about to leave them when they are ill, not even for the safety of Scotland. So she told Thomas to send for me."

"You were sick, too," Cat said softly. "You are better now?"

Madeleine's eyes, green as grass, were tragic to see. "I am— glad to have something to do, anyway," she told Cat.

"Is Anne here?"

The older woman shook her head. "Gone to stay with friends. I was afraid if she came . . . oh, it is foolish, I know, to go on keeping the truth about Rene from her. But on the heels of her father's death . . . and she adores Rene so. I just keep hoping that—that *something* will happen."

"Such as what?" Cat asked, her voice unaccustomedly harsh. "That de Baliol's forces will triumph?"

"God, no! I cannot bring myself to wish for that, not even for Rene's sake. Can you?"

Cat started to say yes, but it was a lie, and she stopped. "I don't know. I doubt, though, that I should have come running to Edinburgh at the request of the man who banished my own son, to make poison for arrows that are going to be shot at him."

"Do you think I don't know that?" Madeleine wrung her thin white hands. "I must be the unhappiest woman in the world, I fear."

Cat bit her sharp tongue and hugged her, holding her closely. "Either you or I," she agreed.

That something will happen.

Madeleine Faurer's tortured words kept running through Cat's head in the next few weeks, while she worked to help provision the Scottish army for the coming confrontation, while she stood through endless fittings of the gowns for Janet's wedding, while, with everyone else in Scotland, she waited for word that Edward de Baliol had made his move to cross the Channel. The invasion, it was generally agreed, could come at any time. Janet was cool as a cowcumber as she planned for her marriage, even though, as Jessie had pointed out time and again, all their preparations could very well prove for naught if de Baliol sailed early. It might not be her wedding, but Jessie was nervous enough for any ten brides. The ceremony would be in Edinburgh, not at home in Douglasdale, because Edinburgh was where, in those hectic days of late summer, nearly all Scotland was.

Tess arrived in the last week of July, fresh from her forty days of forced confinement and, she noted triumphantly at her first gown-fitting, not one jot bigger in the waist than before her pregnancy. Baby Jane had been left behind. "But she is scarce six weeks old," Jessie said in disappointment at this news. "Don't you miss her?"

"Of course I miss her," Tess declared. "But Edinburgh's no place for a baby now, with de Baliol attacking. She has her nurse, and Gill's mother. She'll be fine. Janet, did you order me shoes?"

Like Rawley, Gill would be riding with the army. Tess faced the prospect with equanimity. "Worrying about him won't do any good, will it?" she noted. "It is all in God's hands." The oldest of the Douglas girls had always been practical, but marriage and motherhood seemed to have made her downright nonchalant. Cat was in awe of her. How, she wondered, would Tess have reacted to *her* true love's banishment?

To her surprise, Tess broached the subject herself, when they were alone in Cat's shared room one evening, sewing red-and-gold badges for King David's troops to wear on their caps. "You are being rather cruel to Jessie these days, don't you think?" Tess asked, licking her thread to a point as she sat in an armchair.

"Me, cruel to her?" Cat looked up with wounded eyes. "What about what she has done to me?"

"According to Jessie, all she did was mention to Malcolm Ross that you'd been seeing Rene. Everything else that happened was Malcolm, and that wild Robbie Stewart."

"But if she hadn't said what she did, it would not have happened."

"Oh, you flatter yourself, Cat," said Tess, astounding her.

"What in the world do you mean?"

Her sister stuck her needle in the pincushion and leaned forward. "That fight wasn't about you dear; it was about politics. If Rene was stupid enough to show up for the coronation—"

"Rene is not stupid!"

"Well, reckless, then. He tried the same thing at my wedding, didn't he, with that toast he raised?"

"That was *not* political," Cat said with great certainty. "It had to do with his father. He hates—hated—his father."

"Did he? What a tremendously appealing trait in a man."

Cat's anger flashed. "Oh, it is easy for you to sneer, isn't it, when you are sitting pretty with your Gill, and Jane?"

"I *am* sitting pretty," Tess declared, with the complacency Cat always found so annoying. "But do you know why? Because I went out and found myself a good man, an honorable man I needn't be ashamed of. And do you know what, Cat? We are happy. That is what being in love should do for you—make you happy, not all craven and miserable, sneaking about behind your family's back."

Cat could think of nothing whatsoever to say to that, so she shut her mouth and went on sewing—in, just as Tess had said, utter misery.

Fourteen

Janet's wedding would be held in St. Margaret's chapel, the tiny freestanding building where the mother of King David I had worshiped three centuries before. Only Rawley's family, including his grown children, and the bride's more immediate relatives—with an effort, Janet had convinced her father to keep the list below fifty—would be present, along with a handful of honored guests. In deference to Archibald's standing in the realm, these would include King David and Queen Joanna. Also invited was the regent Thomas Randolph, earl of Moray. When Cat found that out, she considered refusing to take part.

In the end she acquiesced, for Janet's sake and because doing so was so much easier than taking a stand. She felt these days as if the fight had gone out of her, like a drained flask, a limp doll. She could foresee no end to her grief—with Rene gone from Scotland forever, what end could there be? And when getting out of bed each morning to confront the new day seemed to take such an effort, how could she possibly summon the energy for a full-fledged row?

Rawley gave a dinner at the abbey below Castle Hill, Holyrood House, on the eve of the wedding, for more guests than would be present on the morrow. Janet looked very beautiful in a gown of pale lawn, her gold hair plaited and piled high on her head. The food was excellent—a bisque of salmon, eel soup, roast venison and veal, little squab stuffed with bread and oysters, eight kinds of cheese, and a compote of fruits brought all the way from Spain.

Archibald was in a jolly mood at these edible proofs of his

new son-in-law's largesse. He had contributed the wine—two tuns of German Rhenish, two of French red, and a small but precious cask of Italian brandy—and the ale, his own favored brew from Castle Douglas's stores. Everyone drank and ate too much, except for Rawley, who was talking loud and fast already—with nerves, Tess jested, though perhaps it was true even though he had been through this already twenty years before. Jessie developed a crush on one of Marjory's cousins, a dark-haired M'Donald from the north of Scotland, and spent the whole evening getting up the courage to speak to him. When she finally did, she learned he'd left his wife and two young children home in Muir of Ord.

Still, she was in good enough spirits as the guests climbed the steep hill back to the castle, close to midnight. It was, she pointed out to Tess, her own fault, for not taking the time to gossip of him with the rest of the party, as was her wont. It was a warm, still night, with haze in the streets turned silver by a big full moon.

"Mind your purses, friends," Marjory's brother Jean cautioned at a turn in the narrow wynd. "There are plenty of pickpockets lurking in the Edinburgh shadows." Cat looked about curiously. This was a city of shadows, what with the tall houses crammed up against one another and the breakneck stone staircases running in dark alleys between them. She wasn't afraid—as much noise as the Quillan clan was making, they would frighten any thief away—but it was a bit spooky, to think there might be evildoers hiding anywhere.

"I am out of breath," Rawley declared when they were still well short of the walls of the castle. "Let's stop a bit and stargaze."

"Nae, nae," the company chorused, and the M'Donald cousin grinned and shouted, " 'Twill bae good practice fer ye t'morrow, Rawley, ye auld turnip, to bae exertin'! Keep movin', keep movin'!" Rawley laughed and pressed on, with Janet holding to his hand.

Cat was hanging back a little from the others, with some of her older cousins and Janet's mother and stepfather; since she had little merriment to lend to the occasion, she thought it best to make herself inconspicuous. Janet's stepfather was complaining loudly that had he been in charge of the wedding, things would have been done very differently—but then, what could one expect of that savage, Laird Douglas? Archibald was turning now and then to glare at the earl as he expounded; Tess had his arm and was doing her best to keep him under restraint.

At the castle gates, Rawley, evidently having caught his breath, proposed that everyone come to his chambers for a last round of drinks. As the company trooped after him, Cat took the opportunity to slip away to her rooms. The moonlight spilling through the windows there was so bright that she had no need to light the candles, even with the especially intricate lacings of the bodice of her yellow damask gown. The primrose shade reminded her of the dress she'd borrowed from Madeleine and worn at New Year's once upon a time, when Rene had kissed her so sweetly . . .

Just before he'd betrothed himself to Eleanor. She put *that* memory from her mind.

She undressed in front of the windows, slowly; the bedchamber was three stories above the ground, so that even the parapets were quite a way below, and no one could see in. It was lovely to have a bit of privacy. A major disadvantage of being one of the infamous Douglas girls, she reflected, was that people expected to see her and her sisters together—and most often, they obliged. Well, that had changed a bit when Tess had married. It would change even more after Janet was wed on the morrow.

She had her nightdress bundled up in her hand; before putting it on she paused and touched her breast, trying to remember why it had felt so wonderful when Rene had done that. It was only flesh, no different from her arm or knee—but then, when Rene had touched her arm or knee, that had been splendid, too. Had Janet and Rawley slept together already? she wondered idly, shaking out the nightgown and tugging it over her head. It seemed likely. As practical as Janet was, she would want to make certain there were no surprises for her in store that way. What was it really like, that act of love which Tess had once described to her so matter-of-factly? Would she ever find out? *If it isn't Rene I make love to,* she thought, *I don't want to know.*

On summer nights like this, with the yards cloaked in moonlight, it sometimes seemed as if everyone in the whole world was sleeping with somebody else, as if she was the only soul left alone. Well, not Jessie, she reminded herself, pulling open the hangings on the bed and dragging the step stool over from the dressing room, where her sisters had been using it in hemming their gowns. The beds here at Edinburgh were too high for the thick feather mattresses Archibald had brought with them from Douglasdale; they made one feel like an eagle perched upon its nest in a tall pine tree.

Something moved in the corner of the room, by the wardrobe. "Jess?" Cat said in surprise. She hadn't heard the outer door. Then the shadow came closer, so that she saw it was too tall for Jessie, and closer still, until the moonlight fell across Rene's face.

"No. Me," he said, smiling at her.

Cat reached back for the sturdy substantiality of the oak bed-frame, steadying herself. "Jesu in heaven. What are you doing here?"

"Paying a call on my own true love."

"No, no. I mean, here in Scotland!" Her heart was pounding wildly. Had his banishment been rescinded, and no one told her?

"I had business that could not be conducted from France. So I—sneaked in."

He was staring at her, his eyes dark in the moonlight. Suddenly self-conscious, Cat drew the nightdress close around her. "How long have you been there?" she demanded, nodding toward the wardrobe.

"Long enough to have the pleasure of seeing you undress." He crossed to her, reached out, and stroked her breast through the sheer dimity nightgown. "And to watch you do this. I hope that you were thinking of me." She lowered her gaze, felt her cheeks flood crimson. "Ah, so you were!" He laughed and went to kiss her, but Cat drew away.

"You must be gone from here," she whispered, glancing toward the door. "You are dead should anyone find you! Jessie will return any moment."

"Nay, she will not. Rawley Quillan will keep the lot of them drinking with him until dawn."

Cat's green-gold eyes widened. "How did you know about that?"

"I followed you up the wynd. I thought to take you into one of those alleys along the way, but with so many drunkards surrounding you I did not want to risk another sword fight."

Damn him, Cat thought, for his insouciance. "It is easy to see your banishment does not weigh heavy on you," she said bitterly, going to the window, putting her back to him.

"You are wrong there, Cat. It does. More than you could know." He came to stand behind her, his hand gentle on her shoulder. "Not for the forsaking of Scotland, but for the forsaking of you." He bent to kiss her throat, but she twisted away from him. "Love, what is wrong?"

"There's no use in it, Rene. Can't you see?" Her voice was low and strangled. "I cannot bear for you to come to me like this and then go away again, and me not knowing where you are, if you'll ever return. . . ."

"Don't you love me anymore?" he asked quietly.

She hung her head. "My God, I have tried not to. But I cannot seem to help myself."

"Then you have naught to worry about."

Cat whirled on him. "Oh, you've a bloody damned nerve, telling me not to worry! 'Love will find a way,' is that what you intend to tell me? 'Trust in me, Cat. Be true to me and all will be well'—I don't believe any of that any longer!"

"Neither do I."

Startled, she stared at him. "Then what brought you here?"

"I wanted to tell you that I've come back to speak to Moray. To apologize and ask his forgiveness."

Cat's battered heart had stopped beating. "Oh, Rene. Not really."

"Aye. The fact of the matter—" He shrugged, smiling, looking like an abashed little boy. "I find I cannot live without you, Cat Douglas. Everything else—kings and countries and wars and all—just fades to nothingness beside that."

To apologize. To have his banishment annulled . . . it was beyond her wildest hopes. She never had dared dream that proud

Rene Faurer would humble himself so far. "But . . . will he forgive you?" she whispered fearfully.

"I think so. Did you know that when he was young, he was captured by the English in battle and went over to their side? He helped them hunt down the Bruce. Then your uncle James took him prisoner, and he came back to the Scots again."

Cat had heard that story, a long time ago. A small wedge of hope slipped into the door to her heart, propped it open just a wee bit. "Perhaps, then, he will understand."

"Besides," said Rene, laughing as he stood in the moonlight, "they say he loves his wife. And you know what a rareness that is in a man!"

For her part, Cat was crying, crying tears of fearful joy. "Love, what's the matter?" he asked, coming to put his arms around her.

"I am afraid. . . ."

"Of what?"

"I do not think I am worth the sacrifice you are making," she said miserably.

"Oh, Cat." He kissed her nose, very lightly. "My dear Cat. I do."

He tipped her chin up with the tip of his finger, his arm tightening around her. He had the smell on him of summer, of green fields and ling flowers and wide blue skies, and his eyes were silver-blue in the moonlight, like star-spangled lapis lazuli. His mouth when he kissed hers was warm and taut with longing. "I have missed you," he murmured, caressing her cheek, "more than I can say." His hand slipped down to her throat and then to her breast, stroking her softly. Her flesh seemed to flame at his touch, even through the pale nightdress. He sighed with pleasure as his fingers toyed at her nipples, and he told her, "God, you set me afire. I thought I would go mad from wanting you while I was away."

"I feared you were angry with me," she whispered, her arms twined about his neck.

"Oh, I was. At you, at your father, at that blasted Malcolm—you haven't been seeing him, have you?" She shook her head. "Has there been . . . anyone else, in my absence?"

"Of course not."

"I would not have blamed you." His mouth teased her ear. "My damned bloody temper . . . you are the one with the right to be angry."

"How would I dare be angry now, when you are giving up so much for me?" His English lands, his conscience, his beliefs . . . her knowledge of the cost, of all he was renouncing, weighed her heart like a stone. She had been unwilling to abandon her convictions for him. *I must strive,* she thought, *to make this great sacrifice worthwhile for him. . . .*

"You have won, Cat," he whispered. "You have got what you wanted."

She stepped back from him and, hands trembling, pulled her nightdress up over her head. "So have you."

Stunned, he stared at her as she stood naked before him, drenched in the moonlight. "Oh, Cat. Do you mean it?" When she nodded, her head held high, he yanked off his cloak and unbuckled his belt, stripping with startling swiftness. "I don't intend to give you time to change your mind."

He lifted her into his arms to carry her to the bed, groaning as his flesh met her flesh. "Wait," Cat whispered.

He laughed and shook his head. "Too late."

"No, I only meant—what will we do when Jessie and Janet come back?"

"Didn't I tell you I know every inch of every castle in Scotland? There's a hidden passageway back of your wardrobe. How the devil do you think I got in here?"

Cat glanced at the wardrobe, then up at him. "How the devil indeed."

He lifted her onto the bed and then climbed up beside her. His naked body was so different from her own, Cat thought—the clean hard lines of muscle and sinew at his shoulders and chest, his taut belly, his manhood, already sticking straight up, like a flagpole. She stared at it in fascination, then hastily averted her eyes.

He noticed, and grinned. "We missed you, he and I. Christ, this is like sleeping in a bird's nest, isn't it?"

"Papa's feather bed," Cat said in explanation, and then caught her breath a little. There was something strange and uncomfortable about giving herself to him on a mattress that Archibald owned.

Swiftly he kissed her. "Don't think about it. By tomorrow, he may have forgiven me, too."

"Tomorrow is my sister's wedding."

"I know. So you will have two causes for celebration."

But Cat felt a sudden cold shiver run along her spine. What was it that her uncle James had always jested that meant? Someone, somewhere, was walking upon what was to be your grave . . .

Rene put his arms around her, pulling her close. "There is nothing to be afraid of any longer."

"I can't seem to help it. We have been so unhappy for so long—"

"All that is over." He sealed the promise with a kiss, long and lingering. "From now on, we will be together, Cat, whatever happens. I won't ever leave you again."

In the moonlight he let his hand trail down to her breast, then followed with his mouth, claiming its tip between his tongue and teeth. Cat sighed as she felt a kindling in her belly of the near-forgotten fire his caresses always raised in her. Timidly she let her own hand slip over his chest and waist, then lower still, to that hard, straight rod, so encitingly unfamiliar. As her fingers brushed its smooth head, he grunted and wrenched back. "I'm sorry," she said, chastened. "I thought you might like that."

He laughed, but the muscles of his face were tight. "Christ in heaven, I do. But I vowed long ago if I ever did get you into bed, I'd take my time, go slow. And to have you touch me—"

"Go slow some other night. I am too afraid my sisters will come back." Her fingers inched toward his manhood again.

He caught her hand in his and held it firmly. "No, Cat. I don't care if Archibald himself comes through that door. We will do this my way."

His way was to stroke her with infinite gentleness, kiss her with infuriating patience—her throat, her ears, her mouth and breasts. At first Cat lay quietly beneath his ranging lips and hands, but as the long-dormant embers inside her flared to brightness, she could not help clinging to him, returning his kisses, arching against his lean, strong body with a heightened urgency. His touch was feather-soft and yet burning, like velvet fire.

When he finally laid his hand on her belly, she caught her breath. "Spun gold," she heard him whisper, smiling against her mouth as his fingers played in the tight curls capping her mound of Venus. "Red gold . . ." He made a line of fluttering kisses down her throat until he reached her breast, his mouth closing on her nipple just as he slipped his hand between her thighs.

She tensed at the unfamiliar sensation. "Sooth, sooth," he murmured, holding her tightly, brushing her loose, tangled hair from her eyes. "Sooth, Cat. Let me in." He parted her knees with his own knee, turning onto his side while his fingers played against her pale skin. Then he reached lower, deeper, to the bud of her desire.

"Oh," Cat cried as he stroked her sweetly, softly. "Oh, God in heaven." There was a lump of fire deep within her, a knot of red flame. Her arms closed around his neck, pulling him toward her. "Rene," she whispered, her eyes on his.

"I'm not hurting you, am I?"

"God, no!"

He let the pressure of his finger increase, quickened the motion of his hand. Cat threw back her head as the knot turned liquid inside her, running like a river, setting all her blood ablaze. "Oh, Rene. I want—" What did she want? He was up on his haunches now, throwing his legs across her. The stars beyond the window were moving, shimmering across the sky in fiery waves. He paused to kiss her breasts, taste them, warm them with his tongue. Then he arched back, rising above her, a rainbow, a bridge to those distant stars, and entered her.

As that thick shaft pierced her, Cat froze, hands clenching into fists. He coaxed the fear from her as he withdrew, laying a torrent of fierce kisses on her mouth and throat. "Let me inside you," he whispered again. He rose up, blocking the sky, and eased himself down.

Cat gasped at the sensation. There was no pain, only an unfamiliar ache as her body opened in new ways, wondrous ways, to accommodate him. She slipped her hands along his smooth back to his buttocks; this time when he arched away, she followed with her hips.

He thrust harder, pulled up, thrust again, pulled up. She could hear him panting, knew that he was holding back for her sake. But there wasn't any need; she wanted him as much as he did her. She tilted her hips to meet his thrust, taking more of him inside her, and he groaned his gratified surprise: "Oh, Cat. I want this to be so good for you—"

"It already is."

He kissed her mouth, reared back, and then slowly sank his shaft deep inside her, until it seemed that they lay bone to bone. He stayed there, his breath coming fast, while Cat clutched him tight. So that was it, she thought through a fog of satisfaction. How splendid it had been! Rene raised himself up on his knees and smiled—

And fell on her like a man possessed by ten thousand devils, hammering his manhood into her over and over again, crushing her thighs and breasts with his weight. "Cat, come with me," he cried, his voice roughened with need. "Come with me, Cat."

"I am here, love," she told him, bewildered.

"Come with me now, Cat. Now!" They were rocking together, locked in a clenched embrace, and all of a sudden the river of fire in Cat's belly reignited, hotter than ever, and soared straight upward like a beacon.

"Oh!" she screamed, clinging to him in wild wonder. "Oh, Rain!" Whatever he cried out was wordless, but she felt the hot flush of his seed pouring into her belly, and knew that what they had shared would join them, heart to heart as they'd been body to body, till the end of time.

He fell against her, panting, drained, his fingers twined in her long, loose hair. Cat lay beneath him without moving, stunned by what had just transpired between them. Had he felt what she had? Was it for him, too, as though until this moment he had not really been alive?

At last he raised his head, and his eyes were shining. "Oh, Cat. I *never . . .*"

"It was all right?" she asked anxiously. "I . . . I pleased you?"

He laughed and rolled onto his back, pulling her atop him,

his fingers running through her long, fiery hair that the moon-light had tamed. "You pleased me, Cat. Yes."

"I am glad. Was I . . . as good as a French whore?"

"Jesu, Cat, what kind of question is that?"

"A very logical one, knowing you. Was I?"

"You were better than the best French whore. There, does that satisfy you?"

She nodded and snuggled happily against him. "Do you re-member the first time you kissed me?" she asked dreamily.

"No man in his right mind has ever said no to that question." She poked him sharply with her elbow. "But of course I do."

"What made you do it?"

"Annie."

"Annie?"

"Aye. I was so glad to see her laughing again . . . I was grateful to you. I never in my life could have imagined it would lead to this." He stroked her cheek, staring up at the ceiling. "A better question would be why you ever looked twice at such a misan-thrope as I."

"Oddly enough, it was Annie. Or, rather, the way you went to her at Tess's wedding, when the news came that your father was dead. Oh, Rene, she will be so glad to have you back. So will your mother."

"I wonder. I have caused them such grief." There was a tremor in his voice. *They are the chink in his armor,* Cat realized with sudden insight, *that is every bit as steely as the metal suit his father wore—these females that he loves. Madeleine and An-nie . . . and now me.*

She nestled closer to him in the soft feather bed, and his arms tightened around her. "You cannot imagine," he told her, "how often I have dreamed of this—holding you thus, having you sleep against me while I wait for the dawn—"

Just then there was a clatter in the corridor beyond the closed doors, the sound of stifled giggles, and someone—Janet—call-ing Cat's name. "Go!" she told Rene in horror, but before she even got the word out, he was gone from the bed, catching up his clothes and making for the wardrobe. "Cat!" Janet cried again. The latch rattled, and then they burst in—not just her sisters, but a whole passel of people, men and women both. Cat, with her eyes clenched shut in feigned sleep, could make out Rawley's voice, and her cousin Andrew's, and Jean Quillan's, and, of all folk, Malcolm's. They all of them sounded as though they had one sheet to the wind.

"Cat, we are going on a picnic for the wedding breakfast," she heard Janet announce. "We are going right now. Come along with us, won't you?"

"She is sleeping," slurred Rawley.

"No one could sleep through this," said his son Jean.

"She is, though. Look." That was Jessie. Cat fought to keep her breathing even and steady as they all trooped closer. She could feel lamplight through her eyelids. There was a clatter, then a thud, then a gasp from Jessie. "What was that?"

"A belt," Rawley declared. "Which one of you gentlemen has lost his belt?" Andrew hooted with laughter. Cat, her heart pounding, dared peek from beneath her lashes. Christ, it was Rene's. It had to be.

"Let me see that," said Malcolm.

"Why, man, are your breeches loose?" Grinning, Rawley spun the thing above his head, turning in a drunken circle. "Who's for a whipping, then?"

"Shh!" Tess said sharply. "Gill, go and stop him. If Cat can sleep through all this, we ought to let her sleep, poor thing."

"Give me the belt, Rawley." Gill came toward his future brother-in-law.

"I want to see that," Malcolm said again.

"Here you—Christ!" Another thud, a loud one. Through her lashes, Cat saw Rawley trip as Gill lunged toward him. The belt sailed through the air, past Malcolm's outstretched hand and right out the window into the yards below.

Surprise brought a sort of order to the inebriated crowd. "Rawley Quillan, I'll wager you a hundred marks you couldn't do that again on a dare," Janet told him, laughing.

"I can't take your money, darlin'—not when 'twill all be mine soon enough!"

"That's enough, everybody!" Jessie hissed, trying to herd them away from the bed. "Out, all of you, out! Leave Cat to her

peace. Though I must say I would like to know where that bel—
ooh!" She squealed as the handsome M'Donald cousin came out
of nowhere to scoop her up into the air. "What are you doing?"

"Every man take a lady," he said in his thick Highlands burr,
" 'n' th' last one to the river gaes in't! Come alang, then!" Giggling and hushing one another, they trooped out as noisily as
they'd come in.

Cat lay and listened to her heart pound, loud as the drums that
called the army to order. Slowly, slowly, the commotion in the
corridor died away. There was a scrape of stone against stone
from the direction of the wardrobe; then Rene, laughing, was
climbing up beside her again.

"There is nothing to laugh at!" she said angrily, her heart still
wild in her ears. "You might have been caught—and your belt!
How could you have dropped your belt there?"

"That was careless of me."

"Careless? It might have cost you your head! Will you please
stop laughing?"

He kissed her, shoulders still shaking. "Forgive me, love. But
what happened to it?"

"Rawley threw it out the window. Malcolm was reaching for
it—" Despite her shattered nerves, a giggle escaped her. "Oh,
really, it was too droll. Malcolm was so suspicious. I shall have
to come up with some sort of story to explain, I suppose."

He put his arms around her, drawing her close. "They are
gone now, till morning. We have the whole night together." His
mouth brushed hers, gentle and winning. "What shall we do
first?"

The whole night . . . it seemed a lifetime. "I don't know," Cat
whispered, suddenly shy.

"Well, I do." He sat up among the feathers, leaning against
the headboard, pulling her up, too, so that she lay across his lap.
"Tell me everything that has happened to you since I have been
away."

They talked for a long time, of matters weighty and inconse-
quential, of war and of kittens, of heartbreak and new gowns and
the weather in France. It seemed an unspeakable luxury to Cat
to be able to touch him whenever she chose to, have his fingers

twine through hers, reach up and stroke his hair. After a while, their touching became more urgent; they made love again, with mad, furious passion. After that, Cat felt tired. "Go on and sleep," he told her, kissing her cheek. "I would like to hold you while you are sleeping."

Cat shook her head. "I don't want to waste the time sleeping. Talk to me some more."

"What of? I know. How many children shall we have?"

At length they decided on six boys and six girls. Cat thought that sounded a lot, but Rene pointed out they'd have great sport in the making. "Better to strive for too many than too few," he said, leering, and then took her once more, with an inspired energy that made her thighs feel deliciously sore.

"When I am with you every night, I shan't be able to walk," she told him, laughing.

"I will carry you everywhere."

"Then you will tire of me."

"Never," he said, so fiercely that she caught her breath. "Don't you know, Cat, how lonely I was until I found you?"

"You had Eleanor," she pointed out, only half teasing. The memory of the blonde tormented her; had they slept together this time, in France? Had her rival ever lain with him this way, all through the night?

"Forget Eleanor. I have."

"Are you certain?"

"Cat Douglas," he said with exasperation, "I have risked life and limb to come to you here, haven't I? I am willing to bend my knee to that idiot Moray for your sake. If it was Eleanor I wanted, why would I be here? I'd be safe back in France!"

"I know." She nibbled her lip. Put in that light, her fears truly did sound absurd. "I think perhaps I am just . . . afraid to be so happy."

He leaned down to kiss her. "You must get over that, you know. I intend to see that you are happy for the rest of your life." He kissed her again, a slow kiss, warm and lingering, that grew in intensity and strength until she was clinging to him, hips moving against him, her belly on fire, desperate for him to fulfill her wild need.

The night seemed to last forever—and, at the same time, to be gone in a heartbeat. When the first rays of dawn ignited the sky, Rene sat up from the small, tight cocoon they had built of their dreams and hopes, and sighed. "I had better be going. Your sisters . . ."

"Aye," Cat acknowledged in a whisper.

He laughed a little, tossing back his black hair. "It is not as though we are really saying good-bye. Once Moray pardons me—"

"I know." Why was her voice so shaky?

His mouth touched her lips, bruised from this long night of passion. "I love you, Cat. Remember that."

"Why must I remember it? You will be right here."

"I meant—remember it always. Whatever may happen to us, all through the years."

"I love you, too."

He cupped his hands over her bare breasts, caressing them one last time before going. Cat put her hands over his, looked up into his eyes. In this faint light, they were dark as midnight. "Moray is the easy part," he said. "It is your father I am really worried about."

"I know. But it will be all right, I am sure it will. In the end, Papa always gives us girls what we want."

"He spoils you, you mean. His little princesses." He silenced her indignant reply with a kiss. "I shall spoil you, too, never fear."

The sky was brightening moment by moment. "You really had better go," Cat warned him.

"I will." He did not move, though.

She laughed. "Are you so loath to ask forgiveness of him?"

"Let's just say it goes against my natural grain."

Cat felt a small flutter of foreboding. "You will be deferential to him, won't you, Rene? You won't do anything stupid?"

"Have I ever mentioned that I find your confidence in me one of your most endearing traits?"

"Your past record doesn't give one much cause for confidence, dear." She kissed him. "Mind your temper, please?"

"I shall be a perfect pussycat." He rubbed against her. "Mi-aow."

There were footsteps in the corridor. Cat grabbed for her night-dress in the tangle of covers. He kissed her breast and then her mouth. "Later," he said, and sprinted, naked, for the wardrobe, vanishing just as an exceedingly weary-looking Jessie and Janet came through the door.

"Well, where the devil have you two been?" Cat demanded, stretching as though she'd just awakened.

"Picnic." Janet yawned, making a dive, fully dressed, for her bed.

"At this hour of the morning?"

"All night long. Down by the river." She yawned again. "Rawley fell in."

"My God! Is he all right?"

Janet nodded, head already on her pillow. "It sobered him considerably."

"You slept through all the excitement, Cat," Jessie said with a hint of smugness. "We drank wine and ate salmon and peaches, and Gill and Jean Quillan got into a huge big row, so now Tess isn't speaking to him—not Jean, I mean, but Gill. Malcolm didn't come for the picnic—he must have been cross that you weren't there. And Rawley did fall into the river, and it took six men to fish him out, he was so drunk—"

"He kept calling for me to join him," Janet interjected from her bed. "You left out, Jess, about how you mooned over that M'Donald fellow all night."

"He's very charming."

"He's *married.*"

"Well, we didn't do anything *wrong.*"

"Maybe not, but it's a waste of time. Just like you, Cat, with that Faurer fellow. What is the point? You had both better settle down and find some suitable men. After all, one of you is going to have to lose the bet."

"Not I," Jessie said promptly.

Cat, fresh from her night of wild lovemaking, smiled serenely. "The wedding is in five hours, you know. You two had better get some sleep."

Fifteen

Considering that she had a truly monstrous headache, Janet could not have looked more lovely in her wedding gown of peacock-blue satin, with a girdle of white roses and lady's mantle, and plumes of sweet rocket in her long, loose hair. "But I *feel* like bloody hell," she kept groaning, as Cat and Jessie and Tess fussed over the minute details of her dress.

"Chin up," Tess told her. "Gill says Rawley looks *and* feels like bloody hell this morning."

"Well, that's what a twenty-year age difference will do for you," said Janet. "Christ, Jessie, try not to pull my hair. It feels as though my head will roll right off."

"I *could* say something about the virtues of going to bed early," Cat began, "getting plenty of rest, and—"

"Aye, but if you did, you know we'd strangle you," Tess said. "Now be a good girl and run—since you're the only one of us who *can* run—and ask Papa if they are ready for us in the chapel yet." Cat curtsied, grinning, and started off; Janet grabbed her arm.

"And for the love of God, bring back some milk from the kitchens to settle my stomach, or I shall retch instead of saying 'I do.' "

"Of course I will, you poor thing."

Outside the apartments, the day was brilliant with sunshine; bees buzzed lazily in the yards, and the sky was jewellike, flawless blue. Cat found Archibald pacing the cobblestones just outside the chapel. "Hello, daughter," he grunted, stooping to kiss her. "I hear ye war the only one o' my offspring with sense enough to shun last night's bacchanal."

"Did you go to the picnic?"

"Hell, nae. I went to my bed. Let Rawley prove how foolish it bae fer a man our age to try 'n' act as though he bae twenty again."

"How is he?" Cat asked anxiously.

"He'll live. But I'd wager fifty marks he'll do naught but sleep on his wedding night. How bae the bride?"

"Pale," Cat said. "But she'll live, too. Are you ready for her yet?"

"Nae, nae. We bae still missin' ain or twain o' the guests. I've sent to tell 'em we bae ready. Give her five minutes more."

Cat peeked through the open doors of the chapel. "It looks lovely, Papa."

He surprised her by kissing her cheek. "Sae d'ye, Catriona. Ye look—happy again. It makes my heart glad."

"Papa . . ." She wanted so badly to share her wondrous news with him. But no—let it come from Rene. It would mean more to Archibald that way.

He was waiting, watching her, smiling. "Aye, pet?"

"Nothing." She reached up to return his kiss. "I'll go and tell Jan."

She caught up her skirts and ran back into the castle, up the broad stairs from the Great Hall and then up another set, narrower, to the apartments. "My milk!" Janet wailed when she saw her coming, empty-handed.

"Oh, damn. I'll get it now." Back down the stairs, two flights, and up again. "I can't help but wonder, Jan," she said breathlessly as she presented her sister with the pitcher, "whether you are really certain of marrying Rawley, when you got yourself so drunk last night."

"I am sure of Rawley. It is my stomach I'm uncertain about." Janet downed the milk in four long gulps, then stood and waited while it took effect. "Better," she announced at last. "What did Papa say?"

"Five minutes more. But it must be past that by now."

"I'll go down, then."

Tess had gone to the window and was looking into the yards. "There's Rawley going into the chapel. Papa's still outside, though."

Janet smoothed down her bodice, shook out her skirts, and took a deep breath. "I am ready."

"Hold on," said Tess, still at the window. "There's some sort of commotion."

"What do you mean, commotion?" Janet came and stood beside her. "Who's that talking to Papa?"

"Just a servant," Tess told her. "But an excited one."

Cat and Jessie came to look, too. Even as they watched, Archibald left his post at the chapel doors and headed for the castle at a dead run. The liveried boy who'd been speaking to him darted into the chapel. After a moment, Rawley came running out, too. "Lord, I would not have thought he could move so fast today," Janet noted, bemused.

"Why are they ringing the bells?" Jessie asked, as the quiet morning air filled with a sudden clanging. "They are supposed to ring the bells *after* the wedding, aren't they, Jan?"

A whole host of soldiers came swarming from the barracks at the foot of the hill and fanned out through the yards, moving in pairs, pikes at the ready. "Christ," Tess whispered, "what is happening?" Below them, the soldiers were ducking into every doorway, probing bushes, trotting up and down the stairs.

"They've blocked the gates," Janet noted, pointing to the arched entrances at the east and south ends of the yards.

Cat giggled. "Perhaps Rawley is trying to escape."

Janet wasn't laughing. "I am going down," she announced.

"You can't!" Jessie told her. "What if you run into Rawley? It is bad luck for him to see you before the ceremony."

"This looks like bad luck anyway to me." The bride-to-be marched grimly through the doors. Her sisters exchanged glances, then trailed after her uncertainly.

The Great Hall was in chaos. Soldiers and servants were everywhere, banging into one another; captains were shouting orders that couldn't be heard above the general noise. Tess was the first to see Archibald, off in a corner, standing on a stool and waving his arms to try and quiet the crowd. Rawley was close beside him, looking very pale, with the priest, Father Joseph, who was to perform the wedding ceremony.

"Gill!" Tess had spotted her husband in the throng and was frantically motioning him toward her. "Gill, what's the matter? What is going on?"

He pushed his way between two rows of milling soldiers, calling something to her. Tess shook her head at him. "I cannot hear!"

"Did he say 'dead'?" Jessie asked. "Did you hear him say 'dead'? I am sure he said 'dead.' "

"Who's dead?" Jessie and Janet cried to Gill in chorus. He detoured around a little thicket of bewildered serving boys to reach their side.

"The earl of Moray," he gasped out breathlessly.

"Moray? That nice old man?" Jessie cried. "What a dreadful shame!"

"More than a shame," Gill told her, his eyes very grim. "That's why there's all this hubbub. They found him poisoned in his rooms."

"Jesu!" Janet said in shock. "Poisoned? By whom?"

"No one knows yet. But they are combing the castle. They'll find the cowardly bastard, never fear for that." His arm still around his wife, he reached for Janet's hand. "Your father will have to see to the search. I don't know what will happen about your wedding. I am sorry."

Janet shrugged it off. "It doesn't matter. If Papa is needed— who do you think it was, Gill? A de Baliol man?"

"Who else? One thing is certain—this means the invasion will come any day now. They must be hoping to throw us into confusion by murdering the regent. Well, it won't work, that's for—what is the matter with your sister, Tess?"

Cat was standing all alone on the top of a very high mountain, with snow swirling so thickly around her that she could not see. Her teeth were chattering with cold; if she moved, took a single step in any direction, she knew she would go tumbling off the mountaintop into an endless white abyss. . . .

"Cat? Cat!" Jessie was patting her hand, her cheek. "Cat, can you hear me? Why don't you answer? Jesu, catch her, Gill!" Her brother-in-law hurried to do so, just before she hit the floor.

"Take her to our rooms, Gill, please," Janet ordered. "It must be all this noise and confusion . . . Jessie, you go with her. I am going to see if there is anything I can do to help Papa."

"I'll come with you, Jan," Tess decided. "But do come back quick, Gill." She gave him a peck on the cheek as he bore Cat away, followed by Jessie, who was shaking her head in wonderment:

"I cannot understand what's gotten into you, Cat. Why, you scarcely even knew the man!"

Sixteen

"Thank God you came."

Madeleine Faurer unfastened her riding cloak and looked beyond Jessie Douglas's anxious brown eyes to the bed. "How is she?" she whispered.

"The same. She's asleep now, but it won't last long. She is so troubled by dreams—" As though she'd heard Jessie's words, the figure on the bed suddenly writhed and cried out, a strangled, tortured sound that made Madeleine cross herself in horror.

"Poor soul! But I do not understand—why have you sent for me?"

Jessie had dipped a cloth in cool water and was pressing it to her sister's ghost-pale forehead. "She has been asking for you, in those brief moments when she is herself."

"For me . . ." Madeleine's small white hand fluttered against Cat's cheek. "Did she say why?"

Jessie shook her head, her eyes on Cat's rapid, shallow breathing. "She either won't or can't."

Madeleine reached for a small leather bag she wore on her girdle. "I have herbs that may help her. Can you bring me some oil and wine?"

When Jessie returned to the bedchamber, Madeleine was crushing the herbs in her palm. "How long has she been thus?" she whispered.

"A week," Jessie whispered back. "Ever since the earl of Moray was found dead." Suddenly her tears spilled over. "Oh, it's all been such a terrible muddle—Janet's wedding ruined, the army called out, Papa upset that the earl of Mar was named regent instead of him, and Cat so sick on top of everything else . . ."

Madeleine gave her a hug, letting her cry on her shoulder. "It sounds as though it has been dreadful for you. Where are your sisters?"

"Tess has gone back home to baby Jane. Janet and Rawley are gone for two days to Pencraig." She sniffled. "A honeymoon."

"Then they did get married."

"Aye. But it was not much of a wedding."

"Still, it is good to know that love has a way of triumphing."

"Has it triumphed?" Jessie asked through her tears. "They say de Baliol will invade any day now. Rawley will go with the army. Poor Janet may wind up a widow before the first month of her marriage is out."

"Let's not dwell on the worst that can happen," Madeleine said mildly. "How is your father?"

"He is worried for Scotland. And worried for Cat."

"They have not caught the man who murdered Moray?"

As Jessie shook her head no, Cat cried out from the bed again. Madeleine went to her, smoothed back her tangled curls until after a moment she lay still once more. "Well," Madeleine said, "you look as though you will take ill yourself, Jessie Douglas, unless you get some rest, and some food. My orders are that you hie yourself to the kitchens for a good warm meal, and then into a bed."

"I don't like to leave her," Jessie said fretfully. "I don't understand it. Cat's never been ill in her life, not like this."

"It won't do anyone any good if you make yourself sick as well. Go and rest. I'll stay here."

"But you must be tired, too," Jessie protested. "Your long ride—"

"I am fine. Go on, now, or I'll make you take some of this." She held the herbs under Jessie's nose, and the girl recoiled.

"Phew! What a stink! Very well; I am going, then. But I'll be back in an hour."

"Two hours," Madeleine commanded.

"Two hours." Jessie smiled wanly. "Thank you again."

When she'd gone, Madeleine made a poultice of the herbs and oil and held it to Cat's forehead. "Can you hear me, Cat?" she asked softly, gently. "It is I, Madeleine." The girl stirred a little, and Madeleine held the cup of wine to her mouth, dribbling it in. "It is Madeleine, Cat. I've come."

Cat's eyes fluttered open, and Madeleine saw with shock that the green-gold irises, once so lively, were dull and chalky. "Lord in heaven, Cat, what has happened to you?"

"Madeleine?" Cat's fingers fumbled toward her over the bed-clothes. "Is it really you?"

"Of course it is."

"I'm so glad. No, I'm not." Cat grasped the older woman's wrist, her grip tight as death. "Oh, God, I don't know what to do!"

"Tell me about it, Cat," Madeleine urged.

"I cannot tell anyone! I can't! I thought I could tell you, but now . . ."

"Is it about Rene?" Cat said nothing. "Have you had word from him, Cat?" Suddenly his mother went pale. "God in heaven. Is he dead?"

"No!" Cat said quickly. "No, he isn't dead. I know he isn't, for I've seen him."

"Seen him?" Madeleine was astonished. "Where?"

"Here. Here in the castle. He isn't dead, but—but somebody else is. And I am so afraid . . ."

"When did you see him, Cat?"

Those strange dull eyes rose to meet her gaze, slowly. "On the night—the night before the earl of Moray died."

Madeleine sank down beside her on the bed. "Who else knew he was here?"

"No one. Only me."

"But why had he come?"

"He said—he told me he had come to make his peace with Moray. It was the night before Janet's wedding was to be, and all the rest had gone to the river on a picnic. And he came to my room—he knew a hidden passageway. He said—"

"He knows every royal castle in Scotland," Madeleine whispered, "like the back of his hand."

Cat nodded miserably. "He—he—we—"

"He made love to you."

Cat's fingers were wringing the coverlet into tight coils. "Aye. He was here all night long, until Janet and Jessie returned. I was so happy. *We* were so happy. The next thing I knew, the soldiers were swarming, and the bells were ringing alarum, and Gill said that Moray was dead."

"And you think Rene killed him."

"What else can I think?" Cat asked wildly. "Everyone was always telling me he is such a hothead. If Moray refused to revoke his banishment, refused to forgive him . . ." Her voice trailed off in a sob; she buried her face in her hands.

Madeleine sat motionless for a long moment. Then she crossed herself slowly and asked, "Have you told your father, Cat?"

"How can I tell him?"

"Oh, my dear child. You must."

Cat sat up straighter. "How can you say that—you, his own mother? Don't you love him?"

"I love him—more than life itself." Madeleine's green eyes burned with a dark fire. "But there are some laws that cannot be broken, Catriona. The Lord said, 'Thou shalt not kill.' "

"Men kill all the time," Cat cried in desperation. "They kill each other in battle—your husband must have killed hundreds, thousands of men!"

"That is different," Madeleine said steadily, "and you know it. If Rene poisoned Thomas Randolph, it was murder. And Rene—" She swallowed, hard. "He will have to pay the price."

Cat recoiled from her, horrified. "They will hang him!"

"Aye. They will."

"But—but—but—" Cat took a breath. "Perhaps he did not do it after all. Or perhaps it was in self-defense." Grasping at any straw, she pictured him as he'd been when he left her, so merry and loving. "He could not kill in cold blood. Could he? Do you think that he could?"

Madeleine sighed. "I think that it has been a long time since I truly knew my son. Children—when they are infants, you do everything for them. Their thoughts are your thoughts. Every need that they have, you fulfill. Then they grow up, and away. I failed Rene somehow—I, and his father. He is so like his father. But of course, he can't see that."

Cat was reminded suddenly of Rene telling her about Michel Faurer: *I know he liked to kill people. . . .* She shivered helplessly. Madeleine saw, and pulled the blankets up around her. "No matter what he has done," Cat said suddenly, fiercely, "I still love him. And I cannot betray him!"

"Think, Cat," Madeleine urged softly. "Will he ever touch you with those hands that you will not remember that old man dying? Will you have children by him—the children of a homicide?"

"I thought you would defend him!"

"How can I defend him if he is a murderer?" His mother shook her head. "No, Cat. You must tell your father. You must do it today."

"I cannot. I—" Cat broke off as the door behind Madeleine's back suddenly swung open. It was Jessie, looking very pale. She blinked in surprise to see Cat sitting up in the bed.

"Cat! I never in my life expected you would be awake." She eyed Madeleine with wonder. "There must be magic in those herbs of yours."

"I thought I told you to rest," Madeleine said sternly.

"I was going to, but I just went quickly to tell Papa that you had come. And while I was there—" She stopped suddenly. "But I mustn't upset Cat."

It didn't matter; she could guess. "Edward de Baliol has landed."

Her sister nodded. "Aye. At Kinghorn, in Fife."

Madeleine folded her hands, lips moving in prayer, before she murmured, "So the war begins . . . again."

Jessie was chewing her lip. "Papa says there is naught to worry about. The invasion force is small—just de Baliol and the dispossessed Border barons. Edward of England sent no men to aid him. Shall I bring Papa in to you, Cat? He would be so glad, I know, to see you looking so much better . . ."

Madeleine was watching Cat closely. "There was something you had to tell your father, wasn't there, my dear?"

Cat nodded up and down slowly, as though in a dream, a trance. Madeleine turned to Jessie. "Go and get him, then, now. Tell him it is most important that he speak to Cat."

Puzzled, Jessie looked at her sister. "What is it that you have to tell him?"

"Just run and fetch him, Jessie," Madeleine said again, "quick as you can." It was as though she feared at any time Cat would change her mind.

Jessie hesitated a moment longer, then left them. Cat leaned back against the pillows on the bed, closing her eyes. Madeleine took her hand. "It is what you must do," she said softly. "There is no other choice."

"I know that." Her green-gold eyes opened. "But oh, it is hard!" Madeleine took her into her arms, and they cried together, mother and lover. Then Cat roused herself, wiping her tears, pushing the older woman away. "You go, too," she said. "I need a little time by myself before he comes."

"Very well. But I will be right outside the door if you need me."

Cat kissed her. "Thank you for coming. Thank you for . . . everything."

Madeleine went out, quietly closing the door, and then leaned against it in weary exhaustion. Poor child, she thought, for she knew only too well what it was like to be betrayed by one you love. There was a spark of something in her mother's heart when she thought of her son that was frighteningly close to hatred. *Oh, Rene, Rene. What have you done?* she thought in desolation. A million pictures played themselves in her mind: the moment of his birth, his first teetering, triumphant steps toward his father, his pride when he'd seen his new sister . . . For the first time since that dreadful night in Douglasdale when Angus had brought the news, she found herself glad that Michel was dead, that he was spared this pain.

Archibald came soon enough, huffing up the stairs, stouter and more grizzled than Madeleine had remembered. He kissed her on both cheeks when he saw her. "I bae glad to see ye, Madeleine. Ye heard about de Baliol?" She nodded. He shook his head, frowning. "On top o' Cat taken ill . . . These girls o' mine—"

"Women," Madeleine broke in softly.

He grunted. "Whichever. I dinna understand 'em, either way. What bae it that she has to say?"

"She will tell you herself." Madeleine caught his hand as he turned for the door. "Go gentle with her, Archibald, please. Whatever she might say . . . remember you were young once, and did things you were not always proud of. God knows I did."

"Christ! Got herself wi' child, has she?"

"It isn't that."

"Hmph! Well! Anythin' short o' that we can live with, can we nae?" He grinned crookedly and went in.

He came out again but moments later, forehead knitted. "Women!" he growled. "I said I dinna understand 'em, 'n' now I see it bae God's truth."

"What are you talking about?" Puzzled, Madeleine looked past him through the open door.

"Why, there bae nae one in that room at all."

help me upstairs. Why," he murmured, "you're all of gold.
How do I call thee, lady?"

"Isobel," she told him as she said in a low, just-above-
a-breath voice, you may.

"What .. . Isobel, belove . .." Whatever it was he came here

Seventeen

Edward de Baliol's camp was a rough, rude place, thrown together in the course of a night to give the invaders a base in which to rest, and observe what movements Scotland's royal army might be making across the calm blue waters of the Firth of Forth. De Baliol guessed that the enemy, thrown into confusion by the untimely death of the regent, would be in no great rush to engage his forces, and he guessed correctly; his spies reported that the new regent, Donald, earl of Mar, with Sir Archibald Douglas, was still amassing men and arms at Edinburgh. In the breathing space thus so thoughtfully provided, de Baliol laid his plans: he would march as close to Scone, the traditional site of Scottish coronations, as he could before fighting. That way, he jested, if he were unhorsed in the battle, he should still be able to walk to have the crown of Scotland laid upon his head.

Despite the advance reports, de Baliol kept close watch on his encampment's boundaries; in this land of wild men, of Douglases and Wallaces and Stewarts and M'Donalds, it seemed all too likely that some warrior, sanctioned or unsanctioned, would seek to breach his palisade and end the conflict prematurely with a dagger to his heart. So when a figure emerged from the white mists lapping the Firth one evening at twilight, it was promptly challenged. "Who goes there?" de Baliol's sentry demanded, holding up his torch. The figure threw back the hood of its dark cape; firelight glinted on a gleaming mass of curling red-gold hair. The sentry moved closer, and laughed. "Why, 'tis naught but a slight bit of girl! How the devil came ye here, darlin'?"

"I witched it o'er the water," she said in a low, sultry voice. "Did ye not see me, then?"

"Nay, but I can near believe it. What would yer business here be?"

She shrugged off the cape to reveal a close-fitting red satin bodice, cut low enough that it clearly showed the white swells of her breasts. The sentry raised a brow and whistled in appreciation; she winked lashes darkened with walnut juice and pursed her painted mouth. "I bae looking fer a man."

"And here I am, then!" he said eagerly.

She laughed and tossed her curls. "Later, luv, later. First I've an account to settle wi' one o' yer mates, that I spent the whole bloomin' night wi' in Ayr last year afore th' bastard stiffed me. Up 'n' left wi'out payin' me, can ye believe that?"

"Ye don't say so!"

"Aye, that he did."

The sentry's eyes narrowed slightly. "Ayr, is it? Last winter? That's a long time past and a long way come for so small a debt."

"Well . . . if the truth be told, though he left nae money, he did leave a little somethin' fer me to remember him by." And she scratched her nether regions through her flimsy skirt.

"The pox!" The fellow jumped back from her as though bit.

"Aye, aye, the scurfy devil."

"Lord, there's a pity," the sentry said feelingly, "a pretty little thing such as ye."

"True, true, fer he's ruined me, ye see, fer my chosen vocation. Though, mind ye, now 'n' again I find a fellow willin' to brave the risk—mostly those that has already got it." She sauntered closer, put her hand on his arm. "How about it, mate? Bae ye sae brave?"

He shuddered and withdrew his arm from her grasp. "Nay, not on yer life. Not for the crown of Scotland itself."

There was a rustle in the bushes, and another torch flared. "What's going on there, Beaton?" a neighboring sentry demanded. His eyes lighted on the visitor, and he grinned. "Lord, look at this! A New Year's gift! Come fly into my nest, little bird!"

"Don't touch her," Beaton warned, "for she's told me herself she be poxed. Come here to find the fellow what passed it on to her."

The second man laughed. "A bit like lookin' for a needle in a haystack, wouldn't that be?"

"I know his name," the harlot said, mouth twisting. "It bae a French name. Rene Faurer."

"Captain Faurer?" Beaton's eyebrow arched again. "Are ye certain?"

"Bloody damned right I bae certain."

"I would never in my life have guessed that man be poxed," Beaton murmured.

"Then ye don't know him like I do, mate," she said, so viciously that the two soldiers exchanged glances.

"Carryin' a weapon, are ye?" the second one asked.

She shook her head and held out her arms at her sides. "Care to search me?"

He did so, quickly, though he did take time to give her breasts a squeeze. "Well," he said then, rocking back and forth on the heels of his boots. "What d'ye say, Beaton?"

"I say 'tis a bloody damned shame, that's what I say."

The other man nodded, fingers inching involuntarily back toward the harlot's bodice. She smiled seductively and scratched herself again. His hand withdrew. "Go on and take her to him, then, why don't ye?"

"Me?"

"Well, ye found her, didn't ye?"

"He won't be pleased," said Beaton dubiously. "Still, I suppose justice is justice. Cover for me, mate, until I get back, won't ye?" He crooked a finger at the girl. "Come along."

He led her through the woods to the edge of a clearing where bonfires were burning. The air smelled of moss and fern and roasting venison. She pulled her hood back up, but curious stares still followed her across the camp. Halfway along, he stopped and pointed toward a man sitting outside a tent, methodically drawing a whetstone along his sword blade. "There he be," he hissed to her. " 'N' if he asks how ye found him, I'd be grateful if ye'd forget my name."

Rene still had not looked up. Cat stood for a moment and watched him, trying to quell the turmoil in her heart. He was dressed like any soldier on campaign: leather breeches, boots, a loose shirt open at the throat, with no embroidery on it. His black hair, caught back in a thong, seemed longer than she remembered. Christ, had it only been a week since she saw him last, since she had spent the night in those strong brown arms? He looked very at ease handling the long, bright sword blade. Like his father, she thought. Much as Rene might have tried to deny it, these Faurer men were made for war. What, she wondered briefly, might he have been like had he been born in a country—if there were such a country—where peace reigned? She felt suddenly like crying, picturing him moving the whetstone with such calm methodicalness over the edge of a scythe, or the share of a plow.

She glanced over her shoulder. Beaton was standing at the very fringe of the clearing, watching her curiously. It would not do to have him doubt her now. She squared her shoulders, gave the guard a little wave—he, bless him, nodded encouragement, motioning her onward—and paced across the grass that had been crushed by the hard tramp of soldiers' feet.

He saw the edge of her crimson skirts first, and raised his eyes, wary. Cat had a strange sense that she was not who he expected to see when he did. His shock when his gaze reached her face was more than genuine enough to placate Beaton. "Cat," he said hoarsely, tightly.

She leaned down and slapped him, hard as she could. It felt grand. "Give a girl the pox, will ye, ye stinkin', louse-covered bastard?" she cried robustly, and hit him again. "Ruin an honest girl's livelihood wi' yer filthy disease?"

"For God's sake, Cat!" He warded off another blow; the soldiers all around them were laughing. Hastily he grabbed her wrists and yanked her into his tent.

It was dark inside. Unable to see him, Cat listened to his quick, shallow breathing. He was still holding her hands. "Christ," he said, "I've never had such a start in my life!" In the darkness, Cat felt his mouth brush hers. She wrenched away.

"Why did you do it, Rene?" Her voice was harsh and grating, like iron dragging over stone.

"What, give you the pox?"

"This is no jest, Rene! Why did you kill that old man?"

He didn't answer for a moment. Then he said, very quietly, "Don't you think it might be well to ask me first *if* I did it?"

"Oh, really! Do you think me so stupid? You go alone to the rooms of a man everyone in Scotland knows you hold a grudge against, and that day he's found poisoned?"

"He was dead when I got there."

In the sudden silence, Cat heard the thud of her heartbeat. "What?" she whispered.

"He—was—already—dead—when—I—got—there," he said very distinctly. "I did not kill him. I found him dead."

"But," she began, and stopped. "But—"

"Hit me again," he hissed at her.

"What?"

"Hit me again! If you are going to begin a charade, Cat, you must carry it through to the finish." She didn't move. He slapped himself, loudly, and yelped. "Ouch! Stop that, bitch! What makes you think it was me?"

"Who—who else could it be?"

"Any man with a prick and tuppence in his purse, so far as I can tell, you witless whore."

Cat's head was spinning; she could no longer tell what questions he was asking or she answering. He moved to the tent flaps and yanked at them; she caught a glimpse of the bonfires through the angled opening against his hard profile. Then he shut them again and lit a candle. Cat had never been so glad for light.

He squatted on his haunches, motioning to her. "Get down."

"Why?"

"The candle will make shadows on the tent. Get down!"

Dutifully she sat. "Is that true—what you said about Moray?"

"Of course it is true."

Cat put her hands to her forehead; they came away streaked with the paint she wore. "But why didn't you sound an alarum?"

"You said yourself—everyone in Scotland knew I had cause to hate him. Who would have believed that I did not kill him? *You* did not believe in me."

She hadn't—and was still not sure she did now. She began to weep. "There, there." He patted her shoulder. "This is ridiculous, Cat. We can't talk here. You ought not to have come."

"I had to, Rene. I had to know for certain—"

"It sounds to me as though your mind was made up."

"Christ, why not? Your own mother counseled me to tell my father you had been there."

"You told my mother?"

"I had to tell someone! I was alone, and afraid. She was the only soul on earth I could trust with a secret like that."

"And she thought me guilty." He sounded saddened, and bitter.

"What else were we to think?"

"Everythin' all right in there, Captain Faurer?" a bemused voice called from beyond the tent canvas.

"Aye, aye, mate. Just calming down the wench." He lowered his own voice, grabbing for Cat's hand. "Come on. We need more privacy than we can get here. When we go out, act as though you aren't satisfied. Protest. Do you understand me?" She nodded. In a single motion he pulled her to her feet and out of the tent.

"Get on with you now," he said loudly, dragging her by the elbow across the encampment toward the wood. "You can't prove 'twas my fault—"

"Ye know in yer black heart it war!"

"And I'll not stand for blackmail."

"I'll give ye blackmail! This bastard here," Cat cried to the men who were watching their performance, "gave me the bludy damned pox!" Rene clapped one hand over her mouth and moved more quickly toward the forest.

"Need help, Captain?" one of the onlookers offered, grinning.

"Nay, man, she's a small sort of pest. Come on, you." They left the clearing and passed the line of sentries.

"That you, Captain Faurer?" one of them challenged him.

"Aye, Caley. Just ridding the camp of vermin—" His hand

had slipped from Cat's mouth; she closed her teeth on the meat of his palm. "Bitch! She bit me! Can you believe that?"

"I'd believe anythin' of a woman, Captain!"

"Aye, so would I." Leaving the unseen guards laughing, he hauled Cat toward the river, with her kicking and fighting all the way.

At the riverbank he stopped, and set her down. "We should have some space here. But keep your voice low," he warned. "How did you get here?"

"I paid a man to row me over the Firth."

"No, I mean—how did you get out of the castle? What did you tell your sisters, your father?"

"I didn't tell them anything. I went out through the passageway behind the wardrobe."

"You went into the tunnels?" He was astonished. "Alone?" Cat nodded. "Weren't you afraid?"

"Not particularly. I had a candle with me. I did have a devil of a time finding a way to get out, though, once I was in. They seemed to go on and on. I never knew they were there. Who built them, anyway?"

He shrugged his shoulders. "Who knows? Most old castles have them. They are part of the fortifications. Some of them, I think, are older than the castles. Older than time. From back when our ancestors went naked and painted themselves blue. But, Cat, they are dangerous. You could have gotten lost—"

"But I didn't. I popped out of a sluiceway just below the gate. I almost bumped right into a guard." She giggled, remembering how she'd stopped just short of his boots and waited till he moved on. "I wonder does Douglas Castle have them?"

"I only know the royal castles. I used to look for them wherever Father took me. I would spend days just exploring. . . ." He stopped himself, seemed to shake away the memories. "Your boatman—did you pay him to wait?" She shook her head. "How will you get back?"

"I did not think of that."

"We'll worry on it later." A moon, big and half-round, had risen in the east; in its yellow light she saw him grinning. "You did well back there in the camp."

She returned the smile. "So did you."

He stood looking down at her; his hand faltered toward her loose curls. "So you think me a murderer."

"I—I did not know what to think. Everyone tells me so often what a bad man you are. Perhaps I simply started to believe them."

"Well. Some nights, before the dawn, I have thought that perhaps you betrayed me, Catriona—that you set me up to stand for Moray's killing."

"I would never do such a thing!"

"I know that, in my heart. But one's mind can play dangerous games . . . you told no one else that you'd seen me? Only my mother?" She shook her head. "I thank you for that."

"You should have stayed!" she cried in misery. "We could have made them believe you, you and I."

He gathered her in close against his chest. "No, my poor sweet Cat. The trouble is, we have gotten caught up in something far bigger than our love for each other. Something is going on around us that I cannot yet fathom, cannot understand. When I saw Moray sitting dead at his desk, I knew that much for sure."

"And so you came back to them—these quarrelers and traitors you serve now," she said spitefully.

"Where else could I go? At least with de Baliol I knew I'd be returning to Scotland—that I would have a chance to see you again."

"How? All of you are going to be killed in the battle by King David's forces."

"Don't be so sure, Cat. De Baliol could very well triumph."

She stared at him, her eyes very gold in the moonlight. "That is absurd!"

"Spoken like a true, faithful Scottish lass." His smile was rueful. "But he could win, Cat. I have watched him plot and plan for this moment for years now. He is not about to let it slip away easily."

Cat, accustomed to thinking of de Baliol as a pesky nuisance to be swatted away like a fly, could not conceive of it. "But—but—that would mean . . ."

"The Border lairds would all be attainted—your father among

them. They'd lose their homes, their lands. Some might lose their heads."

"I don't believe it for a moment," Cat said stoutly, and then asked in a much more tentative voice, "What would become of King David?"

"I would think—I would hope—de Baliol would let him live."

His uncertainty made Cat shiver. She tried not to think of the little king lying dead, but the image kept pushing itself into her mind. "Is that why you came back to his side?" she demanded. "Because you believe de Baliol will win?"

"I . . . there are things I cannot explain to you yet, Cat. All I can do is ask you to trust me. To go on believing in me." She looked away. He tilted her chin back toward him with a fingertip. "Is that so hard to do? You've kept faith so far."

"You will be fighting against Scotland's true king," she said through a sob.

"Oh, Cat." His mouth brushed her cheek. "What does it matter who is king of Scotland, so long as you and I have got each other?"

But it was not so simple as that. How, she wondered, could she ever explain to him that when you were a Douglas, Scotland and the Bruce were like bread and meat to you—that you grew up dining on them every day? She thought of the castle in Douglasdale, its walls were covered with hangings showing the daring exploits of her ancestors, all the great lairds of Douglas; their stories were as familiar to her as the rhymes she and her sisters had learned in their nursery. She thought of the land her kin had fought and died for, the high green hills and rolling fields surrounding the fortress that the English had captured and recaptured, but that the Douglases always took back in the end . . . she thought of her father, who might have contented himself at his age with hunting for hart and dandling his grandchild upon his knee, and instead had taken on himself all the headaches and heartaches of the fight that faced him. Archibald had said it himself more than once, proudly: The Douglases *were* Scotland. How, though, could one explain that to a man who hated his own father? Who had no feeling at all for the country his parents had adopted as their own?

She sighed. "I only wish that you could care for *something,* Rene—some ideal, some goal." She remembered Anne's words to her, long ago. "That you had got a—a passion."

"I have. I've got you."

"I'm sure that's very nice of you to say, but it is hardly enough for you to build a life on."

"Are you so sure of that?" The moon made his eyes burn with intensity. "Why shouldn't I cast my lot with the side I think will win, if it means a better life for the woman I love, and for the sons and daughters I hope, by God, to have by her someday?"

"Because you need to have something bigger," she tried again to explain, "something grander!"

"As my father did?" he demanded, his voice suddenly harsh. "He had all that, didn't he, Cat—goals and ideals? The flower of chivalry, they called him. And what did it mean for my mother and Anne? Lives spent admiring him from afar. My mother with her bloody damned embroidery . . . would it have been so ignoble for him to have given a little of his love for bravery and truth and justice over to *them?* To dedicate some portion of his life—just a jot, mind, a smidgen—to their needs, their happiness?"

"Someone has got to have the dreams, the visions, Rene!"

"This world has got no lack of grandiose dreamers, Cat; it won't want for me. I've got but one dream—to lie with you in a warm bed this winter, with a roaring fire in the hearth, and know that you are safe from fear and want and war. I'll fight for *that* dream, by Christ—fight to the death for it. I am sorry if you do not think it a worthy goal."

He was angry with her. Cat put her hand to his cheek. "Not worthy, perhaps," she said softly, "but flattering."

He seized the hand and kissed it. "You are all I want, Cat. I don't care for the rest of it. I only want to be with you." His arm tightened around her waist, fingers reaching for her bodice. "Do you remember the last time we were together on a riverbank?"

She nodded, laughing. "At Perth. You and your sailboat, so jaunty, and Malcolm's uncle so enraged—"

"I meant after that. When we were alone." He stroked her breast through the crimson silk. "Where the devil did you get this—this whatever it is you are wearing?"

"It is Jessie's best petticoat. Do you like it? I tarted it up with a bit of sewing as I crossed the Firth, to make it like the gowns worn by your harlots back in Ayr."

He winced. "You would remind me of them."

"I had the hardest time getting the top to stay up. I fear the boatman thought me mad."

"I am surprised he did not fall on you himself, seeing you look so wanton."

"Oh, he was an old man. Past the age of desire."

"No matter how old I get, I shall never stop desiring you." He kissed her, then drew back, rubbing his mouth. "Pah! You taste of rouge and paint. Where got you that?"

"Jessie has been experimenting. Though a bit more subtly." She tried to wipe the paint away with the hem of her gown. "Is it coming off?"

He looked. "Nay. We shall have to wash it."

"Wash it? Where?"

"There is a great deal of water close by, in case you hadn't noticed." Cat followed his gaze toward the river. "Can you swim?"

"Of course I cannot swim."

"Some women can, you know. My mother is a very fine swimmer."

"I never had the inclination to—Rene!" In one swift move, he'd yanked her cloak and the makeshift gown right over her head. "What are you doing?"

"Taking you for a moonlit swim." He grinned, seeing her fold her arms over her breasts. "There isn't much more showing now than there was in that gown." He removed his own clothes just as hastily, stepping out of his boots and breeches and kicking them aside. "Here, let me take your shoes."

Seeing him naked made her flesh tighten and tingle, set her heartbeat racing most alarmingly. "Won't it be cold, though?" she asked, looking at the dark, calm water.

"Not with me in there with you." He pulled off her shoes and stockings and caught her up in his arms.

"You won't drop me?"

"Trust me." She settled back and let him carry her into the estuary.

He had lied; it was cold. "Oh!" she cried as the water covered her toes. "Rene, stop!"

"It is best to plunge in all at once."

"Says who?"

"You'd better keep your mouth closed."

"Rene—" Her protest came too late; he'd already dipped her under the surface. She came up soaked and sputtering.

"I warned you to keep your mouth closed." He was grinning at her, his feet firmly planted on the bottom, the water running in rivulets from his slicked-back hair. "Still cold?"

"I am too shocked to be cold." The water had tightened her nipples; he ran his palm over them appreciatively.

"You look lovely wet. Feel lovely, too." He rubbed his groin against the side of her thigh as he held her. Their flesh was slippery and cool; it was wildly exciting. Cat twined her arms around his neck and kissed him, pressing tight against him. The river lapped at them, pushing gently back and forth, raising her up in his grasp and then drawing her away again. "God," he groaned. "Oh, God, I can't hold back, Cat."

"I don't want you to."

He took her swiftly, cleanly, kissing her mouth as he came in a surge like the current. He tasted of the river water, green and cold; the tide washed the smell of war and campfires and iron on whetstones away from him. As he clutched her, calling her name, his seed bursting within her, Cat felt happier than she ever had in her life. They *did* have each other; that was what mattered. All the rest would get sorted out somehow.

She knew in her heart he was wrong about Edward de Baliol. King David's enemy would not triumph. Her father's dream, the dream of so many good Scotsmen and women for their nation, would not die out so easily. After the battle to come, once Rene saw de Baliol vanquished, it would be easy enough to bring him 'round to her point of view.

If, that is, he was not killed in the fighting. The thought made her shiver in his arms. "Are you—a good soldier, Rene?" she asked fearfully.

He laughed, his manhood still inside her. "As it happens, I am. Blood is thick. My father's legacy to me . . . but what makes you ask that?"

"If you should die—"

He cut her off with a kiss. "I won't. Not when I have you to live for." But she was still trembling. "You are cold, that is all, love." He smoothed back her soaked hair and put his lips to her forehead. "I'll carry you in."

He bore her to the shore and wrapped her in his shirt, that her own clothes would not get wet and chill her. Then he sat on the riverbank and cradled her in his arms, tight to his breast, like a mother with her child. The sound of the water running to the sea was the sound of ten million silvery bells. The willow trees sang in the wind, their long gray-green branches sweeping the ground.

"I must dress," she said, but with no great conviction. She loved the way his bare flesh felt against her legs.

"I suppose it would be best," he agreed, not moving, although she felt him kiss her tangled hair. "And I must get back to the camp."

"Yes, I suppose you'd better." She leaned into him, though, and his hand brushed her breast. Even that small caress was enough to send a wave of heat rippling through her. The degree of her newfound want, her need for him, was astonishing. She twisted in his arms to face him, kissing him full on the mouth.

"Cat?" he said in surprise as she straddled his thighs.

"Rene. Take me again," she whispered, reaching for his manhood, feeling it come alive in her hand.

"You greedy girl! Isn't once enough?"

"Never."

"It is for me." He let himself fall backward onto the soft, warm earth of the bank, watching her through half-shut eyes, a smile teasing his mouth.

"Is it?" She bent over him, letting the tips of her breasts brush his chest, her fingers still tight on his manhood. A groan escaped him even as he nodded resolutely.

"Aye."

"Then why have you got so hard of a sudden?" Cat asked, and raised herself up on her knees.

"I don't—oh, Christ!" She'd slid his rod into her warm, slick sheath with a suddenness that made him gasp. "Oh, Cat." She was moving against him in slow, gentle circles, her hands on his shoulders, pressing down on him and then drawing upward, down and up. "What are you *doing?*"

"I have no idea," she admitted. "Isn't it wonderful?"

"Wonderful," he grunted, grabbing her buttocks, pulling her down on him so far that she thought he would pierce her through.

Bestriding him was a wild, heady sensation; she felt wanton and daring, and the emotions gave a sharp edge to her desire. She loved having him so deep inside her, loved being the one to set their pace. He was holding tight to her, trying to urge her to climax, craning his neck to reach her breasts with his mouth. But she held him off with her fists on his shoulders, still moving slowly, sensuously in circles against him. She heard his breath begin to come in short, quick gasps.

"Cat, I," he began, but stopped as her motions suddenly quickened, as her nails dug into his flesh. Head thrown back, she let out a long, silent scream of pleasure. God in heaven, how could anything feel so fine as this?

He clasped her and held her, pumping against her, that long rod plunging up and up and up while she bore down, her teeth bared, hair wild, all else forgotten but this desperate drive for fulfillment. He came first, unable to stave off his seed any longer, but she no sooner felt the burst of its white heat inside her than she climaxed, in great incredible rolling waves that swept her head to toe. "Oh," she cried over and over again, "oh, oh, oh, oh!" She arched back and strained down one last time as the waves swelled to a peak, then broke and exploded, showering both of them with shards of moonlight and stars.

Then she collapsed against him. "Cat Douglas," he whispered at her ear, sounding awestruck, "you amaze me."

"Mm. I amaze myself." She hugged him and kissed him, hard. "That was *good.*"

He laughed, returning the kiss. "That's not for you to say! Are you ever going to let me back on top again?"

"I shall think about it." His arms were sure and strong around her. To her horror, Cat yawned as he came toward her for another kiss.

"Go on. Sleep," he told her, rolling onto his side with her, drawing his cloak around them.

"I'm not tired," she insisted. "I don't want to waste precious time with you asleep."

"Then just rest for a moment." He made a pillow for her of the crook of his elbow. "Close your eyes." He shut them with his fingertips, very gently. "I love you, Cat."

"I love you, Rene."

Sighing, she nestled against him. *Forever,* sang the song of the river, ebbing and flowing beneath the night sky. *Forever,* sang the rustling willows with their silvery leaves. *Forever,* promised the white moon high above them. Safe in the circle of her true love's arms, Cat shut out the world and slept.

Eighteen

Light broke on the water, sparkling twice as bright for its dazzled reflection, as the sun rose over the far-off headland at North Berwick. Cat woke instantly, sitting up on Rene's lap with a dismayed cry: "I have slept the whole night through!"

"Aye, that you have," he said, smiling.

"Oh, I am sorry!"

"Why? I'm not. I liked holding you, looking at the river." He lifted her onto the bank beside him and then stretched out his legs. He was still naked. Cat laughed as she saw his manhood, already hard upright.

"Don't tell me there are things you would not rather have spent the night doing!"

"We'll have time enough for that in the years to come. But not this morning," he said, a little apologetic as he reached for his breeches. "I'll be marked down a deserter if I don't return to my men." Cat pulled her arms from his shirt; he sighed in longing at the sight of her white breasts. "Christ, it would nearly be worth it." Then he shook himself, splashed a bit of cold river water over his face. "But I can't. About getting back to Edinburgh, Cat. You can hire an oarsman at Inverkeithing; it is only a mile or so from here. But I can't take you there, I'm afraid."

Her green eyes, very gold in the new sunlight, slanted toward him. "I could come back to the camp with you," she offered shyly.

"No. It wouldn't be safe. You'll be better off in the castle at Edinburgh." He reached for the purse on his belt. "I'll give you money for the boatman."

"I brought money with me."

"Oh." He stood, pulling on the breeches, and then put his hands to his hips, staring down at her as she lifted the crimson petticoat over her head. "On second thought, I will go with you. I wouldn't trust any man in Scotland who saw you in that thing not to ravish you."

"I'll keep the cloak wrapped tight around me. I will be all right. Look here." She showed him a knife she had tied to the lining of the cloak with a ribbon. "Besides, I have the pox, remember?"

He laughed, but the sound was a little strained. "I am glad you came, Cat. I am glad . . . that you believe in me."

"Well, there have been moments when I wondered." She stood on tiptoe to kiss him. "And I still say you are dead wrong about de Baliol. He'll be whipped out of Scotland before St. Bartholomew's Day."

"We'll see. But whatever happens, stay at Edinburgh, love. I will come for you there." He returned the kiss; she wrapped her arms around him, pressing close to the length of his strong brown body, molding herself to him, feeling his manhood, still rock-hard, against her thighs. "Oh, no you don't!" Laughing again, he thrust her away. "Get on with you, you hussy. You'll find the road to Inverkeithing just there, beyond the willow trees. Follow the river inland. Go on, now, before some sentry finds you and claims you for booty." He gave her a pat on the buttocks, sending her on her way.

She turned when she reached the thicket of willows; he was watching her go, the sun rising behind him, the river sparkling like diamonds. "Cover your hair," he called, motioning for her to pull up her hood. "It's too beautiful to let it be seen!"

"Stop fretting about me!" she called back.

"Never!" He waved to her.

Cat blew him a kiss from her hand. "When will you come for me?"

"God knows, as soon as I can!"

Satisfied, she took one last look at him and then pushed beneath the weeping branches of the willow trees.

* * *

Inverkeithing was easy to find, and very nearly deserted; fear of the invaders was keeping the populace inside. But as she passed a baker's shop, Cat smelled bread, and was suddenly ravenous. Inside, she asked for tuppence' worth of currant buns from a woman who was stacking dark brown loaves in a wooden box.

"I'm surprised to find you open," Cat told her, "with the enemy so near."

"Folks need bread even in wartime, pet," the woman said philosophically. "Anythin' else?"

Cat looked over the baker's wares; she felt hungry enough to eat the shop bare. "One of those sugared loaves, please," she said, pointing. "A small one. And what sort of tarts are they there?"

"I hae got cherry 'n' blackberry." She winked. "Blackberry bae better."

"One of the blackberry, then, by all means." Cat shrugged back her cloak to reach for her purse. "And could you tell me where I can hire a boatman to take me to Edinburgh?" Busy with counting coins, it took her a moment to realize that the woman hadn't replied. "I said—"

"I heard wha' ye said." There was an altogether new, not at all friendly note to the woman's tone. Surprised, Cat glanced up at her, saw that her round, pleasant face had gone hard. She was staring at Cat's low-cut red gown, her mouth pursed tight. "Got up an appetite, did ye, sinnin' wi' the enemy?"

Cat laughed. "Oh! You think that I—no, no, no. It isn't like that at all. I just—"

"Spare me yer explanations," the woman said coldly. "It bae sixpence in sum." She wouldn't touch Cat's hand to take her coins, so Cat dropped them on the counter and took the paper-wrapped parcel of sweets. "Good riddance," she heard the woman hiss above the cheery jangle of the doorbell as she went out again.

So she wouldn't make the same mistake twice, Cat held the

purse in her hand as she made her way to the quays, munching the juicy berry tart. Then, with her cloak carefully clasped together, she asked a passing man where there were boats for hire, and followed his directions to the proper dock. Half a dozen boatmen came toward her, clamoring for her patronage as she approached. She chose one at random, and he led her to his trim little sailboat, then put his hand on her arm as she started to step in.

"Wait," he said, and nodded toward the river. "No sense goin' until that lot bae landed." Cat followed his gaze, and saw a big boat, perhaps forty feet long, tacking toward the quay. There were soldiers on the deck, and they weren't wearing David's colors. "De Baliol's men," the boatsman said, and spat into the river. "Like to see 'em turn over 'n' drown, I wuld."

Behind the soldiers stood a little bevy of women, ten or a dozen perhaps, all in fine cloaks and lace caps. They were chattering animatedly to one another; their accents were hard English, with none of the softness of Scotland. "Who are they?" Cat asked the boatman, staring.

"The English captains' women," he said darkly, yanking at a knot he'd been tying in the rigging. "Come o'er from Bamburgh, I reckon, to spend a day in the camps."

Cat could not tear her eyes from the elegant ladies. They looked so carefree and gay, as though they were heading for a river picnic instead of a war. *As though they know something we Scots don't about the fight to come,* she thought, and shivered, remembering how certain Rene had been that de Baliol would win.

The big boat scraped the dock; the sailors sprang to secure her and lower a plank. A handful of the braver townsfolk had come out of their houses to watch the landing; Cat saw the woman who'd sold her the buns give a little hiss as the first of the soldiers came ashore. "Gae on back to bludy England, why don't ye?" a man shouted, shaking his fist as the troops filed past him. Two of them turned to him, pikes at the ready, and he ducked through an alley, disappearing from sight.

The women were disembarking now, looking like bright butterflies in their fluttering silks and ribands. "Whores," Cat heard

the intrepid bakewife mutter under her breath. The Scottish boatmen were making rude whistling noises, but the women didn't
deign to hear them; their dainty wood-heeled shoes clattered on
the plank as they went on chattering away. Cat was still staring
at them in fascination when a familiar face beneath a handsome
blue bonnet made her catch her breath.

Quickly she turned away, averting her eyes—but not quickly
enough. High wood heels came clicking toward her across the
dock. "Well, as I live and breathe," said a familiar, detested voice.
"Is that you, Catriona Douglas?"

Trapped, Cat turned back. "How are you, Eleanor?"

"Oh, *very* well, thank you. But what in heaven's name are you
doing here? I should think you'd be with your father at Edinburgh, preparing to get your tails whipped by my uncle Edward."
Her laughter floated like little tinkling bells on the morning air,
echoed by the rest of the women.

Cat's chin came up. "Your uncle won't win."

Eleanor smiled patronizingly. "Wait and see. But why are you
clutching your cloak so tight around you, dearie, on a hot morn
like this?" Her white hand flicked toward the cloak. Cat jerked
back, but Eleanor's fingertips had caught a pinch of the cloth,
drawing it open to reveal the indecent crimson petticoat beneath.
"Oh, my, my." Eleanor clucked her tongue, her smooth blond
eyebrows raised. "How the mighty Douglas girls are fallen! Well,
I suppose 'tis no more than could be expected; it *was* your mother,
wasn't it, was the tavern wench?"

"You haven't changed a bit, have you, you bitch?" Cat raised
her hand to slap the supercilious smile off that hated face.

"Uh-uh-uh, dear." Eleanor caught her hand and held it, her
grip surprisingly tight. "You wouldn't hit a woman, would you,
who is bearing a child?"

Astonished, Cat looked at her more closely, and saw the unmistakable swelling across the belly of her sumptuous gown.
"I—I beg your pardon," she stammered. "I didn't know."

"Come along, Eleanor," called one of her companions; they
were trailing after the soldiers away from the docks.

"In a moment!" Eleanor cried brightly, waving them on, and
then turned to Cat again. "Well, it isn't surprising, I suppose,

that you wouldn't have heard. We've been keeping the news very close to our chests. I don't believe Rene has even told his mother."

The world around Cat suddenly went silent. She could not hear the soldiers marching, or the cries of the seabirds circling overhead, or the muttered grumblings of the townsfolk filing back to their homes. But there was a roar like thunder building, slowly building, in the back of her head. "Rene?" she whispered.

"Of course! We were married last April. And he is just thrilled about the baby. Well, I must be going. Rene is always so glad to see me when we've been apart. He's such an *animal,* you know." She winked and waved coquettishly, taking one last look at Cat's tawdry gown. "And best of luck to *you,* my dear, in—in whatever it is you are doing. I'm sure you're very good at it!" With one hand on her burgeoning belly, she smiled smugly. "Adieu, Cat, dear!"

Nineteen

Edward de Baliol's army marched inland toward Perth in the second week of August, 1332, in searing heat punctuated by thunderstorms that ripped open the skies. The royal forces came out to meet them under the command of Donald, earl of Mar. They met head-to-head on the twelfth, soon after dawn, close by Dupplin Moor.

In the months to come, King David's ministers would expend much vigor attempting to ascertain what went wrong at Dupplin. By the time the sun set on the twelfth, though, only this much was sure: Mar was dead, the royal forces were routed, full half of the king's cavalry lay waiting to be buried, and Edward de Baliol had claimed himself the crown.

Survivors straggled back to Edinburgh for days after the battle, grimy and famished and in shock at the suddenness of their defeat. Tess's husband Gill was one of the early arrivals, with a badly wounded Robbie Stewart slung across his saddle. Robbie's banishment had been rescinded early; Scotland needed all the warriors she could field. But it hadn't made a difference, in the end. "I don't know what happened, sir," Gill reported to Archibald, tears bright in his eyes. "They had the high ground, right enough, and their archers took a fearsome toll. But even so—our horse were all uncertain and chary. We had the numbers, sir. I fear that what we lacked was heart."

Archibald put an arm around his young son-in-law and hugged him tightly. "Sure 'n' ye fought yer best, lad."

"But that's just it!" Gill cried. "I don't think we did! It was as though—" He screwed his face up, remembering the horror.

"As though the men were marching all out of rhythm, hilter-skilter. Like our ears were stopped up, so we could not hear the drums."

Archibald shook his white head. "I reckon we bae feelin' the lack now o' my brother James—'n' of Michel Faurer. Well, Mar did wha' he could, God rest him. Next time it will be my turn." Clumsy but well-meaning, he patted Gill's hand. "Gae hame to Tess 'n' the baby, Gillie. Try not to dwell on wha' ye hae seen."

But Gill had no home any longer, and neither did Archibald Douglas—not technically, at least. Edward de Baliol's first official act after having himself crowned at Scone in September was to forfeit the lands of every Border laird who'd sided against him in the fight, signing them over once more to the English usurpers who had held them two decades ago, before the rise of the Bruce set his countrymen free. Tullibardines, Stewarts, MacPhersons, MacAuliffs, Laniers, Culbertsons, Hartins, Graemes, Grants, and dozens of others were by royal decree declared unhoused and unfarmed—lock, stock, and barrel—from their ancestral grounds, effective immediately.

That was the end to any organized fighting, for the men of Scotland rushed off to defend their families on the homeground, while the English barons who'd come over with de Baliol pressed southward, too, to make good by force of arms what the new King Edward I had decreed.

Archibald straddled the fence for a time, anxious to do right by his new post as regent of the realm but also in a fury lest some Englishman install himself in Douglas Castle. Only after he'd seen young King David and Queen Joanna safely settled at Berwick did he agree to return to Douglasdale.

It was mid-October, two months after the Battle of Dupplin. Rene had not come to Edinburgh by the time the Scots abandoned it.

Two months. Surely, Cat had kept thinking as the days ticked by, he would hold to his promise. Surely what Eleanor had told her about him and the baby was a vicious lie. But as time stretched and stretched, she was deviled with doubt. It could be true. It might be. It would certainly explain why he hadn't come for her, as he'd sworn he would.

She ought to have followed Eleanor's bobbing blue bonnet

back to the encampment that very morning, she thought over and over again. But she simply hadn't dared. What if Eleanor denounced her to her uncle's men, and she was taken prisoner? Archibald had troubles enough already. So she'd stepped into the waiting boat and let herself be rowed back across the choppy waters of the Firth, in which, only the night before, Rene had taken her with such passion. She would not voice even to herself the seed of fear that kept her from the camp: if she had seen them together there, she would have died of shame. Better, she reasoned, to await Rene in the city, just as they'd planned. They'd have a good laugh together about Eleanor's absurd claim when he came.

But he did not come. And with each passing day, Cat inclined more and more toward believing what Eleanor had said. He knew the Edinburgh tunnels; he could have gotten inside the walls. He could have written to her, sent a message. He didn't. Either he was married to Eleanor—either all the loving words he'd said to Cat were naught but a charade—or else he was dead. She wasn't sure which she wished. And she had run out of excuses to give her father as to why he should stay at Edinburgh.

So they returned home to Douglas Castle. Archibald looked older than ever as he tramped through the open gates to find that the English had indeed preceded him there. They hadn't stayed— perhaps in so many years of trying to hold those ancient towers against the Douglases they had learned something. But they had shattered every pane of glass and burned every plank of wood, every scrap of leather, every store of corn and oats, every book, every harp, every drapery and hanging, leaving the place a stinking, smoldering shell.

"Look on the fair side, Papa," Cat told him, picking her way through the ruins of what had been her bedchamber; some charming marauder had defecated in the middle of the floor. "We have our mattresses still; thank God they traveled with us!"

"Aye, 'n' that bae near all," he growled, surveying the wreckage with furious blue eyes. "The cowardly bastards would nae even stay to fight." He kicked a charred bit of rafter across the room. "I hae a gude mind to leave the wagons packed 'n' just keep on goin'."

Cat went and put her arm around him, leaning onto his shoulder. "Nay, Papa. We shall stay and build it all back up again."

"Wha' bae the sense in't?" There was a grief in his voice she'd never heard before, not even when the news had come about Uncle James. "I bae worn down, Kit-Cat. War bae a young man's game. All my bludy life I hae been chasin' the English from my house, 'n' them chasin' me out in turn. P'raps it bae time fer an endin'. P'raps I should let them have the cursed place. There bae nae joy left in't fer me."

Jessie was with them; she looked worriedly at her sister. "I hate to say it, but he may be right, Cat. It isn't likely the English won't be back. And we lost so many men at Dupplin . . . I'm not sure we could defend even the keep, much less the lands."

"Nonsense," said Cat. "It takes but two men to defend Douglas Castle. Don't you remember, Papa, how you and Uncle James held it against three hundred troops for two weeks, until the Bruce came to relieve you?"

The Douglas smile, slow and unwilling, creased Archibald's lined face. "Aye, that we did—'n' could hae held out longer, save that we war scarce o' ale."

"And what of the time you and he dressed in sheepskins, and had Walter Stewart drive you inside the walls in the midst of a herd to retake the keep?"

The grin widened. "La, that war a bonny trick. But 'twar a young man's trick, lass, 'n' I bae an old man now."

"Too old to dress again in women's clothes and stuff your bodice with cloth to get the English guards at the gate to let you through?"

Now he was laughing. "If the moon war new, p'raps, I might try that once more! Faith, if ye could hae seen th' looks on their faces when I drew my sword out o' my skirts!" Then the laughter faded. " 'Twill bae hard, though, without James at my side. James, 'n' the Bruce, 'n' Donald Mar 'n' Michel—sae many gude man gone now . . ."

"But more raised up each day to take their places," Jessie said softly. "You've your grandchildren now to keep Scotland free for." Tess had sent a messenger to Edinburgh just before they left there, to tell them she was once more with child.

"Aye, that I hae." She came to him, too, to put an arm around him, and he hugged her and Cat tightly. " 'Twould please me nae end to hae ye two wed safe 'n' sound before some English arrow finds me."

Oh, Rene, where are you? Cat's battered heart cried, just as a timid knocking came at the place where, before the English had arrived, there had been her chamber door. It was the houseboy, Pippin, grown some since last they'd seen him, and with a new, adult wariness of the world in his eye.

"Gude m'laird." He swallowed. "Sae help me, sir, we did our best to fight 'em—"

"Fight 'em?" Archibald laughed, his good humor restored. "I hope to hell ye ran fer the hills, lad! When ye grow as old as me, ye'll ken—walls can always bae built up again. It bae life that counts." And he ruffled the frightened boy's hair.

"There war sae many o' em, sir," said Pippin, looking relieved. "A fierce ruddy lot. Came swoopin' in just at nightfall. We'd nae more time than to sneeze afore the place war on fire."

"Dinna fret yerself, laddie. Unless—" And Archibald glared at him. "Unless they found my secret ale stores."

"Nae, nae, m'laird. The ale bae safe 'n' sound."

"Praise God fer that! Gae 'n' draw me a pint, then, will ye, whilst I chew o'er where to begin wi' this mess?"

"Right away, m'laird." Pippin turned, then felt the front of his doublet and turned back. "Beggin' yer pardon, but this came fer Lady Catriona." He pulled out a sealed parchment.

"When did it come?" she breathed, reaching for it with trembling hands. The seal bore a scrolled F. For Faurer . . .

"A fortnight or sae past. I kept it safe fer ye, till I should ken where to send it."

"God bless you, Pippin." Cat started to slide her thumbnail under the seal, then noticed that her father and Jessie were looking on curiously. Well, what the hell, she thought, and yanked the letter open anyway.

The writing wasn't Rene's, but Madeleine's, lovely and dainty. *He is dead,* she thought, and blinked back a rush of tears. But better to know than to keep on wondering. She scanned the page quickly, searching for the dread news but finding instead a familiar, detested name. Startled, she worked back to the beginning of the paragraph.

"My dear Cat," Madeleine had written, "I did want to assure you Anne and I are well. But there is other news I thought you should have. Eleanor de Baliol has written to me to say that she and Rene were married in Paris in April. I am sorry. I knew that you would want to know."

"Bae that fro' Madeleine Faurer?" Archibald asked, trying to crane to read it.

"Aye." Cat refolded the letter and slipped it into her sleeve.

"Well, wha' does she say?"

"That she and Anne are safe at Langlannoch. De Baliol's men did not reach so far."

"I bae glad to hear it. Wha' else?"

"Nothing," Cat told him. "That's all." She took a breath, amazed at her own steadiness. "You know, Papa, you may get that wish for me and Jess to be married sooner than you think."

Jessie looked at her, startled. "Do you know something I don't?"

"Nay. But it is just a matter, isn't it, as Tess says, of taking stock of what's available and then making up your mind?"

"Best take stock fast," Archibald said, grinning. "War has a way o' cuttin' down eligible men."

"But those that are left will still be fighting each other to wed Douglases," Cat said, bringing her chin up.

Her father cocked a brow at her, squeezing her hand. "Glad I bae, Catriona, to hae ye thinkin' like a Douglas again. That night ye slipped out o' Edinburgh Castle to pray at Holyrood did ye a world o' gude."

That was the excuse she'd given him for that last night she'd spent with Rene. Resolutely she pushed from her memory the sound of the river, the mist in the moonlight, the whispering willows, and that wild ride she'd taken atop him. . . . "Aye, Papa, it did. But 'twould do me even better to have you whip Edward de Baliol back over the Tweed to England with his tail between his legs."

"After, of course, you get the castle back in *some* sort of order," Jessie put in.

"That bae wha' I shall do, then," Archibald announced. " 'N' whilst I do, ye twain must concentrate on finding husbands."

"It will be our pleasure," Cat said with a curtsy.

Her father chucked her chin. "Nae more moonin' about o'er traitorous scum like that Rene Faurer?"

Cat's green-gold eyes glinted. "Nay, Papa. You have got my word on that."

As soon as he and Jessie had left her, she burned Madeleine's letter to ashes, and watched them whisk away on the wind that breezed through the castle's breached walls.

In that autumn of recouping and rebuilding, Jessie did find herself a man. He was, granted, not so grand a catch as Gill Tullibardine or even Rawley Quillan; he was a Highlander, and Highland families, even those as ancient as Diarmot Mac-Dugall's, tended to be poor. But from the moment she laid eyes on him—he'd come to Castle Douglas with a message for Archibald from his father, chief of Clan MacDugall—Jessie was smitten to her core.

"Do you think he is handsome?" she would ask Cat. *"I* think he is handsome."

"That's all that matters then, isn't it?" Cat diplomatically replied. Diarmot didn't fit her notions of beauty; he was altogether too gangly, and his hair was fair, which she had never cared for in a man.

"You *don't* think he is handsome."

Cat smiled at her. "All right. He's the most handsome man in the world. Are you satisfied now?"

"Not at all." Jessie shuddered. "You might try to steal him from me."

"Well, you can't have it both ways, pet!"

"It doesn't matter." A true sign of love, Jessie's mood these days could change from hope to despair in an eyewink. "I'll never see him again now that he's returned north. I know it."

He was back in a fortnight, with another message to the regent, of such sublime unimportance that Archibald accused him out-

right of coming solely to court Jessie. The shy young Highlander
shamefacedly admitted as much—whereupon Archibald clapped
his back and bade him stay on at Douglasdale for as long as he
liked. A week after that, he proposed to Jessie. "He may be a
mite bashful," Archibald noted with bemusement, "but he kens
wha' he wants!" A wedding date was set for July, only eight
months hence.

"Splendid planning," Cat told her sister. "Even if he gets you
with child now, you'll more than likely be married before you
deliver."

"Oh, Diarmot isn't like that," Jessie said very gravely. "He's
a gentleman. There'll be none of that until we are wed."

For one fleeting instant, Cat thought of telling her sister what
she was missing by waiting; just for that moment, she let herself
think of Rene, of his sweet weight bearing down on her, setting
her flesh afire . . .

"I *said*," Jessie repeated, shaking her head at Cat's inattentive-
ness, "it looks as though you are certain to lose the wedding bet.
Unless, of course, you give the nod at long last to Malcolm."

"Malcolm?"

"Malcolm Ross, you fool. He'd marry you in a snap of your
fingers."

"Oh, him." Cat laughed. "I can't marry him. Lord, I can barely
recall who he is. He is blond, isn't he?" The boy who'd picked
the fight with Rene at Perth that Robbie Stewart finished . . .
He'd been at Edinburgh, too, for Janet's wedding, hadn't he? It
was hard to remember. She'd been so blind in love then. . . .

"You said yourself it was only a matter of taking stock and
then picking one," Jessie reminded her, twisting her gold-and-
garnet betrothal band around her finger.

"Aye, so I did. But it is a little more than that, isn't it? Even
for Janet, I think that it was."

Janet and Rawley had visited at Martinmas. Shocked though
she was at the state of her family's home, Janet had never looked
happier. Even Archibald had noticed it right away. "Ye did well
by yerself with Rawley, did ye?" he asked his daughter, stroking
her blond hair.

"Better than I thought, Papa," she confessed.

Tess and Janet, and now Jessie to be married, too. *I am the
youngest,* Cat reminded herself defensively. *It's to be expected
I'd be married latest.*

And first, of course, her shattered heart would have to mend.

Archibald was governing Scotland from the towers of
Douglas; Diarmot MacDugall was far from the only messenger
knocking at the gates that fall. When he wasn't trying to raise
funds from the pope, the king of France, the princes of the rich
Low Countries, and anyone else he thought might be sympathetic
to the nation's troubles—or, at least, antagonistic toward Edward
the Third of England—the chief of the Douglases was coordi-
nating the maneuvers of the remnants of the Scottish army. They
had one clear objective: to find Edward de Baliol and put an ax
or arrow through his heart.

Gill rode with these raiders, after for safety's sake moving Tess,
now three months along, and baby Jane back to Castle Douglas.
So did some of the old Templars who'd ridden in Michel Faurer's
cavalry at Bannockburn. Cat remembered these from her New
Year's holiday at Langlannoch—grizzled Tomas, tongueless Guillaume, cheery, garrulous Brant. Malcolm Ross was willing to give
up the defense of his uncle the earl's estates to join, but when he
came to Castle Douglas he was sent home again, after Angus
MacPherson argued eloquently to Archibald that the Ross estates
were too strategically vital to risk their loss. Cat was unspeakably
grateful to Angus; the band of elite warriors was at Douglasdale
far more often than she wanted Malcolm to be.

They were elite, but they were not infallible. De Baliol continued to elude them in the game of hare and hounds, staging
raids on the smaller strongholds in Strathclyde and Lothian and
the Southern Uplands, always falling back to one of the Border
castles he held. There was no question on either side of another
pitched battle—not yet. Archibald needed time to reconstruct his
army; de Baliol hoped to pick off enough fortresses to build a
wide wedge of safety northward of the Tweed. But when the next
battle did come, it seemed sure to come near Berwick, where a

hand-picked corps of soldiers was guarding the young king and queen.

Archibald had so much on his mind that his daughters rarely saw him. He took an occasional meal with them—so, he jested, he could listen to Jessie's dire warnings about the dangers of his diet—and twice or thrice stopped by their rooms to catch up on the news and make a fuss over Jane. But the country had first claim on him—which is why Cat and her sisters were all surprised when the serving boy, Pippin, came to them at supper one evening in November to report that their father wished to speak to his youngest daughter immediately.

"Uh-oh, Cat," Tess teased. "What have you done now?"

"Nothing that I know of." For once, that was true. "Did he say why, Pippin?" The boy shook his head.

"Only one way to find out," Tess told her.

Cat folded her napkin and got up. "Come with me, Jess, and we can ask him about that collection you wanted to take up for the orphans in Lanark."

Pippin spoke up then. "He said ye should come alone, mum."

"Oh," said Cat. So she did.

He was in his study, sitting at his desk. Usually the room was crammed with soldiers, and his big oak desk covered with a litter of maps and missives and the remnants of meals taken there. It was spotless now, though, Cat noted.

"Sit down, Catriona," her father said.

God, he looked weary. Cat perched on the edge of the chair across the desk from him, wishing she could do something to ease those lines of care from his brow. Some sort of treat, she mused. When she and her sisters were little, sometimes they would put on pretend pageants for him, complete with costumes and music of sorts, with Tess puffing the bagpipes and Janet dancing, Jessie playing flute and Cat banging a drum. Archibald had always laughed until he cried to see their antics. Perhaps they could do that again. Or would he think it too silly and childish? No, she decided, he'd enjoy it. Janet wasn't here, of course, but they could work around that. . . .

Archibald opened his desk drawer and drew out a leather belt.

Cat smiled. "It's a bit late in our lives, don't you think, Papa, to begin whipping me?"

He didn't smile. He took a single sheet of parchment from the drawer, laid it beside the belt, and then pushed both toward her. "Read it," he commanded, in the hard voice he used sometimes to his troops.

Puzzled, Cat picked the parchment up and turned it over. There was a single line of writing on the other side. ASK YOUR YOUNGEST DAUGHTER WHO WORE THIS BELT IN HER BEDCHAMBER ON THE NIGHT MORAY DIED, it said.

"Well?" Archibald Douglas asked.

Cat's mouth had gone bone-dry. She licked her lips to wet them. "How came you by this?" Her voice still came out cracked.

"A messenger brought it in a packet."

"Whose messenger?"

"He wore nae colors. He left it 'n' went." His big hands were clenched atop the desk. "Wha' o' it, Catriona?"

"I have no idea whatsoever what this is about," Cat said bravely.

"Ye hae nae, hae ye?"

"No, Papa."

He unwound the belt. Cat saw there was a buckle, a silver buckle worked in a design of acanthus leaves. In the center was a small medallion bearing two initials: RF. She caught her breath.

"I'll ask ye once more, Catriona. Whose belt bae this?"

"I—" Cat swallowed; there was a dreadful sour taste in her throat. "I—" But she could not go on, could not bring herself to lie or to admit the truth.

"It dinna matter," Archibald said then. "We both of us ken whose it bae." He leaned back in his chair, his keen blue eyes narrowed. "Eighteen years past, when I got a letter fro' yer mother sayin' she war bearin', my brother James counseled me to gae wary. A tavern wench, he said, that ye dallied but a few days with? It bae likely she has heard o' the others, 'n' bae out fer wha' she may get o' the bairn. I wuld nae believe him then." His hands unclenched slowly. "I believe him now. Ye bae nae child o' mine."

"Papa!" Cat cried in horror. "You cannot mean that!"

"Wha' else can I think, when yer deceptions run sae deep?" He counted off on his fingers. "Ye hae betrayed me—well, that bae the least o' it. Ye hae betrayed the house o' Douglas, more the shame to ye. Ye hae betrayed Scotland, 'n' poor wee King David—'n' ye hae betrayed God in yer wanton lusts. Nae blud born o' my blud would hae done this thing."

"Your blood! Why, you old hypocrite, you spread your seed over all Scotland!"

"The occasional Douglas may hae betrayed God," he said evenly. "But the others—name 'n' country 'n' king—never in a million years." A fire was burning low in the hearth. He tossed both belt and letter onto the embers. "Pack up yer things. I'd hae ye gone fro' the castle at dawn."

"Gone?" Cat echoed. "Where would I go?"

Archibald shrugged, reaching to pour himself whiskey from a vessel on the sideboard. "To yer traitor lover, o' course, who has taught ye sae well all those virtues ye hae shown me: lyin', schemin', fornication—"

"Papa, please!"

"Bae the word too bald fer ye, then? Pity ye dinna think sae o' the act."

"How can you be so cold?" she whispered brokenly.

"Me?" He laughed. "Me cold? Wha' o' ye, that could lie wi' a man in my own feather bed, then send him off to make a murder—"

"I didn't know he'd commit murder! Anyway, he told me that he didn't do it."

"Did he, Catriona? When did he tell ye that?"

"When I went to—" Too late, she faltered. "I mean . . . I . . ."

"Sae, ye saw him afterward as well," Archibald said relentlessly, "this homicide. When? On the night ye told me ye war prayin' wi' the holy sisters down at Holyrood?"

Awash in her shame, Cat began to cry. He could not mean what he had said about not being her father, could he?

"Yer tears dinna move me," he told her, his visage stony. "Get out from under my roof."

"Papa—"

"Nae langer."

"Papa, listen to me! I did all those things that you accuse me of. I even went to him at Inverkeithing, after—after Moray was dead. I went because I could not believe Rene had killed him." Her mouth, the Douglas mouth, so like Archibald's, tightened. "I believe it now, though. I would believe that man capable of anything at all."

" 'N' wha' has brought ye round to this conclusion at lang last?" His voice was clearly skeptical. "Bein' found out in yer sins by me?"

Cat hesitated. On top of the betrayals he'd listed already, did she need to add adultery? She pictured in her mind Eleanor's smug, cool smile of triumph on the docks at Inverkeithing, heard in her head the vow Rene had made to her that very morning— *Wait for me at Edinburgh,* he'd told her. *I will come for you there. . . .* Oh, you bastard, thought Cat, and then looked straight at her father. "I just know it, that's all." Her small face crumpled like a dying flower. "Don't cast me off, Papa. I'd have nothing to live for if I didn't have you."

"Ach, Kit-Cat." He sighed heavily. "Wha' bae I to do wi' ye, my headstrong, hapless daughter?"

She caught her breath in a tremulous sob. "Does that mean— you don't believe what Uncle James said about my mother?"

"James war a bludy fool when it came to women. On top o' that, he ne'er met Marguerite. Nae soul who did could doubt her. She ne'er spake a false word in her life." He shook his head. "I always thought ye took after her, Cat, that way."

She always had, before Rene. "I don't know what to say to you, Papa. I don't know how to explain it. He was like—like a sickness in my blood that I could not be rid of. Like a leech on my heart." That took and took, and never gave anything in return . . .

"Ye hae ruined yerself fer the husband ye will hae someday, God willin'."

She dropped her shamed eyes, the gold swallowed by tears. "I know."

"Still—" He smiled, a faint smile. "Ye do bae a Douglas. P'raps 'twill suffice fer ye in that, too."

Cat scented forgiveness in that smile—sweeter than eglantine, than the small, wild dog roses. The sweetest smell she'd ever smelled in her life . . . "If you can find it in your heart to forgive me, Papa, I swear on—on Mama's grave that I'll never give you cause to doubt me again."

"Forgiveness cannae bae given sae freely, lass. It must be earned."

"I'll make it up to you, then," she said quietly but fiercely. "Just wait. You will see."

He took a draught of the whiskey in his cup, then stared into the musty amber liquid. "D'ye know, Catriona, why neither yer uncle James nor I e'er married?"

"Why—you didn't find the right women, I suppose."

"Nae, lass." Another small smile. " 'Twar on account o' findin' too many o' them. Early on we knew—dinna ask me how—we war nae fitted out fer baein' faithful. We war Douglases, after all, 'n' where'er we went, there war nae shortage o' lassies ready to tumble to our pleasures. Sae it seemed the noble thing to us to forswear marriage—to ne'er speak a set o' vows we knew we could nae keep." He rolled back his sleeve, showed her a tiny scar on his thick wrist, right where the blue veins ran. "We sealed the pact, ain to another, in blud. I war all o' sixteen."

"I never knew," Cat breathed.

"We ne'er spake o' it. James—sae far as I ken, James ne'er regretted the takin' o' that vow, right up to the day that heathen ax blade felled him there in Spain."

She looked at her father, at his worn face and care-bleared eyes. "And you?"

He barked a laugh. "I war sorry afore the blud clotted on my arm. But wha' could I do, then? I had given my word as a Douglas. I wuld nae sully my name."

"Oh, Papa," she whispered. "How awful for you."

"I dinna tell ye, pet, to earn yer pity. I told ye—well, I suppose, fer this: each thing we do in this world, good or evil, casts a shadow. It bae like—" He had screwed up his face, concentrating. *He has not,* Cat thought, *much practice in speaking like this, from the heart, no audiences, no admirers.* The realization filled her with a great swell of sadness. How lonely he must have been all these years.

"Like rainwater," he went on finally. "Like a lane drop o' rain that falls from the sky onto a windowpane. It lands 'n' touches another, runs into another, 'n' another, 'n' each ain it touches, it changes, sae that neither ain can e'er bae the same. Ach—" He swallowed more whiskey. "James 'n' I knew nothin' o' that then; we were feckless boys. But I hae thought on't since—o' how that ain act has made others suffer. Yer mother, Jan's, Jessie's, Tess's—'n' I pray the Laird in heaven will nae take account o' how many more. But I hae suffered too fer it. I suffer now, wi' all this great weight o' governance upon me, 'n' nae mate to share the burden wi' me."

Then break your vow, Cat wanted to urge him. Rawley is newly wed at your age; you could be too. Uncle James is dead. No one would ever know . . . but he would not. She felt it in her heart, sure as sorrow, as death. He had given his word as a Douglas. There was no more to say.

"I'm so sorry, Papa," she whispered.

He reached across the desk for her hand. "Then be chary, pet, in wha' ye do fro' here on. P'raps, by the grace o' God, the sluice o' water ye hae let loose wi' that knave will nae turn to a flood. Ye may bae more lucky than—" There was a knock at the door, very timid. "I said I wuld nae be disturbed, dammit!" he roared at the wood.

Pippin's voice, hesitant: "Aye, gude my laird, but—"

Then the door flew open. "It bae my fault, nae the lad's," growled Angus MacPherson, grimy from the tips of his boots to the top of his red head—on him, a very long way. He was nearly as dirty, Cat thought, staring, as he'd been on the day of Tess's wedding, when he'd burst into the hall with the dreadful news about Uncle James. . . .

Her father must have been remembering that day, too; his knuckles had turned white gripping his whiskey cup. "It wuld nae be gude news, wuld it, Angus? That always can wait."

"Nay, Archibald. It bae Gill. He war taken by de Baliol's men yestreen."

Twenty

When Jessie heard that Gill had been taken prisoner, she fainted outright. Tess, on the other hand, was a rock, a mountain—Ben Nevis, Ben More. With the curve of the growing seed her husband had planted in her belly just beginning to show, she stood for a moment in silence, her black head lowered, then excused herself: it was time to put little Jane to bed.

Her sister's courage, coming so hard upon Archibald's discovery of her own shameful deceit, moved Cat fiercely. Lord, how selfish she had been, thinking only of her own wants, her lustful desires, while all around her the men and women of her country were making sacrifices such as she could not imagine. What impossible fortitude it must have taken for Tess to tuck her tiny daughter beneath the covers that night without dissolving in tears.

Archibald took two steps in quick succession. First, he set into motion a formal request to de Baliol for an exchange of prisoners. Then, by less official channels, he spread word throughout Scotland that he personally would pay a bounty of ten thousand marks for de Baliol's head. "You haven't got that kind of money, Papa," Tess pointed out calmly.

"I could raise it if I had to, lass. Mortgage a house or twain, sell off some land . . ."

"Gill would not want you to ruin yourself on his account," his oldest daughter told him.

"It bae nae fer Gill alone," he said grimly. "It bae fer every Scots man 'n' woman 'n' child wha' has suffered at that bastard's hands."

Because even official correspondence to the country's self-declared king had to be routed through England—"What kind of monarch," Jessie demanded in fury, "is so afraid of the people he governs that he will not even let them know where he is?"—it would be at least three weeks before a response came to Archibald's request for a prisoner exchange. He had in the keeps at Douglasdale and at Berwick bait he trusted would serve to effect the trade—two sons of the earl of Northumberland who'd been taken at Dupplin, a couple of minor de Baliol cousins, half a dozen assorted barons and knights. While he waited, Archibald ordered that the men he held be fed lavishly, with white bread, ham, salmon, butter, fresh fruits, and all the mead and ale they could drink—though this largesse meant his own troops went without. "When they gae back to that bastard, let them tell him there bae nae lack o' victuals here," Archibald explained to his men when they grumbled. "It may put a touch o' fear to him."

There was fear aplenty in Douglas Castle. Jessie's Diarmot had taken Gill's place riding with the Douglas raiders, much to everyone's surprise and his intended's chagrin. "Ne'er thought I'd see the day when a Highlander war contented to take orders fro' any man exceptin' his chief," Angus marveled. But Diarmot did all he was told to, with a sense of discipline quite foreign to the reputation of his rowdy clan.

"Either he bae true in luv," Archibald said of his future son-in-law with dark humor, "or Scotland bae worse off even than we think."

But Jessie saw nothing amusing. "What if he is taken prisoner, what then?" she fretted to Cat. "Papa has offered all his *good* hostages to get Gill back; there'll be no one left to trade for Diarmot's life!"

Cat hid a smile; love had made her sister considerably less saintly. "He won't be taken," she tried to soothe her. "You cannot take a Highlander captive; didn't you know? They're all sorcerers; they change into black cats and slip off in the night." The way Rene had slipped into and out of Edinburgh Castle, she thought idly, looking down at the heads of Archibald's hostages, who were taking the air in the yard below. She must remember to tell her father of Rene's boast that he could sneak into any royal castle in Scotland; it was dangerous indeed to have such a man at loose amongst the enemy. Once he'd even said, hadn't he, that he could scale these well-defended stone walls if she bade him to?

She caught her breath. Jessie glanced at her, curious. "Cat? What is it?"

"Nothing," Cat said quickly, pushing away the thought that had sprung into her mind at that memory. Impossible. She would never have the nerve to see it through.

The idea gnawed at her, though, through those long days of awaiting de Baliol's reply. She even took to strolling through the yards each morning when the hostages were let out of their cells for exercise, trying to decide which she would approach if she had the courage to. There was one, youngish, quite handsome, with a softness to his hazel eyes that made her settle on him finally—all in theory, of course.

Then, at last, de Baliol's messenger arrived with a proposal. Archibald swore roundly when he read the terms—the usurper was asking three of the regent's hostages for every one he released—but had no time to quibble, not with the glacial pace of the negotiations so far. Always thorough, he sent Angus and six more of his best raiders out to trail the messenger leaving Douglasdale with his letter of acquiescence, in the hope he might lead them directly to de Baliol. They returned two days later to report that de Baliol, equally thorough, had his courier take ship for England in Kirkcudbright; they'd not be tracking him that way.

Still Tess waited, never giving a sign of the awful anxiousness that had to be hounding her. In the end, it was her sister's unflagging strength that gave Cat heart for what she had to do.

On the day before the hostages were to be exchanged, she went down to the yards with some needlework—a hoop holding a linen clout for Jessie's dowry chest. Then she took a seat in a wall niche out of view of her father's soldiers, and waited for the hazel-eyed hostage to pass by.

"Good milord." His head jerked 'round as she called him. "Don't look at me, I pray you," she said, her voice trembling. "I have . . . a boon that I would ask of you."

Obediently he kept his eyes trained on the soldiers, standing and stretching his legs and shoulders as he replied: "Good milady, what boon could a lowly prisoner possibly perform for one of the lovely daughters of our host here in Douglasdale?"

So he knew who she was. Cat's heart sank a little; she'd been hoping for anonymity. Too late for that now . . ." I have a message," she whispered. "A letter I would—" She stopped; Angus MacPherson was approaching.

"A mite chill out here for that sort o' thing this mornin', bain't it?" he asked, nodding at her sewing. The prisoner had unobtrusively sidled away and was bending his knees low, touching his toes.

"I—I wanted to see the colors of the threads by daylight," Cat told Angus.

"Ye should nae bae in the yards whilst yer father's prisoners bae loose."

His broad, grim face nearly sent her scurrying. But she had come this far. . . ." Oh, Angus," she said, and sighed. "I know that. But I get so tired of being cooped up indoors, doing nothing day after day, while you and the other men are risking their lives so bravely." That was it; play to his vanity. "You don't know how I envy you."

"D'ye, now? There bae men eno', I reckon, wuld sooner sit hame sewin'."

"Not me. I would ride with the raiders if I could. I would find Edward de Baliol and stab him straight through the heart." That, at least, rang with conviction.

Angus's pale eyes had turned thoughtful. "Some wuld say, ye ken, that de Baliol's death wuld spell disaster for Scotland."

"Why, how could it?" she asked in surprise.

"Edward o' England bae contented right now to let de Baliol fight his own battles. Were his poppet-king dead, he might feel he maun enter this fray. 'N' de Baliol's murder wuld gi' Edward leave to murder King David in turn."

Cat gasped. "David is only a child."

"But he bae the blud o' the Bruce. Sae lang as he lives, his father's dream lives, too."

Cat's prisoner was making for the other side of the yard. "Papa can protect King David," she said stoutly. "If he says 'tis best to find de Baliol and kill him, then it must be."

Angus shrugged. "I only say wha' some will say." He looked at the hoop and cloth she held, and then back into her wide cat's eyes. *He suspects something,* she thought, fighting off panic, doing her best to meet his gaze unflinchingly. "Ye spake o' women 'n' men," he said finally. "Women hae their part to play in this conflict."

"Of course we do. Like your wife, that makes the arrow poisons—"

He went on as though he hadn't heard her: "That part bae to sit 'n' wait, whilst those wha' ken better how the warld bae made wage the wars 'n' such."

She laughed a little. "I never would presume to think that one of my sex could have any impact at all on—"

"It dinna take sae much force as ye might think to wrench the course o' history." He was speaking softly, staring at the sewing on her lap. "It has been done, I reckon, sae often wi' a skein o' silk or hank o' hair as wi' a lance or sword. Look at young Rene Faurer."

"What?" Cat could have bit her tongue; she'd sounded far too startled.

"Why, de Baliol's niece has got him into wedlock, has she nae? 'N' he the son o' the brawest, truest soul that e'er served the Bruce. . . ."

So it was no secret, then, Eleanor and Rene's marriage. Cat hoped that in the blaze of morning light, the blush she felt might not show.

Angus looked right into her eyes. "Leave war to the men, lass, 'n' stick to yer sewin'. That bae the best way."

"I had no intention of doing anything else, Angus."

"See that ye dinna, then." Someone was calling him from close by the castle gates. "Mind ye get back inside, now."

"I will."

Angus hesitated, then started toward the gates at a slow lope, turning more than once to look back. Cat took a moment to wind up her skeins on her fingertips.

"You asked a boon, milady?"

The prisoner's soft voice made her jump. He'd come back toward her and resumed his exertions, eyes trained on the soldiers. Cat licked her dry mouth, the Douglas mouth. Should she? It would be her last chance. . . . *Leave war to the men,* Angus had warned her.

She shrugged his words away, still winding the silk. "I have a letter I would send," she whispered. "To someone who is . . . on your side."

His hazel eyes widened a little, but remained on the guards. "Can you not send it through regular channels, milady?"

"I'm afraid it's rather delicate. A—an affair of the heart."

"Ah." There was a long pause, during which Cat's heart pounded. Had she misjudged him? Did he fear some sort of trap? When he spoke again, his voice was very low. "To whom might your missive be addressed?"

"To Captain Rene Faurer." She held her breath. Would he scruple at carrying a billet-doux to a married man, the husband of his leader's niece? "Do you know Captain Faurer?"

"I know of him, naturally." He could not keep from looking at her now. She let her face show all her desperation, past the point of pride, and shifted her 'broidery hoop to reveal the sealed parchment hidden beneath.

"Will you take him this for me?"

Another pause. "We're to board ship for England, milady. I have no way of knowing when, even if, I might see the captain."

"I know that. But you could try. All I ask is that you try."

His hazel eyes regarded her with undisguised curiosity. "Can you tell me, milady, why you think I would even consider such a thing?"

"For the sake of one you love," she whispered, "who might need to send such a letter someday."

He hesitated. Then his long arm stretched to snatch the letter and tuck it in his doublet front. "I'll do what I can."

The guards were shouting for the prisoners to return to their dungeon. On the edge of their deliverance, the scent of freedom in their noses, they were slow to assemble. "God bless and keep you," Cat told the man who'd taken the letter. "I am forever in your debt." As he moved off, not looking at her again, she was seized by a sudden fear. "You would not read it, would you?" she called after him. His back straightened; his voice drifted toward her over the hubbub in the yard:

"Milady, that you would even pose such a question fills me with chagrin."

Relief sagged through her; she had not misjudged him. If there were any way on earth to do so, he would get her message to Rene. After that—well, best not to think of what would come after that. For now, there was nothing left to do but wait.

Gill came back to Douglas Castle a fortnight later, gaunt and drawn but grateful to be free. "Would that bastard de Baliol had your wit, Archibald," he told his father-in-law with a grimace when he learned how all the dainties in the countryside had gone to feed his former captor's men. "Bad gruel was what we dined on—and, God help me, not enough of that."

Tess hugged him, laughing; he had Jane on his knee. Seeing them together, a family reunited, happy, filled Cat with wistfulness. After all the mistakes she'd made, could her future possibly hold any such sweet contentment? She remembered what Archibald had told her: forgiveness is not given, but earned. Watching Gill caress Tess's swelling belly, she thought of the machinations she had set in motion. "For you, Gill, and all the others who have suffered . . ."

He glanced at her, grinning. "What's that, Cat?"

"Nothing. I didn't say anything."

"Cat's been very mysterious of late," Tess told her husband. She could not stop touching him, his arm, his back, his hair, as though to reassure herself of his substantiality. "Very meek and quiet."

"Hmm! Not like you at all, Cat. Are you unwell?"

Jessie was sitting in a corner of the hall beside her shy Highlander. "She's pondering joining a nunnery, I think," she put in, "now that she's lost the wedding bet."

"I still have six months," Cat pointed out, "before you and

Diarmot are wed." But her heart wasn't in the banter; her mind was a long way away.

Tess was speaking to her; she forced herself to listen, concentrate. ". . . come home with Gill and me to Tullibardine for Christmas," her sister was saying. "Do us all good to get away from here for a bit. And at least there, one doesn't always have soldiers tramping through the solarium—not to mention the smell of cinders. No matter how many times I clean this hall, I swear, it still stinks of that burning. Well, what do you say?"

"Oh, I can't leave," said Cat.

"Why in heaven's name not?"

"I . . ." Christ, how she longed to tell them what she'd done, let them know this prodigal daughter was finished with straying. But she didn't dare. Too much was at stake. "I can't, Tess. That's all."

Not even to herself did she voice her deepest, her most secret fear, much less to her sisters and their lovers.

She was terrified that at the final assay, with so much in the balance, she might weaken and fail.

Twenty-one

Christmas at Douglas Castle was marked by a three-day holi-day used by most of the soldiers in residence to visit their fami-lies, and triple rations of Archibald's minuscule ale stores—from a supply he'd cannily tucked away inside a cavern in the hills above the castle, just in case of English invasion—for those who stayed. Jessie and Diarmot had gone with Tess; Janet was at home with Rawley, whose gout was troubling him again. Cat went to Mass with her father, then shared with him a hurried meal of roasted acorns and a goose, donated by one of his cousins, before he stomped off to study his charts and maps for clues to de Baliol's whereabouts. Food was growing more and more scarce as the winter set in.

Everyone was to return to Douglasdale for the New Year. Cat spent that week trying to scavenge provisions and gifts, crafting a doll out of fabric, with a dried-apple head, for Jane. As she worked, she found herself remembering that other little girl for whom she'd once made a New Year's gift—Anne Faurer. She would have turned ten in September. Had Madeleine told her the truth about her brother yet? Cat hoped not. It would have broken Anne's stout heart.

And Madeleine—how was she faring? It had been good of her to come to Edinburgh at Jessie's bidding. Cat never had apologized for disappearing on her the way she had, nor answered the letter with the news of Rene's marriage. *I ought to write,* she thought now, watching a few weighty flakes of snow drift from the dull gray sky outside her window, and even went so far as to try to remember where her quill was laid. But the snow made

her think of the storm she'd ridden through with Geordie onc
upon a time, and the sound of bells through that great rush o
whiteness signaling that Rene had come for them, that she wa
saved.

Saved? *Saved?* Ruined, rather. But even as her mind forme
that thought, her heart was far away, beating wild and fast again:
Rene's chest as he bared her breasts to the moonlight, lying o
the hard crust of snow by the seawall at Langlannoch.

Two years past on the morrow, she'd begun the long down
ward slide toward the loss of her innocence, traded for a sprin
kling of sugared words and that wretched, traitorous fire h
raised in her loins. Christ! Even now, after all that had passe
to remember him striding her, riding her headlong toward pas
sion, raised a want in her that brought a hot flush to her cheek
Mandrake could do that to a man, Madeleine had once tol
her, or henbane, with the seeds of red poppy—put a cravin
for more in the soul that, once tasted, could not be stayed
Appalled, she cranked open the window and let the frigid win
sweep through her chamber, while she just as coldly tried t
calculate whether Eleanor de Baliol—Eleanor Faurer—migh
be brought to childbed as yet.

The New Year's Eve feast Archibald had planned was gran
by the proportions of wartime. There were three deer to b
roasted—small ones, granted, that in happier days would hav
been beneath the bowmen's notice, but the smell of the meat a
it turned on the spits was the same. There were casks of fisl
brought from Kirkcudbright, for the bounty of the sea wasn'
stayed by fighting; Cook stirred them up with wild onions an
her last precious threads of saffron into a *soupe de poisson* tha
would have been fit for the Bruce himself. Rabbits went int
pies, thin-crusted for the lack of flour but nonetheless tasty, an
Diarmot's father the chieftain, God bless him, had sent as a gif
a treasure beyond words—an entire cask of dark, peaty *uisque-
bauqh*. Cat had had wine hidden in her room ever since the exchange of prisoners; now she siphoned off a beaker of the spirit:
in secret, nervously listening for Cook's footsteps, transferred i
to a leathern flask, and tucked it in her bed.

The company was gay that night; the toasts were clever and

lengthy. Cat felt uncomfortably conspicuous at the long table, each of her sisters having a man at her side. When her father, well-meaning, laughing, raised his cup to her as the last of the Douglas girls—" 'N' th' sole one loyal enough, it seems, to stay hame with her father!"—she knew her face went crimson even as she tried to smile at the jest.

Tess, four months along with child, was radiant. Janet had a new coif for her blond hair, braids drawn back into lustrous loops, to show Rawley's New Year's gift to advantage: eardrops of red gold and Scots pearls. Jessie was leaning into Diarmot's wide shoulder, her gaze on him always, utterly adoring. Cat drank more wine than was her wont, though she was wise enough to shun the whiskey's fire.

After the feasting she helped Cook to clean up, retrieving beakers clenched in the fists of drunken soldiers, tossing the scraps to the dogs, stirring the rushes to cover the worst of the litter. *Like some old spinster,* she thought, *content not to rush to my empty bed . . .* Her sisters had long since disappeared with their men. Jessie, of course, had told Cat she and Diarmot were saving themselves for marriage, but Cat doubted more and more that they would. Who could blame them, with the turmoil of war all around them, for seeking a bit of solace in each other's arms? Perhaps tonight would be the night for Jessie to discover what she had been missing. What sort of lover might Diarmot be? Cat wondered as she threw a coverlet over Angus MacPherson, who was snoring madly on a bench a long way from the hearth. Shy as Jessie's intended was, most likely hesitant, very gentle. Different from Rene—she threw that thought from her like a bone to the mastiffs. You can't be sure for Diarmot, she decided judiciously. They did say still waters ran deep.

Her head felt thick; her feet were aching. She took a final glance round the hall, snuffed all the candles but her own, and trudged up the stairs.

She'd left the window open; the clean smell of snow singed the air. But no, she saw, crossing the room; she hadn't. The latch was pulled tight. Then how—hands suddenly trembling, she turned to the curtained bed, knowing her prayers had been answered. "You came," she said.

"How could I not, to such a pretty summons?" He was grinning, leaning against her father's feather mattress, still in his wet cloak and boots. His beauty struck her as it had that first time, in the hall she'd only just left below—black hair curled with the cold, eyes like the midnight sky beyond the window, his mouth—God, his mouth! *The most handsome man,* she thought, with a spark of pride, *that I ever have seen . . .*

"I wasn't sure it would reach you."

"It reached me. I came as quickly as I could." He held out his arms. "Aren't you going to kiss me? Or perhaps—are you angry about Edinburgh, Cat? As I love God, I meant to meet you there. But I took an arrow in the fighting, and they hauled me back to Bamburgh to have it out of me. It gangrened, and by the time I got to the castle, you were long since gone."

"An arrow! Christ, where?"

"In my—" Still grinning, he twisted and pointed. "Right here. It only hurts when I sit. But I figured I'd not do much sitting on a visit to you."

"You took an arrow in your . . ."

He nodded. "The very definition of a flesh wound."

Cat began to laugh. "You told me you were a good soldier!"

"And so I am. A bad one would have let the thing find his heart. How about that kiss?"

She went to him. Along with snow, he smelled of sweat and leather. When his mouth closed on hers, she began to cry. "Cat, Cat," he murmured, stroking her hair, holding her tight to him. "Don't cry, my fierce little Cat. I'm here now. I love you. Everything will be all right."

"It happened just as you said at Dupplin," she said brokenly. "How did you know? How did you know who would win?"

"A lucky hunch."

She stiffened in his grasp. " 'Tis nothing to jest at! Good men died—"

"Good men died on both sides. Christ, Cat, I didn't ride half-way across Scotland in a snowstorm to quarrel with you!"

There was an unaccustomed edge to his voice. She raised her gaze, looked at him more closely in the candlelight, and saw that the handsome face was haggard, taut with lines of care. He was thin, too; she felt it in his arms. No brawn left, only muscle and bone. "Forgive me," she whispered. "Has it been . . . hard?"

"It has been bloody hell," he told her evenly.

"I'm sorry. What—how can I help you?"

His grin returned, though she saw now how it stretched his skin. "I know I should say all I need is to make love to you. The truth, though—" He coughed a little, without noticing, as if it had become habit. "Have you any food?"

"Of course. Wait here." She drew a key from her girdle. "Lock the door after me. I'll knock once, then twice, when I return. There is wine on the sideboard there. Oh, and—" She drew the leather flask from beneath her pillow. "Whiskey."

"God be praised."

"Go soft, though, if you haven't eaten," she said, chewing her lip.

His kiss cut off her fretful gesture. "Then hurry with the food."

Down to the kitchens she flitted, blessing Diarmot's father for the whiskey, that kept the soldiers in the hall hard asleep. Without light she found what she was searching for: one of the pies, two or three thick slices of venison. In the pantry, she hesitated over the meager choices. Cook's sharp eye would notice anything missing. But by then it would not matter. She took a crock of cherries potted in brandy, grabbed a heavy loaf of bread, and bundled the lot in her skirts to carry it upstairs.

He took the venison first, devouring it. Cat picked up the whiskey flask on the excuse of moving it out of his way. It felt considerably lighter. She sat on her haunches at his feet, anticipating his needs, keeping his wine cup filled. He ate the entire pie, polished off the bread, asked for another draught of whiskey. By then he was slowing, breathing between bites. "Where have you been, then, that they feed you so ill?" she wondered aloud.

He shook his head at her, mouth filled with cherries, then swallowed. "You know I cannot say."

"Have you seen your mother and Anne?"

"Nay."

"Oh, Rene. Written to them, even?"

"There is nothing to say." Sensing her disapproval, he scowled. "Did you summon me here to chide me for that?"

She looked at him, her green gaze steady. "I summoned you because I love you. Because I could not live any longer without seeing you." She was handing him the wine cup; his fingers closed over hers.

"Forgive me," he said softly. "Forgive my vile temper. I have missed you . . . more than I can say."

Cat leaned against his knee. The cloth of his breeches was threadbare; his left boot had a hole in the shaft big enough to fit her fist into. "You need clothes. I could find you some in the armory."

"Nay, thanks. I'll have the devil's time as it is explaining where I've been."

"Had you a long ride, then?"

"Long enough."

His answers were so wary. Was it just the natural caution of a soldier, or did he suspect her of something? "I'm sorry," Cat said, and surprised herself with how unhappy she sounded. "I don't mean to press. But I've worried so about you. I can hardly believe you are here." She nestled even closer to his boot; he set his wine cup down and drew her into his lap.

"Nor can I." He kissed her, tasting sweet, like the cherries. "You can talk, though, even if I can't. Tell me all that has happened since you left me in the woods at Inverkeithing. Oh, by the by!" He snapped his fingers. "An odd thing. Eleanor showed up at our camp that day. Eleanor de Baliol. Did you happen to see her, perchance?"

Supercilious smile above the smug curve of the blonde's belly . . . "Nay, I cannot say that I did." So Eleanor hadn't told him of their meeting at the docks. When she reflected on it, that made sense. Rene's wife wasn't completely certain Cat hadn't been with him, and evidently did not want to know.

She'd been quiet too long; he was watching her, his blue eyes veiled. She laughed. "I was just trying to think where to begin! There was a woman selling cakes in the town there who thought me a harlot; that was rather droll. Gill was taken prisoner—but

I suppose you knew that." He nodded. "It was hard on Tess. She is with child again. But so brave . . ."

"I tried to get him released sooner, but that damned Harry Percy was holding out for his big, stupid sons."

Cat's eyes widened a little. "Are you so tight to de Baliol, then, that you could ask a boon like that?"

"Well—" He shrugged. "Anyone can ask a boon, of course. You can see what asking that one got me."

She twined her fingers through his. "Still, it was good of you to try."

"It's as I've said all along, Cat—there's no reason not to be civilized on both sides. We are going to have to live together anyway once all this is done."

"Yes, that's true."

He was stroking her breast, tracing small, tightening circles around the bud of her nipple through her velvet gown. Cat had spent much of the weeks since she'd sent the hostage off with her letter wondering just what she would feel if he touched her that way. The answer was a familiar aching low in her belly; her heartbeat quickened; her breathing turned shallow and fast.

He set his wine cup on the floor beside his chair. "More?" she asked, starting to move from his knees to fetch the pitcher.

"Much more." He held her fast, unpinning her hair.

"I meant the wine."

"Ah. Nay, no more of that. I feel groggy as a green boy. Which did you drug, the victuals or the drink?" Drugs. Why the devil hadn't she thought of that? "Christ, Cat, 'twas but a jest!" He tweaked her nose, seeing her pensive face.

"If you're weary, you should sleep."

"Would that I could! But I cannot risk it, cannot stay. A wee brief visit . . ."

She laid her palm on his breeches. "How brief?"

His manhood throbbed against her hand. "Oh, Cat . . ."

"I forgot to lock the door." She got up to do so.

"Catriona," he said at her back.

He never called her that. She turned, the key still in her hand.

"I have something to tell you." His eyes were obsidian-dark, his voice low and distant. "But to do so I must break a vow—the gravest vow I ever made." Then he shrugged. "Well, what of it? I cannot go on this way. And you are worth having my body sliced in twain for, my bowels burnt and scattered to the winds."

Cat shivered, staring at him. She'd thought he meant to confess his marriage to her. But what sort of heathen oath was this he had taken? It had the scent of sorcery. . . .

"You know my father was a Templar." She nodded slowly. "The world thinks the Order of the Knights Templar no longer exists. But it does, under a different name, a secret name. More than exists—it flourishes. It is dedicated to the cause of freedom—to Scottish freedom."

"Under de Baliol?" she asked, astonished.

"Nay. Under the son of the Bruce."

"And you have made a vow . . . to exterminate this order?"

He laughed. "Nay. I joined it, Cat."

She felt a sudden need to sit, groped her way to a stool. "I don't understand," she whispered.

"I'll explain. When I was a boy, I was . . . aware that my father and his friends kept a secret. How could I not be? They met at Langlannoch often enough. Not just the old Templars, but Scotsmen, too—the Bruce, the earls of Mar and Moray . . ."

"Uncle James?" she broke in. "My father?"

"Oddly, nay. The order demands that you swear allegiance to it above all else but God. And for the Douglases, the clan comes next God—perhaps, even, above God. They did not join. I'm not even sure your father knows of the order's existence."

"He is regent of Scotland!"

"Aye. But the members of the order are not bound by oath to the king. Only to one another, and to their leader, their Grand Master."

"Who is the Grand Master?"

He shook his head at her. "Don't ask me questions like that, Cat. I've said more than I should have as is."

All the wine she'd had to drink at supper seemed to have swum to the center front of Cat's brow. "You say you belong to this secret society that supports King David, yet you fight for de Baliol?"

"Don't you see? I'm a spy." He nodded at her incredulous

expression. "That's right. My assignment has been to insinuate myself into the de Baliol camp and learn all I can of its plans."

Cat passed a hand over her forehead. "When did all this begin?"

"On the night I knew I was in love with you. Two years past, at Langlannoch, there by the seawall. I knew that night I had to have you. But I would have to prove myself worthy." His blue eyes were blazing. "I swore to myself I would."

"But it was the next morning you declared yourself betrothed to Eleanor!" she cried.

"Aye. After you went to your bed, I went to Tomas and told him—'Whatever it is that you and my father and the others have, I want in.' I swore my oaths that night. I promised utter obedience to the Grand Master. Then I asked what I might do to serve the cause. And Tomas told me—I should betroth myself to Eleanor as soon as I could, then go to France and openly cast my lot with her uncle Edward."

"And you were willing to do so?" she demanded. "Despite what we had shared that night?"

He rubbed his forehead with both hands, as though to ease the lines of care there. "What else could I do, Cat? I had just vowed on my life to do whatever the order might require of me. Could I then say—'Oh, no. Please. I beg you. I will do anything but that.' "

"You might have explained you were in love with me!"

"It would have made no difference to the order. These men—they are made of steel, single-minded in their aims. They are all—like my father. Cold as ice. Immutable as stone."

From across the room she stared at him. "The odds were I would never speak to you again."

"A risk I willingly bore. I was in love with you. If I succeeded, I knew someday we would sit together this way while I explained what had happened. If I failed, if I was found out by de Baliol—well, it would not hurt you, I thought, to have someone you hated die." He smiled a little. "It was meant to be a sort of holy crusade, my redemption. Pure and untainted. I did not reckon on the craving my flesh would come to have for your flesh."

"The duel at Stirling," she whispered.

"Staged with Robbie Stewart. He is one of the brothers. Though that bloody fool Malcolm Ross damned near ruined everything by poking his head in. *He* would have killed me; he's the best bloody swordsman in Scotland."

"But why go to such lengths?"

"Eleanor was being . . . difficult. I wanted out of the betrothal. So the Grand Master came up with another way of assuring the world I'd be Moray's enemy forever—my banishment."

"Who is—" she started to ask again, but stopped, knowing he would not say. Everything he'd told her dovetailed so neatly, so perfectly. Too perfectly. "Are you and Eleanor married?"

"Christ, no!" he said explosively. "Where did you get that notion?"

"There have been rumors," Cat said slowly. She had already denied seeing the woman at Inverkeithing; it would have been hard now to explain why she'd lied. Besides, there were other parts to his story that she did not comprehend. "But . . . if what you say is true—"

"If?" Beneath his weariness she sensed mounting outrage. "I risk my life to reveal this secret to you, and you don't believe me?"

"Sooth, Rene, sooth! What am I to think?" she demanded, with a touch of temper of her own. "You shally in here with a tale that turns topsy-turvy every word you've ever said to me in our lives, and I'm to swallow it whole just because of your say-so?"

"That was enough for you once." His jaw was tight.

"Aye, so it was—and now you tell me all that was lies!"

"Ach." He grinned a little; it eased the lines that soldiering had made 'round his eyes, made him look less forbidding. "You have me there, Cat. Ask what you will."

"Well, then. If you are for King David, why don't you just murder de Baliol some night while he sleeps?"

"The man has two sons here and one still safe in France. Killing him would not end this."

"Papa says it would."

"I am sorry to be the one to bring you this news, love, but your father does not know everything in this world."

She was angry again. "All right, then tell Papa where he is. March on into his rooms and say where that bastard is hiding."

Rene shook his head. "If Archibald didn't kill him, he'd surely chase him back over the border to England. And that's to be avoided at all costs."

"Why?"

"Because if he goes back to England, then Edward the Third will surely come out for him; he'll not see his puppet-king so shamed. He'll raise up a force, a mighty one, to back de Baliol. We are not ready yet to risk that sort of battle. And if Edward captures David, he will not let him live."

"David is married to Edward's sister," Cat pointed out, shocked.

"Edward's mother had his father murdered. Honestly, do you think a Plantagenet will scruple at killing a rival king? So long as David Bruce lives, he is a threat to England. His life must be preserved at all costs."

That was what Angus had told her, too, Cat remembered. But if Rene was arguing it . . . "Papa's not afraid of King Edward," she told him defiantly.

"He bloody well should be."

She looked at him with suspicion. "If you were spying for King David, what went wrong at Dupplin? Why was our side defeated?"

"God only knows. I did my part. Mar knew when de Baliol was marching, knew with how many men, knew everything but the color of his bloody damned underbreeches. We ought to have won. But the men were fighting all unsteady, out of kilter. Perhaps 'twas the lack of your uncle James."

Gill had said the same thing, Cat remembered. "Well—whom did you fight for?"

"I did my best to aid the Scots," he said carefully.

"What the devil does that mean? Who did you aim your ax at?"

"At de Baliol's men." He saw her disbelief. "In the mishmash of battle, it is not so hard a thing to manage as you might imagine. Though I would not relish living through it again. It was an arrow from de Baliol's archers, by the by, that nicked me."

"Good God, Rene." He helped himself to more whiskey. Cat nibbled on a fingernail, weighing what he'd told her, trying to decide . . . "Are there members of this—this whatever it is you belong to among Papa's advisers?" she asked finally. He nodded over the rim of his cup. "And they have told him what you have told me?"

"Aye, time and again. But he will not take it into that great, swollen Douglas head of his. He says England's Edward is too busy with his squabbling nobles to pay heed to Scotland."

"And isn't he?"

"Think, Catriona! What better way to silence such squabbling than to get all the quarrelers united in a war, fighting for one cause?"

"You need not speak to me as though I am some sort of stupid child!" Stung by his impatient tone, she swallowed hot tears.

"I am sorry." He sighed; it turned into a yawn that he covered with his hand. "I have been living in the midst of all this deception for too long. It takes a toll on me." His blue eyes met her gaze. "Why do you sit so far off? It makes me think you don't still love me." He patted his knee. "Come here."

Cat rose from her stool, but slowly. "Tell me this last thing. If I went to one of the others—to Tomas, or to Robbie, and asked him to confirm what you've said—"

"They'd deny every word," he interrupted her. "And I would be dead for having broken my oaths. These are not men to be toyed with." Nor was he any longer, she sensed; there was a hardness to him now like the edge of a blade. "You have to trust me, Cat."

That much he said easily, as though, with his having bared his soul, there was no question she would.

She crossed to his chair, took the whiskey cup from his hand, and set it on the sideboard. Then, standing before him with her fiery hair unbound and hanging nearly to her knees, she unlaced the bodice of her velvet gown, slipped out of the surcoat, pulled down the sleeves—

"Oh, God," he whispered, his voice unsteady. "If I live to be a thousand, Cat, I'll never see any woman so beautiful as you. Your hair, your skin, your mouth—I never see your mouth that

I do not ache to kiss it." He traced its fullness with a fingertip. "The most beautiful mouth in the world." *My father's mouth,* Cat thought, and pushed the thought away. "And your breasts . . ." He sighed against her pale, blue-traced flesh as she bared them, thumbs brushing against the rosy buds that crowned them so that they grew tight and round.

"My sisters say I am too skinny."

"What do sisters know?" He put his arms around her narrow waist, drawing her toward him, and put his mouth to hers. Tucked between his spread knees, she felt the bulge of his manhood hard at her thighs. "You are the only woman I have ever wanted with such a fire, a burning. I have longed for you, love, as the black stag longs for the hills." Desire was gleaming in his eyes, tensing his muscles, rippling sinew and vein. "And you—did you miss me?"

She nodded, not trusting herself to speak. He kissed the side of her face, then her throat, then each white breast in turn. His hands slid over her shift to her buttocks, raising her up, pressing her to his loins. Cat circled his neck with her arms; against his strength, the passion coursing through him, she felt very small. Hesitantly she kissed his forehead as his tongue teased the bud of her nipple; instantly he tilted his head up and claimed her mouth with his own. "So shy, my little one," he whispered, holding her close, hands running over her hips. "Have we been so long apart that you've grown strange with me?"

"It is just that . . . here, in my father's house . . . this room, these walls . . . it seems so odd," she told him softly "As though you've come into a part of my life where you never were."

"And so I have. But if the newness distracts you—" He caught her up in his arms, rising from his seat. "That feather bed, at least, I know I've seen before." He carried her there, lifting her easily, like gossamer, like down. "We'll shut the curtains, Cat, and shut out the world . . . for a little while. They can't take that from us." He kissed her fiercely, sinking atop her onto the soft bed.

"You smell of forests," she whispered, catching the scent on him of leaf mold, moss, lichen. Was that where de Baliol was hidden—in one of the great woods, in Galloway or Annandale?

He laughed, sitting up, pulling off his road-worn boots. "I had no leisure to bathe before I came."

"I was not complaining. I like the smell." Mushrooms, acorns—that was an oak leaf, brown and sere as bone, tangled in the back of his hair. There were no oak trees on the moors. It had to be a forest. Unless—perhaps he'd only ridden through one, then, on his way to her. "But I am used to having you smell of the sea, and I miss that." He was pulling off his shirt, unbuttoning his breeches; she put out her hands to help. "Two years past, on this night—do you remember the sea, Rene, down below in the moonlight, and the way the snow was crusty beneath us?"

"I remember it all—every jot of it. It is burned on my memory by the fire you raised in me." He was naked now, brown and honed hard, no trace of boy's softness to him. He looked like his father, Cat realized, a vision of the dead warrior rising suddenly in her mind. He looked lethal, and frightening.

"I would like to see the sea again; I am weary to death of these walls." She untied her shift at the waist and let it fall to the floor, so she was naked, too. "Has it been long since you have seen the sea, Rene?" *God, let it rest, Cat,* she thought; *stop wondering, stop probing.* Shut out the world; wasn't that what he'd said?

He didn't seem to have heard her; he was running his fingers lightly over her shoulders, down her throat, over her breasts and belly. His touch made her skin tingle; she caught her breath in a little gasp as he riffled the red-gold thatch of curls between her legs. His manhood was stark at attention, swollen with his life's blood, his seed. "I love you, Cat," he told her, his eyes very dark, very grave.

"I—I love you, too."

Those restless fingers hovered at her waist, smoothed back her hair, traced circles on her thighs. "I wonder will we ever lie together for days on end, Cat, only getting up to fetch something to eat, a sweetmeat, or refill a wine cup. . . . Why must there always be so little time?"

"You will stay till dawn, surely."

"I cannot. I should not have come at all."

She put her palm to that thick, pulsing shaft, closed her hand on it, felt the pump of his blood, heard his indrawn breath. "Are you sorry you did?"

"Lord in heaven, how could I be?" He laughed behind clenched teeth, arching his back. She inched downward on the cold linen sheeting, kissing his shoulder, his sternum, following the vee of curling black hair leading to his waist and then lower . . . "Cat, what are you doing?"

"Sooth, sooth." She touched a kiss to his manhood, saw it spring in surprise. She let her tongue trail along the end—smooth, fleshy, tasting musty and oddly sweet. A bit of juice spurted from its tip. His seed. She licked it away. He groaned, put his hand to his mouth and bit down.

"I'll wake the house if you are not careful."

"I am being very careful, Rene." Around and around went her tongue, while her fingers gripped the shaft. Arousing him so, she found, was setting her afire. He had his leg thrown over her waist, and the feel of his weight atop her made her clench her thighs tight. His hand found her breast and kneaded it with mounting pressure, teasing her nipple between his thumb and forefinger. Tentatively Cat took his manhood into her mouth, just an inch at first, then a bit more as he grunted his astonished pleasure.

"Cat, you needn't—"

She raised her head. "I want to."

"I won't argue, then."

He lay back against the feathers, watching through narrowed eyes as she put her mouth to him once again, sliding up and down along the shaft, slowly first and then more quickly. The muscles in his belly were taut, pulled tight as bowstrings with his effort to hold back his release. When she looked up at him from beneath her lashes, she saw sweat beading on his brow.

"No more, Cat," he said hoarsely.

"A little more—"

"No." With a sudden movement he turned her over onto her back and knelt above her. For a moment he waited, to draw her red-gold curls from her eyes. Then he entered her with a sharp, quick stroke that took her breath away.

Heat spread from him as he thrust inside her, heat and light;

though she closed her eyes, she could see bright figures etched within her lids. He had his hands on her buttocks, pulling her up as though he meant to fuse her with him. Then he drew back, arching high above her, and she opened her eyes.

"Do you love me, Cat, for aye and for always?"

"You know that I do."

He smiled and drove deep inside her. Beneath the pounding rhythm of his loins, Cat could hear his heartbeat, ragged and wild. He jerked her upward, plunged into her. Cat saw a little flurry of feathers rise in the air; they'd made a hole in one of the pillows. The bits of down went swirling around them as he thrust into her again and again. . . .

He was grunting her name. A swell of that red-hot flame swept through her, engulfed her, made her cling to his shoulders and bury her face at his neck. "Rain, Rain, Rain . . ." Her nails were burrowed into his flesh. "Oh, God, Rain—"

Satisfied, he bent his head to her breast, kissed it, and then loosed his seed in a frenzied burst that burned her to her core. She was still shuddering with the long, slow waves of her ecstasy when he rolled over again, pulling her atop him, holding her tight to his heart. Feathers settled gently around them—a soft, warm snow.

"Christ," he murmured, his voice thick with whiskey and spent passion. "Christ, you make me want you out of all reason."

"And you I." That was heaven's own truth.

He was smiling, leaning back against his crooked elbow. "What do you think, then—will it be better when we can take our leisure at this, love, or will it want the edge of danger?"

She twined her fingers through the black curls on his chest. "I cannot imagine ever being free to love you openly."

"It will happen someday, Cat." He raised his head to look at her. "You do believe that." She nodded. Satisfied, he lay back before he could see her green eyes fill with tears. Another yawn escaped him. "God's blood, I could sleep for a week."

Cat stroked the tense, coiled muscles in his arm. "Rest, love. Just for a little while." He had coaxed her once to do the same, on the riverbank at Inverkeithing.

"I dare not. I must be gone."

"Surely an hour's sleep would do no harm. I'll wake you far before the dawning." She could feel his muscles slacken, just a bit, at her soft, even touch. "These winter nights are long."

"I would that I could. But I must away."

"To what? A cold saddle, and then a colder pallet?" Cat let petulance creep into her tone. "Why are you ever in a rush to leave me?"

He laughed groggily. "Christ, if you knew what I'd give to lie the night with you . . ."

"I'm not asking for the night, am I? Just for an hour or two." Her silken strokes were steady and even. She felt him drift away from her, then rouse himself with a start:

"Lord, have mercy, Cat! What's to keep you from falling asleep yourself?"

"The fact that I have got your life in my hands." She laid them on his heart, palms down, light as the feathers. "Trust me. Isn't that what you are always telling me?"

He laughed again, his voice grown distant: "Aye, so I do. . . . An hour, then? No more?"

"As God bears my pledge."

"Well, then . . ." He kissed the top of her head and was instantly asleep.

Cat lay very still and listened to his breathing, felt the warmth from his naked body steal throughout the cocoon they'd made from pillows and blankets. When he started to snore she pulled herself up sitting, and looked at him for as long as she dared. He really was beautiful, she thought, and remembered what she'd said to her father when she saw him on the night of Tess's wedding: "Papa, it is real this time. . . ."

She touched his cheek, very softly.

He never stirred.

Stealthy as a mouse, she climbed down from the bed.

As she padded through the silent castle, she found herself thinking of the story her father had told her, of the oath he and her uncle James had sworn, one to the other, and that Archibald had never broken despite his unhappiness. An oath sworn on their name of Douglas . . .

Sometimes to be a Douglas was a dreadful thing.

He wasn't in his bedchamber. Surprised—he'd not been sparing of the whiskey himself—she sought him out in his study. He was sprawled asleep atop a map of the Border Counties spread out on his desk.

"Papa," she whispered.

He was awake in an instant, though dazed. "Who—wha'? Wha' bae—Catriona?" He blinked at her in the light of her candle; his own had burned down.

She put a finger to her mouth—the Douglas mouth, so much like his. "Rene Faurer is here," she told him.

He came close to falling off his chair. "Here? Where?"

"Upstairs. In my bed." She held up a hand to forestall him. "I'm to wake him in an hour to send him on his way. If you follow him, he will lead you to de Baliol."

He was already reaching for his boots. "Who hae I got that bae nae blithered wi' whiskey? Diarmot; he ne'er drinks o' excess. Gill—though I bae loath to roust him out o' his bed. Angus—Angus drank eno' to keep a horse asleep for a week. But Paidy, sure, 'n' Colin—" He looked up from his lacings. "I'll nae ask ye how ye got him there, fer I dinna care to know." His eyes took in her loose, tangled hair, the rumpled robe she'd pulled on so hastily that she wore nothing beneath. "I would ask ye, though—why?"

"He . . . he just lied to me one too many times, Papa." Biting back tears, she raised her chin. "Besides, I'm a Douglas."

Boots on, he stood and kissed her pale forehead. "Aye, lass. Sae ye bae."

Part Four

Edinburgh
May, 1333

Twenty-two

"Treaty-breaker," Archibald Douglas growled, and glared at the parchment in his hand so balefully that the English messenger stepped back two paces. "Bludy double-dealin', lyin', thievin' son of a ditch-drinkin' scurfy bitch . . ." He ran on in that vein for some time, while the messenger stood with his hat in his hands and the nobles and clerics packing the receiving chamber of the castle shuffled in their places. But all the oaths in the world would not change what Edward the Third of England had set his seal to on the sheepskin page: In consideration of the persistence of certain Scots brigands in transversing the border between their two countries for the purpose of harrying and pillaging the peace-loving people of England, the terms of the Treaty of Northampton were as of this moment declared null and void.

It was a terrible blow. The Treaty of Northampton was the precious document, secured by the Bruce's great victory at Bannockburn, in which England had, after centuries of warfare, acknowledged Scotland's independence. The parchment Archibald now gripped in his white-knuckled fists served to wipe out all the brave sacrifices made in that hard fight for freedom—and set Archibald, as regent, at the head of the meager forces that must win it back again.

If they could. "I dinna think he would gae sae far," Archibald muttered, shaking his great leonine head. *Poor Papa,* thought Cat, watching, with Jessie beside her, from the far side of the room. He'd been riding such a crest of high opinion from the nobles and commons ever since his daring dawn raid four months ago had driven Edward de Baliol over the border to England, still in his nightshirt, that the fact of the most dire warnings of his more cautious councilors coming true was a grave shock to him.

"It bae war," the old earl of Ross said softly.

"I ken bludy well it bae war!" Archibald snarled at him.

"P'raps we went too far in raidin' Bamburgh," Angus MacPherson said worriedly.

"Ach, there bae little sense in harpin' on that song," the regent told his faithful captain. "Wha' bae done, bae done."

"Is there any response to His Most Glorious Majesty?" the English messenger asked, with a flitting smile.

"Ye can tell his right ruddy glorious majesty fer me," Archibald began, and then stopped, reluctantly, seeing the archbishops of St. Andrews and Glasgow shaking their heads at him in unison. "That I'll need time fer the digestin' o' his missive's contents," he finished, and glanced at the archbishops, who were now nodding. His big hand crumpled the parchment as he let out a sigh.

Cat knew why. This role of regent, that he'd been so anxious to take on, was proving naught but a headache. Archibald was not a man made for the slow, tangled wiles of diplomacy. Since his heady rout of de Baliol in January, matters of state had left him little time for the action he loved so well. Instead there were more of the deferential letters to the crowned heads of Europe— would they not support young King David in his fight against the English Goliath?—the thicket of taxation to plow through, and a dull but deadly siege laid against Bamburgh, meant to tempt the invaders away from their own siege at Berwick.

"He looks so old, Cat," whispered Jessie, and she nodded grimly; that he did. *Rene Faurer was right,* a small voice said from inside her head. *It was chasing de Baliol from Scotland that has brought the fist of Edward of England crashing down on us like the tide.* But Cat would not listen to that voice; betraying Rene had meant her redemption in her father's eyes, and she would have purchased the sweet taste of that forgiveness at any price.

The English messenger dipped a hand into his packet. "There is one message more, then."

Archibald slid his horny thumbnail under Edward's royal seal. "What is it now?" wondered Jessie. The peers were pressing forward, equally curious. Cat watched her father scan the letter, saw his white brows knit. "It bae a challenge," he said then. "Edward would set a date to end the siege he has laid at Berwick. If we hae not relieved the city by the feast o' St. Margaret, he proposes, then the garrison there must open the gates."

A flurry of comment went up from the crowd. Cat felt a prickle of foreboding, understanding the reason for the buzz. It was the same scenario that had led to the triumph of the Bruce at Bannockburn—only in reverse. There, nearly twenty years before, it had been the English who held Stirling Castle, and the Bruce's mad brother Ned who made the dare to the English commandant which Edward of England posed to her father now.

"Refuse it, Archibald," the earl of Ross urged quietly. "Ye hae naught to gain."

"Refuse it," the young earl of Moray, successor to his poisoned father, echoed.

"I wuld counsel th' same, Archibald," the long-bearded archbishop of St. Andrews said.

"Wuld ye, then? Why?" the regent demanded.

"The wee king 'n' his queen bae at Berwick."

"D'ye think I dinna ken that? Edward kens it, too." There was a dangerous edge to Archibald's tone.

"Why, where bae the sense in't, man?" That was a cousin of the earl of Mar, who'd been bested at Dupplin. "It bae but a veiled invitation to pitched battle. 'N' God love ye, Archibald, but ye bae nae the soldier yer brother war."

Cat caught her breath. Jessie gasped beside her. Their father's face had become very red. He surveyed the company surrounding him with glinting blue eyes. "Bae that wha' ye all say?" he barked, letting his angry gaze rest on one after another of the nobles. "That James war my better? That I cannae lead my countrymen?"

"Faith, Archibald," said the Mar cousin, highly embarrassed. "I misspake myself. Ye ken I dinna mean—"

"I ken bludy damned well wha' ye meant, John Mar!" Archibald rose from his chair and yanked the regent's sash over his head, holding it out in his hand. "Ye think ye can do better, d'ye? Here, then, take it!" He was shaking with his rage. "Gae on, take it!" Mar lowered his gaze. "Who amongst ye will hae it, then? Ye, Moray? Ross? How about ye, Atholl? Or ye, vaunty William Campbell? Where bae the man among ye who would hae my place?"

The nobles were silent, motionless in the shafts of spring sunlight that slanted through the chamber's high windows. Archibald muttered something to himself that Cat, straining, could not hear. She was frightened for her father; she had a growing sense that he was in this over his head. But if the realm's peers shared her intuition, they recognized that in his shoes they'd be in above their own heads, too. There was not a soul among them who'd not lost kin in this endless battle against England—sons, fathers, brothers, cousins. Edward's abrogation of the Treaty of Northampton, raising as it did the specter of a full-scale invasion, buckled all their stomachs.

Archibald gave his grand gesture a good long moment to sink in. Then he tugged the regent's sash back on, and took a step toward the English messenger, who'd been watching all the to-do while smiling his small, polite half smile.

Archibald's hand at his throat wiped the smile away. "Ye listen to me, ye pooty wee lapdog," he growled, hauling him up by his spotless lace collar. "Trot hame to yer master on yer skinty legs, 'n' tell him this fer me: I accept his bludy challenge on behalf o' King David o' Scotland. Berwick shall be relieved by St. Margaret's Day."

Cat felt a flush of pride in her father. What if the act was reckless? It was grand all the same. Jessie squeezed her hand, and she knew her sister shared her emotions. Then Archibald looked their way above the heads of the crowd. "Catriona," he called out. "Jessie." He beckoned them toward him. "Come here."

Perplexed, Cat nonetheless came forward. The nobles and churchmen made a path for her and Jessie, straight to the front where their father stood, still with his big hand grasping the messenger's collar. "My daughters," he grunted, close to the Englishman's face.

"Very—very honored to meet you, miladies." The messenger did his best to make a bow.

"Now, when ye see yer King Edward, laddie," Archibald went on, jerking the man's head toward him again, "d'ye tell him this, too. Wi' the grantin' o' permission from the siege commandant, I'll bae sendin' these twa daughters o' mine into Berwick till St. Margaret's Day, just to show how certain I bae that the Scots will prevail."

"Papa!" Jessie started to cry out, but Cat stopped her, digging her nails into her sister's wrist with all her might. Jessie whirled on her, eyes wide, aghast. "But what about Diarmot?" she hissed. "We are to be married!"

"Shut your mouth," Cat hissed back, "and hold your head up."

"But—"

"Not one word more, Jess! Do as Papa says!"

Archibald wasn't finished. " 'N' if I bae wrong—if yer king takes the city . . ." He paused, that grim fire still in his eye as he surveyed the company as though daring them to stop him, to interfere. Then his gaze came 'round to the messenger again. "Ye tell him he bae welcome to do wi' my girls wha' he will."

A gasp went up from the assembly. Jessie, openmouthed, swayed on her feet. "Papa, for the love of Christ! 'Tis an invitation to—to ravishment!"

At the least, thought Cat. But she made certain Jessie was leaning on the archibishop of St. Andrews' arm, took a step toward her father, put her hand in his, and stood on tiptoe to kiss him. "We'll be waiting for you, then, Papa," she said in a voice loud and clear enough to be heard throughout the room, "there in Berwick." And she smiled defiantly at the Scots lairds—the Douglas smile.

Twenty-three

"Senility," pronounced Janet, as Cat calmly carried a stack of neatly folded underdrawers to the trunk she was packing. "That's the only explanation. The old man has gone soft in the head."

"Well, you are the authority on old men, Jan."

"Honestly, Cat," Jessie cried, "how can you jest about a thing like this? He has thrown us to the English like—like Daniel thrown to the lions!"

"Daniel came out of that unscathed, if I remember aright."

"Still." Janet frowned, picking a bit of thread off Cat's best surcoat as it lay in the trunk. "It really isn't like Papa at all, to risk putting any of us in danger."

"You weren't there, Jan," Cat told her. "You didn't see him, didn't see his face. They'd boxed him into a corner, all of them, Scots and English alike. That bloody stupid John Mar . . . you know Papa can't stand that anyone should think him less of a man than Uncle James was. He had to do something to save his pride."

"What about my pride?" Jessie asked tearfully. She hadn't stopped crying, not altogether, since Archibald had made his infamous response to Edward of England a fortnight past. "I was supposed to be married, and instead now I'll be handed over to a passel of savage English soldiers, to be raped and tortured and God only knows what else—"

"You forget," Cat interrupted her tirade. "That will only happen if Papa can't relieve the siege in time."

"Well, scant comfort that is!" Jessie said.

Janet's blue eyes were thoughtful. "Rawley says the English muster is fearful strong."

"So? It was fearful at Bannockburn, too," countered Cat.

"Aye, and the Bruce had a deal more experience commanding armies than does Papa."

Cat's chin came up. "Are you doubting Papa?"

"I am just trying to understand what possessed him to take such a chance with your safety."

That was no mystery to Cat; she understood how desperation could make a soul do wild, reckless things. She thought of what Rene had said to her on the night he'd come to Douglasdale: *I am sorry to be the one to bring you this news, love, but your father does not know everything in th' world.* Well, Cat knew a secret now: Archibald, for the first time in his life, perhaps, was aware of that, too. And he was running scared. He could not resign the regency; his Douglas pride never would let him. All he could do was make crazed stabs back at high-handed Fate, like this flamboyant gesture of sending her and Jessie to Berwick. They were to leave on the morrow; by the night after next, they'd be barricaded within the besieged city's walls.

"And to think I saved myself for after I was married to Diarmot," Jessie sobbed brokenly, her eyes puffy and red-rimmed. "All for what? For nothing! So some bastard English soldier could take my maidenhead!"

"Oh, Jess." Janet looked at her pityingly. "Did you really? You bloody little fool."

"Well, it's easy for you to say, isn't it? When the English march into Berwick—"

"*If* the English march into Berwick," Cat murmured reprovingly.

"You'll be safe and sound at home, won't you, Janet?"

"She'll be worried sick about Rawley and Papa, and you and me, too, Jess."

"You!" Jessie whirled on Cat, furious. "What have you to fret about? Your Rene Faurer will come marching in with them, won't he, with his arms open for you? You'll have everything you ever wanted at last!"

Cat laughed. "Not bloody likely."

Something in her harsh voice made Janet raise her head. "Why do you say that?"

Cat hesitated. There was no sense anymore, was there, in keeping secret what she'd done? And perhaps it would give Jessie courage for what was to come. "You recall when Papa chased de Baliol back over the border to England last winter?"

"Of course I do."

"Well, how do you think Papa learned where he was?"

"A lucky guess, he said."

"It was a bit more than that. I had written Rene a letter asking him to come to me at Douglasdale. I sent it off with an English hostage. When he came, I got him drunk and made love to him. Then, when he fell asleep, I went and told Papa to be ready to follow him back to de Baliol."

Her sisters stared at her in disbelief. "Sweet holy Jesu," Janet said, with a little whistle. "You've bloody well burned your bridges there, I guess."

Jessie found her tongue at last, so shocked she'd finally stopped crying. "How in God's name *could* you, Cat?"

"Which part of it offends you most? Getting him drunk?" Janet asked, bemused even in her surprise.

"You know. M-making love to him and then . . ."

Janet and Cat exchanged glances. "I'll wager making love was the easy part," Janet said.

Jessie was shaking her head back and forth. "I really cannot fathom you, Cat."

"What did Papa say when you went to tell him?" Janet wanted to know.

"He—he asked why I'd done it."

"And why did you?"

Cat took a breath. "Because he'd gone and married Eleanor de Baliol, and got her with child, and he never even told me."

Jessie's blue eyes had gone even wider. "The bastard!" she said.

Just then, the door to their antechamber opened wide. Tess strode in, with Jane hanging tight to her skirts and the new baby, a boy, Robert Archibald, screaming, slung on her hip. "What are *you* doing here?" Jessie cried in astonishment. "You're supposed to be in Tullibardine; your forty days aren't up!"

"Did you think I would sit there in my home while my sisters were made into sacrificial lambs? Not likely. Take Jane, will you, Janet?" Janet scooped up the toddling girl while Tess sank into a chair and opened her bodice to nurse. Robert Archibald fumbled for the nipple for a moment, then latched on. "Blessed peace at last," Tess said gratefully.

"Why in the world are you doing that?" Janet asked, nodding at the suckling baby. "Couldn't you find a wet nurse?"

"Aye, I could have. But with all this coming and going, I just thought it would prove easier." She shrugged. "Besides, with the way this country is going, he may prove to be the last child I ever have. If Gill should . . ." She paused, his minute fist wrapped close 'round her finger. "I just wanted to, that's all."

"Oh, Tess." Jessie looked at her, swallowed. "Does Papa know you're here?"

"Of course he does; I've just come from talking to him. And try as I might, I could not get him to listen to reason. I had everything all arranged. I'd even found the girls for him, one red-haired and one brown."

"Found what girls?" Cat asked her.

"To take your and Jessie's places, naturally. Just local girls from Gill's estates—you know, peasants. They wouldn't fool a Scotsman for a moment into thinking they were Douglases, but since the English believe we are all uncouth savages anyway, they would have passed. I know that they would. But Papa wouldn't even—"

"Just a moment," Cat broke in. "Let me get this straight. You were going to send two peasant girls into Berwick pretending to be us, just in case Papa can't relieve the castle?"

Tess glanced up from her contented baby. "That's right."

"Oh, Tess. How awful!" Janet made a face that made little Jane laugh.

"I don't see why. I was going to pay them quite handsomely."

"Money can't buy everything, Tess Douglas." Even Jessie was offended by her sister's proposal.

"Very well, then, you and Cat go ahead, and see how you like

being an evening's diversion for an entire English battalion."
That launched Jessie into tears again.

"Damn you, Tess," Cat shot at her, going to hug Jessie's quaking shoulders.

"Why Aunt Jess cry?" Jane demanded to know.

"Because she hasn't got the sense she was born with, and neither has your grandpapa," her mother told her, and appealed to her sisters: "What exactly is wrong with my idea?"

"It is utterly disgraceful, that's what!" Jessie said through her tears.

"Good for you, Jess!" Cat cheered.

"So Papa said, too, though I honestly don't see why. Noblemen pay all the time to have someone else go into battle for them. It's called scutage. Why shouldn't women?"

"No Douglas," Cat said darkly, "ever did such a thing."

"Oh, Douglas, Pouglas. It is being Douglases has got you into this mess. You can't tell me that at this moment you wouldn't rather be any MacSomething lass from Aberdeen."

Cat searched her heart. "No, Tess. Not I. Anyway, we cannot help our birth." Someone had said that to her once, a long time ago. Rene . . .

"Now tell Jessie you were only jesting about the battalion," Janet chastised their sister.

"Oh, I was. The English care to think themselves so bloody civilized, they'll likely just pat you on the bottom and send you on your way."

"You don't believe that," said Jessie.

"No, I don't, as it happens. But no one seems to want to heed my advice." And she burped Robert Archibald emphatically.

Cat laid a nightdress atop the growing pile in the trunk. "There's all I'm taking, Jessie. You had better get started." As Jessie, sniffing, moved toward her wardrobe, Janet caught her sleeve.

"If you want, Jess, I'll go in your place. I am not afraid."

"Hmph. You only want to go so you can find out what it is like to have a young man take you—or ten or a dozen," Jessie said.

"Who's to say I didn't try old and young before picking Rawley?" her sister retorted.

Cat was so glad to see a smile on Jessie's wan face that she wanted to dance. "The English only ravish virgins, anyway, Janet," she put in.

"Really? Then why are *you* going?"

Tess had been sniffing the baby's tight-swathed behind suspiciously. "Say, here's an idea, Jess. Why don't you spend tonight with Diarmot, just to sort of even things up? It would serve the bloody English right to get nothing but tainted goods."

"What a perfectly execrable thought," Janet told her. "You *are* your mother's daughter, aren't you?"

"Takes one to know one," Jessie murmured.

Cat had her hands on her hips. "Who are you calling 'tainted,' Tess?"

"If the shoe fits, put it on."

Cat reached into the trunk and hurled one at her instead.

"You haven't even heard about how she seduced Rene Faurer right in Castle Douglas last winter," Janet told Tess.

"How she *what?*"

"Little pitchers have big ears," Cat said meaningfully, looking toward Jane.

"We all ought to go." Jessie started to giggle. "We ought to stand on the battlements at Berwick in the altogether and shout at them: 'Come and get us, you ninnies! Last one up the tower stairs gets the clap!' "

"What do you know about the clap?" Tess demanded.

"What do *you?*"

"I clap," declared little Jane, and did so, with gusto. Robert Archibald let out a hiccup.

"It will be an adventure," said Janet.

Jane looked from one sister to another. "Why aunties laugh?" she said.

Twenty-four

The castle at Berwick was perched atop an abrupt slope rising from the flat, wet ground at the mouth of the River Tweed, commanding a view of the surrounding countryside for miles on end. This vista had been the cause of constant battles between Scots and English for the keep and the town; from Berwick's towers, one could see border raiders coming—in either direction—a long way off. Its vantage also meant Cat and Jessie glimpsed the bleak walls that were to enclose them hours before they arrived.

"We shall have a nice view of the sea in the other direction," Cat ventured to her sister. They were riding side by side, accompanied by a handful of Scottish soldiers led by Angus MacPherson; they'd made their farewells to Archibald and the rest back at Edinburgh.

"Pity we'll only have until St. Margaret's Day to admire it," Jessie replied. Cat was proud of her sister; now that push had come to shove, she was proving quite brave.

"You cannot tell. Papa may come to rescue us before the deadline."

"Papa will need every second of time until then to prepare for the battle, and you know it, Cat."

Brave, but not optimistic. Cat looked again at those dark, distant walls, still two hours away.

Angus glanced down at them from atop his tall war-horse. "Time ye war stoppin' to eat somethin', lassies. There bae a siege where ye bae goin'; victuals'll bae few 'n' far between.

"I couldn't, Angus," Jessie told him. "I'm too afraid I'll be sick when you hand me over to the English commander."

"I'm not hungry either," said Cat. "But if you and your men want to stop . . ."

"Hell, we bain't stayin' in Berwick. If ye dinna want to rest, we'll ride on." The big red-haired man looked at Cat. "Hae ye somewha' to defend yerself wi', then, if it comes to that?"

"I've a dagger in my boot, and one tied in my cloak." She opened it to show him. "Jess wouldn't take anything, though."

"I'm not accustomed to weapons," her sister explained. "I would only poke a hole in myself, I fear."

"Ye should hae somewha', lass."

"I'll stick close to Cat."

He cleared his throat. "It bae a bold thing ye do, the twa o' ye, fer yer father. I hope my own girls, when they bae grown, will bae sae strong in their love o' me."

"I hope you'll never give them cause to need be, Angus," Jessie said wryly.

Cat glanced at him as he rode a little behind them, ramrod-straight in his saddle. They'd known Angus all their lives, seen him come and go in Douglasdale on the Bruce family's business for as long as she could remember. She let Jessie canter ahead and then turned to him. "Angus," she said very softly, "have we got a chance?"

"I'll get ye safe to Berwick, ne'er fear." He seemed surprised.

"I don't mean Jessie and me. I mean Papa. Scotland. Can we beat Edward this time?"

"Ach, lass. That I cannae say."

His guarded answer—no vaunty boasting there—brought home to Cat just how desperate her country's plight was. "Is it—because of Papa?" she asked, knowing Angus wouldn't lie.

"Nae, nae, pet. There bae nae man in Scotland I'd sooner follow int' battle than Archibald."

Cat swallowed, thinking of the warning he'd given her in the yards at Douglasdale—*Leave war to the men, lass*, he'd told her. But she hadn't listened, had sent her letter to Rene and then sent her father after him, when she knew Angus was sleeping, too drunk to waken, in the castle keep. She'd felt guilty every time she'd seen the redheaded giant since then. "Angus," she said, and he smiled at her.

"Aye?

"There's something I should tell you."

"About yer visitor New Year's Eve last?"

Cat felt her mouth drop open in surprise. Papa hadn't told anyone who had brought Rene Faurer to Douglasdale, and never would, she was sure, to shield her from disgrace. "How did you know?"

"I hae my ways."

She looked at him more closely. She'd always thought of Angus as a faithful soldier, a follower, stolid, simple, whose role in life was to take orders and see them through. Now, for the first time, she saw a glimmer of something more in him, something steely and hard as obsidian. Into her mind there came a snatch of Rene's conversation to her on the night she'd betrayed him: *These are not men to be toyed with,* he'd told her of that supposed band of Templars to which he belonged. But all of that had been lies. . . .

"If ye bae thinkin'," Angus interrupted her thoughts, with a grin so breezy that she blinked away the dangerous image she'd had of him a moment before, "that all o' this bae yer fault, pet, one might as well say it bae mine, fer drinkin' too much o' Diarmot's daddy's bludy whiskey that night. But I doubt my voice could hae dissuaded yer papa fro' followin' Faurer. He war dead set, Archibald war, on doin' it his way."

"Well, someone must be to blame—God, I suppose, if no one else."

"Nae, nae, lass. Life bae nae sae neatly sorted as that." He glanced her way, his gaze curious, appraising. "If ye care to hear, I'll tell ye wha' I think."

"Go ahead, then."

"Well, I think that nations hae their moments, some gloomy, some grand. Ye take England. The first Edward, that war this one's grandfather—la, he war a fearful fighter. 'N' wha' came after him? That poofter son we beat at Bannockburn. Now comes the third Edward, 'n' I fear the tide bae turnin'. We had our glory wi' the Bruce. I dinna think any o' us will live to see that sort o' victory again."

"You—you do think King David will be a good king, don't you? When he grows up, I mean."

He was a long time before answering. "I hope sae," he said carefully.

"He is the blood of the Bruce."

" 'N' England's second Edward war the son o' his father. See wha' it gained him—done to death by his own nobles and wife."

Angus MacPherson's views on the inheritance of greatness seemed oddly akin to Rene's. "But you would not prefer de Baliol," she said, suddenly fearful, "just because David is unproven."

"Christ, no!" he said vehemently. "One way or t' other, David maun hae the chance to show his mettle. His father's service to this country has earned him that."

They rode for a few minutes in silence. "But Papa *could* relieve Berwick," Cat said finally. "Despite the odds against it."

"Oh, aye, sae he might. Ye ken Madeleine Faurer." She nodded, surprised. "Michel used to say she told him life war like a big wheel, always turnin'. Those wha' bae at the bottom now will spin 'round to the top someday."

Cat looked at him through her lashes. Who would ever have expected this soldier to view history with such a philosophic bent? "But if that's true, Angus, if it all just goes 'round and 'round, what's the sense of trying? Of fighting? Of living and dying?"

"The battle gives a man his chance o' redemption," he told her with grim, grand grace.

His mention of the Faurer family made Cat think again of Rene's fable about the Templars. Was there any grain of truth, she wondered, in what he had said? "Angus, do you know anything about a secret society of Templars that is sworn to serve the Bruces?"

He threw back his heavy head and laughed. "La, bae that old chestnut tossin' about again?"

"You—you've heard talk about such a society, then?"

"Ever since Michel Faurer led the horsemen at the Bannockburn. Folk will wish, won't they, fer some sort o' savior?"

"So you don't believe it."

"Nae, I dinna—on twa counts." He held up a finger. "One, I spent my life wi' the Bruce, 'n' ne'er saw nae sign o' such Templars. 'N' twa—if there war such Templars, why wuld this nation bae in such a sorry state?"

Cat laughed, making Jessie swing her mount back toward them. "What in the world are you two whispering about?" she asked Cat. "Some plot to escape and leave me behind?"

"I'd never leave you behind, Jess."

"Hmph. So you say. Angus, how much longer now?"

"Five mile or sae."

"Tell me again what will happen when we get there."

"I'm t' present ye both t' th' English commander. It bae up t' him t' arrange fer us t' pass through the gate."

"Who commands the English?"

"The earl o' Northumberland. He bae a fair-minded man."

"And remember, Jess," Cat put in, "how well Papa fed his sons when they were his prisoners back at Douglasdale."

"Ye see, lass?" Angus smiled at her. "It all gaes 'round 'n' 'round."

"What does?" asked Jess.

"Everythin'." The redhead squinted off into the distance, then looked back down at Cat. "Th' Bruce himself used to say there bae more than one sort o' victory. Ye might chew o'er that, lass, while ye bae eatin' siege-bread in Berwick."

Just as the sun was slipping down behind the hills at their backs, they met the first English sentries: half a dozen of them, armed cap-a-pie, stepping out on chargers to challenge them as they came 'round a bend in the road. "Who goes there?" one barked, and Cat could not repress a small shudder as she heard his harsh, foreign-sounding speech.

Angus didn't seem intimidated. "Angus MacPherson, envoy from his honor the regent o' Scotland, Sir Archibald Douglas. Move back, there, laddie," he cautioned one of the soldiers who had ridden close to have a better look at Cat and her sister. "Laird Douglas has sent his girls here to bae taken into the city."

"Aye, we had word of it," the leader of the sentries replied. "We're to bring 'em along to His Grace, the Earl of Northumberland."

The man whom Angus had cautioned was sidling closer again. "I reckon they'd be counted a right bit of relief from a siege, wouldn't ye, mates?"

Cat saw Angus's big hand go toward his sword hilt; she met his eyes, shaking her head, and looked the soldier in the eye. " 'Twill be a fair day in hell before you breach these walls, *mate*. Now move aside and let us go to your commandant." Knowing Jessie would be frightened, she reached back for her sister's bridle and started down the road, with Angus grinning beside her. But despite her brave words, even she felt a qualm of terror as the Englishman snarled from behind her back:

"We'll see if she's so bloody high-and-mighty *after* St. Margaret's Day."

The curious eyes of scores and scores of soldiers followed them across the plain toward the walls of Berwick. They appeared settled in for a good long stay, Cat thought, noting the huts and palisades the invaders had raised. They even had a mill wheel installed in one of the tributaries of the Tweed that burbled toward the sea, and a system of buckets on ropes to bring water across the camp. The men seemed bored but confident—professional, accustomed to the tedium of siegefare. But underlying their unhurried pace as they went about their duties she could sense tension, taut as a string stretched to fraying, ready to snap when they were at long last let loose upon their enemy.

Northumberland's pavilion was a grand one, with flags of his own arms and those of King Edward hanging limp from poles atop it, waiting for breezes. Even at dusk, the day was hot for late May. Cat ran her glove over her forehead as Angus dismounted, rummaged in his saddlebag for the official letters Archibald had sent, and then entered the tent. Without the red-haired giant she felt suddenly bereft, exposed. Jessie brought her mount closer to Cat's in the gathering darkness, and reached for her hand. Cat turned toward her. Her sister's face was very pale. So far, though, she was holding back tears.

The tent flaps suddenly snapped open to reveal a tall, beefy man whom Cat could tell from his bearing had to be the mighty Harry Percy, earl of Northumberland. He had the air as he stepped from the tent, followed by a parcel of retainers and the faithful Angus, of being annoyed. Cat faced him bravely, wondering what he was like, this man whom her uncle James and father had spent so many years harrying on his Border estates.

He wasn't one, apparently, for niceties. He bestowed on Cat and Jessie a scant nod, signaled to one of his lieutenants, and barked, "Fetch a horse and take them up to the walls." Angus moved toward his own horse; at an almost imperceptible nod from the earl, his path was suddenly blocked by a pikestaff.

Angus turned to Northumberland. "I gave their father my word I'd see 'em safe inside, gude m'laird."

"Ye're about to break yer word then, soldier. I'll not have ye and yer men dashing in there and then claiming the city's relieved."

"Oh, honestly," Cat murmured. But it was a clever idea; she wished she'd thought of it. She glanced at Angus. Perhaps her father had?

She could not tell from looking at him; all he looked was stubborn. "Nor bae I about to risk sendin' 'em there wi' yer men, who might sneak across 'n' claim the city taken."

"Fair enough," the earl said after a moment. "They'll go alone."

Angus turned anxious blue eyes toward Cat. "Bae that all right, lass? Ye should bae safe eno'."

"Of course, Angus. It's certainly far preferable to riding with *them*." She tossed her head, indicating the Englishmen.

Northumberland wasn't amused. "I'll have ye know, young lady, this bit of folderol with ye and yer sister is just what I'd expect from a Douglas. A fine lot of trouble for a windy gesture, that's all it is."

"I couldn't agree more," Cat said. "After all, what's the sense of sending us to Berwick when Papa will be chasing all your pretty little soldiers back to England in a month or so? Still, I daresay King David will have his opinion of the English confirmed by this treatment of us. My father, at least, has always treated his hostages with courtesy. How fare your sons, milord?"

He had the grace to flush. Angus let out a little chuckle. "Well spoke, Cat. I see I need nae worry fer ye. God gae wi' ye, the twain o' ye."

"And bide with you, Angus. Give our love to Papa."

Ready to wheel her horse around, Cat tried to loose her hand from Jessie's. But her sister was holding on tight. *Christ,* Cat thought, *what a time for you to go dicey on me, Jess!* Annoyed, she turned to give her a pointed look, just to let her know what was expected of her, and was surprised to see her sister's eyes fixed on the little knot of courtiers behind the earl. Truth to tell, Cat hadn't given them a second glance. She did now, though— and had to fight off another swell of surprise as she recognized Rene Faurer in the dusky gloom. His face, handsome as ever, betrayed no emotion. But his blue eyes burned so fiercely that her heart stood still.

"You," she breathed, and felt a sudden burst of fury as she looked at him, standing so at ease among the men who'd come to conquer her country. "It wasn't enough for you to serve a Scots traitor, then, you dog, but you must go begging for scraps at an Englishman's feet?

The courtiers around him were laughing. "Know the wench, do ye, then?" Northumberland drawled. "Well, ye won't have long to wait now before renewing yer acquaintance. And I'm sure ye'll find plenty of yer mates clamoring for introductions." The soldiers hooted with glee.

"Come on, Jess," Cat said sharply, yanking their horses about and urging them forward across the plain toward the besieged city. At their backs they heard English soldiers' whoops and cat-calls, and Northumberland's loud, harsh voice raised above the ruckus:

"We'll be seeing ye, ladies, come St. Margaret's Day!"

Twenty-five

Life under siege, Cat was soon to discover, was composed of equal shares of tedium and want. There was an initial flurry of excitement upon her and Jessie's arrival, as they were greeted like heroines by the residents of Berwick. But that soon died down, and everyone resumed their regular occupations of worrying whether the water in the wells would hold out and blaming the city burgesses for not having laid in sufficient stores of oats and wheat. There was still enough food for the people of the town, but just barely. The governor, a huge, pompous man who was perpetually sweating, had calculated that the ale and bread would give out by the first week in July—barring, of course, any wave of cholera or summer fever that reduced the population within the walls significantly. Cat didn't trust him. She suspected he'd have opened the gates to the English in a moment just for the chance to maintain his big bourgeois belly, in which he took such pride.

She wasn't alone in that thought. Robbie Stewart had expressed the same sentiment to her and Jessie, in a low voice, at their first audience with King David. She'd been surprised to find Stewart there, and even more astonished to discover he was now in charge of the city's defenses. He was quick to explain, with ingratiating self-deprecation, that his post was strictly a result of happenstance. The earl of Albany, who'd originally been posted there with the king, had been struck down by dysentery six months after Dupplin, and the veteran sent by Archibald to replace him was turned back by Northumberland's troops, who were by then in place. King David's soldiers welcomed taking orders from the Bruce's nephew, even though many of them were twice or more his age.

Stewart looked older than Cat remembered from the previous autumn. So did young King David, who had grown a half a foot at least. "I keep telling Robbie I am ready to fight with the army," he told Cat when she and Jessie came to pay their respects to him. He was all of nine.

Cat met Stewart's gaze above the king's head, remembering how she had hated Robbie for his duel at Perth with Rene. "Well, Your Majesty, there's no sense talking of fighting until my father can relieve the town."

"No, but once he does, don't you think I am old enough?"

This frail little boy, the only heir the Bruce had left to Scotland . . . *If aught befalls him,* Cat thought, hiding a shudder, *what's to stop de Baliol then? We'd all be Edward of England's lieges faster than you can say pie.* "One step at a time, pray Your Majesty. Is the queen well?"

"Aye—though unhappy that we're at war against her brother again." *How confusing all of this must be to these children,* Cat thought. *God knows it is to me.* "She is learning to do tapestries. Lady Madeleine is showing her. Do you know Lady Madeleine?" That was how Cat found out Madeleine and Anne had been caught by the siege in Berwick.

"We came with the king and queen from Edinburgh after the battle at Dupplin," Madeleine explained when Cat sought her out that night. "Anne and Joanna have become quite good friends—I think the queen is relieved to have someone who is even half-English about! I knew we should leave—it was clear enough a siege was coming. But somehow I didn't like to abandon King David. I kept thinking that perhaps somehow I might be needed." She shrugged her slim shoulders. "Foolish of me, I suppose. Still, one never knows. Now you tell me—what in the world was your father thinking, to send you to Berwick?"

"Oh, you know Papa. John Mar dared to insinuate he might not be as good a soldier as my uncle James, and the next thing Jess and I knew, we were on our way!" She gave Madeleine a hug. "You can't imagine how glad I am to find you here."

"Well, I wish you were safe home in Douglasdale. Still, Anne will be delighted." They looked at one another, each wanting to raise the subject of Rene, neither wishing to cause the other pain. Then, "Have you," they both began at once, and stopped, and laughed.

"No," Madeleine answered first. "Though truth to tell, I don't know how he would send word to me. I doubt he has any more idea where I am than I of where he is."

"He is out on the plain with Northumberland. I saw him today."

"With Northumberland!" Madeleine had gone pale. "With the *English?* Are you sure?"

"Oh, very sure."

His mother turned and paced across the room. "Lord, it was bad enough to think of him with those turncoat Scots. But with the English . . ." She shook her head. "Still, it is something just to know he is alive. Did you—how did he look?"

"He looked like . . . Rene." Like a god, just as he always did. If you could ignore the blazing anger in his gaze.

Madeleine reached for her hand. "I loathed being the one to tell you of his marriage."

"I already knew when you wrote me," Cat said quietly.

"He confessed it himself? Well, I am glad to learn he has that much honor at least."

"Not exactly. I saw Eleanor. Last August, just before the battle at Dupplin." Cat squeezed her eyes shut, trying hard to block the rush of anguish the memory engendered—the imprint of Rene's lips on hers scarce vanished, his seed warm within her, and that detested blonde smiling smugly: *Rene is always so glad to see me when we've been apart.* . . . "It was then she told me about their marriage and the child."

"The what?"

"The child."

"The *what?*" Rene's mother was staring, openmouthed.

"Didn't Eleanor tell you in her letter?" Madeleine shook her head. Cat smiled wanly. "Well. Congratulations, then. You are made a grandmama by now."

"Impossible!" Madeleine blurted. "No! Rene would have told

me!" Regret and wonder were dancing an odd dance across her face.

"You said yourself—how could he, if he did not know you are here?"

"A grandchild!" Madeleine's green eyes were filled with wonder. "Oh, God, her child!" She made a moue of distaste. "I never could abide her. But I shall have to learn to live with it, I suppose. When did you see her, August? How far along was she?"

"Truth to tell, I didn't ask. Perhaps three months, or four."

Madeleine was counting on her fingers. "You did not waste any time at it, did you, Rene? Let's say three. That would have made it February that she delivered. Lord, I hope the child is well." She crossed herself quickly. "A boy or a girl? How I wish I knew! It will be five months old now, and I never have seen it!"

"I did not mean for the news to distress you."

Madeleine laughed. "Oh, I am not distressed! I am just . . . well, aye, I am. I should have been much happier, Cat, if the child were yours."

"There was never any chance of that, I'm afraid."

"I thought there was, once upon a time." She sighed, her green eyes haunted, distant. "Michel would have loved having grandchildren. And yet—perhaps it is better he is gone. To have his blood mixed with de Baliol's . . ." She stayed staring into space for a moment, then reached for her sewing basket. "St. Margaret's Day is six weeks hence. One way or another, I shall see Rene then. I can get started on a few bits and pieces for the baby. A gown or two—those can be for either a boy or a girl; I simply won't make them too fancy. And hats—it will need hats." Then she looked up at Cat, stricken. "Forgive me, my dear. I did not mean to gloat. It is just that—"

"I know. The birth of one's first grandchild is a momentous occasion!" Cat forced her voice to lightness. "I remember how proud Papa was when Tess gave birth to Jane."

"I am not proud of my son." Madeleine's fine mouth was tight. "I am ashamed of him, and ashamed for him. For what he's done to Scotland. But even more, for what he did to you."

Anne had heard the news from her mother by the time Cat

saw her the following day. She was a good deal less sanguine. "How *could* he?" she cried, and promptly burst into tears.

"Oh, Annie." Cat put her arms around the girl. She'd grown too, in these months; their heads were nearly at a level. "You must be glad for Rene."

"Well, I'm not. How can I be? He was *supposed* to marry you!"

"I could not marry someone of his politics."

"I know that, Cat. But I kept hoping he would come to his senses. Or that—" She screwed up her small face, just budding now into the sort of breathtaking beauty that had been her mother's in youth. "Or that it all would turn out to be some kind of mistake. I still can't fathom that Rain . . . but a baby makes it all rather final, doesn't it?"

"Aye," said Cat. "It does."

Malcolm Ross was at Berwick. "Lord, this place is full of the last people one would expect, isn't it?" Jessie marveled the first time she and Cat glimpsed him, marching with Robbie Stewart's men in drill through the center of town. "Well, at least you will have someone to court you."

"I don't care for him. I never have. I thought you were rather sweet on him once, though."

"He is very nice, Cat. Not so nice as Diarmot, of course," she added loyally. Then she frowned. "With my luck, you will fall in love with him and be wed right here, under siege, and I will lose the bet."

"Honestly, Jess. With all that has gone on, how can you still care about that silly wager?"

"You only say that because it is near certain you'll lose." She raised her kerchief to wave it. "Yoo-hoo! Hallo, Malcolm!"

"Jess!" Cat grabbed for her sister's hand, but it was too late; he'd seen them and broke ranks, starting toward them at a trot across the cobblestones.

"Ladies!" He swept a bow, still running, pulling off his hat and ruffling a hand through his corn-white hair. "I'd been hoping for an opportunity to tell you how much I admire your bravery in coming here."

"We hadn't really got any choice," Jessie told him. "But won't you get in trouble for leaving the drilling?"

"Not likely. I'm a captain now. Less through worth than from attrition, though. There weren't many officers here when the besiegers arrived." He grinned disarmingly. "Robbie tells me congratulations are in order for you, Jessie. Can't say I know the fellow, but I think him lucky." His pale gaze went to Cat. "And you, Catriona—no such announcement to make?"

"Oh, no," Jessie burbled, beaming at the two of them. "Our Cat's still footloose and fancy-free."

Malcolm bent low over Cat's hand. He'd grown a mustache, bristly-thick, that tickled. "Well, in that case I must say—I'm suddenly delighted that we're under siege."

"Not *again*," Cat groaned a fortnight later, when she heard that Jessie had asked Malcolm to dine with them in their chambers.

"What is the matter with you, Cat? He is perfectly lovely company."

"Not every evening, for God's sake!"

"It is only the third time this week," Jessie said complacently. "And anyway, he always brings something to make the meal special. Those splendid radishes the one time, and real French wine the last—"

"I should like to know where he gets those things. It is supposed to be share and share alike in a siege."

"Oh, Cat, don't be such a spoilsport. How far would that handful of radishes have gone amongst five thousand people?"

"They ought to go to the sick and the old, then. Those who have most need of them. Where does he get such stuff, anyway?"

"The people in the town give it to the soldiers, in hopes they might get special protection when the English come."

"I do wish you'd stop saying 'when,' Jess. If Papa's own daughters don't have faith in him—"

"Very well, 'if.' And if you are thinking of telling me how shocked you are by the townspeople's behavior, spare your breath. They are only trying to look after their own—as anyone would do in such circumstances. Except Papa, perhaps."

"Well, the soldiers ought not to accept what they're offered. It isn't right."

"You're a fine one to lecture others about right and wrong," Jessie muttered darkly.

Cat cocked her head. "I must say, I'm not certain falling in love with Diarmot has been good for you. You used to be the most gentle, generous soul I knew."

"At least falling in love didn't make me betray everything I was brought up to believe in," Jessie said snappishly, and then, as Cat stared at her with wounded eyes, clapped her hand to her mouth. "Lord, I am sorry, Cat! I don't know what has got into me, to make me say such a thing."

"Too much siege-bread," Cat told her, setting the dense loaf that was their evening's ration on the table; it bore a faint, sick-sweet smell from the mold that had invaded the meager flour stores. "And too little Diarmot. You must forgive me, Jess. I forget how much harder being here is for you than for me. After all, I've got nothing to lose."

Jessie hugged her tightly. "You mustn't talk that way, Cat. You're still so young; you still have all of life ahead of you. If you would just try a little harder, put yourself out a bit to make new friends . . ."

Cat let the familiar litany wash over her like warm rain, that one did not even pull up one's hood for. Her sister meant well, she knew, but the truth was that she did not feel young; she felt old as Methuselah, as the rocks in the walls, as the roiling sea, guarded by English warships, that beat against the cliffs below the battlements. She would fall in love again someday, she supposed. And yet she knew, with a great swell of sadness in her heart, that it would not be the same. She thought of how she'd given in to Rene's sweet kisses in the snow at Langlannoch, in the hay-sweet barn at Perth, in broad daylight on the banks of the Firth of Forth—Christ, how wild and desperate and reckless they'd been! It would never be that way for her again. It never could. "Innocence" might be a strange word to choose to describe those heady months of love, but innocent was what she had been. Innocent enough to believe that what she and he felt for one another could surmount any obstacle, to think that love was all the troubadors and harpists and poets claimed it: hope and salvation, the one bright light toward which the human soul yearned.

And though, on the morrow, she might in theory meet and fall in love with a wonderful, a splendid man, she would never have her heart to give that way again—green and dewy and mint-new. It was a loss that seemed to her incalculably more grave than that of her maidenhead.

Well, there were different kinds of love, she tried to console herself. There was Janet's love for Rawley, half her father, half amour; he gave her security, protection, and she warmed his bed and soothed his gout. There was Tess's love for Gill, practical as rain-shoes, wound 'round now with the strong threads of child-birth, of fretting over fevers and rashes and celebrations of the milestones of first teeth, first steps. There was Jessie's love for her shy, gentle Highlander, and whatever sort of love Archibald had had for each of their mothers, and they for him. . . .

If circumstances had been different, if she and Rene had been free to marry, chances were that by now they'd be as well-worn and comfortable together as Tess and Gill, talking mostly of the children, the blinding fire in their hearts burnt down to a slow, steady glow. Perhaps it was better, she mused, not to marry one's first love; this way she could keep their passion like a shrine in her memory.

But no. If their love would have burned down, she wanted to have had the chance of finding out what it would have burned down *to*. Considering how hot it had been to begin with, she guessed they would have gone a good many years before becoming lukewarm. And even a comfortable old love with Rene would have been better than new love with anyone else; she was sure of that—

"What are you thinking of, Cat?" Jessie asked softly.

Cat shook out the napkins with a flap. "Nothing in particular. Why?"

"You looked all sort of dreamy. I thought perhaps you were reconsidering about Malcolm."

"Not likely."

"Well," said Jessie, "you never do know. Sometimes you can look and look at someone for years without ever really seeing them. And then one day—zing! It hits you like an arrow that he's the man for you." Seeing Cat's expression of utter skepticism, she laughed. "Well, who are you to say? I mean, it *could* happen."

"And pigs could fly," said Cat.

"The world is full of miracles," Jessie told her solemnly. "Who knows? They might."

Twenty-six

One after another after another, the days in Berwick crawled by with numbing sameness. Cat thought often of Janet's words on the eve of their departure—"It will be an adventure"—and wished that she could tell her sister: it was not. People were suffering, all in different degree. Robbie Stewart's new plan for food distribution favored women expecting or nursing children, the infirm, and—an ominous innovation—men capable of bearing arms. Clearly he intended for the city to aid in its own defense. He also set a bounty of a farthing for every seabird brought to the castle—money being less scarce than food—prompting the boys in the city to spend every waking moment in the squares and streets with stones and slings. The birds smelled and tasted like old fish, and everyone was sick to death of them in a week, which was about when they began to learn how risky it was to alight anywhere in Berwick.

Every morning Cat climbed to the western parapets and looked down on Northumberland's soldiers, still camped out on the plain awaiting Scotland's army. Only another week until St. Margaret's feast . . . Robbie had told her that on the day she saw the men in the field take down their tents, she'd know her father had come. She thought of Archibald often, imagined him drilling his troops, penning final pleas to Europe's princes, sitting in his study at Douglasdale worrying whether he had done, would do, the right thing. Cat dearly hoped he would not come to regret sending her and Jessie to Berwick, as he'd told her he regretted that other impulsive act, when he had sworn never to wed.

Robbie Stewart came that evening to the room she and Jessie were sharing—the thirteenth of July. It was late; they were close to retiring, and Cat had already taken down her hair. Jessie opened the door to him and then hesitated, not certain whether it was proper to ask him in. "Hallo, Robbie," she said, and glanced back over her shoulder. Cat nodded to her. Hell, in another week's time, if the English prevailed, they might all be looking at each other's entrails; it didn't seem to matter if Robbie saw her in her shift.

"I am sorry to come so late," he apologized, hat in his hands. They were freckled hands, Cat noticed, the fingers narrow and tapered. Robbie did not look the part of a soldier, not with his snow-pale skin and true-red hair. And he was so young to have so great a burden as defending the king laid upon him—a year younger than herself, Cat had calculated with Jessie's help. Scant eighteen . . . yet he seemed ages older. His energy was never flagging; he worked passing hard at finding ways to alleviate the suffering of the city's citizens, unlike the mayor, who did nothing but whine and grouse. If he ever was unsure of himself, ever doubted he would do right by his responsibilities, he never gave a sign.

She had come to admire him in these past weeks, despite the hard knot of resentment that lay deep within her for what he had done at Perth to Rene. Well, the sentence of lifelong banishment had been Moray's doing, not Robbie's. And perhaps, considering the web of falsehood Rene had since then woven, Robbie had done her a favor by sending him out of her life when he did. Robbie Stewart was the sort of man she ought to have fallen in love with, she thought, still looking at his graceful hands, if she'd had any sense.

"Could ye come with me, please, ladies?" Robbie said now.

Jessie clutched her heart, looking weak-kneed. "Good God. It's come, hasn't it? Papa's been defeated."

He grinned at her. "Nay, lass, not yet. There's just one or two matters I'd mull over with ye and a few others about what will happen when the battle does come."

Still uncertain, Jessie looked again at Cat. "We shall have to dress . . ."

"Oh, honestly, Jess, put a robe on and have done with it. I'll wager even the queen of France suspends the rules of etiquette when she is under siege."

Robbie grinned again, meeting Cat's gaze as Jessie, looking huffish, vanished behind a screen to don her dressing gown. He had a nice, raffish smile, Cat thought, not bothering to turn as she shrugged on her own robe and tied it at the waist. His eyes were greenish gray, like willow leaves . . . like the leaves of the willows weeping over the firth at Inverkeithing. *Damn you, Rene Faurer, will you haunt me so?* she thought in wrath, and let her own smile blaze at the redhead. He wasn't so good-looking as Malcolm, she supposed, but she liked the way he bore himself, so sleek and vaunty. And Lord knows he was brave; the wounds he'd taken at Dupplin, she recalled Gill saying, would have killed three ordinary men. She remembered how well he had acquitted himself in the duel at Perth against Rene—dammit, Rene again!

"Your buttons, Cat!" Jessie hissed, scandalized, as she came around the screen to find her sister lost in thought, her robe still unfastened to the waist.

"My what? Oh." Reaching for the buttons, Cat glanced up at Robbie again and found his willow-green gaze trained on her bodice. One would not have to be in love, she mused, just to have a dalliance. It surely would relieve the tedium of the siege. . . . Was that what had led her mother into temptation with Archibald, she wondered—the long, dull winters at Craignure? Boredom could be a very dangerous thing, she decided—but took her time doing up the buttons, Robbie's eyes on her all the while.

They followed him into the corridor, Jessie's arm on Cat's holding her back a little way from him. "Did you see the way he was looking at you?" Jessie hissed.

"Aye. What of it? You told me I should put myself out, make new friends."

"Not by lolling about undressed in front of eligible young men! You'll get a reputation," Jessie intoned, making it sound worse than plague.

"Well, it won't last long, seeing as within a week we'll both

be raped and murdered." As Jessie gasped, Cat could see Robbie
Stewart's broad shoulders quake with his laugh.

They were climbing a long, narrow flight of stairs that led
away from the main rooms of the castle. "Where—where are we
going?" Jessie asked nervously as Robbie pulled a torch from
the sconce at the top; beyond that point, there was no more light.

"Ye'll see. But pay attention, both of you. Ye maun need remember the way. Down this corridor, right at the end, then up,
left, down, and follow that to the end. Got it?"

"You must be jesting," said Jessie.

"Right from our rooms, up at the end of that corridor, straight,
right, up, left, down, and on to the end," Cat repeated. Robbie
turned around to look at her, the torch bobbing.

"Very good," he said.

Jessie was peeved. "I must say, I don't know why there has
got to be all this mysterious climbing about in the middle of the
night."

"Ye will, soon enough." The corridor in front of Robbie
stopped dead at a stark wall—no doors, no turns. "Watch," he
said. "Third stone from the top, two in from the left." He gave
it a shove, and a section of the wall swung into the darkness.

Cat took a few steps forward, inhaled the dank smell of mold
and unmoving air. "Just like the tunnels at Edinburgh," she whispered, standing in the stillness.

"What the devil d'ye know about the tunnels at Edinburgh?"
Robbie asked at her back.

"I was in them once. . . ." On her way to meet Rene, make
love to him on the mist-shrouded night riverbank—

"What is wrong with yer sister?"

Robbie's voice whipped her 'round. Jessie was shrinking back
against the wall, looking scared and stubborn. "Come along,
Jess," Cat coaxed her.

Jessie shook her head. "Maybe you are willing to trot along
to wherever it is he wants to lead us in the middle of the night,
Cat, but I am not. I'll not go one step farther until I know what's
going on."

Cat sighed. "If you don't come along, Jess, Robbie and I will go on without you. And we'll take the torch. Do you want to find your way back to our rooms in the dark?"

"No, but—"

"Then come on."

Robbie had a brow raised. Cat took the torch from him and started walking away from Jessie, who let out a little burble of fright and then ran after her, clinging to her arm: "Don't leave me here!" she cried.

Cat took pity on her. "I would not have left you. But soldiers must learn to take orders without asking questions, isn't that right, Robbie?"

"I'm not a soldier," Jessie sniffed.

"We are all soldiers now, Jess." Cat gave the torch back to Robbie and held her sister's hand.

They'd been going steadily up; now they were going down, down, down, along a crumbling, moldy staircase so lengthy, Cat thought, that it could only have lain within one of the battlement walls. Something splashed in the darkness ahead of them, making Jessie jump: "What was that?"

"Likely a rat," said Robbie, and when she screamed amended: "Well, it might have been a fish."

"I warned you not to ask questions, Jess," Cat said.

Then they were at the bottom; the torchlight glistened on water, pitch-black, smelling of salt. "I'll carry you across now," Robbie told them, "but when the time comes, if you have to, you can wade through."

"When *what* time—" Jessie began, and stopped as Cat poked her.

"Put yer arms around my shoulders," Robbie told Jessie, handing Cat the torch. He lifted her in his arms, walked through the murky water to deposit her on the far side, and then turned back for Cat. She'd taken off her slippers and hiked up her robe, and was already more than halfway across.

"Oh, God, Cat, how *could* you?" Jessie squealed. "In bare *feet?*" But Robbie was once more eyeing her approvingly. She put her hand on the wall to steady herself as she put her slippers back on, and something slithered down, very close to her fingers, and vanished into the water in a flurry of bubbles. Jessie gathered in breath for a scream, and Robbie clapped his hand over her mouth.

"From here on, we have to be very quiet," he told them, and the urgency in his voice silenced even Jessie.

Cat could guess why from the salt tang of the air and water; they were close to the seawall, with the English warships anchored not too far away. Her heart was racing, not with fear, but with excitement; at least, at long last, there was something to *do*. It was a pity Jessie was being so squeamish. Well, it couldn't be helped. She, at least, intended to do well by the Douglas name.

Up one more flight of stairs they went, with the scent of the sea growing stronger. Then that flight ended at a door. "Fourth stone down this time," Robbie told them, and another hidden door swung wide. In the small, square chamber beyond there were candles, and ewers of wine on a table, and, in high-backed chairs, Madeleine Faurer and two soldiers whom Cat did not know but recognized by sight from Douglasdale.

"Well, fancy seeing you here," Cat told Madeleine, who laughed.

"Did you enjoy Robbie's tour of the castle?"

"I did. But I'm not sure about Jess."

"Won't someone please tell me what is going on?" Jessie begged, looking nervously at the soldiers.

Robbie closed the door behind them. "Certainly. Sit down. Mick, Nate, pour the Douglas girls wine. D'ye know Mick Jonas, Cat, Jessie, and Nathan MacGuinness?" Cat and Jessie shook their heads. "They are good soldiers, and good friends of mine. You can trust them utterly. Madeleine you know, of course. Shall we begin?"

The soldiers had stood to pull out chairs for the two sisters. Jessie collapsed into hers; Cat perched on the edge, her heart still beating fast. Robbie sat too, poured wine for himself, and took a long swallow. "Now. Ye know nothing would please Edward of England more than to get his hands on our King David. He's a stout lad, the king is, with plenty of heart. Yet the time is not yet come for him to fight his own fight. So we must make provisions for him and the queen, in light of what's to come. Drink up, ladies, drink up."

"I couldn't possibly," Jessie told him. Cat took a sip, though.

"It may be," Robbie went on, "that Scotland will prevail in the fighting. If so, God be praised, for the king will ride free out of these walls. But if we do not prevail—well, that's what I would speak to ye about tonight. King David must not be taken. I've put my mind to the problem, along with some friends"—he looked to Mick and Nate—"and here's what we've come up with. Now, then. We'll have a watch in the towers, of course, to see what can be seen of the battle. If it comes clear the day will not go to Scotland—"

"But it will go to Scotland," Cat interrupted.

"Sure and it will, lass. But we still must have a contingency. If it comes clear Scotland's losing, Nathan will go to the king's chambers. Lady Madeleine and her daughter will be there. Nate will bring them here, to this room, with the king and queen. Mick will come and get ye, Lady Jessica, Lady Cat. Ye'll come here as well."

"If Mick's to come and get us, why did you want us to memorize the way?" Cat asked him.

"Things have a fashion of going wrong in battles. Better ye should know yerself how to come."

"But *why* must we come?" Jessie asked plaintively.

Robbie looked at her. "I thought ye understood. Yer father's challenge to King Edward puts ye in grave danger. After the king, ye and yer sister will be the first folk the English seek." Jessie stared at him, blue eyes very wide. "I'd have ye well away before they come for ye, lass, that's all."

Cat saw her sister was crumbling. Lord, they'd jested often enough about what the English would do to them. Hadn't she realized? Or perhaps it had just not hit home. "What will we do once we get here?" she asked Robbie, squeezing her sister's hand.

"Sit and wait, all of ye, until I come for ye."

"Will we be safe?" Jessie asked, her voice trembling.

"As safe as ye could be anyplace in Berwick. There's no way in but the one I showed ye. Mick and Nate can readily defend that narrow stair."

"What if you don't come?" Cat wanted to know. "What if something happens to you? How will we know? How long do we wait?"

"Cheery thought—but a good one." He grinned. "There's food and wine and water here, and air enough if the door's kept open. Ye could stay for a week."

"A *week?*" Jessie was apoplectic.

"Not that ye'll have to," Robbie said hastily. "Nate and Mick will get ye out long before that. Can—uh—can you ladies swim?"

"Not a stroke," said Cat, while Jessie shook her head.

"Well, we'll have to think of something else, then. What's important is that ye stay put. Have faith. I will be coming for ye."

"So you say," muttered Jessie.

"Sooth, 'tis far preferable to having that battalion of Englishmen have its way with you, isn't it?" Cat asked her sister.

Jessie looked about at the dank walls and shuddered. "I'm not sure it is."

Madeleine leaned forward across the table. "If you are frightened, Jessie, just think how it must be for the king and queen. We must be brave for their sake."

It was the perfect appeal; Cat was reminded again of how wise Madeleine was in knowing people's hearts. Jessie would not allow herself to be shown up by a nine-year-old, even a nine-year-old king. "Well, of course," she said, and squared her shoulders. "As you say, we must do all we can."

"So," said Robbie, setting down his empty cup. "Ye understand now what I need from ye. Have ye any more questions?" Cat shook her head. Jessie glanced at her uncertainly, and then did the same. "Good!" he told them. "We'll see ye back to your rooms now. Do pay attention along the way."

They trooped out of the little room with Mick in the lead, followed by Madeleine, then Nate, then Jessie and Cat and last of all Robbie. At the edge of the pool of black water, Cat started to reach for her slippers, but Robbie's hand forestalled her. "No need of that," he said, and scooped her into his arms to carry her across.

"I really don't mind wading," she told him.

"Well, I really don't mind carrying ye. Small as a feather ye are." He smiled down at her, then set her down on the far side. "A wee brave lass."

"Jess will be brave too, when the time comes. Just wait and see."

"Ach, I'm sure she will."

Cat had thought of a question. "You don't think we'll prove a hindrance, Jess and I, to getting King David safe away?"

"If I thought that, I'd leave ye here, English soldiers or no English soldiers." There was a touch of steel in his easygoing voice. Cat nodded, satisfied.

No one said much as they made their way back through the maze of doors and tunnels and stairs to the castle proper. Cat was concentrating on committing to memory the sequence of their escape route; Madeleine looked weary. Cat could only imagine what Jessie must be thinking at this latest turn of fate. Robbie accompanied the sisters as far as their rooms. Jessie darted inside as though the hounds of hell were nipping at her heels. Cat paused on the threshold, turning to smile at Robbie. Christ, he did look old, with all this burden laid on him.

"I'm grateful to you for thinking of us," she said softly. "For including us."

"I could not leave ye here to be ravished by Englishmen, could I?" He cocked his head, grinning.

"Still, considering everything else you've had laid on your plate . . ."

"Ye did not ask to be here, did ye? Ye are only doing what yer father expects of ye."

As was he, Cat realized. As the only son of the late, valiant Walter Stewart and the Bruce's daughter Marjorie, he had a family obligation at least as weighty as hers to discharge. It was a relief to find someone who didn't shirk such a duty. For a fleeting instant she thought of Rene, his unreasoned hatred for his father, the suffering he had caused to Madeleine, and her temper flared.

Robbie touched her hand. "I hope the fierceness in yer eye is not for Archibald!"

She laughed. "Oh, no. I'm not angry at Papa. He only did what he felt he must do."

"That's all any of us do, isn't it?"

"There's some won't even do that much," Cat told him darkly. She was thinking of Rene again. Suddenly she remembered what he'd told her about the duel he'd had with Robbie at Perth. "Robbie," she said impulsively, "the fight you had with Rene Faurer—" But she did not have a chance to finish:

"Bah!" Robbie said, and spat on the fieldstone floor. "Don't mention that black traitor's name to me! I only hope the devil does not catch him by the heels before I do; I'll finish with him what we began at Perth." He looked at her, his willow eyes sharp. "I heard once ye were sweet on him."

"I . . . was, a little. Long ago." She blushed, embarrassed to admit as much to this stalwart Scot. "I did not know then what manner of man he was."

" 'Twas plain enough, I thought, from that toast he made at yer sister's wedding. I ought to have finished him off then and there—and would have, too, if yer father had not stopped me."

Cat smiled, recalling how he'd torn off his doublet and rushed at Rene. He smiled back, and to her great surprise she felt flare up in her soul a small bright spark of desire, of craving nearly forgotten. Perhaps it was just the circumstances of their being here at Berwick, both of them, drawn by the cause of duty. Perhaps it was simply the surprise of finding someone who took allegiance to family and nation as seriously as she. Whatever it was, she found herself wanting Robbie Stewart with a passion that suddenly made her draw in breath.

He looked down at her, hearing her soft, startled gasp. Still riding the crest of astonishment, Cat reached up on tiptoe to circle his neck with her arms and press her mouth to his.

He sprang back as though he'd just embraced fire, reeling, stumbling in his haste. Cat felt a wretched telltale flush rise in her cheeks, ride straight up to her hair. "I'm sorry," she whispered, eyes on the floor as she groped for the door latch.

"No! No, I'm the one who—I didn't—" He took a breath, a deep one. "Christ! Ye just surprised me."

"Not a very welcome surprise, I gather," she could not keep from murmuring.

"Don't get me wrong, lass. It isn't that I don't want ye—Christ, what man wouldn't? Lovely ye are, and brave, and true-hearted . . ." He shook his head as though in wonderment. "And a union of Douglas and Stewart—ach, there would be a legacy for Scotland. Can ye imagine it, Cat? But . . ."

"But?" she echoed miserably.

"But—" His voice was very gentle. "This is not the time, nor the place. There are other claims on us both, Catriona, strong claims, that we must satisfy first. Ye ken what I'm saying?"

She nodded, swallowing her embarrassment. "I only thought—to make the waiting easier."

"La, it would do that!" The words were rich with a regret that belied their jocularity. "But we have too much, too many folk, depending on us. And I'm much afraid, Catriona Douglas, that loving ye could make a man forget all about country and king. So I'll naysay ye for now—*with* the understanding that when all this is over, if it ever is over, I reserve the right to claim my prize." He reached out and tipped her chin toward him. "Agreed?"

"You make me ashamed," she whispered, "to have been so selfish."

"Well, ye make me think I must be daft to be so bloody damned noble, seeing ye standing there in yer nightdress! Now get on to yer bed, before I come to my senses." He pushed her toward the door. "Good night, Cat."

"Good night, Robbie." She slipped into the room. Jessie was already asleep; she heard her soft, steady breathing. Not wanting to wake her, Cat stood by the door, getting her bearing, collecting her thoughts. Christ! What a hell of a night.

When she was certain Jessie wouldn't awaken, she tiptoed across the room and climbed up into the bed, feeling utterly exhausted. *Please God,* she thought, *don't let the battle come tomorrow; I shall sleep straight through it, and never reach the rendezvous . . .*

Robbie had been kind—and wise, she recognized. The times were too uncertain for love. Look at poor Jessie, torn away from her Diarmot. Who would want to suffer that way?

Tired though she was, her thoughts chased 'round like hares in a circle, not letting her sleep. It wasn't till a long time later that she heard the sound she realized she had been waiting for— Robbie's bootheels moving away from her door. That only gave her more to think on. Finally, toward dawn, with the sky arching over the sea beyond her narrow window showing streaks of vermilion and gold, her thoughts wound themselves up into skeins of regret and sorrow and resignation, and she slept.

Twenty-seven

Time had a strange way of passing that last week before the feast of St. Margaret. During the day it crawled impossibly slowly, so that everyone scrambled to fill it up with minute tasks just to keep from dwelling on what lay ahead. Cat saw women in the town scrubbing the stairs of their houses, wiping doors and windows, sweeping off the streets, as though their fate in the confrontation might be determined by sheer cleanliness. Jessie fell prey to the same sort of compulsion, ceaselessly straightening bed linens, rearranging the scant clothes in her wardrobe a thousand times. Cat thought she understood: in the face of such uncertainty, one needed to feel there was *something* that could be controlled, even if it was only the direction of a broom or the sequence of one's gowns on hooks.

Women weren't the only ones tending their nests. Each morning Robbie's soldiers made another round of the town walls in search of breaches, of loose stones and mortar, of some overlooked exigency that might make a difference in the battle to come. They could not seem to stop marching; hour after hour, they formed and re-formed and went tramping back and forth across the yards. Yet despite all these best efforts to stay busy and useful, hours dragged like lead—until the night fell, when folk looked at one another in surprise and murmured, "Another day gone by already? Doesn't time fly!"

And each morning Cat climbed to the towers and looked down on the sea of enemy soldiers surrounding the city, baking in the early summer heat, drenched by the showers that never fell long or steadily enough to replenish the drinking water stores inside

Berwick's walls. And each day, seeing that the Englishmen had not struck their tents, she wondered anew whether she was glad or sorry that they had not moved—whether it was better to go on living in this odd suspended state for yet another cycle of dawn and darkness, or preferable just to get on with the fighting and find out what the end would be.

She wondered, that is, until the morning when she saw the soldiers pulling up stakes, saddling horses, donning mail and helmets, all amidst an eerie, unaccustomed silence, the usual bold banter of the camp, which had carried so clearly across the plain, conquered by nerves and prayer. For a moment she stood on the ramparts and watched, and knew that in her heart that she had been wishing this day never would arrive. Then she raced back through the castle to tell Jessie. It was the nineteenth of July, 1333— the day before St. Margaret's feast.

Jessie already knew. She looked up as Cat burst into their bedchamber, breathless with her news; the expression on her face was wan and worried. "Robbie's already been to tell me," she announced, "though I think he was looking for you."

"Where are the English headed?"

"I don't know. Oh, he was all full of speculation, but the truth is, I wasn't listening. I just keep thinking of Diarmot—and Papa."

"They'll be all right," Cat said soothingly.

Her sister turned on her, blue eyes flashing. "You don't know that, do you? It is an easy enough thing to say, but you don't know what will happen to them. They could both of them be maimed, or killed—"

"For God's sake, Jess!"

"Well, it's true! Robbie was the same way, all pats on the shoulder and confident smiles, but the fact is that the world as we know it could be ending, and there isn't a thing we can do about it except sit and wait!"

"It won't be the end of the world," Cat tried to reason with her, "no matter what happens. And we'll be safe enough. We have got Robbie's plan—"

"Robbie's plan?" Jessie's voice rang with scorn. "So far as I can tell, Robbie's plan is to have us sit in a hole in the ground with the king and queen of Scotland until all of us die of rot! *That's* Robbie's plan!"

Cat looked at her sister and saw she was shaking all over, tiny little shakes that she could not or would not bother to control. "What is it, Jessie? What in the world has got into you?"

"Nothing," she said, but the word tripped over a sob. "Yes there is. I had a dream last night of a raven knocking at the window." Her pale eyes were wide. "They do say, don't they, that always means death?"

"Oh, Jess." Cat went and hugged her. "With all the real worries we have got, I shouldn't think you'd need to go looking for omens in dreams!"

"I can't seem to help myself. Ever since Robbie came, I've been thinking . . . about Papa and Diarmot. I keep wondering—if one of them has got to die, which would I rather it be? I love them both so terribly . . . but it really does seem unlikely they will both come through this. And it just keeps chasing 'round and 'round in my head—which one do I want saved?"

Her plaintive sincerity gave Cat chills. She crossed herself. "Thank God, it isn't for us to decide such things!"

"I know that. But I wonder if I should concentrate my prayers on one or the other. I wouldn't want God to punish me for being greedy by taking both of them."

"I think you'll have plenty of time to pray for them both, Jess, and for everyone else. If the English are only now breaking camp, it's not likely there will be fighting today."

"That's what Robbie said, too. Tomorrow, then." She forced a smile. "Papa waited right up until the last moment, didn't he? Hoping for a miracle, I suppose."

"He may get one yet." At least she'd stopped shaking, Cat noted. "I should like to go and find Madeleine and Anne, Jess, if you will be all right without me."

"Do you mean, am I going to throw myself off the parapets? Not yet—but I'll reserve the option. I'd almost sooner that than descend into those tunnels again."

"Don't forget—we only have to hide ourselves if Papa is losing."

"Of course," said Jessie, but the words were hollow, with resignation echoing beneath them like the overtones of a bell.

The same air of impending grief cloaked the king's chambers, though Madeleine Faurer was doing her best to dispel it. She'd brought a lutist in to perform for the children, and the queen's spaniels had been let loose to rollick beneath tables and across the bed. Anne was playing draughts with David; she looked up as the guards at the door admitted Cat. Her green eyes showed the toll of uncertainty, but her voice raised in greeting was so carefree and gay that Cat felt awed by her strength. What a pity it was, she thought, for Scotland's children, that this fight for freedom made them grow up so fast—not least of all King David. Madeleine had drawn his curtains over the windows, but he took the excuse of Cat's arrival to go to the casement and look out over the fast-emptying plain.

"I should be out there fighting," he muttered.

"Come and finish the game, David," Queen Joanna said mildly. "It isn't fair to quit just when Anne has nearly got you beat."

"How has she almost got me beat?" Indignant, he returned to the checkerboard. As she listened to their wrangling, Cat found herself wondering what outcome Joanna might be hoping for in her heart from this battle. David was her husband, true, but at their ages that meant no more than playmate. Edward of England was her brother, lord of the land she'd been plucked from while still so young. Whose banner would she rather see flying over Berwick? Where did her sympathies lie?

"Robbie was here?" she asked Madeleine quietly.

The woman nodded. "But I would have known anyway. On the eve of battle there is something in the air—I recall it well from Bannockburn."

"You were there?" Cat asked in surprise.

"Oh, aye—eight months along with Rene. But I would not have missed it for any prize." Her eyes were far away, remembering. "Everyone expected we would lose. I was certain that Michel would die."

"Jessie would be glad to hear that," Cat said wryly. "She is convinced that either Papa or her betrothed will not live through the battle."

"Is she, poor thing?" Madeleine frowned at her daughter, who was crowing in triumph over having bested David in the game. "Anne, it isn't becoming to gloat."

"He always gloats when he wins."

"Do not," said David. "Let's make it best out of three games. Set the board up again."

"Madeleine," said Cat, "what do you think is going to happen?"

"Oh, I know what is going to happen. God's will." Then she shook her head. "But what that is, I could not tell."

Cat spent most of the day there in the king's chambers; playing with the children was better than brooding over things that could not be helped. Jessie came and went, unable to leave off worrying enough to enjoy storybooks or charades. The two guards Robbie had set to accompany them all into hiding, Mick Jonas and Nathan MacGuinness, stopped by at suppertime, making the king choke a little on his bread. But, "No, no," they said, suddenly aware of the impression their arrival had made. "Forgive us, Your Majesty." After that, they stayed away.

David retired early, though Cat wondered if he would sleep. She returned to her chamber to find Jessie praying—"For everybody," she told Cat, "just as you said." Cat joined her, and stayed on her knees at the smooth-worn prie-dieu even after Jessie had crawled into bed—no longer praying, just staring out over the dark waters of the North Sea.

She missed her papa. She wished she could be with him, though she knew he would be far too busy on this night to tell her the stories she was longing to hear, of his exploits with Uncle James and of all the triumphs of the house of Douglas. Somehow she felt those timeworn tales might give her courage for the ordeal to come. "Ye bae Douglases," she could almost hear Archibald saying, "that will suffice fer ye." Lord, she hoped it would!

But she felt weary and scared and impatient all at once. *Perhaps this is how a soldier feels on the eve of battle,* she thought, *mind all jumbled . . . but it depends on the soldier, I guess. Some*

*of them, no doubt, are cool as cowcumber—those who haven't
got any heart.*

And that, alas, made her think of Rene, a topic she'd been
doing her damnedest to avoid. Oh, hell, she thought, getting up
from the prie-dieu with the almost unconscious realization that
it would not be fitting to kneel in prayer while he was on her
mind. Instead she perched on the window seat, arms hugging
her knees, and allowed herself the forbidden luxury of memory.

Because I think I love you, he'd shouted at her on the street at
Perth, making those two old ladies turn and goggle. She could
smell the sweet, cool hay in the barn there as he'd kissed her,
recalled his frantic impatience: *I need you.* . . . And how she'd
wanted him! Still, she'd staved him off, until that night in Edinburgh. The night before Janet's wedding, the night before Moray—

But she would not think of that now, nor of that other night
when she'd made love to him so sweetly and then betrayed him.
She would think only of the good times. *Oh, Christ, Rene, there
were such good times!* she thought, tears flooding her eyes. *When
we rode up into the hills in the snow with Annie, and the whole
world was silent—do you remember that moment, Rene? Do you
ever even think of me?*

The night sky stared back at her, moonless, a few stars gleaming. There were clouds, she realized. Perhaps the morrow would
bring rain, a great wild deluge of rain that would sweep Edward's
army back to England and sweep Rene back to her arms. . . .

Come the morning, she knew, she would have to be strong
and brave and practical—for Madeleine and Annie, for King
David, for Jessie. But on this night, with the fate of the world
seeming to hang on a mere wisp of starlight—

On this night, by God, she intended to dream.

Twenty-eight

From the walls of Berwick, one could not clearly see the battle that began in the early morning hours of the next day against the slope known as Halidon Hill, some three miles north and west of the city. At that distance, all that could be glimpsed was a sort of roiling of colors, red and blue and yellow and brown moving in waves against a backdrop of lush summer green. The trumpets could be heard, though, sounding attack and alarum, marshaling the masses of men and horses into what, to Edward's mind and Archibald's, must have been a plan. The bodies of troops marched closer and closer together, and as the gap between them diminished it seemed to Cat, straining her eyes beneath the overcast sky, that the wave that was Scotland's hope was being thinned considerably.

It must have seemed that way to Robbie Stewart, too. He passed by her just as the chimes of the Bell Tower were ringing ten of the morning. "Get inside," he snapped, and moved on.

Cat stared across the plain once more, whispering a prayer for her father. Then she obeyed, returning to her rooms.

Jessie wasn't there. Gone to be with the king and queen, no doubt, Cat thought, and hurried toward their chambers. On her way she saw young Mick Jonas starting up a stair to the parapets; he gave her a wink and a nod, nonchalant as a man heading for a game of golf. Robbie chose cool ones, she thought, in him and Nathan, and then realized it was well he did. If it came down to a lengthy stay in that dungeon below, God forbid, they'd need the guards' brash insouciance.

Malcolm Ross was stationed at the king's door. He spoke some nicety or other as he let her in, but Cat just nodded and smiled, her mind on other things. Madeleine had the children playing tag, running and chasing each other all around the antechamber, Anne and Joanna with their skirts kirtled up at the waist. "Come and play, Cat!" Anne invited, and after a moment she did, though it felt a bit like fiddling while Rome burned.

"Have you seen Jessie?" she called to Madeleine as King David pursued her with outstretched arms.

"Not since this morning's breakfast. Isn't she in your rooms?"

"She wasn't when I left for here. Do you think I'd better look for her?"

"I suppose so."

"You can't go, Cat!" Anne and Joanna chorused. "We need you to play!"

Madeleine and Cat exchanged glances; then Anne's mother shrugged. "I don't suppose it matters. Mick will find her should anything happen."

"Anything like what, Mama?" Anne asked. She and Joanna hadn't been told of the plan to hide them, lest they give it away to someone. But the secret couldn't be kept much longer.

There were half a dozen servants, as well as the king's gentlemen and the queen's ladies-in-waiting, in the antechamber. Madeleine glanced at Cat, one black brow raised as if to say, "Now?" But Cat shook her head. It was still so early. There was still hope, wasn't there, for Archibald and his men?

Just as she formed that thought, Nathan MacGuinness appeared in the doorway. Cat felt the blood drain from her face, saw Madeleine reach for Anne in a hug that had to it an edge of desperation. "Mama, what is it?" the girl demanded, impatient that her game was interrupted.

"So soon as that," Cat whispered.

Nathan met her gaze, his dark eyes sympathetic, before turning to the king. "Yer Majesty. Won't ye please come this way?"

David was no fool; he knew not to question or argue. "Joanna." He held out his hand to the queen. "It is time to go."

She spun in a circle, flustered. "Now? Where? What about my dogs?"

David looked to Nathan, who shook his head. "The dogs will have to stay here for now, I'm afraid," the king told her.

"Oh, very well. Constance, fetch my trunk," she ordered one of the ladies, "and you, Adelia, start packing. I'll need my red velvet, and the green damascene, and the—"

"Joanna."

Her eyes were so frightened. "Aye, milord?"

"All of that can wait. We must go." David put out his hand to her again, and this time she took it like a queen, like Edward of England's sister.

"Farewell," she said to her ladies, her voice trembling only a little. "God be with you."

"And with you," they chorused; Lady Constance was crying. Then they followed Nathan through the wide bronze doors.

Madeleine and Anne came next, mother leading daughter, and then Cat. The corridor was deserted except for the guards. "Nathan," Cat called, "I am going back to my rooms to get Jessie."

He pursed his mouth. "I think it better if ye come with us, milady. Mick will see to yer sister."

Cat wanted to argue—Jessie was so overwrought already, and Cat wanted badly to be with her—but she didn't like to set a bad example for the children, so she simply nodded and followed along. The route to the tunnels was different from this part of the castle, of course. Nathan set a quick pace, glancing about from time to time to make certain they weren't being seen, but the castle seemed empty. *Everyone must be up on the battlements,* Cat thought, *watching the fighting.* She was glad Nathan was moving so quickly; it kept her from dwelling on exactly what their hasty flight meant. Defeat for Scotland—but how had it happened so precipitously? Poor Papa . . . she stumbled a little, thinking of Archibald, and Madeleine caught her elbow, helping her up. "Are you all right?" she asked. Cat nodded and moved on.

They were into the tunnels now, climbing one of those dank, steep staircases, following the bobbing light of Nathan's torch. The queen was having trouble with her dress, and Madeleine moved forward to take the hem for her. In the near-darkness, Cat felt Anne's small fingers grope for her hand and clutch tight.

"Wh-where are we going, David?" Joanna whispered. The

sound carried a long way behind them, bouncing off the ancient stone walls.

"Someplace where we will be safe, of course." He sounded so trusting. Cat could only pray his faith would be justified.

Down and up and then down again, that last long descent with the smell of the sea in the air, and the pool of black water . . . Joanna balked even at having Nathan carry her, and Cat couldn't blame her; for all one could tell, it might have been a hundred feet deep. But finally they all made it across, Cat and David and Anne, bless her, wading, so that Nathan had only to cart Madeleine and the queen. Then Nathan fumbled for the stone that was the key to the door of their hiding place; it clanged open with a frightening racket that made everyone jump. David laughed at their nerves; the door closed again, and they were inside.

"It is not very big," said Joanna, her lower lip trembling as she stared about in the wavering torchlight.

"It doesn't need to be," Nathan told her. "We won't be here long."

"There's everything we need," Madeleine said reassuringly, showing her the stuffs on the floor. "Food, wine, water, even games—see? Dice and draughts, and a chessboard—"

"What will we need all that for," she demanded, "if we won't be here long?"

"I think it is exciting," Anne declared stoutly. "Like something in a story. Hiding out from the enemy—"

"We don't *need* to hide. Edward wouldn't hurt us," the small queen insisted.

"He wouldn't need to hurt us," said David. "All he would have to do is take us prisoner. Then I wouldn't be king anymore, and you wouldn't be queen. You like being queen, don't you?"

"Not if it means being cooped up in here I don't."

David drew himself up to his full height. "Well, I intend to be king. So it would be best if you just stopped complaining and decided what you want to play first. That's an order, Joanna." The queen, two years older and half a head taller than he, stared for a moment. Then she flounced down in a chair, crossed her arms over her chest, and spoke one word:

"Chess."

Cat, who'd been hoping Jessie might have preceded them to the secret chamber, watched as Madeleine turned over an hour-glass. "Half past ten, Nathan, wouldn't you guess?" she asked the soldier, who nodded. "Anne, you must help me keep track of the time; you know how forgetful I am."

"I will try, Mama."

"Do you want to be black or white, Joanna?" asked David.

"White."

Madeleine had brought needlework, the bodice of a summer gown for Rene and Eleanor's baby, to be covered in violets, four shades of purple and five of green. Watching her ply the threads, Cat found herself remembering the shirt Rene had worn at Tess's wedding, its collar pricked out with subtle white-on-white 'broidery. Did he still wear the clothes his mother had made for him, even as he betrayed everything she believed?

"Could you please stop tapping your foot that way, Lady Cat?" David asked, his voice apologetic. "It is rather hard to concentrate."

Cat did so immediately, sneaking a glance at the hourglass. Christ, not a single hour gone and already they were fraying one another's nerves! And where the devil were Jessie and Mick?

"Shouldn't they be here by now?" she appealed to Nathan, who had settled down by the door with a knife and block of wood for carving.

"Not if Mick had to go to the battlements to find her. There was an awful crush up there." He sliced a few long, neat curls from the sweet-scented fir block, paused to contemplate its shape, then began whittling again.

Cat wished she'd had the foresight to bring along something to busy her hands. Instead she wandered over to the short stack of books that had been provided. The Bible, of course—*and* a Psalter. Something in Latin by Cicero—she would have to be a good deal more calm before tackling that. A volume on the lives of the saints . . . that should be cheery, she thought, opening it at random to an illustration of St. Sebastian pierced through with arrows. And one of Anne's favorites that she remembered from Langlannoch, full of tales of Arab princesses and princes overcoming huge odds to be united in final bliss. Somehow she hadn't got the heart for such tales right now.

Across the small room, Anne rose from the chair where she'd been watching David trounce Joanna at chess. "The hourglass, Mama."

"Oh!" Madeleine let her needle fall and reached to turn it over. "Thank you, dear."

An hour. Cat felt panic rising in her throat, tightening her bowels. *Oh, Jessie, where are you?* She looked at Nathan, whose woodblock had already taken on the form of a bird, with outstretched wings crudely shaped. "We'll give them one hour more," he said softly. "Then we'll deal with it."

She would not have guessed an hour could pass so slowly. The worst of it was knowing that she must not, could not alarm the children, had to maintain utter calm for their sake. She took up the Psalter and stared, simply stared, at the same page, unable to read. Anything at all might be happening outside this little refuge. If that damned shifty mayor had opened the gates to the city, the English could have overrun the castle already. Jessie might be—but no. She wouldn't even think it.

"Lady Cat," said David. She glanced up in surprise. "Your foot. You are tapping again."

For the final minutes she gave up all pretense and stared at the sand cascading down in a lopsided pile, ears strained for any sound from beyond that stout door. The instant the last grain fell, she was on her feet. Nathan put down his carving and stood as well. "What did ye think to do?"

"Go and find her, of course!"

"But if Mick can't—"

"She is not Mick's sister."

"I could go instead."

Cat shook her head, impatient. "No. Your task is to stay with them."

He nodded. "All right, then. Here." He handed her a torch, and a candle to put into her purse. "Ye have a tinderbox?"

"Aye."

He laid his hand on her arm. "If Robbie should come for us while ye are gone, we will not be able to wait."

"I know that. I would not have gone anyway without Jess."

Nathan lowered his voice to a whisper. "And if the English have come to the castle—"

"Then I take my chances out there. I understand. I won't lead them here."

She would have liked to embrace Madeleine and Anne, but with her nerves so wrenched she feared she might start crying. "Your Majesty," she said. "With your permission, I'll go and look for my sister. She was to have come down here with us."

"Very well," David said airily. "Check, Joanna. And mate."

Nathan unbolted the door, held a torch aloft, and scanned the outer cavern. Then he moved aside for Cat. "Have a care," he told her. She looked to Madeleine and saw her green eyes swimming with tears.

"Hurry back, Cat," said Anne.

"I will." She stepped out into the echoing cave.

Her torch threw shadows high on the walls. Nathan stood in the doorway and watched her for as long as he could, down the first stairs and across the black water—she didn't bother this time to take off her shoes, merely hiked up her skirts. On the far side she paused and looked back. He held his hand out, palm up. She waved in return and mounted the second staircase. Then he was out of sight.

One thing was certain, she thought as her wet slippers slapped on the stones: in this dead silence, if anyone else was afoot in the tunnels, she would hear them from a long way off. It was lucky, too, that the dark had never made her frightened, for the darkness that her torch made a weak stab at lessening was black as the pitch in the barrels Robbie had made ready to spill onto invaders from the parapets. Even so, each time the passageway branched, the new openings yawned like gaping maws, and she had to steel her nerves to slink past.

She made one wrong turn, and had a bad time of it until she realized what she must have done and retraced her steps. The error threw her off-kilter; she began to imagine she heard sounds behind her, and when she stepped on something squishy and slimy, she nearly screamed. *Damn you, Jessie,* she thought, not daring to look down at whatever it had been, *you had better have*

*a bloody good excuse for not having been where you were told
to be!* She hurried on through the first of the hidden doors, pulled
it shut behind her, and paused to catch her breath, her heart wildly
pounding. At least if there was something in back of her now, it
wouldn't get through.

At the second hidden door, the one giving onto the castle
proper, she waited as long as she could bear to, listening, before
cracking it open. The stairway was deserted. She crept down it,
saw that the corridor was also empty, and ran headlong to her
bedchamber door.

It was locked. "Jess!" she cried, and pounded on it. "Jess, are
you in there?" The door flew open, and she fell into her sister's
arms. "Christ in heaven, Jessie, where have you been?"

"Where have I been? Sitting here twiddling my thumbs for
hours and hours; where do you think? Where have *you* been?"

"I was in the king's chambers when Nathan got there, and he
insisted I go below with them. Didn't Mick come for you?" Jessie
shook her head. "I can't understand that. It was just ten o'clock
when Nathan—"

"Ten o'clock! Why, Papa's men had barely started up the hill
by ten o' . . . ." Her voice trailed off as Cat stared at her accusingly.

"You said you were here, Jess!"

"And I was, honestly I was! From half-past ten on I was right
in that chair!"

"And where were you till half-past ten?"

"Up in the towers—and I won't apologize for it, either! I still
think Robbie Stewart acted too quickly in deciding Papa was
losing, and I told him as much when he brought me down here!"

With that admission, Cat could piece together what must have
happened: When Mick came to the room for Jessie, she was up
on the parapets. By the time he'd returned to the parapets, she'd
been back down here. But where had he gone next, and where
was he now?

It didn't matter. Jessie was safe, and Mick could look after
himself. "Come on," she said, grabbing her sister's hand.

Jessie was even more jumpy in the tunnels than Cat had been.
"Stop," she kept whispering, holding fast to Cat's sleeve. "I hear
something. I know I do."

"We can't stop. They'll be waiting for us, worrying for us."

"But I heard something, truly I did!"

After the fifth round of this, Cat turned on her sister. "Listen, you," she said, her voice carrying through the passageway. "If you'd been where you were supposed to be when you were supposed to be, you could have trooped down here with a good strong man to protect you. But since you weren't, you've got only me. And I'm too tired from chasing you about to listen to any more nonsense. Keep walking, and hush!"

"Well!" Jessie huffed in indignation. Then she clamped her mouth shut.

The silence lasted all the way to the pool of black water that ran through the cavern. Jessie stopped at the edge and began to tuck her skirts up into her girdle. "You can ride on my back if you like," Cat offered, regretting that her rebuke had been so sharp.

"I wouldn't dream of it," Jessie snapped, stepping in up to her ankles. Cat had just drawn up her own gown when her sister began to scream.

"Hush, Jess!" she cried, but Jessie went on screaming, pointing down into the water. Cat brought the torch closer and gasped. Close by her sister's foot was a human arm.

"Jessie, you've got to be quiet!" Cat conquered her own horror, remembering Robbie Stewart's warning; this was the place where the sea smell was so strong in the air. "Here, hold this." She thrust the torch at her. "Bite down on your hand—"

"Oh, God, look at *his* hand!"

"Or on your skirts or something. For Christ's sake, Jessie, get a grip on yourself!" Cat pushed her toward the opposite shore, leaned down, and tugged on the arm.

Jessie squealed again. "Lordy, Cat, don't touch it!"

At their backs, the door to the secret chamber had swung open. "Who is out there?" Cat heard Madeleine call.

"It is Jessie and I, Madeleine! Keep the children inside!"

Madeleine promptly shut the door. *Thank God for someone who does what you tell them,* Cat thought, and gave the arm another yank. It was attached to a body, heavy as lead. At least Jessie had stopped screaming; now she was standing halfway up the stair, watching Cat with saucer eyes. "Just leave it be, Cat," she begged.

"I can't leave it be!" Giving one more mighty heave, Cat flopped the body facedown onto the stone. It wore a soldier's clothes.

"Who is it?" Jessie whispered.

With her toe, Cat pushed the head to one side. Mick Jonas gaped at them, bug-eyed, a silken cord knotted round his neck.

"Holy Mary and Jesu." Jessie made the sign of the cross. Cat sank down on the staircase, trying to think, trying to blot out the sight of that ghastly, bloated face.

"Go on up to the chamber," she told Jessie. "Send Nathan down here. Don't tell anyone about this. And, Jess, for the sake of the children, try to be calm."

"But how could he have—who could have—"

"I don't know! Maybe Nathan will." Feeling impossibly weary, Cat rose to her feet again and stood with her sodden skirts spread, to block the corpse from the view of those inside the room.

The door opened to Jessie's cries, but it was Madeleine and not Nathan who descended a few moments later. "What is wrong, Cat?" she asked. "Nathan has already—dear God." She'd glimpsed Mick.

"Nathan has already *what?*"

"He came out here," Madeleine said faintly. "Half an hour ago."

"But why?"

"Anne heard—we all of us heard—some shouting. He thought there must be trouble. You don't think he did this, do you?"

"Of course not!"

"Then who—" They looked at one another, wide-eyed, and then at the stone walls around them, realizing for the first time that the murderer was very likely still about.

"Unless Nathan has chased him off," Cat said in a whisper.

"I don't think that's a chance we dare take. Whoever did this is out to harm David!"

Cat nodded. "I know. Let's get back inside."

"What about—" Madeleine glanced at Mick's body.

"We'll have to leave it for now. Come on."

They hadn't climbed two stairs when they heard it: footsteps somewhere in the tunnels beyond the black water, quick ones, growing louder. "Nathan?" Madeleine mouthed.

Cat reached for her dagger. "Only one way to find out," she said grimly, and then called out boldly, "Who is there?"

The footsteps stopped abruptly; there was only silence. Madeleine gripped Cat's arm; Cat gripped the knife. Then a voice that was reassuringly Scottish called back: "Is that you, Catriona?"

Not relaxing her grasp on the weapon, Cat repeated, "Who is there?"

The footsteps started running. "It is I, Catriona! Malcolm! Malcolm Ross!"

"Thank God," Madeleine whispered, sinking onto the stairs.

They saw the light of his torch first, bobbing against the walls of the passage, and then his shock of white-blond hair. "Nathan sent me," he panted. "He found Jonas's body, and went to tell Robbie. But he didn't like to leave you alone." He sloshed into the water, stopping to stare at the corpse, then quickly crossing himself. "I see you found it, too."

"Who does Nathan think did it?" Madeleine wondered.

"Who knows? But it wasn't the English. They haven't come into the city yet."

"How goes the fighting?" Cat asked him.

"Not well. The last courier to get through reported that our forces were routed." There was pained sympathy in his gray eyes as he gazed down at her. "I have more bad news, I fear, Catriona."

But that look had already told her. "Papa is slain."

His arm slid around her shoulders as he nodded. "Aye. The rider said he fought like a madman. He was fighting for you and your sister."

"He was fighting," Cat said softly, "for the Douglas name."

Madeleine squeezed her hand. "I am so sorry, my dear."

"As am I. But do you know, I am not surprised. He never could have lived with the shame of defeat. Someone would surely have brought up the specter of Uncle James."

Archibald dead. She tried to absorb the fact, feel it, but her heart seemed numbed. Too much had already happened on this doleful day.

Malcolm touched her forehead with his mouth, his arm drawing her closer. "I am here if you need me, Catriona. Until the end of time."

Faithful Malcolm. *Jessie always did tell me,* Cat thought hazily, *that I should be in love with him.* It felt good to have a man to lean on. Suddenly it seemed to Cat that she had been fighting her battles alone for a very long time.

At their backs, the door to the chamber creaked open a crack. "Cat?" Jessie called tentatively. "Are you there, Cat?"

Cat glanced at Madeleine and then Malcolm. "Don't let's tell her yet."

"Whatever you wish," Malcolm murmured.

"I am here, Jess," Cat answered her sister. "Everything is fine."

Jessie's brown head poked around the edge of the door. "Who is that with you—Nathan?" Malcolm raised the torch to show his face. "Oh, Malcolm! I've never been so glad to see a soul in my life!"

"It is good to see you, too, Jessie. How fare their majesties?"

"Well . . . everyone is getting rather curious as to what is going on," Jessie said helplessly, just as King David came to the door and demanded:

"Just what *is* going on?"

Malcolm gently pushed Cat toward the stairs, giving her shoulders a last reassuring squeeze. "Go on, both of you. Get inside and lock the door. Tell them whatever you think you must. But whatever you do, don't open up again until I tell you to! I will wait outside here for Robbie and Nathan."

"Will you be safe?" Madeleine asked worriedly.

He touched the long, bright sword at his belt, his pale eyes glinting with determination. "Safe enough. Don't fret about me."

Cat and Madeleine climbed the stairs to where David waited, tapping his small royal foot. "Something's gone wrong, hasn't it?" he said with a hint of accusation.

Madeleine looked to Cat, who closed the door behind her and drew down the bolt. "Aye. Something has."

"What sort of something?" asked Joanna.

The children were frightened; it showed plainly on their faces. The truth, or a lie? Cat considered. Young they might be, but they were king and queen of Scotland—and Annie was so brave. "Someone hurt Mick Jonas," she told them. "So Nathan went to fetch help. Malcolm Ross is standing guard outside until he or Robbie comes back."

"Hurt him how?" asked David.

"Killed him," Cat said, after a pause.

David grasped his sword. "I am going out there."

"You mustn't, Your Majesty!" cried Anne. "Don't you see? Whoever killed Mick was trying to get to you! If you put yourself in danger, then Mick's death was in vain."

"I want to help Malcolm!" the king insisted. "How do you think it makes me feel that men are out there dying for my sake, while I sit on my fanny with a bunch of girls?"

"But if you leave," said Madeleine, "who will look after us? You are our last line of defense." And, Cat could have sworn, she batted her black lashes at the young king.

David paused. "I hadn't thought of that."

"Well, you had better," said his queen, "for if you leave, I swear, I shall be too terrified to live!"

Slowly David resheathed his sword. "Oh, all right. But what are we to do while we wait? I'm sick and tired of games."

"Do you suppose we might eat?" Jessie said shyly. "Isn't anyone else hungry?"

"I am," Annie announced. "I'm *starving*. What have they got in here?"

Cat smiled gratefully at her sister. She doubted Jessie had any more appetite than she herself did after having seen Mick Jonas, but food would calm the children down. And rummaging through the provisions gave them something to occupy themselves. "All this potted meat," Joanna was muttering. "You would think we would be here for a month!"

King David had come upon a glass jar of lemon drops and horehound ropes and licorice pastilles. "Look! Sweets!" he cried, digging in delightedly.

Exhaustion was stealing through Cat. She curled up on a cush-

ion in a corner, looking for the hourglass. In the muddle, no one
had remembered to turn it; it sat with the sands all run through.
Perhaps we are better off not knowing, she pondered, *how slow
the time creeps by.*

Archibald was dead. The knowledge lay like a stone at the
center of her being, weighting all her feelings and thoughts. She
closed her eyes and tried to imagine it: No more Papa. Impossible
to conceive. *I hope,* she thought, *he died at the start of the battle,
before the English rout began.*

And what would happen now to the house of Douglas? With
de Baliol, there would be English once again in Douglasdale.
Who would chase them away? She had a sudden strong intuition
of an era passing, a great river flowing onward, never to return
to the same point again.

"See here, Joanna!" David crowed. He had come upon some
almond cakes.

Cat closed her eyes. She felt as though they'd been open for
a hundred years. The solace of the darkness seemed soothing,
suitable for mourning. She would have to tell Jessie the truth
soon. But not now. Not right away. There was time just to sit by
herself in the darkness for a little while.

Twenty-nine

Cat thought for one wild moment when she wakened that she'd gone blind; opening her eyes made not one whit of difference between the bleak blackness outside and that within. Then she heard out of the silence around her the soft sounds of sleepy breathing, and realized what must have happened: the torches had burned out. Christ, first the hourglass unturned, and now this! A fine lot of guardians she and Madeleine and Jessie were turning out to be.

Her tinderbox was in her sleeve; she found it, struck a spark, blew the flame to brightness, and reignited one of the wax-soaked cattails hanging on the wall, tiptoeing among her companions. David and Joanna and Anne were curled up all together, like kittens in a heap. Madeleine, looking very pale, was seated at the table, her head on her arms. Jessie was nearest the door; Cat suspected it was she who'd fallen asleep on watch.

Well, no harm had come of it, and God knows they all needed rest. Was it day or night outside these thick walls? she wondered. How long now had they been there? The stillness in the chamber was a little frightening. *It is like a tomb,* Cat thought, and then wished she hadn't, for that made her remember her father, and then poor Mick Jonas, with his eyes, once so bright and alive, popping out of his head.

It would be nice if someone else awakened, she thought, suddenly feeling lonely. She'd left the book of the lives of the saints on the table; she tried now to read it, but the light from the torch was too little, and she did not want to risk a candle with the rest asleep.

Being alone with her thoughts, though, was uncomfortable; they kept turning to Archibald, to what the end might have been like for him. Think of happy things, she told herself, watching the shadow from the torch flicker against the far wall. But the image that rose up in her mind at that was of Rene as he'd looked arching over her on the banks of the Tay, his eyes wild with desire, before Pauly's ball ran into the bushes and she'd sent him away. Those had been happy times—before all his betrayals, before the murder of Moray and the lies about Eleanor. He—

Cat jerked up her head at a sudden soft but unmistakable chink of stone rubbing stone.

Her gaze flew to the door. It was still bolted; she could see no movement. Where, then—

The sound came again, a little louder, and the flame on the torch dipped and swayed in a gust of wind. Where was it coming from? She let her eyes sweep over the walls of the chamber even as she reached for the dagger in her girdle. Was there another entrance to this place?

Scrape. Scrape. Scrape. Suddenly she pinpointed the sound, staring upward. A section of stone was sliding back right over her head.

She shrank against the wall, willing her skirts not to rustle. Her hand on the dagger was shaking; she rewrapped her fingers on the hilt, finding a better grip. Scrape. Scrape. The hole in the ceiling inched wider. Cat's heart was beating like a hammer. Should she call out, challenge whoever was up there? It might be Robbie—but if it was Robbie, why hadn't he come through the door? More likely it was Mick Jonas's murderer. If she cried out, she might frighten him away.

Or she might give away for certain that someone was down here. Women and children . . . not much to stop a murderer. If she summoned Malcolm—but to do that, she would have to cross the room and open the door. By the time she did so, he'd be on her. *God help me,* she thought, panic thick in her throat. *I don't know what to do. . . .*

Scrape. Scrape. Blackness loomed beyond the growing gap in the stones, big enough now for a body to squeeze through. The scraping stopped. There was silence, as though whoever was up there was staring down. Cat pressed flat to the rock at her back. Could he see her? She could see nothing.

Then she saw a muddy black leather boot appear in the hole, followed by its mate. Toe and then heel, then shaft, then the patched knee of brown breeches . . . he was as tall as Robbie, whoever it was; his legs seemed to go on forever. Even so, there would be a moment when he had to drop from the ceiling to the floor. And his back was to her. Cat braced against the rock, readying herself.

He let himself go.

Cat lunged at him.

The knife hit just between his shoulder blades—a perfect strike, or so it would have been if the tip hadn't skittered off to the side with a *clink*. He was wearing mail beneath his shirt, Cat realized, and cried, "Damn!" as he whirled to face her. Eyes blue as mountain gentians in the faint torchlight, black hair tumbled over his forehead, mouth wide and sensual, but hard, unforgiving . . .

Rene came at her, grabbing for the dagger. She slashed out again, and this time struck where he was unprotected, in the meat of his forearm. Blood spurted from the wound she'd made. "Christ," he muttered, and wrenched the blade away with such force that she fell to her knees.

The sounds of the scuffle had wakened the king; he pushed himself up from the floor, bleary, blinking, rousing Anne and Joanna in the process. "What is—"

"If anyone speaks one more word," Rene said very softly, "I will slit her throat. Do you understand?" He had Cat pulled tight against him, the knife tickling her breastbone.

"Rain?" said Anne, looking very small and pale as she sat up in the pile of blankets. "Is that you, Rain?"

"Hush, Annie," he told her. But her voice had wakened Madeleine, who raised her head from the table, saw her son with the knife to Cat's throat, and instinctively moved backward toward her daughter.

"Hallo, Mother." Rene's voice was a whisper. Madeleine said nothing, just folded Anne against her side with one arm and the

queen with the other. "I want you all to listen to me, very carefully. I am not going to hurt anyone."

"Then why," Cat began, and he gripped her more tightly, his
bloodied arm across her throat so that she could not speak.

"Because I need you to listen to me. You are all in great danger."

Cat started to laugh, the sound muffled by his sleeve. "Not
from me," he went on quickly. "From the madman out there."
He jerked his head toward the door.

"Malcolm?" his mother said in disbelief. "But . . . Nathan
sent him . . ."

"Nathan is lying in the tunnels with a silk cord around his
neck," Rene said very distinctly. "Whatever else that bastard
Ross told you about why he is here is a lie."

His mother stared at him. "But then—why is he here?"

"For the same reason he poisoned the earl of Moray. Because
he is in love with Cat."

She moved in his grasp, letting out a garbled protest. He held
her tighter. "It is true, Cat. It has to be. I *know* no one in de
Baliol's camp could have done it. And someone took my belt
from the yards that night after Rawley hurled it from the window.
I tried to retrieve it before I went to Moray. It was already gone.
Ask your sisters who left the picnicking before then. I'll wager
ten thousand pounds it was Malcolm Ross."

Anne spoke up then. "If you are not going to hurt any of us,
why are you holding that knife to Cat?"

"Because if I know Mistress Douglas, she has likely got another weapon hidden on her somewhere. And she would not hesi-
tate to use it on me—even in my back. Am I right, Cat?" Still
grasping her roughly, he ran his hand over her bodice, down
against her skirts to her slippers—"There." He raised the hem
of her gown and yanked away the knife she had strapped in a
sheath at her calf.

"Cat wouldn't hurt you," Anne protested. "She loves you."

"Aye—loves me enough to seduce and then to betray me."

"Rene," his mother cautioned, "the children . . ."

"It is her fault the children are here." Cat felt his breath against
the nape of her neck, angry and hot. "You just couldn't do as I

asked, Cat, could you? You could not trust me. You had to send your father after me, and bring all this down on our heads."

King David looked dazed. "I don't understand what is happening," he said plaintively. "Whose side is this man on?"

They had all of them forgotten about Jessie, sleeping close to the door. She sprang up now, threw the bolt back, hauled at the iron handle, and screamed into the dark cave: "Malcolm! Help!"

"Damn you!" Rene pushed Cat aside and lunged for her, but he was too late; Malcolm's burly shoulder shoved the door wide open, and he leaped inside, sword already drawn.

"Kill him!" Jessie screeched, finger lowered at Rene. "Kill the traitor!"

"It will be my pleasure," Malcolm told her, torchlight gleaming on his blade. "What a surprise, Faurer, to find you here. But a welcome one. I'll finish the job of killing you that Stewart botched at Perth."

"I'll gladly fight you, Ross," Rene said evenly, reaching for his own sword. "But not in here." He gestured toward the doorway. "Out there."

"Why? So you can hie your coward's tail out into the maze, like the rat you are?" He kept coming on.

"Mother." Rene's voice was sharp as he kicked Cat's daggers toward her across the floor. "Have an eye to the king. Ross has killed three men already for Cat that I know of. He could try anything."

Malcolm's pale eyes were narrowed. "Lady Madeleine. If you would save the king *and* Scotland, help me put a blade through your son's black heart."

Cat looked at Madeleine. She was clutching the knives, her lovely face twisted with doubt. "Surely you don't believe Rene!" Cat cried out. "What he said about Malcolm murdering Moray— why, that's absurd!"

"Is it, Cat?" Rene's words rang from the rocks. "He knew that you would think I'd done it. He thought it would turn you against me once and for all."

"What in God's name are you blathering about, Faurer?" Malcolm demanded. And he rushed at Rene with his sword.

Joanna screamed, burying her face against David's shoulder.

Jessie was still by the doorway; as Malcolm's blade crashed against Rene's with a deafening clang, she edged toward the back of the chamber, where the others were huddled. There was a bright gleam of pride in her eye. "Don't worry, Cat," she declared. "Malcolm will whip him."

"Oh, Jessie," Anne said tearfully, "you've made a dreadful mistake! If Rain says milord Ross is dangerous—"

"Hush, Annie," Cat said sharply. "You are simply too young to understand some things."

Anne looked at her with wounded green eyes. Rene had beaten off Malcolm's thrust and countered with a barrage of blows that backed his opponent nearly to the doorway. "Never mind, Annie," he called to his sister, not turning. "It is good to know that *someone* still believes in me."

Furious at him for playing so shamelessly on Anne's blind trust, Cat reached out to Madeleine for the daggers. "If you won't help Malcolm, I will."

But Madeleine would not relinquish the weapons. "They are to defend the king."

"Defend him against whom?" Cat cried. "We know who is the enemy!"

Madeleine's grip on the knives was unbudging. "Are you sure?"

Frustrated, Cat turned back to the fighting. Rene had told the truth about one thing: the chamber was too small for this battle. Neither man could swing freely, closed in as they were by the piles of stores, by the table and chairs. Blood was still oozing out of the cut she'd made in Rene's forearm. It was his sword hand that was hurt, she saw, and was glad she'd helped Malcolm in that small way.

"Cat!" Jessie hissed. Cat glanced at her sister and saw her beckoning at the wine casks ranged against the wall. She made a little pushing motion with both hands, and Cat understood: they could use them to trip Rene. As she nodded and edged toward her sister, Madeleine moved to stop her. Cat shook her off.

"You do what you must," she told the older woman, "and so shall I."

Rene started to turn to see where she was going, but a vicious flurry of blows demanded his attention. Cat joined Jessie by the casks, and together they crouched there, waiting their moment. As Malcolm drove Rene backward toward them, Jessie cried, "Now!" They shoved at one small barrel, sending it careening over the stone floor straight at Rene's legs. Only the awful racket it made coming saved him, making him leap aside.

"Dammit, Cat!" he shouted, just barely evading Malcolm's sword. "Listen to me! Use your head! It didn't work when he murdered Moray, did it? You still came to me at Inverkeithing. So he tried something else. I don't know what it was, but you do. Something that made you hate me—did he tell your father I was at Edinburgh when Moray died? Was that it, Cat?"

"Come on, Cat," Jessie urged, maneuvering another barrel into position. But Cat was frozen still, remembering that awful meeting with Archibald, when he'd shown her the belt and the parchment that had come with it. Was it possible Malcolm had been behind that trick? She looked at him, trying to imagine his motivation. Rene had said it was because he loved her. But he'd never been forward with her, had hardly even touched her . . .

"For God's sake, don't listen to him, Cat!" Jessie grabbed her and shook her. "Hasn't he done enough to you already? Don't fall for him again!"

Malcolm was dancing impatiently back and forth, trying to reach Rene through a palisade of chairs. "Come on, Faurer," he taunted as his opponent evaded him by leaping onto and across the table. "Stand and fight like a man." And he made a lunge that just barely missed nicking Jessie.

"A man doesn't endanger innocent women and children," Rene countered grimly. "Come out into the cavern." He himself was moving that way.

"Push him out, Malcolm," Jessie proposed, "and I'll slam shut the door!"

"I'll not leave any of you alone in here with him," Rene vowed, edging backward, parrying another blow. "I tell you, he's a lunatic. That's why the Grand Master would not let you join the brothers, isn't it, Ross? Because he knew you were mad. Because he did not trust you—"

Malcolm made an animal sound of outrage, low in his throat,

and rushed at him. "Because he saw into your black soul," Rene finished, raising up his sword. As Malcolm charged past Cat, she had a glimpse of his face, and it shook her to the depths of her being. He *did* look mad; his eyes had gone so pale they seemed white, and his mouth was twisted into a horrible rictus of fury and hate. "Come on, boy," Rene said softly, the edge of his blade teasing Malcolm onward. "Come and get me."

Malcolm sprang. Madeleine let out a little cry of fear, but Rene sidestepped him adeptly, turning to give him a shove so that his momentum took him straight out the door.

Quicker than flame, Rene followed. From inside the chamber, all one could hear was the chaos of scuffling, hard breathing, and then the sickening thud and slide of a body falling down stone stairs. "Rain!" Anne cried, running for the doorway.

"Anne, come here!" Madeleine called frantically. But Anne was already backing away. Malcolm loomed up in the torchlight, his pale gaze trained straight on Cat. There was blood on his doublet, blood on his sleeve.

"You won't have to worry about him anymore, my dear heart," he said tenderly. He smiled at her, a crooked smile, gentle and winning, and in that moment Cat knew that what Rene had said was true.

"My God," she whispered as he took a step toward her. "You did kill Moray."

His smile broadened. "Catriona, I would do anything for you."

"Malcolm?" Jessie's voice was hesitant, uncertain. "Malcolm, you didn't . . ."

Out of the darkened doorway, two hands suddenly reached to grasp Malcolm's ankles and haul him away.

"Rain!" Anne cried again, but this time in joy.

"Give me the daggers, Madeleine, please," Cat said, her voice newly steady. Madeleine handed them over without a word.

"Cat. Don't," Jessie pleaded. "You'll be hurt. And you cannot be certain—"

"I am certain," said Cat, "that I should have stopped listening to my family a long time ago."

She paused in the doorway. By accident or design, Malcolm's torch had gone out, and the light from the chamber did little to dispel the thick blackness. They were in the water at the foot of the stairway; she could hear their boots sloshing. The clangor of their swords reverberated crazily from the stone walls. And just where Robbie warned us to be quiet, too, Cat thought regretfully. Well, there was nothing to be done for that now.

The king had come to stand at her shoulder. "What are you going to do?" he asked hesitantly.

"Kill Malcolm Ross," she whispered, "if I get a chance to. Get back with the others."

"You've got two knives there. Give me one."

She looked away from the shadowy duelists, into his small, proud face. "What will you use it for if I do?"

"Just what you said."

Cat passed it to him, hilt first, and they crouched together at the top of the stairs.

"Die, you bastard," they heard Malcolm mutter, and then Rene's voice:

"Not unless I take you with me." But Cat heard the strained undercurrent to the words, and knew he was wounded more than just the stab she'd given to his forearm. Where? How badly? Did Malcolm realize it, too?

Their blades snicked and sang, water splashing in the darkness. "You are slowing down, Faurer," Malcolm declared with satisfaction. "Where did I get you? Was it the knee?"

"You haven't touched me, lunatic."

"Don't call me that." A furious burst of fighting, followed by a little space as the two men drew apart, drew breath. Someone else had come to stand behind Cat.

"Here," said Annie. She had brought a torch, held it aloft. "Does this help?"

Thin light shimmered down on the combatants. Cat gasped as she saw the sword gash running down Rene's cheek. "So, it was your face." Malcolm sounded delighted. "Too bad, pretty boy. But I don't suppose it will matter anyway when you're dead."

It was worse to be able to see, but Cat could not turn away. Rene was faltering badly, more than could be accounted for by the face slash; he could barely meet Malcolm's blows. He must be wounded someplace else, Cat thought, someplace that did not show. He was going to lose this fight.

King David had evidently come to the same conclusion. "I am going down there," he announced.

"Wait." Cat put her hand on his sleeve. "Malcolm!" she called. The name bounded from stone to stone to stone. Both men paused, staring up at her as she stood framed in the halo of light from the doorway. She could hear the waves around their feet slowly lap in circles against the rocks. "I love you, Malcolm Ross!" she sang out. Their faces, like ghostly white flowers opening out of the darkness, bore twin looks of stunned disbelief.

Then Malcolm started to smile at her. "Catriona," he whispered, and made it a saint's name, a prayer. It was then that Rene ran him through, from side to side, just below the hinge of his mail.

"Holy Jesu," the king whispered as Malcolm fell to his knees in the water, his body twitching and jerking. Rene stood over him with his head bowed, then pulled his sword free and wiped it clean on his soaked breeches leg.

"I could have taken him without your help, Cat," he said, reproach in his voice. Then he collapsed, falling atop Malcolm's body in a cascade of waves.

"Sure you could have," Cat muttered as, followed by Annie and David, she hurried down the stairs to him before he drowned.

Thirty

"Over here," said Madeleine, helping to half drag, half carry her son to the blanket she'd laid on the stone floor. It had taken all of them together to haul him up the stairs. "Cat, help me get his mail off him." Madeleine, unbuttoning his shirt, stopped dead. "My God."

"What is it, Mama?" Anne crowded close to see.

"He is wearing your father's armor." Cat, leaning in, saw it was true; she recognized the finely made silver-gilt links as part of the equipage she had brought to Langlannoch so long ago. "I did not even know he had it." Then Madeleine shook herself from her thoughts. "Here, unfasten the ties. . . ." As the front-piece fell away, she gasped.

"And wounded in the same place as Papa." Anne raised frightened eyes from the gash in her brother's chest, made through one of the thin ribboned seams that let the mail move more freely. "Will he die, Mama?"

"I hope not." Madeleine probed the ugly tear with her fingertips. "But this is not a new wound; the blood here is dried." She reached into her purse for herbs, already crushing them in her fist. "Bring wine and water, Annie, quick as you can." Anne hurried to fetch her a bowl of each.

"Should I close the door or leave it open?" David wanted to know.

"Open, I think," Madeleine decided, after seeing that Cat was too busy pulling Rene's bloodied shirtsleeve from his arm to answer. "But pray you keep good watch, Your Majesty."

"I will. Anyone who isn't Robbie Stewart will taste my knife before he makes it upstairs."

Madeleine was daubing Rene's chest with a cloth. "It isn't so deep as I feared," she pronounced of the wound. "Still, he has lost much blood. Cat, how is that arm?"

"I did less damage than I thought. But as you say, the bleeding . . ." It felt so strange to be touching him again.

"Anne, give him just a bit of wine," her mother ordered. "Make sure you prop up his head."

The strong Rhenish poured down his throat made him choke and sputter. "Too much, Annie!" Madeleine cautioned. But Rene's hand stopped his sister as she withdrew the cup.

"Not . . . enough," he said hoarsely. "Hallo, crumpet."

"Oh, Rain!" Anne was crying. "I was so afraid you were going to die!"

"Nay, not I; I am tough as nails." His blue eyes found Cat as she knelt beside him. "You gave me . . . a bad moment there. I was afraid you meant it . . . about Malcolm."

"Perhaps I did." Cat's heart felt as raw as his wounds. In all the agonizing excitement of the fight, she had almost forgotten the unbreachable barrier that stood between them.

"And who would blame her if she did?" Madeleine demanded, cleansing Rene's wound vigorously.

"Dammit, Mother, that hurts!"

"Good! I am glad! When exactly did you intend to tell her—not to mention me—about your wife and child?"

"About my what? Mother, stop it!"

"I don't know why I am bothering to save you." Madeleine punctuated each word with another brusque push of her dampened cloth. "I am so ashamed of you! To have to learn of your marriage from that—that woman! I had to grit my teeth with every stitch I made embroidering your linens."

"Embroidering my—ouch!" He caught her wrists. "What in God's name are you talking about? What woman?"

"Your wife!" she nearly spat at him. "The mother of your child!"

Rene blinked in the torchlight. "Am I delirious? Have I got a fever?"

"Not yet," Cat told him, "but there's always hope."

"I really don't understand you, Rain," his sister told him, shaking her head. "Why in the world would you want to marry Eleanor de Baliol when you could have had Cat?"

"Marry Eleanor?" He stared at Anne. "Who says I married Eleanor?"

"Oh, honestly, Rene," Madeleine said in exasperation. "She herself wrote me a letter with the news. And she told Cat about the baby all the way back in August, at Inverkeithing."

He turned his blue gaze on Cat. "You told me you had not seen her at Inverkeithing."

"Aye, well, you told me you were not married to her. So we both lied."

"No! I told the truth." His puzzled brow cleared. "But that was why you set that trap for me at Douglasdale. 'The fact that I hold your life in my hands, Rene. I will wake you in an hour, Rene, and see you safe on your way'—aye, with half a score of Archibald's men following behind me." His voice was rising, bitter. "And I never even once looked back, Cat—because I trusted you. Because I loved you so."

"Eleanor told me you were married to her!"

"You asked me if I was. I said no. Yet you believed her, not me."

"She'd written to your mother with the news." Cat heard the hitch of uncertainty in her own voice. "And Angus knew all about it."

"Angus! Christ! Angus told you I was wed to her?" Cat nodded. "Oh, Angus, you hard-hearted bastard!" He began to laugh. "When was that?"

"Just before I sent you the letter with the hostage."

"What is so amusing?" Madeleine demanded of her son.

"He must have suspected Cat might try to trick me as she did, to lead her father to de Baliol. You know how adamant he was that Edward of England not be brought to the battle, Mother, for David's sake."

"I know," Madeleine said slowly. "But how do you know?"

For answer he shifted on the floor, reaching under his doublet, and drew something out—a folded bit of hide. A sheepskin.

Madeleine's green eyes grew wide, and a look passed between mother and son.

"You," she whispered, and then said it again, in wonder: "You?" He nodded. "Oh, Rene! When?"

"Ask Cat. I told her all about it, didn't I, Cat, on the night I came to Douglasdale? But you sent your father after me anyway."

"Why would Eleanor lie about a thing like that?" Cat demanded hotly.

"I bloody well don't know. I only know that I trusted you—and you betrayed me."

Madeleine had finished bandaging his chest and thigh; now she beckoned to Anne and Joanna, who were watching this argument, wide-eyed. "Come away, children. Over here," she said sharply. They didn't move. "Anne! Joanna! Come and have something to eat. Let them be." Reluctantly the two girls moved toward the table. "And what are you grinning about, little miss?" her mother asked Anne suspiciously.

Anne did indeed look gleeful. "Sometimes you and Papa used to fight this way," she whispered. Madeleine swallowed a laugh.

As for Cat, she was verging on tears. "I was in an impossible position, Rain! Someone—it had to be Malcolm—sent your belt and a note to Papa, telling him you were with me that night in Edinburgh. Papa said I wasn't his daughter. He told me to get out of his house. And Eleanor had said . . . I hadn't any cause to doubt her, not with the letter to your mother, and Angus saying the same."

Rene had pushed himself up to sit, wincing only a little with the bandaging. "I risked my bloody life to come to you at Douglasdale. And then I told you things . . . confided matters to you that I had never shared with another living soul."

"I had to prove myself to my father," Cat tried to explain, "to show him I was truly a Douglas."

Rene stood, so as better to roar down at her: "I am sick to death of that damned bloody name!"

"And I am sick to death of your lies! Who are you, Rene Faurer?" She stood, too, squared off against him, her hair a tangled red-gold mane as she craned her head back to see him. "What is it exactly that you think is worth fighting for?"

"I told you once." His voice faltered, just a little. "You, in my lap of a cold winter's night, before a blazing fire."

"I don't know, Cat." That was Jessie, silent all this time. "I think he means it."

"Of course I bloody mean it!" He glared at Jessie. "And if it weren't for you and Tess and Janet, I'd have had it a long time ago!"

"Don't you *ever* shout at my sister!" Cat said, so haughtily that Rene began to laugh.

"Christ," he said, "I'd have done better to fall in love with a tiger than a Douglas girl!"

Cat's back went stiff in a very feline manner. "You," she started to say, but he cut her off with a kiss, bending her backward over his arm, his mouth covering hers, tasting, delighting, exploring. The girls went wide-eyed again, and even Jessie let out a breathless, "My!"

Anne began to dance a little dance. "If you aren't married to Eleanor, Rain, does that mean you and Cat will be wed?"

Her brother ended the kiss with reluctance, raising Cat to her feet again. "You should have to ask Cat that."

She looked into his blue eyes, saw that they were afire. "Are you proposing marriage to me?"

"No, I am asking you to go fishing. Of course I am, Cat!" Then he scowled. "But perhaps you think such a proposal isn't fine enough for a Douglas girl. Perhaps you would like me to get down on one knee—" He proceeded to do so, awkward with his bandages and bad leg.

"Rain," she said, "stop it."

"And take your hand and kiss it—"

"You are mocking at me. . . ."

"And say, 'Catriona'—what the devil are your other names?"

"You had better stop!"

"Edith," Jessie helpfully supplied, "and Agnes."

"Edith Agnes?" Anne squealed.

"I hate you, Jessie," Cat declared.

"Catriona Edith Agnes Douglas," Rene repeated, with only a hint of a grin, "will you do me the very great honor of marrying me?"

She looked down at him. "I really cannot think of one good reason why I should—"

"Oh, Cat!" Anne cried in dismay.

"—besides the fact that I love you. I always have loved you."

"Does that mean yes?" he asked. She hesitated, thinking of her father. But Archibald was dead.

She nodded.

"It's about bloody time," he growled, and kissed her again, a kiss like a promise, searing and tender.

"Rene, the children," his mother chided, but she was smiling.

"Tell the children to go play." He pulled Cat into his arms. "My love. My passion."

King David cleared his throat in the doorway. "Someone is coming."

"Christ!" Rene let Cat go abruptly, reaching for his sword. "Who?"

"Robbie Stewart."

They heard Robbie's bootheels on the stairs, and then his voice: "Yer Majesty!" He bowed and came past David, eyes sweeping the chamber, stopping when they saw Rene and going very wide. "Jesus," he whispered, and slowly raised his hand to make a sign across his chest, palm downward. Rene repeated the gesture, and Robbie ran to embrace him, clapping his back so hard that Rene gasped and clutched his ribs. "Jesus!" Robbie said again, this time with stunned joy. "I scarcely dared hope to see ye again after de Baliol put that price on yer head!"

"What?" Madeleine cried, but Robbie had rushed on:

"I saw Malcolm Ross's body outside. What has gone on here?"

"It was so amazing, Robbie!" David told him breathlessly. "Malcolm had killed Mick, but he told us he hadn't, and then Nathan went out to find Mick, and this fellow dropped from the ceiling and Cat tried to stab him, and there was a sword fight, and Malcolm said he killed my uncle Moray, and then this man killed him!" His dark eyes were bright with excitement. "And then he asked Cat to marry him, and she said yes!"

"Congratulations," Robbie told Rene, and cocked his head at

Cat. "Perhaps ye understand now why I made ye the answer I did the other night."

Cat flushed red, recalling her bold proposition to him. "What, pray tell, was the question?" Rene demanded, raising an eyebrow at her.

Robbie grinned. "It doesn't matter now." Then he turned grave. "Nathan never made it to me on the ramparts."

"No. I found him dead in the tunnels." Rene's voice, too, was grim. "Ross must have been good, to get close enough to kill them."

"He *was* good. I had a hard time myself crediting what ye told me about him killing Moray. But the Master never was fooled by him, thank the Lord." He turned to Madeleine, saw the sheepskin she was holding. "Good to have yer son home again?"

"Better to know he never left us," she said, eyes aglow. "But what is this, Rene, about de Baliol putting a bounty on you?"

"That's how far I was from married to his niece," he told her. "I only barely escaped from Bamburgh last March after one of my contacts told me de Baliol had secretly put the word out he was willing to pay five hundred pounds for my head." He looked down at Cat. "I thought perhaps you'd informed him I was responsible for leading your father to him."

"I might have," she admitted, "had I thought of it."

"So where have you been these past months?" Robbie asked curiously.

"With Northumberland's men. Even if de Baliol had found me out, I figured I might keep tabs on the English. Angus knew—but you won't have heard from him since you are under siege. I told them I was a disinherited Campbell. I was scared to death, Cat, you'd call me by name when you saw me out there on the plain."

"You ought to have stayed in the tent!" Jessie exclaimed.

"I couldn't bear to. I had to see your sister again."

"Even if it meant your death." Jessie sighed happily. "It is so romantic! I never dreamed you were that sort of man."

Madeleine had been counting on her fingers. "March—that is when Cat thought Eleanor's baby was due. Why in the world

would she write me she was married to you, and tell Cat she was
having your baby—"

"And then let her uncle try to hunt me down?" Rene shrugged.
"I can't hazard a guess. De Baliol shipped her back to France
after Dupplin Moor. I'd heard no inkling of any of this."

"Perhaps she was lying—"

"I *know* she was lying!" Rene protested.

"About being with child," his mother finished. "Could she
have been, Cat?"

Cat clenched her eyes shut, summoning up every detail of the
encounter on the docks that she had fought so hard to forget. "I
don't think so," she said slowly. "You saw her at the camp,
though, Rene. What do you think?"

"I spent the day avoiding her. We'd scarcely spoken after she
made such a scene when I broke off our betrothal. That's why I
can't fathom—" He shook his head, perplexed. "Christ, she's
slept with half the officers in the camps. Why in God's name
would she want to pin the child on me?"

"If her uncle knew her reputation, perhaps that's why he
wanted you killed," Robbie suggested. "A dead man can't dispute
paternity. And better a widowed niece than a disgraced one, if
you hope to be king." He frowned. "Speaking of that, how did
you fare on the field today?"

"You were at the battle?" David asked eagerly. "Is there any
good news?"

"If there were," Rene told him gently, "I would not be here.
The day's gone to Edward of England. Their numbers were too
strong."

Cat looked at him. "Malcolm told me my father—" Then her
green eyes gilded with hope. "But perhaps he lied!"

"If he told you your father is dead, love, then he spake true."

"No," Jessie whispered. "Oh, no! Poor Papa!" She turned on
Cat with tearful accusation. "You knew and did not tell me?"

"I needed you to be strong, Jess, for the others." Cat went and
hugged her closely. "You *were* strong. Don't fail me now."

"Angus and I were with him when he died," Rene told them.
"He nearly fell off his horse to see me turn my ax against de
Baliol's men. He fought . . . as you'd expect from a Douglas.

Hand to hand, no one could have stopped him. But an arrow found its mark."

"Was it quick?" Cat whispered.

He nodded. "Very quick. He had time, though, to ask me to tell all of you that he loves you. And to send Cat this." He reached for his tattered shirt and pulled something from a leather purse sewn into the side. A bit of cloth, Cat saw—a corner torn from the Douglas banner; it still bore one star. Something was scrawled across it in mud, dipped with a finger.

"What . . ." Jessie squinted, trying to read the hasty letters.

Cat was smiling through her tears. BLESSING, it said. "But why didn't you give me this before?" she asked Rene.

"Because I needed you to marry me because you love me," he said fiercely. "Not because the laird of Douglas bade you to."

Cat clutched the cloth to her heart. Jessie looked at Rene with fearful blue eyes. "While you were on the field . . . do you know the man I am betrothed to—Diarmot MacDugall? Did you see him? Please God, is he alive?"

"He was with your father," he said soothingly. "I left him hale and well, and full of worry for you. But I promised him Robbie and I would see to your safety." Rene grinned a little. "He said that if I didn't, he would cut the arms and legs off me and feed me to his father's dogs. A mite bloodthirsty, isn't he, for such a soft-spoken man?"

"He did not mean it." Jessie's pretty face was flooded with relief. Then it turned thoughtful. "Do you remember, Catkin, a long time ago, at Tess's wedding, when Papa said it would be the happiest day of his life when he saw the four of us well wed? If he knew Diarmot lived, and if he gave you and Rene his blessing . . ."

"Then he got his wish," Cat said softly, "on the day he died." Rene took her hand in his, and she leaned against him, her mourning for Archibald tempered by piercing joy.

"I am sorry about your father, Lady Cat, Lady Jessie," King David told them. "His death is a grave loss to Scotland." Then he turned to Robbie. "But how are we going to get out of here?"

"We need to wait for darkness—and for Rurik's ship. He's to

be in the harbor mouth, just by the claw point, every night at midnight until we come."

Annie glanced up from the chessboard where she was setting up the pieces. "Not Uncle Rurik!"

"I wouldn't expect any other," her brother said. "Not really an uncle," he explained to Cat, who'd raised an eyebrow in question. "An old friend of my father's. He is a corsair."

"A pirate!" David's dark eyes lit up. "We are going on a pirate ship! Did you hear, Joanna?" Joanna looked horrified.

"The sun was already down when I left the ramparts," Robbie told them. "I'd guess we have another hour, perhaps two, before the rendezvous."

"How will we get onto the ship?" David wondered.

"There's a skiff hidden down by the cliffs! I am glad Rene is here to sail it out to meet Rurik." The two men exchanged glances, and Cat, watching, caught a glimpse of just how risky an undertaking this was likely to be. She remembered the English warships that had dotted the harbor. Would they still be there? Rene would be running a gauntlet, with death on either side. . . .

Jessie had sidled close to Rene. "I just wanted to say—I was wrong about you, very wrong, and I'm sorry."

"You can hardly be blamed for thinking me a villain when that was the role I was playing." He bent down and kissed her cheek. "Your sister here, though—she ought to have known better."

"I don't know how she kept faith in you as long as she did, the way all of us hounded her about you. And Papa"—she shook her head—"Some of the things Papa called you were really quite dreadful."

"He was only trying to protect his daughter." His arm tightened on Cat's waist. "I imagine when we have a daughter, I will be the same."

Madeleine had seen the children settled around the chessboard with ale and biscuits and cheese; she smiled at her son. "I was so glad today to see you wearing your father's armor. He would have been so proud of you for all you have done."

A familiar stiffness tightened Rene's features. "I had need of mail, Mother, and this fit me. Pray don't make more of it than that."

Cat tilted her chin to see him, astonished. "Don't tell me after all this that you still bear him grudges!"

"You make it sound like a schoolboy feud," he said tautly.

She raised a brow again. "Well?"

He turned away from her. "I have caused enough pain to my family already. I'll not compound it by speaking of this."

"But he was your family, too," Madeleine told him softly, sadly. "Oh, Rene, why must you hate him?"

"For the wrong he did to you and Annie."

"What wrong?"

He waved a hand at her. "This is not the time, Mother, nor the—"

"Don't you dismiss me, damn you!" Cat stared; Madeleine was dug in for a fight, her fists balled. "After all that you have put me through these past three years, don't you *dare* dismiss me! What wrong did he do me?"

He faced her once more, with his own spark of temper. "Very well, then. Where shall I begin? He built you that house on that godforsaken little spit of land in the middle of nowhere—"

"And do you know why he built it there?" He hadn't time to answer. "Because I asked him to! Because that 'godforsaken little spit' happened to be the place where he and I first made love after not having seen one another in more than two—"

"Mother, please!" Rene hissed, with a quick, reddening glance at Cat.

"What? If you can speak so freely of hatred, why can't I of love? That was where I wanted my house, and so he built it there!"

"Well enough," Rene said, his jaw tight. "But he did not have to keep you shut up there."

"Keep me?" Madeleine laughed. "What makes you think he kept me?"

"You never came to court with him."

"Because I did not care to! I'd had my fill of court life when I was young; it was a duty I was only too glad to leave behind."

"You preferred sitting by yourself, sewing tapestries?" Rene's voice was richly ironic.

"As it happens, I did." Her green eyes blazed defiance. "I had Anne to tend to. Besides, I like being alone. I always have. It was why I nearly joined a nunnery once upon a time. But you don't know about that, do you? You know very little about me, because all your life you have set me up on some sort of—of pedestal, made me the heroine of your little imaginary tragedy, and your father the villain. You never even *asked* me about such things; you would not let me explain—"

"You missed him, though," he interrupted, accusing. "All those endless battles, all that time away—will you deny that you missed him?"

"Does the sky miss the sun at nighting? Does it dream of morning? Of course I missed him. I miss him with every breath I take to this day. I loved him"—she paused, gathered herself in—"with a love beyond telling. And I know as I know God lives, that is how he loved me."

Her son stood, arms folded over his chest, jaw still set but with the first faint glimmer of uncertainty in his blue eyes. "He ought to have been better to you and Annie—"

"Never mind me and Annie; we loved him." She stood squared off against him. "What is it you would have had him do for you, Rene?"

And Cat, wide-eyed, saw him falter, saw her great, strong lover with tears on his cheeks. "I don't know. . . ."

"I do." The quiet voice was David's; he had come up beside Cat. "I mean . . . I think that I do. You wanted him to tell you that you had done well. That he was proud of you." He shrugged a little, boy's shoulders early grown accustomed to weight. "That is what I always longed for from my papa, anyway."

"Oh, Rene." Madeleine looked at him, stricken. "You do know that he loved you, don't you?"

"I . . ." He could not finish.

"Because, God in heaven, he did! I know sometimes he seemed a hard man, a cold man, but that was just his way. He was not good at letting others see into his heart."

"He did not . . . he did not marry you because he had to? Because of me?"

"Is *that* what you think?" Madeleine shook her head. "He'd told me once, 'tis true, that he did not want children. But on the night you were born, he sat down and cried for joy on the stairs."

"Fathers," Robbie Stewart murmured. "Why d'ye suppose it is so hard to be a good one?"

"Because," David Bruce said simply, "it is so hard to be a good son."

"So it goes 'round and 'round," Madeleine said, almost to herself, "generation after generation." She looked at Rene, half-smiling. "If you would get an earful someday, ask Grandpapa why he once delivered your father to the Inquisition."

Anne stared at her, shocked. "Mama! He didn't!"

"Oh, yes he did."

"I should *never* do such a thing to any child of mine!" the girl said with indignation.

"Don't say 'never,' Annie," David cautioned her. "Never is too long a time."

Rene raised an eyebrow at him. "With a few years on you, you might make a middling good king."

Joanna had been rocking back and forth on the legs of her chair. "If we ever get out of here," she noted pointedly.

"Quite right, Yer Majesty." Robbie stood, stretching, looking worn. "I'll go and take a peep in the harbor, see if Rurik is there."

David looked puzzled. "But won't the English see him when he sails in?" he asked Rene as Robbie started for the door.

"Rurik has flags of every nation on earth in his lockers," Rene told him, grinning. "I said he was a corsair, didn't I? And his ship can outrun any vessel afloat. When—" But he broke off abruptly; Robbie had stepped back into the chamber and swiftly but silently bolted the door. "What is it, Robbie?"

"Englishmen," he mouthed, pointing.

"Christ!" said Jessie, throwing up her hands.

"The noise of the sword fight must have led them to the sluice-way," Rene whispered. "Damn! How many, Robbie? Can we take them?"

"If we fight them, they'll know we are here. Better just to slip away." He stood on his chair to hoist himself through the hole in the ceiling, then reached back down. "The queen first."

"Oh, really," said Joanna, "this is just too—" Rene clapped his hand over her mouth and stuffed her into Robbie's arms.

David was next, then Madeleine, then Jessie. Cat waited with her hand curled inside Rene's. The Englishmen had found the door and were battering against it just as he put his hands on her waist and raised her to the ceiling. "Aren't you glad now," David was asking Joanna, "that we didn't bring the dogs?"

"Hush!" Rene said sharply, swinging up through the hole, wincing a little with the weight on his arm, then starting to push the cover stone back into place. Before he had it set, there was a sound like the loudest thunder, so loud that the stones they stood on seemed to shake. "Blasting powder," Rene muttered, settling the stone against a cloud of noxious gray smoke. "The damned fools will bring the castle down on their heads."

Robbie had lit a candle. "Let's go," he said.

In a line they filed through a tunnel much narrower and lower than the ones they had been in before—so low that Robbie and Rene had to double over. These passageways were ancient, Cat realized—perhaps older than Berwick, or Scotland, hewn by the blue-painted men Rene had jested of to her once. The light from Robbie's candle seemed a long way off, but she wasn't afraid, not with her hand in Rene's. Then they turned into a wider corridor; there was more air, and the men could walk upright. "Where are," David whispered, and stopped as Robbie turned on him, his face stern in the glow of the candle; he had his finger to his mouth. In a moment, Cat saw why. The tunnel they were in ran parallel to the outer wall of the Great Room in the castle; through an occasional chink in the mortar, one could actually see and hear the English soldiers questioning the unhappy mayor, who was sweatily insisting that he had no notion where King David might be.

They climbed a stair, a steep one, and Robbie paused at the top to let them catch their breath. Rene bent down to kiss Cat. "I love you," he whispered, brushing a loose curl from her throat.

The words had carried farther than he meant them to in that

echoing stillness. "Tell her when we're safe away, Rene," Robbie muttered, and led them on.

Annie had something to say to Rene; Cat could tell, could see her dancing a little in her eagerness to speak. "Rain," she whispered finally, unable to contain herself. "Rain, I think I know—"

"Hush, crumpet. No more talking." They moved ahead in silence until Robbie, in the lead, breathed a curse and then held up his hand. Cat, standing motionless, listening, heard what he had: a clamor, not too far off, of men's voices and footsteps.

"What now?" he mouthed to Rene, who beckoned for the candle and turned back the way they had come.

But they had not gone more than a hundred feet before he stopped, too, with his hand up for silence. More voices, from ahead of them, and something more ominous: a barking of dogs. Again Rene and Robbie shared glances.

Queen Joanna had begun to cry. "I don't see why we don't just—" Robbie clapped his hand over her mouth.

"Ye know the tunnels best," he muttered to Rene, who was thinking as hard as he could.

"We'll have to go on out to the cliffs," Rene whispered back. "It's the only way."

He started back down the corridor, away from the dogs. Madeleine and Cat herded the children after him, with Jessie close by the queen lest she speak out again. The pace Rene set was a fast one; they were all a little breathless with keeping up. The voices ahead were still distant, but getting clearer. *I hope you know what you are doing, Rain,* Cat thought, those harsh English accents grating in her ears.

Even as he moved forward, Rene began to peel off his shirt and then flung it away. Robbie quickly followed suit, removing his doublet and letting it fall. To confound the dogs, Cat realized, as Madeleine rid herself of her surcoat. Not to be outdone, Cat unlaced her bodice and, ignoring Jessie's horrified expression, shed the top of her gown. If the trick bought them a little more time, it would be worth the damp chill of wearing only her shift.

By now Rene was running. The hounds were howling behind them, and up ahead the voices of the English soldiers sounded so close, it seemed impossible they had not appeared. Cat was frantically reminding herself how noise echoed in the tunnels when Rene found whatever it was he had been heading for and stopped, before a length of wall on their right that looked, to her eyes, not one whit different from the rest. But when he stooped and pushed at the stones, a little opening appeared.

"Christ, Rene," Robbie muttered, " 'tis scarcely enough for a pup to fit through!"

"It looked bigger when I was ten. Go on, all of you. Robbie and I will guard your backs."

For a moment they stood there, no one eager to be first to face whatever was beyond that black hole. On the other hand, those dogs . . . Cat met Rene's blue gaze one last time in the candle-light. Then she gathered up her skirts, knelt down, and pushed through.

The stones were cold on her shoulders and back where her shift left them bare; the smell of sea grew strong. She popped out headfirst into a whipping wind—God, the good fresh air! Someone was shoving at her heels, still back in the hole. Quickly she clambered out onto a ledge of rock and turned to help who-ever came next. It was Annie, scrambling out beside her. "Rain won't fit, will he?" she asked Cat worriedly. "I know that he won't!"

"Of course he will. Stay back against the rocks, Anne." The night was very dark; there were stars, but no moon.

Jessie's head appeared in the opening. Cat put her hands out to pull her through. "My skirt is caught on something," her sister was saying.

"Here!" Cat reached in and gave a yank, and the fabric came free.

"Jesu!" Jessie cried when she saw the narrow rim of rock on which she was expected to stand, high above where the dark sea was breaking against the cliffs.

"Just stay in one place," Cat told her, "and you'll be all right. And keep your voice down. The English ships must be just over there."

David was the next to squeeze through, and then Madeleine. Then there came a lengthy pause in which they all looked at one another in terror. Then at last came Joanna, cross as old Clootie, being forcibly pushed from behind.

Robbie was doing the pushing. He had a hard time fitting through, but he made it. "Good thing Rene took off his mail," he grunted as he stood, "or he'd be doin' so now, and the hounds near on him." Cat put down her head to stare into the hole, and could hear them howling. "Christ," she whispered. "Rene?"

"I am . . . coming." She could hear him scraping against the walls. He'd started through feet-first, so as to pull closed the stone that formed the door. She had never realized quite how big a boot he wore, she thought as they appeared. He had to twist and turn to find the widest point for his shoulders to squeeze through. Then at last he was wriggling the last few inches. Cat reached to help him up, and felt a warm stickiness on his arm. Blood . . .

"Have to move fast," he told Robbie, wrapping the wound again as best he could with the battered bandage. "It won't be long before the hounds find that hole, with the trail I've left. Help me off with my boots, Cat, would you?"

"What are you going to do?"

"Swim for the skiff."

"Can you, hurt as you are?"

"Of course I can."

She eased the boots from his feet, feeling him wince once when she braced against his thigh for leverage. She didn't dare argue, though, when he'd said he could do it. "There's a path you can use to get closer to the water leading off to the left there," he told Robbie. "Handholds and toeholds, mostly."

"Handholds and toeholds?" Joanna shrieked.

"You can do it," David assured her.

"Rain," said Annie, "listen to me. I think I know why—"

"Later, crumpet." He kissed her, swiftly, and his mouth brushed Cat's. Then he dived straight down into the black water below.

"My God," whispered Jessie. "He's a madman."

Cat was watching, hard as she could. She saw him surface, wave, and strike out for the bend in the rocks that hid the English fleet, keeping close to the cliffs.

Madeleine was pulling her by the hand. "Come along, Cat. There is no time to waste."

The path down the cliff wasn't bad, after all they had been through already. There was one spot where the holds were too far apart for the girls and Cat, but Robbie swung them down. With his arms still around her waist, she took the chance to whisper, "You won't ever tell him, will you, what I said to you the other night?"

He laughed. "Nay, darlin'. He'll not hear it from me." Of course, that left her wondering whether she herself ought to confess to him—and then, as the footholds ended and they crouched on the last outcrop of rock, still some ten or twelve feet above the roiling water, with the minutes lengthening, whether she would ever have the opportunity to.

"He ought to be back by now, oughtn't he, Mama?" Anne whispered.

"It just seems a long time, because we are waiting," Madeleine told her quietly.

"Do you see Rurik's ship?" David asked Robbie, scanning the harbor.

"No. But Rene will see it when he brings the skiff 'round." He did not sound completely confident, though, thought Cat.

The wind, already brisk, seemed to be worsening. "A storm is all we need right now," Jessie muttered. Cat expected to hear the hounds baying at the hole in the rock above them at any minute. Where the devil was Rene? What if the English had found the skiff, what then? How long could they hold on here? Come the dawn, someone would certainly spot them. Something splashed against her cheek. Spray, she thought, and then came another spattering. She was shivering in her thin shift, regretting her bravado in casting her bodice aside.

Anne had bent over on the thin ledge. "Annie, what are you doing?" her mother asked sharply.

"He should be here by now," she said stubbornly, pulling off her own boots. "I'm going after him."

"Anne, don't you dare!"

"But, Mama—"

"There he is," Robbie murmured, and Cat, trying to pierce

the night's veil, stared across the water. "No wonder it took him so long. He hasn't raised the sail."

The little boat hove into sight. Rene was using the oars, pulling very slowly, so as not to splash. He was rowing against the tide, and against the wind. "Lord, he must be strong," Jessie murmured in admiration. Cat saw him turn to check how close he was to the cliffs, then haul on the oars again.

"The sail would be much faster," Annie fretted, chewing on her nails.

Madeleine pulled the girl's hand from her mouth. "Don't do that, darling."

"What's the difference? They are all broken to bits anyway." A swell rode in from the night-black sea and sent the skiff spinning toward the rocks, so that Rene had to stave them off with one oar until he could control the boat. Anne's hand promptly went toward her mouth again.

He was very close now, only a dozen yards or so from the ledge. Cat had her heart in her mouth, to see the way he was straining to fight against the water and wind. "Get ready," Robbie said softly. "I'll hand ye down one by one. Ye first, Lady Madeleine." She nodded. As the skiff swept directly below them, Robbie grasped her wrists and lowered her over the edge.

Rene had to let go the oars to catch her. The little boat banged against the cliff face, tilting crazily. Cat glanced at her sister. Jessie's face was stark white.

"Move to the fore," Rene told his mother, and she climbed over the thwarts toward the bow, avoiding the boom and the bundled sail. Robbie was already handing down David. Rene caught him, set him in the boat, and he stumbled, making Joanna gasp.

"I'm all right," he assured them. "It is slippery, that's all. Mind your step, Joanna." He took her hand as Rene put her down at his side, then guided her to a seat beside Madeleine. Then Anne went, smiling at her brother as his arms came around her. Jessie's turn was next.

The wind was getting rougher, and the boat was rocking crazily on the swells. Rene had to stop and take the oars to turn it 'round. Robbie reached for Jessie's hands. "Oh, God," she whispered. "I can't."

"You haven't any choice," Robbie told her, and grabbed her, swinging her over the edge. She let out a yelp as she dangled in the air, before Rene caught her ankles, steadied her, and let her slip into his grasp.

"There, was that so hard?" he asked her. She shook her head uncertainly and crawled forward, clinging to the oarlock. Cat was already in the air when a frenzy of baying announced that the hounds had found the tunnel at last.

Rene dropped her in a heap atop the keel. "Stay down," he said in a tight voice. "All of you, duck your heads and stay down!" Robbie leaped from the ledge, landing with a thud and making the little skiff spin in a way that made Cat's heart reach her throat. Together, Robbie and Rene were hauling at the ropes that raised the sail. It went flying up the mast with a *snap*. Robbie scrambled forward, cleating lines as he went, leaving Rene to stand out over the stern with the sail hung loose to catch the wind. It filled, billowing down to the boom, then collapsed, making everyone in the boat sigh at once, and then filled again. Rene trapped it with a twist of the rigging, and they flew out from under the cliff like some great spread-winged bird.

"Look!" Jessie cried, pointing back. Soldiers had made it through the tunnel to the cliff; they stood out along the upper ledge like a row of toys.

"What will they do to us from there, lass—throw rocks?" Robbie asked with gleeful contempt. Just then something whizzed through the air and struck the water beside them with a loud hiss. Robbie laughed. There was another high-singing *whiz*, and a second missile clattered onto the deck of the skiff. Cat was closest to it. She put out her hand to see what it was. An orb of iron, some six or eight inches across, with a glowing rope hanging out of it—

"Ouch!" she cried; the rope was scorching hot where she'd grabbed it.

"Look out, Cat!" Robbie lunged toward her with his hand outstretched, but she'd already taken the thing and sent it whirling off into the air, high and far as she could, by the rope. As it reached the top of the arc it inscribed over the black water, it burst into flame with a thunderous boom that seemed to shake the boat.

"Christ, Cat!" Jessie cried in terror.

Rene was looking down at her from where he rode atop the taffrail. "Help her, Mother," he said, his voice tight. "She's burned her hands."

Madeleine moved toward Cat, dipping the hem of her skirt in cold seawater. Everyone else kept looking back to the cliffs, but the skiff was cutting cleanly over the waves, and they were beyond the soldiers' range. Rene had them headed due northeast, through the mouth of the harbor.

"Wait a minute," King David called. "Where's the pirate ship?"

"Rurik isn't here yet," Rene shouted back. "We'll have to go and meet him."

"Meet him where?"

Rene, his hands full, nodded toward the vast emptiness that lay ahead of them. "All of us in this," the king said dubiously, "on the open sea?"

"It's a bit late now for anything else," Robbie noted, looking behind them. Their flight had evidently not gone unnoticed; three of the English warships had hoisted sail and were coming after them.

"Lord, this is a nightmare!" Jessie wailed, and pulled her skirts up over her head.

Madeleine was praying while she gently daubed Cat's scorched palms with chill seawater: "Our Father, which art in heaven . . ."

Robbie had moved to the bow of the ship and was perched on the pulpit, staring out at the star-glittered sea. "No sign of him yet," he called to Rene.

"He'll be there."

"Rain," said Annie. "I really have got something important to tell you. I think I know why—"

"David!" Joanna shrieked, leaping up from her seat. "Something is on fire!"

"It's only the powder from the ball that—"

"*No,* David. It smells like hair."

Jessie drew her skirts down to sniff. "She is right."

"Christ!" Madeleine cried, just as Cat heard a crinkling, crackling sound from behind her ears. Robbie leaped toward her, sword drawn, grabbed a great hank of her curls, and hacked. He flung them overboard, and they sizzled as they hit the sea.

"Oh, Cat, your hair!" Jessie screeched, and pulled her skirts up again.

Cat's head felt lopsided. She put a hand up to touch her cropped curls. "Is it out now?"

"Aye," Robbie told her. "I'm sorry. I could not think what else to do. The wick must have singed it." He sounded so stricken that Cat had to laugh. Under the circumstances, like Anne's fingernails, what difference did it make? The English warships were gaining speed, their broad sails white in the starlight. The sea was rougher since they'd passed the harbor mouth, each new wave threatening to swamp the bow, already riding low with all of them aboard. And they were out here at the mercy of a pirate. . . .

"There!" Annie cried, pointing into the darkness at a prick of white on the horizon. "Look, Rain! There they are!"

"So they are." Cat saw the gleam of his teeth as he hauled at the sail, bringing them 'round to head straight for what, to her, looked like no more than a white-winged gull in the distance. But as the skiff skimmed nearer, it grew and grew until it swelled to a ship, a strange one, low-hulled and sleek and oddly foreign, its peaked sails rigged tight. "Come on, Rurik," she heard Rene mutter. The English warships were still gaining. A hundred yards behind the stern, rain was falling on the water—no, arrows. The bowmen had misjudged the distance, but it would not take them long to home in.

And then Rene lost the wind. The sail went limp, and the boom swung crazily, making them all scream and duck. "Damn!" he said, pulling at the loose-flapping lines. "Damn it all!" Another hail of arrows, this one closer, pattered down behind them. The skiff floated on a swell with a calm, rocking motion, like a baby's cradle. The sudden stillness was all the more striking for Rene's frenzy of activity. "Shall I," Robbie began, rising up from the thwart, but Rene cut him off:

"Damn it, just stay down!" He shook the sail out again, teasing the stays in his hands, feeling, waiting, testing—

With a rush, the canvas fluttered and filled, and they were moving again.

"Hooray!" Anne cried, but her mother hushed her. It was no time for rejoicing yet, not with the English bowmen hanging over the warships' rails with drawn strings. The pirate ship had let its own sails droop, riding on the tide. Rurik could come no closer without the risk of smashing into the skiff. Rene would have to reach him.

This time when the archers from the closest ship fired, the fugitives could hear the order as it was given. They got down low as they could, and were glad they had, for two arrows actually zinged into the skiff. Cat, watching the bowmen, was certain that next time they'd hit someone, and they might have, had a row of mangonels on the port side of Rurik's ship not let loose a round of fireballs made of burning pitch. The archers scattered just as the skiff swooped in beneath the overhanging hull of the pirate vessel. Hooks flew down from the deck; Robbie and Rene lunged to secure them. A wooden ladder clattered, rung over rung, to the skiff. "Go!" Rene bellowed, shoving the nearest passenger toward the ladder. It was Jessie; dutifully enough she began to climb. But when she reached the top, she took one look at the gold-toothed, black-bearded, be-earringed ruffian who grabbed for her, his eyes agleam in the light of the ship's torches, and screamed, plummeting off the ladder straight into the sea.

"Jessie!" Cat screamed, rising in the skiff.

"Cat!" Rene roared at her back. "You can't bloody swim!"

He was too late. She'd already jumped in.

The water was unspeakably cold, so cold she lost her breath as she hit. Her skirts clung to her legs like vines, wrapping 'round and 'round, tugging her down, but she struck out with her hands, floundering, willing herself to stay afloat while she clawed toward the spot where she'd seen Jessie vanish under the waves. The skiff rose toward her, frighteningly near, threatening to crush her against the side of the pirate ship. She thrust an arm out as though that might stave it off; it hung precariously close for a long, long moment before the tide swept it away.

But she couldn't see Jessie. "Jessie!" she screamed again, in black panic. Someone grabbed her from behind. Rene—"Let me go!" she cried, fighting him off. "Let me go and get Jess!" He shouted something back at her, but she kept on flailing. "Let me go, let me go—"

He wrenched her 'round toward the ladder. "Robbie has got her!" he roared in her ear. "Stop it, Cat! Robbie's got her!"

She heard him then. "Robbie's got her?"

"Aye, you bloody little idiot! Come on!"

He caught the bottom rung of the ladder with one arm; the other was wrapped around Cat. They lurched upward, into the air, as the men on deck hauled them in. Cat's shins banged against the hull, then against the port rail. "Set the sail!" she heard a gruff voice bellow, and above her head the great white canvas sky filled with wind.

Rene had not let go of her yet. They stood, dripping, on the deck. "Cat!" Her sister ran toward her, hugged her. "Oh, I am sorry, Cat!"

"Never mind, pet," Cat soothed her.

"You bloodly little idiot," Rene said again, glaring at Cat. He was winded, and furious. "What in God's name possessed you—"

"Well, I couldn't very well leave her there; she's my sister!"

"You both might have drowned!"

"Aye," Cat acknowledged, Jessie's hand in hers, "but we'd have gone together."

Rene threw his own hands up in despair. "You Douglas girls are daft!"

His sister came toward him, eyes wide in the torchlight. "Rain! Are you crying again? That is twice in one day."

"Of course I'm not crying," he said, tears streaming down his face as he lifted Cat right off her feet to kiss her.

"Strong love," Madeleine murmured to herself, and smiled at her son.

Thirty-one

"Are you completely, absolutely certain this is legal and binding?" Jessie asked dubiously.

"Of course it is," Rurik Johanneson assured her, his gold tooth gleaming in the light of a long bank of candles. "From time immemorial, a sea captain has been granted authority to perform the sacraments in time of exigency. The blessed St. Jerome wrote in his *Commentary on the Twelve Minor Prophets*—"

"Never mind, Rurik," Rene broke in, grinning as he slipped his arm around Cat. "Mistress Douglas is only concerned about the outcome of a wager she had with her sisters as to which of them would be the last to—"

"Cat! You *didn't* go and tell him about that!" Jessie said in horror.

"Well, with Rain having revealed all his secrets to me at last, I felt I ought to offer *something* in return. Besides, how else was I to explain why I was so bold to him when we met at Tess's wedding?"

"I thought you fell in love with me at first sight," Rene protested.

"Oh, darling, I did. It was the times I saw you after that which made me hate your guts."

Rurik cleared his throat. "Perhaps we should begin? We may have outrun Edward's warships, but we have still a fair way to go." His rich, deep voice still held traces of an accent from his native Norway, and each time he opened his mouth, Cat wanted to laugh at the incongruous contrast between his elegant, precise speech and his maniacal, piratical appearance. No wonder Jessie had her doubts!

Jessie was worrying her lip. "Jest if you like, but I just want to be sure . . ."

"Jessie, the man was a Templar monk for more than twenty years," Madeleine said, laughing.

"Aye, but look what he is now!"

"What?" Rurik demanded. "An honest sailor, plying the seas between my native country and the Mediterranean. Mind you, now and again another vessel confronts me, and I am forced to take steps to defend myself, as any captain would." He grinned his gold-toothed grin, and the purple-faced parrot perched on his shoulder preened and squawked out, "Cap'n! Cap'n! Cap'n!" through its short hooked beak.

Jessie shuddered, and rolled her eyes at Cat. "Why not wait until we are ashore again? You cannot tell me this is the wedding of your dreams!"

"Oh, but it is! Or would be, rather, if only Tess and Janet could be here."

"Wait, then," her sister urged her.

"I told you," Rene said darkly. "That wager . . ."

"Pardonnez-moi, mam'selle." The absolutely most sinister-looking member of Rurik's crew, his first mate, a Frenchman named Pepin with no teeth at all, scars on every inch of his face, and legs so bowed that when he stood at rest they inscribed a perfect circle, took a step toward Jessie, who flinched. "But until your sister and Monsieur Faurer are joined in holy wedlock, I greatly fear they are living in a state of mortal sin. Surely you would not care to endanger their souls."

"Surely, Jess," Cat said briskly, "you don't want to argue theology with Monsieur Pepin, do you? Go ahead, Rurik, please."

Rurik grinned, and did. "My friends, we have come together on this night to join this man and this woman in the blessed sacrament of matrimony—a sacrament instituted by God the Father, sanctioned by his only Son, and perfected by the Holy Spirit." To a man, the pirates crossed themselves. "St. Paul wrote in his first epistle to the Corinthians, 'Love bears all things, believes all things, hopes all things, endures all things.' And so it has been for Catriona and Rene."

There you are, Jessie, Cat thought, smiling at her sister. One could not ask for a more apt text than that. The bank of candles flickered in the night wind that billowed the white sails; overhead, the stars stretched from horizon to horizon in an endless sweep. Rene's arm was around her waist; on her other side, Anne held tight to her hand, her eyes wide and shining. Rurik's smooth, deep voice slid into Latin, the timeworn words of the ceremony echoing across the sea's vast, awesome splendor. No bishop's cathedral in all the world, Cat thought, not even in Rome itself, could feel so sacred as the star-swept deck of this pirate ship.

Rene turned to look down at her, his eyes dark as the sky in the glow of the candles. His borrowed shirt and doublet were too tight, and he'd had to leave them open at the chest; she could see the bandages wound around his rib cage. *He looks beautiful,* she thought, staring at him. *How can a man be so beautiful?* And self-consciously her hand crept upward toward the patch of close-cropped hair at her right temple.

Gently Rene reached out and pulled the hand back to her side.

"If there be any man here present," Rurik intoned, "who knows of any reason why these two should not be wed, let him speak now. . . ." An image rose in Cat's mind of Malcolm as he'd looked in the cavern, staring up at her with his mad, hopeful eyes when she'd said she loved him. The memory made her shiver. Rene tucked his arm around her once more, protectively.

"Our Father," Rurik began to pray, and the pirates' deep voices echoed: "which art in heaven . . ." *Papa?* Cat thought, staring up at the night sky through the billowing sails. *Papa, are you there? Can you see me? Do you know how happy I am?* Her gaze met Jessie's. Her sister was crying, but did not look sad. *She always cries at weddings,* Cat remembered, and felt tears well up in her own eyes. She was going to miss Jessie. "Come with us to France," she'd begged her earlier that day, as they made ready for the ceremony in the captain's cabin.

Jessie had shaken her head. "I'm going to find Diarmot." Robbie was going with her to the MacDugall territory in the Highlands; Rurik would put them both ashore at Cromarty some-

time tomorrow. The rest of them were going on with King David
to the Orkneys, to take on water and stores, and from there across
the North Sea and southward, along the coasts of Denmark and
the Low Countries, until they reached France. King Philip, Rene
said, had offered David and Joanna asylum there.

It was strange, and a little frightening, to think of going to
some country other than Scotland. But, of course, Rene would
be there, so it would seem like home. She tried to imagine living
with him as his wife, lying with him every night, waking to him
each morning, but could not conceive of it; such luxury of time
and place seemed impossible. Why, they would eat together at
table; she could ask him as she dressed, "Do you prefer that
gown, or this?" Well, when she had any gowns she could, she
amended, looking down at the makeshift bodice Madeleine had
sewn to replace the one she'd torn off in the tunnels. It was made
from Captain Rurik's best linen shirt, and somehow Madeleine
had found time to embroider a line of tiny flowers across the
yoke, in thick, borrowed red yarn. A bit of red silk ribbon one
of the pirates had bought in Algiers for his sweetheart served to
lace it; more of the ribbon wound through her hair. Oh, God, her
hair looked absolutely wretched where Robbie had—

"Cat?" Rene interrupted her thoughts, very softly.

"Aye?"

"Are you reconsidering?"

"What?" She looked at him blankly.

Anne was tugging her hand. "It is the part where you're supposed to say you'll marry him," she hissed impatiently. "Rain
already did!"

"Oh! Of course I will. I mean, I do."

"What God hath joined together," Rurik said, his voice low
and solemn through his wind-whipped beard, "let no man put
asunder." Then he clapped Rene's shoulder with awesome force.
"Go on and kiss her, mate!"

He did, to a chorus of hoots from the pirates and sighs from
his mother and sister. Cat's mind was not wandering now, not
with his sure arms around her, and his mouth, tanged with sea
from the wind, crushing down on hers. Man and wife . . .

He pulled away from her a little, to look down into her face, his eyes filled with a love as deep and wide as that ocean. "I told you, didn't I, that someday . . ."

"Aye, Rain, you did."

He kissed her again. Madeleine came to embrace them, and Annie; Robbie shook Rene's hand and kissed Cat's cheek. She turned to look for Jessie, and saw her dabbing her eyes with a kerchief provided by Rurik. "I simply cannot *imagine*," she kept repeating, "what Tess and Janet are going to say."

"Poor Jessie." Cat giggled, braced in Rene's arms, as he carried her into Rurik's cabin and kicked the stout door shut behind them. "Did you see her expression when Pepin told her she was eating seaweed soup?"

"It wasn't bad, though," Rene said judiciously. "All in all, I thought the meal very good. Did you try the albatross?"

Cat shook her head, with a shudder. "Is there anything you won't eat?"

"Of course there is. Your cooking." Cat stuck out her tongue at him, and he pressed his mouth to hers. "Mm. Do that again with your tongue." She did, her arms tight on his neck. He carried her toward the long, narrow bed built into the cabin wall.

Last night, the night they'd come aboard, they'd slept in the hold—but they really had slept, side by side, like nuns, too exhausted to undress, much less to make love. In the morning Anne had been awake and bouncing back and forth between them, full of energy and excitement at this new adventure. They had tried to creep below, unnoticed, after breakfast, but the pirates, all former Templars, had been anxious to speak to Michel Faurer's son. After dinner, Anne and Joanna were napping; then Rurik wanted to discuss plans with Rene and Robbie. Cat swore it was sheer frustration at ever getting her alone that led Rene to ask the pirate to wed them that very night.

"Here we are," he said, standing over the bed. She nodded, suddenly shy, remembering the last time they had been together this way, at Douglasdale, when she'd betrayed him. "What is wrong?"

"Nothing. It is just—that I hate my hair."

He sat on the bed with her on his lap, and started to pull out the ribbons. "I'd rather Robbie take a bit of your hair than take you up on that proposal you made him."

She flushed. "That snake! He swore he would not tell you!"

"He didn't have to. I guessed. Thank God you chose him. No other man in Scotland would have resisted the temptation." A sudden doubt suffused his strong-planed face. "There weren't any others, were there? It has been such a long time . . . I wouldn't blame you, though, if you—"

"I didn't."

Satisfied, he kissed her forehead. "It is selfish, I know, but I'm glad."

She straightened on his knees. "Now you tell me something—and mind you speak truth! Did you *never* lie with Eleanor de Baliol?"

"Never."

"Really?"

"Really. And since that night I kissed you at Langlannoch, there's been no one but you. And since I could count the times we've lain together on my one hand—" He rolled her over onto the bed, his eyes agleam in the light from the ship's lamp that winked overhead. "No more talk of Eleanor, or of anything else. We have too much making up to do."

Just as his mouth touched hers, someone rapped at the door. "Rain!" they heard Annie call. "Oh, Rain!"

He groaned. "What now? Annie, go away!"

"This is important, Rain. Really."

"Nothing is important enough."

"It will just take a moment."

"Let her in, Rain," Cat urged him. "We have the whole night."

"Which is starting to seem shorter and shorter." But he heaved himself up and went to open the door. "What is is, crumpet?"

"It was a lovely wedding, wasn't it?" Anne came and plumped herself down on the bed beside Cat.

Rene promptly picked her up again. "So it was. And if that's all you came to say—"

"It isn't!" She squirmed out of his grasp. "But I just remembered what I meant to tell you back in the tunnels, only everyone kept shushing me. I know why Eleanor—"

"Don't say that name!" Rene howled, hands over his ears.

"Why Eleanor what, Anne?" Cat asked curiously.

"Why she wrote to Mama that she and Rain were married. And why she told Cat she was having a baby. And why her uncle tried to have Rain killed."

Rene rolled his eyes at Cat, then said indulgently, "Very well, let's hear it."

"It was for the land."

Her brother blinked. "What land?"

"All the land that would be yours if de Baliol won," she explained patiently. "Langlannoch, and the crofts, and Mama's inheritance in Devonshire—and don't forget Grandpapa's holdings in France. Remember, Cat, when you first came to Langlannoch, I said Eleanor was only after Rain's money? That she never loved him?"

"So you did," said Cat.

"And that's why her uncle Edward wanted you dead," Anne told her brother earnestly. "Then Eleanor's baby would inherit it all. That's why she wrote to Mama. Mama never would have turned her or the baby away, not if they were all she had left of you."

"But wouldn't she have to prove there was a marriage somehow?" Rene said dubiously.

Anne looked at him as though he was dim-witted. "Her uncle won. He's king of Scotland now. I doubt she'd have trouble finding a priest to swear he married the two of you."

"And after a decent interval," Cat said softly, "the grieving widow would be free to remarry. Her child would bear no stigma of illegitimacy. It could be true, Rene."

But he was shaking his head. "She would not do such a thing."

Cat looked at him. "Still harboring fond memories?"

"Christ, no! I just cannot believe she could be so cold."

"I can," Anne said distastefully.

"You scorned her, humiliated her, when you broke your betrothal," Cat reminded him. "Perhaps this was her revenge."

"She was curious about Grandfather's estates," he mused, almost to himself. "By God, she had me take her out to see his vineyards once, I recall. And she had plenty of questions about Mother's Devonshire holdings. Perhaps her anger at me, and her greed, would be reason enough. . . ."

"It all fits together," Cat said softly. "Pity we'll never find out, Annie, if your theory is true."

"Oh, but we could." Rene's jaw was suddenly tight, his blue eyes filled with anger. "So what if I am still alive? If he was willing to kill me, Edward de Baliol will not scruple at having me attainted. But Eleanor's baby will still inherit; you cannot attaint an heir. As Anne said, how will I prove a marriage never took place? It will all be hers—Grandpapa's lands when he dies, and Mother's English estates, and—"

"Langlannoch," Anne breathed, turning pale. "Mama's heart will be broken."

Rene stared into space. "This is my penance, for ever having courted that black-hearted bitch. By God, I'll get Langlannoch back for Mother. I swear it on my life." Then his voice changed; his stern face turned less formidable. "Don't fret about it, Annie. It will be all right. We've got the true king of Scotland safe away. All we need is to restore him to the throne."

His sister brightened. "I'd forgotten about that. We'll show old Eleanor then, won't we, Rain?"

"Indeed we will." He kissed her cheek. "Now, do you suppose you might leave Cat and me at least a little of our wedding night?"

"Oh! Of course. I am sorry. 'Night, Cat. 'Night, Rain. Sleep tight." She eyed the captain's bunk. "It looks as though you will. That's a very small bed." She left them, with a cheery wave.

But Rene turned sober again once she had closed the door. "Damn it all to hell. What in God's name have I done?"

Cat was sitting, miserably twisting her hands. "What have I done, you mean. If I'd not sent Papa after you at Douglasdale, David would still be sitting on the throne at Edinburgh."

That made him smile a little. "So you think you are single-handedly responsible for the fall of Scotland, love? I would not wound your pride, but I fear you were only a small spur to history. With England's Edward who he is, and de Baliol, and Mar, and your father—the conflict was inevitable. It would have come, later if not now. And the outcome would have been the same. It will be a long time before David is grown enough to prove himself his father's son. And Edward of England is a mighty king."

"Do you mean it, Rain? Because I could not bear to think all of this, even Papa's death, is my fault."

"He did not have to come after me to find de Baliol, did he? He made that choice himself, against very good counsel. Angus—"

"Angus is the Grand Master, isn't he?" Cat interrupted.

"I can't tell you that."

"But he is," she pressed. "That is why he told me you were married. He was afraid I would send for you at Douglasdale, and afraid you would come."

"And he chose to drink himself into a stupor on New Year's night, much to his rue." He chucked her chin. "We all make our own choices. And each one we make sends ripples out through all the rest of the world, and runs into other ripples, altering—" He stopped; she was staring at him. "What's wrong?"

"Papa said something very close to that to me once."

"Did he?" Rene looked pleased. "Well, except in his opinion of me, I always admired your father greatly."

"You did not."

"I did! He was the sort of father I hope someday to be."

Cat laughed a little. "Well, no one could ever call him cold, or distant." Then she started to cry.

He held her close while she gave way to her grief, mourning for Archibald. It was the first chance she'd had to, and her wild tears embarrassed her. She ought not to do this to Rene, not on their wedding night. But he was infinitely patient with her, stroking her hair, kissing her forehead and hands, rubbing her shoulders and back until the tide of her sadness crested and receded, and she leaned quietly with her head in the curve of his shoulder, drying her eyes with his handkerchief.

"I am sorry," she apologized, and sniffled. "That was more like Jessie than like me."

"No, Jessie is far more ladylike when she cries." That made Cat laugh, shakily.

There was a porthole by the head of the bed. Through it she could see the stars, and the wide black canopy of the night. Somewhere out beyond that vast sky lay Scotland, chafing under the thrall of its puppet-king. But David was safe. What was it Angus told her the Bruce had once said? There was more than one kind of victory. And those that were low on the wheel would someday be brought 'round. . . .

"Do you feel better?" Rain asked softly.

"Aye."

He pulled at her bodice laces, his blue eyes ablaze. "Then come and make a father of me. I want to know the sort of love that makes you cry so for him. I want—" He hesitated. "To break that damned wheel. To cherish my children. Daughters *and* sons."

He undressed her slowly, reverently, touching her as though her body was a shrine and he a sinning suppliant, come for healing, absolution, a miracle to cure the soul's woes. When she was naked and reached for him, to ease his shirt over his bandaged arm, his flesh quivered beneath her fingers. "When I think of having done that to you—" She shook her head, biting her lip at the wound she had made him.

"I'd have given my whole arm to have you." And it wasn't a jest; he meant it, absolutely. To be loved so fiercely was a little frightening . . . *and yet,* Cat thought, *I would die for him; I love him that same way.*

Half-in and half-out of his shirt, he was sitting there, smiling, waiting. "Oh, I am sorry!" She started, realizing she'd been lost in her thoughts.

"I've never known such a dreamer as you, Catriona. First during our vows, and now this—"

"I was only thinking of you," she defended herself, finishing with the shirt and then his breeches.

"I know."

"How?"

He put his palms to her nipples, that had gone round and hard. "See? At least, I hope no one else has this effect on you."

"No one else ever has."

He began to stroke her gently. His fingertips were rough, abraded from the stones in the tunnels. The sensation made her catch her breath. "You don't have to dream about me anymore," he told her. "You have got me right here. Forever and ever."

"I can't get used to the notion."

"You have time to grow accustomed to it." He rolled her onto the soft coverlet, and promptly cracked his head on the cabin paneling. "Christ! You can tell Rurik is still a celibate; this bed's not made for two."

"We should fit well enough one on top of the other."

He grinned. "So we should. Who first?"

For answer she slid beneath him, her hands on his back, smoothing his skin, tracing the long, straight indentations along his spine and then the taut muscles of his buttocks as he knelt above her. "Christ," he groaned, and she felt him shudder in her arms. He kissed her, slowly, his tongue flicking against her. "You have got the most amazing mouth," he murmured. "Have I ever told you how I love your mouth? I cannot see it without wanting to do this, and this. . . ."

His tongue was wildly insistent. She parted her lips and took it between them, savoring the taste of him, luscious as plums, tart at the skin and then bursting with sweetness.

"And this." He settled his weight on her thighs, so that she felt his manhood, ready and hard, push against her mound of Venus. The sensation made her weak with anticipation. She gripped his shoulders, her legs opening beneath him. He groaned again and ducked his head to find her breast, take her nipple in his teeth and pull at it with just enough force that she shivered in delight.

"More," she whispered. "Do that again, please."

He did, while he smoothed her other breast with his hand, teased it with his fingers, plucking at its red bud. "I love your breasts, too," he murmured.

"Lord, they love you."

Cat could feel heat building inside her, pulsing in her veins, migrating toward her belly. Rene shifted to trail his hand downward, following the heat to the thatch of red-gilt curls that crowned her womanhood. His long finger stroked, tested, probed, and then pierced her, pushing into dark warmth that was slick and caressing, like a tropic tide pulling at the moon.

He made a noise in his throat, desire strangling him as he touched her. She strained against him, aching for him. He moved his hand, found the small, tight center of her need and rubbed it back and forth, back and forth. Cat uncoiled like a tiger spring-ing, clinging to him, her breath coming in short, hard gasps. "Oh. Oh. Oh . . ." She had her hands on his buttocks again, trying to raise him up, willing him to come inside her. But he made her wait, made her writhe and pant until at last she dug into his flesh with her nails and cried out, "Rain, come to me!"

He laughed and sank his shaft deep inside her, with a sudden-ness that shocked her silent. "God in heaven," he whispered as her sheath tightened around him. He wanted to explode in her then and there, could not believe he wouldn't with the unbearable pressure in his loins for release. Quickly he withdrew, but found that only more arousing—the heat of her, the flow of her, rivers of velvet bathing him in fire.

He thrust into her again. She'd tilted back to gather him closer, opening herself to him like a rose, full-blown, heavy and ripe with dew. He closed his eyes, lost in sensation, her skin soft as chamois against him, her hair a wreath of flame. The sounds she made, quiet little moans of passion each time he pushed inside her, drove him mad with longing. He wanted this to be so won-drous for her, wanted to clear away the years of hurting and hardship he had inflicted on her. He needed to erase from her bright, gilt-edged cat's eyes the doubt and fear he had put there, until only love shone through.

The ship rocked on a swell, pitching up and then down again— or was it only the desire coursing through him that rocked them? He let his hands slide to her buttocks, round and white, impossibly lovely, and cupped them close, held her tight as he could. He was thrusting and pulling back, thrusting and pulling back, but he could hold off no longer. "Cat," he whispered. "I love you." Then his seed erupted from him like shot, fire merging with fire, his wild cry of fulfillment melting into her answering cry.

He fell against her, felt the slow, shifting thud of the world slipping back into place. Her mouth was at his ear; he felt the kiss she gave him, heard her breathless sigh: "Oh . . ."

"Was it all right, Cat? Did you—did I satisfy you?" He didn't realize how plain his anxiousness showed in his voice till she laughed.

"Oh, my love. Yes. You did."

Relieved, he shifted and pulled her atop him in the narrow
wood bunk. She seemed so small in his arms . . . like a child.
Her hair was a tangle of pale fire in the starlight. As he touched
it, he found himself thinking of the first time he ever saw her.

She had been wrong when she told Jessie that evening he had
bared all his secrets to her. He still had one.

The first time he'd ever seen her had been nine years past, at
David Bruce's christening. His father had dragged him along to
a reception—too many folk, too many lights, too much noise for
a solitary, guarded ten-year-old boy. He had hated it there. And
then he'd glimpsed the four Douglas girls, dressed alike in white
dresses, their little feet in cunning white shoes, their smooth
bright hair gleaming. And one's hair had more than gleamed—it
had seemed on fire.

He'd followed her for hours, a shadow to her brightness, drawn
like a moth to that headful of incendiary curls. Her eyes were
bright, too, like the green-gold peridots in his mother's jewel
box. God, he could remember every minute detail of that night—
the way her dress ruffled as she darted through the crowds to
swipe sweets from the cake trays, her laughter, high and careless
and gay, how her stockings had bagged, just a little, behind the
knee as she curtsied to the great king, Robert the Bruce, with a
bird's lithe grace. He'd trailed after her like a cowering dog, pulling at his stiff, tight collar, feeling his face bright with sweat, his
own hair lank and lifeless, his limbs somehow awkward, too long.

And then, when he knew the reception was ending, when the
servants were clearing the wine cups and the weary musicians
were playing with the burst of vigor that meant their evening was
nearly at a close, when he was seized by a sudden, unreasoning
terror that he might never see her again, madness overcame him,
and he approached her as she giggled with her sisters, actually
came and stood before her—Christ, he could feel his knees
knocking, the dreadful clamminess of his palms—and had stammered out something that, miraculously, came forth sounding
like, "Would you give me the honor of this dance?"

And she, the glorious bright bird that was the object of his
vague, abject longing, the lodestone to his ten-year-old being,

the girl he would have laid down his young life for in a moment if only given the chance—

She, Catriona Douglas, the just-discovered core of his wretched, hormone-ravaged, pimpled universe, looked at her sisters, looked back at him, opened the amazingly red, lush-lipped mouth that he'd have sold his soul to kiss just once, for an instant—

And laughed.

It had taken him years, literally, to work up the nerve to ask another female to dance after that. He'd fled to France because of Cat Douglas, and once he was there some friend of Grandpapa's took pity on him and introduced him to the concept of paying for a girl's companionship. No one in the brothels laughed, he learned, when he showed them his purse. His nerve slowly grew stronger. By the time he met Eleanor de Baliol, he knew that the cool insouciance he'd painstakingly cultivated around women would stand him in good stead.

But Lord, he never had forgotten that first excruciating rejection. Was it any wonder that years later, at her sister's wedding, when Cat had approached *him,* he had wanted to hate her, wanted it more than he'd ever wanted anything—except that ten-year-old dance—in his entire existence? Time passing had only made her shine more brightly; she threw off light like a diamond, so filled with life that her fire penetrated even his dark, frozen heart. His bitter, mocking toast had been nothing more than a desperate attempt to wound her the way she had once wounded him. . . .

But you couldn't crush a diamond, couldn't put out Cat's fire with a deluge like Noah's. And now God, in his astonishing mercy, had given her to him.

"And you call me a dreamer." She was laughing, tucked into the crook of his arm. "What in the world are you thinking of?"

"The moment I knew I was in love with you."

"And when was that?"

"When you took Fergus's mug of ale from him so haughtily."

It took her a moment to place the memory. Then she smiled. "Ale, eh? My mother would have been pleased."

It had only been a little lie. And by God, a man had a right to his pride.